THE AUCTIONEER

The Auctioneer

Charles Fernyhough

FOURTH ESTATE • *London*

First published in Great Britain
in 1999 by
Fourth Estate Limited,
6 Salem Road,
London W2 4BU

Copyright © Charles Fernyhough 1999

'The Fountain of Salmacis', words and music by Steve Hackett, Peter Gabriel, Tony Banks and Michael Rutherford. Lyric extract used by kind permission of Stratsong Ltd and Carlin Music Corp, Iron Bridge House, 3 Bridge Approach, London NW1 8BD.

10 9 8 7 6 5 4 3 2 1

The right of Charles Fernyhough to be identified as the author of this work has been asserted by him in accordance with the Copyright, Designs and Patents Act 1988.

A catalogue record for this book is available from the British Library.

ISBN 1-85702-982-8

All rights reserved. No part of this publication may be reproduced, transmitted, or stored in a retrieval system, in any form or by any means, without permission in writing from Fourth Estate Limited.

Typeset by MATS,
Southend-on-Sea, Essex

Printed by Biddles Ltd,
Kings Lynn & Guildford

For Lizzie

... the Agate, the Green and other colour'd Glazes have *had their* day, & done pretty well, & are certain of a resurrection soon, for there are, & ever will be a numerous class of People, to purchase *Shewy* & *cheap* things.

JOSIAH WEDGWOOD
to THOMAS BENTLEY,
5th March 1774

Green

Midnight, December: a man kicks off his clothes and dives into a starry pool.

The first thing is the water, the way its cool force takes him and hangs him there, delirious, in the inexhaustible darkness beneath the night. It's a cold that cuts through skin, a weight that drops him against the tiles then lifts him, drunk and naked, towards the moonlit surface overhead. The sky is unfathomable blue. He breaks the surface with a hiss, believing no one comes here except fellow travellers and friends, and kicks out for the deep end, fighting the boozy darkness arm on arm. On her bench a woman yawns. She is the one he never knew was watching, the one he doesn't even notice until he's breathing fast and reaching for the sill: Anna Ballantyne, the deliberate stranger with dark curved hair, eyes pointing upwards and to the left as if she had word something bigger was on its way. Finn Causley waits for a sign. She sits on her hands, bare knees gleaming beneath the Kandinsky dress, her face a pale secret against the bushes that surround the pool. She glances down and smiles. It's not a smile that expects a lover: it's an accident in the darkness, something in the moonlight on the water that scatters before he can catch her eye. So he keeps it to himself, and never asks why she was watching him – for she'll say she wasn't watching him, she was looking upwards and to the left, to her escape route between the rhododendron bushes, the two flights of steps leading up to the road.

He pushes back and floats, lit by the water he has broken and the glitter that settles around the pool. The colours are green, black, blue. They are the colours of the moonlight and a single streetlamp behind a screen of trees; they are also the colours of Anna's dress, the simple cotton sundress that has brushed bare flesh at hostels and beach parties in all the harbour cities of the world. Five months into her year-long trip, the colours are fading and the hem is turning to fur. But to Finn Causley, with a film of brine on the surface of his eyes, it is as fresh as a new envelope, and Anna has been slipped into his delirium by an invisible hand, to show him how memory begins. How does it end? Seven years later, in a junk-filled room on the other side of the world, will she still look at him with that half-intended smile, as if to say she's only looking because he happens to be here, and the secrets he brought her here to witness – framed prints and rocking horses and crates of household trivia – might interest her but probably don't? No: one thing at a time. One day he'll know who she is waiting for; he'll understand that she didn't come down to the poolside because she really cares who turns up in the water, but because she promised to meet someone, and there are nights in cities when young travellers don't need to be alone.

Breeze ruffles the rhododendrons, gleaming swimmers giggle and slip back into shadows, and Anna takes it in with a patient gaze. Finn tips back his head: more of the cool water, a very dark blue sky, and an inverted snapshot of his hotel-mate Roxanne, neck-deep in water, taking a new lover in her nut-brown arms. It was Rox who started it, left the blue hotel to go skinny-dipping in the public pool, on a night when a young woman's nakedness could charm a city out of its clothes. But it's not her that Anna is looking at now: it's Einar, their housekeeper from Reykjavík, who has seen enough of other people's smoochery and is hauling himself from the water with only one thought on his mind. Anna reckons the gap between the bushes. She knows his next move is to squeeze up close beside her, try to cajole her into dropping the Kandinsky dress and joining him for a few lengths under the stars. But Einar remembers his modesty: a flash of his Viking nudity and he looks around for cover, and Roxanne's cast-off purple one-piece fits him like a rubber glove. Anna checks her watch for the millionth time. Tight as a wrestler in borrowed lycra, Einar lurches towards her, powered by boredom, whisky and lust. Now, instead of rehearsing her escape, she is looking straight at Finn:

it's her first night back in Sydney and she has to look at something, if only to prove to her obscenely budding admirer that the thing she's waiting for has still not come into view. And what happens? Instead of introducing himself as a new member of the hotel clientele, Finn is suddenly aware how much of Finn is obvious; he kicks out from the side and drifts away to the shallow end of the pool.

He drifts for seven years. Friends become lovers, stars change places above the harbour, drunks shiver and stumble back into their clothes. Finn Causley finds other memories to deal in, the sort that make you old before your time, until hair draws back across your forehead and your skull gleams like the light on a swimmer's skin. Even now, I still have it cropped so short that it's guesswork where frown ends and fuzz begins (yes, this is Finn's story, and all those jokes about being bald by thirty are getting painfully close to the truth). I still have the blue-and-green friendship band she gave me on her last night in the hotel; I still get that feeling in the back of the neck when I remember how she watched me: the guarded smile, the perfect stillness of the gaze. Seven years later, I can hardly forget the evening it began, when life was more real than memory, before Bliss became the preferred disorder for a new generation of travellers, and the past was no longer something on which anyone could agree. And although you, Anna, will dispute the details (I know you're watching, I have that affliction in my spine), there are pictures that are truer than any photograph or film: a night at a swimming pool, scrambled messages transmitted through fingertips and skin, and seven years wondering what you would have made of this naked stranger if you hadn't been waiting for something else.

I am happy now. I have a child and my child has a mother. I remember some things with an intriguing certainty, and the rest I'm happy to forget. I like to recall what happened that night at the swimming pool, before the dream that brought us here, before I began to fill this makeshift warehouse with evidence of good lives and hopeless deaths. When my happiness has got me thinking particularly hard, my eyes drift off to the right and my forehead crumples in a frown. You might hear me humming a tune. The problem is History: not the fates of nations and grand impractical schemes, but the sort of history made by cheap useful objects: what's dusty on your sideboard, what's sticky at the back of your drawer. The problem is History, and the solution is Bliss. In the years since it began to stir, Bliss has made happiness an affordable dream for everyone, and, according to my marketing experts, other people's happiness is now my main concern. My business is a great success. I fraternise with scrap merchants, scavengers, antique dealers, fat men in unmarked vans; I provide basic employment for the best of my fellow travellers, those of them (so goes the joke) who still have minds to put to work; I stand on my podium under a fluorescent light and sell the stories of your lives, so that no one goes away without their own little bit of history, a trinket they can prop on the mantelpiece and lie about to their heart's content. I am a simple sort of artist. There is a colour, a very deep colour, which, matched with black and a little blue, is the only colour an artist needs. It is the colour of the bushes around that saltwater pool, of clothes left in a pile on a wooden bench, the screen of water that hid a young man from a stranger's eyes. It is the colour of a particular kind of certainty, a quality of memory that has no historical or biochemical precedent. It is late spring in England, evening light fills the windows of a disused mill, and I'm wearing wintergreen jeans, a green cotton shirt and green canvas shoes. That's my colour. I'm starting now, I am perfectly new.

The Catalogue

LOT
1

It is not beautiful. If the width of the cloth bonnet is reckoned at just under an inch, it is five or six inches tall. The woman is seated at a wooden throwing wheel, attending to a nail in the floor in front of her, hands raised to the frame. Her dress is purplish green. Once you have turned her in your hands and looked at the hand-painted letters on the base, you'll be able to refer to her by name: 'The Silk Twister', modelled by a William Ellis in the year 1832. Don't be too impressed by the date: the first item in the catalogue is not much older than the one who is compiling it. It was bought for my dead mother by my very-much-alive father during a visit to the area in the year of their marriage and my sister's birth. It almost made it back here, too: Dad says he found it in the boot of the family Cortina, which someone else found, wheels turning and engine running, in a windblown ditch with a good view over Blacksheep Moor. You have to take my father's word for it. I know he saw more in it than a symbol of a marriage that always looked outwards more than it looked in, and whatever it was saying, it was more than he wanted to hear. For twenty years it lay wrapped in tissue paper and the greater darkness of our attic, as if he thought the exclusion of light could shift traces of an already faint expression: a cast to the porcelain eyes which, in better light than this, can be named as abiding disenchantment, given shape by recent shock.

For the moment, while I think of words to describe her significance in my life, I have pushed her close up to the window, where the night outside can see as much of her as I can. She can't run away; she is tied to her wheel; it is in the nature of her work. Besides, she belongs here, in a mill built for just this kind of industry, even if it sometimes bothers me to see how much she puts into it and how little she takes out. She twists and twists until her fingers burn and her face glazes with sweat. No one comes to pay her or place a cushion over her wooden stool; her owner admires her with a purely commercial eye, and she is not asked to return his look. Otherwise there is not much to choose between us. We each have our aching eyes and our eternally revolving tasks. I have set myself to find a place for her among the ordinary heirlooms that clutter up our three floors of living space, and she has to twist four silk threads to produce an organzine warp. If I had to distil her essence, I would say she represents two distinct but interdependent industries, without which the story of this patch of central England would not have been a story at all. But only theorists are interested in symbols. I have her here because she is knowledgeable about things I do not understand; she is one of the shapes these empty spaces configure themselves around, and if I can learn her outline I might, just possibly, be able to work out where the two of us have been.

I can't pretend she's irreplaceable. She is little more than a local speciality, one of a fragile army of china statues whose charm brought prosperity to these valleys of coal and marl. In a while I'll be showing you the bottle ovens, grim as pyramids against a smoke-dark skyline, stoked by men with pale skin and blue eyes. We'll drive along the canal and see how the clay came in and the pots went out, to America, India, Europe, wherever tea was sipped and English voices were heard. We'll see how things remember what their makers forget, how the ovens crumbled and nothing was ever thrown away. Then we'll come back here to celebrate a quieter industry, which begins with the mulberry tree and the cocoon of a pale oriental moth, where on certain late spring evenings you can still hear the sound of thread being drawn through steel hoops, as if women in coarse green dresses still twisted from twilight to twilight in each of these purring mills.

We call this place Big Kimberley. 'Why?' says Robinson, remembering that curiosity is an important part of being three. 'What's it for?' says Linden, the day he drives here in his red Y-reg Mustang, leaving a trail of lead fumes and unfinished sentences to a city two hundred miles to the east. 'Couldn't you find anything bigger?' says my clean-shaven and fragrant father, trying to be funny or trying to put me down. 'Why is he always trying to put you down?' says Hen, from the bed across the room; she vanishes, of course, the moment I look up from the screen. 'Where's Hen?' say the others at varying delays, as if her disappearance were a rather tasteless conjuring trick and I a white-faced clown. And Robinson again, the little boy she left with me for safekeeping, the only one of us with any right to an answer, asks: 'When's she coming home?'

No answers but in things. Lot 1, 'The Silk Twister', a five-and-a-half-inch Staffordshire figurine, slightly chipped around the base (First Rule of the Auction: all lots taken strictly as seen), from the catalogue of the Royal Etruscan Manufactory (1962–1967). Big Kimberley has three floors. Every one of them is crammed to the roof with objects, noted down on a list, labelled with a paper tag, recorded in a yellow folder for the day their owners return to collect them or, if Bliss gets there first, when blokes in blue overalls hold them up to an expectant auction room and wait for the bidding to begin. Ceramics from Etruria, kitchen utensils from Sheffield, silk scarves from moorland towns . . . things that would have gone on cluttering up surfaces and casting unremarkable shadows, if events had turned out differently in certain brains. Sometimes, I'll admit, they're little more than lot numbers, items of more or less value in the auction room, worth nothing until someone shows an interest with a respectable bid. At other times, when the light is right and minds are open, they're so full of other people's stories that it's all we can do to remember our own. That's when the bids start flying and our customers go away with creaking cars and faraway smiles. That's the time to wander around the storage bays, try to count the countless plastic crates, cardboard boxes and packing cases, and hear the whispering of ten thousand common objects: did you, were you, was she, tell me, tell me again.

But there are some things, like this figure rescued from the boot of a badly parked car, that are too precious to leave to the chaos of the

---

Lot 1: **Porcelain figurine**, from an early nineteenth-century design, depicting a young woman in a common industrial scene.

storage bays, whose stories are too sensitive to let them find their way in any ordinary sale. They need special treatment: daylight, a room of their own, time for careful observation, until, with a barely audible sigh, they spill their secrets onto a magnetic disc like the one now spinning under my palms. (For ever, said my father, pushing his gift into her hands; and the Silk Twister witnessed her first lie.) They fill the glass cabinet across from this desk, where an oval in the dust on the top shelf marks where this bit of my mother's life belongs. They occupy corners under tables, displace the darkness from cupboards, distress old pine shelves with their accumulated weight. They drive us mad with their stories. They can tell you why a young woman's car came off the road in fair conditions, with no sign of mechanical failure, in by no means the remotest part of the moor. They can explain the expression on the Silk Twister's face: a suggestion of having seen something she wasn't supposed to see, a reason, perhaps, for the accident that bit a mother-shaped chunk from a family and split the remainder along a seam of forgetfulness. They can tell you how one of the children grew up, travelled the world, realised the one thing he wanted from life had other ideas, and became a junk merchant with a three-storey warehouse and a sky-blue van. And, if you really know about patient observation under difficult conditions, and are no stranger to some of the nasty diseases that are going around, you might even find out why, twenty years after that first accident, another little fair-haired boy is looking around for his mother with the same brave hope in his eyes.

On a still May evening in the middle of the moors, with only the odd Manchester-bound lorry to draw a line through the silence, things can speak for themselves. On the creaking drop-leaf table that serves me as a desk, a laptop computer hums and glows. Wait long enough and you'll hear the chatter of the keys, as words are broken down and put back together on the screen, and another seemingly worthless object is assigned a lot number and two lines of dry descriptive prose. Across the flickering streetlamps and slate roofs of Print, and far into the lit-up world beyond the moor, people are falling asleep one by one, or just forgetting they were ever awake, blinking out like candles under an airless sky. Out of sight on other floors, my fellow travellers entertain themselves with memories of waterfalls and canyons, unforgettable nights in boxy hostel rooms. A phone rings in the office on the first floor and is answered after four bleats by a machine. Thank you for calling BK Storage Services. We're sorry there is no one here to take your call.

And others work. People walk past this room and say: He is writing a catalogue, he must not be disturbed, he wants to break the past down into manageable units so that everyone can have a share. He is a democrat. He is a fair boss. Others think the reason he is itemising all this junk is so he'll know what prices to ask, he never used to be interested in objects, it's only the thought of lining his pockets that turns those lips up in a smile. Some say he only seems this cheerful because he never thinks of all the things that are around to hurt him; he reckons he can fill the gaps in his life by shutting his eyes and humming a tune. There are others, people with names, who don't realise he is writing about people as well as things. Jack will walk past, saying something in Middle English which none of us, except Einar, will understand. Einar will answer in the Icelandic of the Sagas, two medieval tongues a-duelling, and their own cleverness will make them grin. The dead also speak, and the half-dead, the people who found the answers to their lives by forgetting the questions, and now have nothing to do but smile. Hen Threadgold, mother of Robinson, sits in a white gown in a room across the moor and remembers saying: 'Of course I want to keep it. He will have his name in the paper. He will be the only man I ever loved.' She remembers saying it but she no longer remembers what it means. And because she can no longer read, because words are nowhere near as interesting as the paper on which they're written, she will never be able to replace what she has forgotten with any new version of the truth. She would rather investigate the properties of natural materials, the textures of surfaces and walls, the way evening light gives a quiet voice to things.

Then when the public dead have spoken, the private dead have their turn. A woman stands in the doorway in a 1970s raincoat, showing every sign of recognising the statue on the desk, recalling the day she took it to be valued in a city ten miles south of here. Her face is in shadow but her eyes gleam. A piano plays a childish tune. She looks around at these cluttered shelves, and remembers her son saying he wanted to be a famous architect, to love a young woman with dark curved hair. But to traffic in objects, quarry for memories in dusty cupboards, try to find meaning in the relics of undistinguished lives? She speaks with her eyes. Ribbons, cushions, silk ties? Medals, birdcages, plates? Is this why you followed me here? Is this what you wanted to find?

When we came here we were already a family. Finn was counting cars on the M6 and wondering why a Kandinsky sundress was still there when he closed his eyes; Hen, who had never worn a sundress in her life, had lost her concentration and her teaching job, and was crossing the broken line (this exit, on the left) for the promise of an entirely new life; and Robinson, the third corner of their love triangle, was strapped into the gap between them, trying out his handful of vowels. The sign said Etruria. The slip road made a tight three-quarter turn, tipping the kid to one side of his baby seat and sending his soft horse flopping to the floor of the van, then a dual carriageway ran straight and hedgeless for one or two miles. If the names on the signposts were familiar, it was only because a curious child had once spent the best light of many evenings with an Ordnance Survey map spread out on a kitchen table, trying to place the spot where his mother began her ascent. The landscape wasn't so different from the affluent south: more hills for sure, and valleys crowded with houses, but where was all this noxious chemical machinery, the nuclear wasteland flashed up on southern TV screens whenever jobs were lost or bodies were found in cars? It began to look as if we'd been misinformed. Then six chimneys shot up ahead and to the left, sunlight shredded on the corrugated roof of a tyre factory and, softened by their own haze, the Towns ran down to meet the road.

Etruria, let's face it, was no more than the idea for a city: the Towns were where people clocked on and clocked off and, when Bliss drove its circus into town, watched the procession with forgetful smiles. The idea, given to the world in a glossy brochure from the development office, was to take a conurbation founded on clay dust and a common industry, put a pin through the heart and call it a city, and hope a new industrial miracle would rise from the cold ovens of the old. Etruria was where the blindfold planner made his mark, the showpiece metropolitan centre that shone out above the warehouses in blue plastic and orange brick. We drove through, looking for clues. You don't have to have been born there to guess they were selling replacement windows and mobile phones, that the car parks looked like shopping centres and the shopping centres looked like factories, and that it would have made more sense if it had been raining, just so the sky could match the skyline, which was the colour of bloody steel. In a downstairs room an old woman cleaned the inside of a window, net curtain tucked into the rail. THERE IS STILL HOPE said the plastic signs tied to three successive lamp-posts; the fourth hung from one corner and dithered in a slight breeze.

And three southerners were smiling, because it was new and they were really lost and, with all the blue skies stretched before them, it was not hard to be leaving some things behind. Anyway, said Hen with feeling, even the thought of sleeping in some long-lost uncle's draughty barn sounded better than that flat on Bristol Street.

'I'll tell you something.' She's always telling me something, with that croaky, insistent voice. 'One more day in that place and they'd've carried me out in a strait-jacket, no a bin-bag, no I mean a body-bag, SORRY AM I BORING YOU?'

Finn starts from a daydream. Behind blue-and-pearl sunglasses her brain spins like a bike wheel, throwing out ideas that her lips will never catch.

'Do you mind? I put a lot of work into that flat. That bathroom was the best thing I ever did.'

'No darling, the best thing you ever did was coming back from Australia and falling in love with me. Isn't that right Robin? Anyway, it was all my design. You just connected up the pipes and slapped on a few tiles.'

'Yeh?'

'Yes. You started as a skivvy and ended as my sex slave. Always said those handcuffs would come in useful . . .'

Our son thumps the side of his seat. A bubble forms between his lips and expands no further. You'd think he was a medieval king, fat and panting after a banquet, cheeks so plump he can hardly see over them, banging down orders with his right arm.

'And now you're going to be working for me . . .'

She scowls behind the shades. 'Oh, I was bored of teaching anyway. All those kids running around and screaming and being sick everywhere. It did my head in if you want the honest truth.'

'Hen?'
'What?'
'I love you.'
'You'll get over it. Thousands have.'

That's how we were in those days: always ready to answer a joke with a joke, never doubting that when the time came to cut the smiles and say what we really meant, we'd have no trouble finding the words. If you'd asked us whether this was what we wanted – the baby, the flat, the two-hundred-mile drive to a new life in an unknown town – you wouldn't have seen us for knowing grins. We'd learned that if you never spoke about the past it didn't bother you; we were in love and could only think of the future; we were in love because we said 'I love you' hundreds of times a day. Even in her absence, which is the sort of steady hum of central heating, I can feel the certainty she put out, this faith that if she'd chosen something it had to be right, for the mere fact of her choosing it. What's more, with her phenomenal memory for every word we'd ever uttered in anger or jest, you really believed she had everything planned.

'Anyway, there was just something about the place. I think it always reminded me of Simon. After all, he was the reason I moved to Norwich in the first place. That absolute utter piece of shit.'

'You know what?'
'What?'
'You can be in a place too long.'
'Oh yes. Very deep.'

She slumps back and bangs her wrists against the steering wheel. With this action – sudden, violent, well-rehearsed – she's trying to remind me of something, something she daren't put into words, from one of the days we no longer mention. I mean the day it all began, a September evening after a smattering of rain, when I went round to the flat with my notebook and tape-measure to find that all she'd told me on the phone that afternoon, about how Simon Hughes had left and taken everything that wasn't nailed down, was true. When? Well, counting back from the day of our arrival in Etruria, maybe two and a half years. I was running a small business from a two-roomed flat in Norwich, giving quotes on all sorts of interior conversions and making up the hours behind a bar. 'You look too complicated for a builder,' she said, clearing books from a chair. 'It's your face, it's like one half of you is smiling while the rest stays, ooh, *totally* cool.'

She told me about her time with Simon: moved to Norwich for the sole purpose of getting off with him ... looked a bit like David Cassidy on the rare occasions when he smiled ... made a fair bit of cash as a lawyer for Norwich Union ... raped some young professional in their supposedly sacred bed while she was telling a class of seven-year-olds about life as a Roman slave. When it was obvious she wasn't going to say any more, I told her about my business – how I'd got into it, what I was hoping for – and felt her amused gaze on my skin. When I said something she agreed with, she nodded in this crook-necked way, as if rubbing an ear on a shoulder to alleviate an itch. I finished my story and looked back at her, waiting.

'Let's get out of here,' she said,

and she drove us in a knackered 2CV to a pub on the outskirts of Norwich, and I could see that instead of cotton sundresses she wore stuff like jeans, a trendy long-sleeved yellow top and silver Viking hair clip, and that she was by no means the sort who'd have me dreaming up attic love-nests on rainy afternoons. She did things, said things, which I knew, preferring my women moonlit and mysterious, would soon get on my nerves. Like this: slumping back in her seat and bringing hands down on the steering wheel, just for the energy of it, to let us know she was there. I told her I'd given up on love affairs the day I lost my hair in a radiation accident. 'That's very funny,' she said, squinting and dropping hands into her lap. Then laughed, tipping back her head as if to gulp a purer layer of air, a rich high ha ha ha.

The pub was pink pebble-dash and fake oak beams. She parked in the sloping car park, turned to me with glimming eyes and asked her question with no expression at all.

'What now?'

'A drink?'

'Not what I had in mind.'

'What did you have in mind?'

She cut the engine and looked across the car park. 'We could always borrow a car.'

'We've got one,' I said.

'It bores me.'

'I think it's all right.'

'Cor, where's your sense of adventure?'

Finn sweated to death in the passenger seat. In the wet twilight she was birdlike, golden, every feature moving as she spoke.

'Bit obvious, isn't it? Prove you're young and reckless by stealing some poor bastard's car?'

She looked at me with the most alluring smile, sweet harmless madness overtaking her and threatening to overtake me.

'I wasn't thinking of some poor bastard. I was thinking of that Ferrari Testosterone over there in the corner. Anyway, what's wrong with being obvious? If I'd been worried about being obvious I wouldn't have phoned up to ask you over. And then where would we be?'

'At home.'

'Oh yes. But in my opinion, if you want something you have to go out and get it. Otherwise, life, ha, it's a waste of time and money.'

I can't say that's what sealed it. But I know that if a certain part of me, something I had always trusted with my most important decisions, had curled up and gone to sleep instead of standing on tiptoe for a better view, our relationship would have ended with her driving me back to my two-roomed flat and wishing me luck in finding a life. Instead she shifted her hips in the seat, smoothed the jeans over her thighs, and little crises of obedience broke out throughout my nervous system. It was bad luck, a rebound case. She was not the type I'd travelled the world to find. But I had a childish curiosity and a list of questions that got longer as the weeks went by. Who taught her to bypass the alarm on a BMW? When did she stop setting fire to bus-stops in sleepy hamlets? Where did she learn to spot a reliable dealer in a crowded pub, when the band was so loud and the smoke so thick you could hardly tell Rona's Surfboard from Hen's hay-fever pills? And who damaged her like that, made her so unwilling to trust anyone in the future; whose past left such a taste in her mouth?

'What odd colour legs she's got! That woman crossing the road. *That woman!* That's what they used to call Mrs Thatcher. Remember her? Course you do. You're humming to yourself, you must be having more of those guilty thoughts. COME ON GRANDAD GET A MOVE ON. Oh, that reminds me, did you say your uncle's got sheep? I hate sheep. They're so ... *disappointing*. And cows! Cor, we'd better hurry up and find a place to live.'

We were headed for the town of Print. Radio Etruria guided us with a report on a woman found wandering in a duvet cover on Blacksheep Moor, claiming to be looking for the sixth Earl of Chester, the testimony of her bloodstream complicated by substantial traces of unnatural phenethylamines. Hen had been found in similar circumstances some few weeks earlier, on the wooded common across the road from St Peter's County First School, having left a class of nine-year-olds to fish for water-boatmen on their own. One of them, a princess named Janice Brown, told a small internal inquiry that (a) Miss Threadgold was drunk; (b) Miss Threadgold's behaviour had, quite frankly, always been somewhat unpredictable; and (c) Miss Threadgold had used one earthworm and three fly agaric toadstools to put a special medieval spell on them so they would never find their way out of the enchanted wood. Well, it was not much of a charge. Lunchtime drinking caused Hen nothing but a pain behind the eyes, and the days we would enhance our love with chemical treatments had ended the day Robinson was born. So it's a surprise to hear her picking up on this story about the woman in the duvet, as if it meant her own attempts to commune with the undergrowth had been more than a harmless blip.

'So I told them, by the time I found my way back to the pond the jam jars were empty and they'd all wandered off. Except they said it was me who wandered off! I'd say it was not amnesia but the repression of a painful memory. I think I was alive at some point in the historical past and something happened to me which I'm still trying to shut out. Don't look at me like that. You're always going on about how I've changed, I'm different, I'm not the girl you first met.'

When Hen went into hospital, there was a moment when all her symptoms, all the eerie silences and enigmatic smiles, seemed to fall together so convincingly that we couldn't believe we'd never noticed the pattern till now. But in the days I'm remembering – when all we knew of St Mary's Disease was another dim warning from the experts, a few more words for what we didn't understand – I was too busy listening for signs of economic recovery to notice the trouble waiting ahead. I had started up in business at the worst possible time, with borrowed tools and little expert knowledge beyond a few tricks I'd picked up over summer holidays working for the family firm. By family, I mean Mervyn with the grey sideburns and the power-tool hands. Mervyn was my mother's brother. I worked for him in my year off before college, and together we ripped out the insides of houses all over Essex and replaced them with airy rooms and heat-efficient windows. I loved the work. I made fewer mistakes but asked bigger favours, and Uncle Mervyn, struck for the millionth time by my likeness to his dead sister, was generous, patient and kind. So when I came to him with my Australian tan and said I wanted to start up in business, he didn't laugh the way my father did: he lent me tools and sold me my first van. It fell apart on me at the same rate as my business did, and it might have taken me even further down the road to ruin if our new family situation hadn't demanded something bigger. We traded it in for a sky-blue twelve-foot box van, another of Mervyn's fleet, with money from my father's second wife. The same money will keep cropping up all over the place, so make a note of its colour and smell.

So we're driving, following the blurry line on the left side of the road. There is a colour here, among the dwindling outskirts of Etruria: Hen's yellow hair. My palette has no other name for it than yellow; my inside information says it isn't bleached, or poured out from a bottle marked Butterscotch or Strawberry Blonde. The only artificial treatment is the lemon juice she rubs in at the sink in the morning, when she still looks too young to be a mother, burying her face in a towel. Against her black hairband, in four o'clock sunlight, it is the colour of a magnificent bird. Trust her to start singing. 'Ask your father if he knows this one!' The rust-red terraces have dropped away, the canal has put in a brief appearance disguised as a ditch, and we're doing fifty for the first time since we left the motorway.

'This is the story of a great Abbey, founded in the year 1214 by Ranulph de Blundeville, sixth Earl of Chester, in the ancient Manor of Print.'

Robinson struggles in his seat. Hen clears her throat, scowls, then is shouting her lesson above the noise of the moor.

'Listening? Ranulph de Blundeville had a grandfather, who was also called Ranulph. Now, before he died, Old Randy had already founded himself an abbey over the border in Wales, but his monks were getting fed up of having to steal their sheep back off the marauding natives, and there's nothing worse than an unhappy monk. Young Ranulph had just had a dodgy divorce and was feeling in need of a bit of penance. You don't know what penance is? Well, wait till you have a little lambikins of your own.'

A baby yawns. Farms flash by on both sides, rising to warm green hills.

'So anyway: it's a stormy night in autumn and Ranulph the younger is taking himself off to bed. He's just got back from the Crusades and he's feeling the cold. The wind is blasting straight through his bedroom and right up his nightshirt. On top of that the pillow is lumpy. He tosses and he turns. Then the wind lets rip with a sudden gust and blows the candle out: puff! Ranulph sits up and looks around. There, sitting in the chair by the window, is the ghost of his grandfather, looking like death warmed up. The ghost starts talking – in French, of course, cos everyone spoke French in them days – but luckily I have a translation:

'"Remember that monastery I founded?" Yes, don't laugh, ghosts really *do* talk like that. "Well, you've got to shift it." "What?" says Ranulph. "The big churchy thing," says the ghost. "But the brothers!" squeals Ranulph. "They've no sense of direction!" "Come on," says the ghost, "this isn't the Dark Ages." And he draws a map on the floor with his bony finger, takes a roll of paper from his pocket and tells him what to do.

'Ranulph's up the chimney with terror. The wind moans and moans. In the morning, over a light breakfast in the orchard, he tells his new wife about his visit. "Why didn't you call me?" she says. "I want to know what the shopping's like." Anyway, they shift the abbey here to Print and decide to call it Dieulacres, which means "Oh my God" in French. There. That's the story. Now, ask your father why *he* decided to bring us here.'

What? All right, I had a dream too. There was no ghostly grandfather or thirteenth-century nightshirt: it was a simple dream of country roads and a badly parked car. This, if you hadn't guessed, is Blacksheep Moor. I've been marking this place on maps since the day in April 1977 (I was a bendy thin-necked nine-year-old) when I realised a mother was not the sort of thing that stays around for ever, like a bald patch or a scar. We're on the north side of Etruria, which, on the road atlas we've been following, shows up as a yellow splodge of civilisation bisected by a thin black railway line. I know the route she took from the city centre, after meeting a man in a collector's shop to discuss a certain porcelain figurine, which is now wrapped in a square of silk and hidden in the boot of the car. I can read the contours on an Ordnance Survey map and see how the bunching of the orange lines corresponds to a sharp drop in the land. Years before I came back here for myself, I could imagine how a particular detour from the main road to Print gave a clear view over the valley and slate-roofed farms. But I had never dreamed the outcome of that decision: pylons, ditches, the colours of sky and road, the sights that met her eyes at the end of this most secret journey, what on any other day would have been a simple trip across the moor.

Look out of the window to the left, and you'll see a road that winds across the moor to the villages of Schyre and Mead. The blue Cortina, polished to a shine by memory, turns into this road, accelerates, and vanishes around the curve. There are dry stone walls and hovering birds. At this point Hen will keep on driving until we find the turning for my aunt's farm, but in my dream of the preceding months, the one that set all this in motion, we followed the blue Cortina across the moor. Or let's just say we turned the corner and there it was, dumped up onto the verge, front wheels turning in the ditch, radio spilling friendly voices into the air. Is that a figure asleep in the driver's seat, or has someone unclipped their seatbelt, put a shoulder to a caved-in door, and crossed a small footbridge into an open field? Shoeless in a strange heat, feeling lush grass and moss between the toes. I am a woman with children, I don't know the area, I cannot explain why I am here.

There is sound, too, in this dream. The music came into my head without warning, reminding me of a song I used to hear. When you're young you are told to gather in a room and make noises with your hands and throat. There is a woman who plays piano music on the television, on the programme you watch when you come home from school. Here they come, Izzy, Lizzy and Joe. She sits at the piano, presses the keys and moves the pedals with her feet. Her lips move as she plays. The words are lost but you never forget the tune; you never forget her long face or her sad anxious smile. Hide, Izzy, hide! Run, Lizzy, run! Twenty years later, the telly is on and my son is dancing to the piano waltz. And my mother is dead, her music comes to me from a place I do not understand, I cannot find my mother anywhere.

LOT
2

How Finn Causley came to be the owner of a redundant silk mill, its idle ghosts and the acre in which it stood; how in the time it took to snap a handcuff into place he was transformed from a slow-witted, even clumsy lover to the single parent of a three-year-old son; how he came to be dealing in other people's memories with as much skill and cool as if he and Uncle Mervyn were still converting cellars or turning garages into self-contained flats; and how, catching sight of a green May oak (green, the colour of his well-worn clothes, the backdrop to his wildest dreams), he came to be thinking about one star-attended evening at an open-air swimming pool when his most trusted helper, Einar Björnfríðursson, was moving in on the girl he loved ... What's the proper order for these questions, and are they really a clutch of notes from which a jazzman with a feel for human suffering could pick out a melody and improvise a life? Einar tends to frown at all such suggestions, which, with foreheads like ours, is not a joke. 'This life of yours,' he goes, 'it's not a Miles solo. It's more like a rock ballad which goes on for ever with enormous guitars. Besides this, Anna is waiting for Duncan – she only *seems* to be looking at you. Maybe you are new, and therefore interesting to her in some way. Or more likely it is the other way up.'

It's his logic I can't stand. And this thing he's holding, not telling me if it's a bunch of violets or a brick. He sort of cups it in his hands and nuzzles it against his cheek, as if he'd like to irritate me further by pretending it wanted to be loved. We're in that part of Brink Farm that smells of carpet and always makes us gloomy, even though the paint on the walls is as white as God. 'Let me look at it,' and he shoves it behind his back.

'It came from over there. Yes mate I have stolen it.'

Bloody mischief flickering in those ice-blue eyes . . . And I might be laughing, if recent events at Big Kimberley hadn't made arguments over property such a familiar sound. It's a matter of days since our friend Linden Smedlund announced to a hushed room that if any more of his possessions were eaten, drunk, moved, hidden or tampered with in any way he would be leaving our little community in his Y-reg Mustang to go and build his avant-garde furniture elsewhere. His huge hairdo quivered with rage. One or two of us coughed. The culprit was back in his own flat-cum-recording studio, amid patch leads and signal processors which most here wouldn't know how to switch on. But less than a week ago Jack was at Big Kimberley, treating two female friends to an impromptu party in the room we call the Chapter House, and between them they finished off half a bottle of Linden's Glenmorangie which he had hidden, one might say carelessly, in the linen press in the corner. We're all honest people, so when Jack, with a typically theatrical hangover, says he'll replace the booze as soon as the money comes through from his European deal, we've no reason to doubt his word. But until then, don't be surprised to see Linden kneeling by his intensive care fish tank and counting off every brilliant pet as though he can hardly believe they're all there.

But this is not about domestic squabbles. This is Einar saying he's been working long enough this morning to deserve a little diversion, which is why he's been pointing at the shelves above the fireplace and yawning like a lion for longer than I care to think. Granted: when there are so many objects around, and at least one word for every object, it's no surprise that I use more of them than I need. It certainly has its effect on my right-hand man. Without constant entertainment he's so quickly bored: his mouth stretches into ever more perfect ellipses, eyelids crumple and brows pile up on his forehead in a crush of pink-and-orange flesh.

'I give up.'

'You were staring out at that tree, I think it is an oak tree, and going on about our life at the Point Hotel as if it is interesting to anyone except yourself. So I think I will commit a crime.'

It changes hands behind his back, allowing me a glimpse of something white and egg-ish. Then more of the slit-eyed smirk. If we stay like this for ten more minutes, with barely enough light to pick each other out against the anaglypta, I can't say I'd complain. It's been a hot and stroppy morning in the downstairs rooms of Brink Farm, sweat soaking into the patch of trouser above the knee, shins banging into crates left in hallways, crammed with the contents of cupboards, drawers and shelves. 'What does your auntie do with all this stuff?' he asks, and I leave a weary sigh drifting down. For he knows as well as I do that there are things we can never hope to understand, the crumbs and sweepings of people's lives which, if it wasn't for this thing that's going around, would only ever be pondered over by spiders and woodlice. Take this box I'm holding: I've counted three packs of playing cards, several marker pens without lids, one wing of a pair of child's scissors, three years of Gardener's Diaries with only the first page (*Yesterday he called me Mary*) filled in. If it was my choice I'd torch the lot of it, unable to imagine a reserve price that would make our presence here worthwhile. But we're expected to be thorough, and Einar's pen is twitching. 'Put it down as Ornament, and we'll let Sarah decide.'

Which means we're houseclearing. In fact, what we have here is a special commission, Don and Sarah Long having been our nearest family ever since Hen and I took over their barn and a small community of rodents, and stayed there until we found Big Kimberley. The aunt's farm I mentioned? This is it. Which means we're making inventories, looking at everything twice. The second item in the catalogue, the thing to which Einar has taken such a shine, is Don Long's painted wooden goose. I'd say it was a pre-war piece, though I have no books on the subject. It's certainly been on the shelf in this gloomy parlour for as long as I've been coming here, getting along famously with the framed photographs of underachieving nephews and the pink-and-yellow figurines. But since my uncle Don is now in a public ward at the Etruscan Royal Infirmary with all the symptoms of St Mary's Disease, and since his good wife Sarah knits her days away in a cat-infested maisonette in one of the uglier parts of Etruria, we're having to find it another home. And you can forget about family ties: everything they've left behind is going to be loaded into that sky-blue van, driven to Big Kimberley and kept in storage until we can sell it off to the highest bidder. Being new to this method of supporting children, Einar thinks it's like robbing graves. But then he hasn't quite got the hang of Bliss.

'In Iceland we call it something else. It's when people's brains are so full of information they must get rid of some of it. It happens to everyone over a certain age.'

'Unless they're called Hen.'

'Hen is obviously fed up with you, and is just pretending to have forgotten who you are. Other women have done the same. Anna, for example. Do you know she is going to be a doctor?'

Hen/Anna/Anna/Hen . . . Even with Einar breathing down my neck, and the mere sound of her name making me want to fight my way out of here with a fucked-up heart, I have to keep my feelings to myself. Which is easier said than done, especially when he's trying to pair them off against each other, like he wants me to believe they're two aspects of the same woman, who in turn is a symbol of what I'm lacking in myself. So instead I humour him, and lap up all this cheap brainology as if it were sugared milk. It's therapy, you see. It calms me down. It makes me believe they're all very simple, all the things that have had me terrified since birth. The truth is that Hen and Anna are as different as this and that, which means it should be possible to love one more than the other and not feel too bad about it. At least, that's the theory. And this is my fucked-up heart.

'Why do you mention her?'

'I have no ideas, because she hasn't mentioned you. She seems to think you have disappeared into outer space.'

Note the technique: the casual name-drop, the efficient *coup de grâce*. It must be said, I didn't hire him for any special aptitude for the job. He's here because of his importance as a witness, or just because his insatiable curiosity about what happened between this Finn and that Anna is guaranteed to keep her name alive. He's bashing away at this defence of mine as if it had a fondant centre: I mean the fact that only I, of all the residents of that blue harbourside hotel, know the truth behind the rumours: what Finn said to Anna when he realised who she was waiting for that night; what Anna said to Finn after the swimmers went home . . .

But how to get there from here . . . I could start with Einar, and how he went from being a housekeeper at a backpacker's hostel in Sydney to an auction handler in a junk-infested English town. By the time Australian Immigration finally caught up with him, he was working as a gardener in Adelaide, passing himself off as my old room-mate Wayne Norrie, and claiming a New Zealander's residency and working rights. This was five years ago, two summers after I came home, and Einar's original working visa was already years out of date. The Bruces could do nothing but throw him in a hot cell for a day or two, empty his bank account and put him on a plane back to Reykjavík. He stayed long enough to pay a visit to his mother, who he'd left three years earlier with a message that he was off to Scotland to get drunk, but also to catch up with his last-but-three lover and what he had always thought was his four-year-old son. 'They say they don't know me. In Iceland women get on very well without men. Therefore you can just fuck who you want and then get on a plane. I go to Canada and make friends with a man who drives a van.'

This man was Jim de Groot, who'd been one of the long-stay residents at the Point Hotel, and whose name had been linked with Einar's ever since they were spotted sucking face on the ferry back from Darling Harbour after a run-in with the bouncers at the Pump House. Jim, like me, was in the building trade. Unlike me, he knew how to get work. On returning to Canada the previous year he'd built himself a two-storey house at the edge of a small lake, paying most of his timberyard bills with the cash he'd saved doing height work on sites in North Sydney. Einar showed up just as Jim was glazing the outhouse, and took the downstairs room at the front from which the view was clear over lake and distant hills. They drank for three days and then went fishing, and it was by the side of the lake, a few hours after sundown, that Jim kissed Einar on the chin and Einar dropped his favourite lighter among the reeds. The Canadian mosquitoes were closely related to the Australian kind, and gave them merry hell with bites to the legs and face. It was for this reason that Einar thought they were back by the harbour, on a bench at the rear of the Point Hotel, listening to the roaring of the lions from the zoo on the next finger of land. Jim hummed one of that summer's international hits; fingertips dithered on bare inside legs. Words: 'How long you staying?' 'How long you got?' It takes five minutes to fall in love. The moon flashed as they walked the lawn back to the house, which, because Jim's skills did not extend to making curtains, was filled with the silvery light of fish.

He stayed for two years. I've never been to Ontario, but I've seen the genteel slopes of mid-Essex, and I know the picture money makes when it accumulates on good land at the base of hills. Parties went on till morning, no one was invited, so no one objected to the conversation (Canadian television, the symbolism of the green shirt on the cover of *Milestones*) or the food (smoked puffin, baroque salads, endless potato-based snacks). Einar has shown me a few snapshots of these occasions, but that always leads to an argument about why I have no photos of my own to share, nothing to prove that what I think happened really happened, and that gets us nowhere. 'I understand,' says that sub-Arctic smirk, and he shows me a deliberate stranger with hand-curved hair, and I make some oh-so-casual comment about the character at the edge of the shot or the architecture of the Point Hotel. Then we're back in Ontario, and he's telling me how the sky was always jasper blue, how it was a bad day if love hadn't struck him several times in the form of a sunbathing teenager, and how dark-skinned children hitched rides to school in Jim's van.

Why does something always have to go wrong? Ever since the heady days of Rona's Surfboard, we'd known about Einar's contempt for controlled substances and those who tried to get a little pleasure from them. The barest whiff of dope would have him lurching off, yodelling, making no secret of his belief that whisky and an unselective libido were the only routes to happiness. Fortunately, the effects of Rona's Surfboard were so private that he could hardly ever tell which of our fellow travellers were travelling, and which of us were just naturally elated to be idle on these beautiful shores. All the same, for reasons we guessed at but never really understood, we kept it quiet when Einar was around. 'You are children,' (we pinched each other guiltily) 'you do not know what this shit can do.'

So that's how the trouble began: with Einar's chemical purity. When the dodgy gear was going around, Jim was as keen for a hit as any of us, which meant it was only a matter of time before the detested aroma began to find its way up his lover's hypersensitive nose. One hot night Jim refused to lie about what he had been up to in his own outhouse, the sweet smoke bore aromatic testimony, and Einar hurled himself from a ground-floor window, arms stretched out like a bird, shouting 'Look where this shit is taking you!' Later, on returning from a two-mile run around the local residences, having tried without success to wake one local teenager for whom he had developed a healthy obsession, he did the unforgiveable: he went through Jim's pockets. There he found papers, roach card, stash box and a bottle of small white pills, whose perfect powdery roundness recalled immortal evenings at the Point Hotel, and no doubt, my fellow travellers, brought a few of your smiling faces to mind. He never explained his dramatic leap into the geraniums. He never stayed long enough to hear what Jim had to say. There was another long flight around the rim of inner space, the lights of sleepless cities twinkling like the stubble on his ex-lover's chin, and Einar, stretched across three seats in the no-smoking section, nursing his broken heart and thinking of the little boy in Reykjavík who would never know his father's name.

Three myths about Einar Björnfríðursson, in order of popularity. First, he loves women but he prefers men. He certainly made more of his relationship with Jim de Groot than he did with the mother of his child, but since when (and Anna looks on with that undecided gaze) was time elapsed such a reliable measure of love? Second, as a member of an Icelandic bar jazz band, he was wanted by police in Norway and Sweden in connection with a number of public order offences. He admits playing the trumpet as a church-going youth, but that's where the story ends. And third, he came to England because he specifically wanted to work with me. I know this one's a lie, because it took him five months to track me down, four of which were spent working as a cleaner at a hostel for medical students in Manchester, drinking in the afternoons and spending most nights in the corridor outside one particular room.

'She is revising for her finals at the time. This is why she seems uninteresting in me. I knock on the door and say, Anna Ballantyne, room service! It is just like old times in the Point Hotel.'

As usual he leaves a generous pause to let the name sink in. It doesn't take long. The more the jittery silence yawns around us, the more the trick of breathing escapes me, and it seems I could wait another seven years and she'd still be looking down from her bench, reminding me that you only lose a love like this once in your life, and never really find out why. Some people are lost before they begin, condemned by the worst of genetic accidents to spend their lives searching for one dream-real thing: a guarded smile, a texture of sun-lightened hair, the face the meddling angels printed in your blood. But the sky is no longer deep blue over Sydney, and I know more about love than I did then. I know how it can introduce itself as one thing and turn out to be something else. In fact, the more I see of it, the more I doubt it's an object that would fit into my catalogue with a line or two of descriptive prose. Besides, I have a child, born long after all this happened, and who looks after the children while their parents play games with the past?

So it seems Einar's first task in England was to find Anna and achieve what he'd failed to achieve all those years before. And how did Anna deal with Einar's advances? She smoked cigarettes. She read none of the scribbled notes he pushed under her door. Once she was back in her room in the evening she had few reasons to leave it, and she was usually gone before he woke. Except for one morning in December, when she emerged humming into the corridor to find him standing up, looking very much awake. 'I have not slept. I play with my zip. She thinks I am about to expose myself. She says, What you gonna do, chase me? I tell her I have been here every night for four months. She says, I know, I heard you snoring. Then she says she is going home today.'

This time it's Einar who loses the thread. The fact that he loses it at such a poignant part of the story is, I promise, more coincidence than anything else. He holds the goose against his chest and stares out of the window with a puzzled, slightly sad face.

'I want to find you, Finn. I hate being a cleaner. Ever since the Point Hotel we are really good mates. I think, What is he doing, my friend Finn?'

He is holding his breath, waiting for a mention of her name, the vowel that opens like a cut.

'Yeh, so you know, I am in this corridor with Anna beautiful Ballantyne, and she is telling me she is going home to her mother and her whatdoyoucallit cat. I say, Have you finished your exams? She says, My surgical wasn't too bad but I made a mess of my viva. In my obs and gynie I think I just about scraped through. Here you see I begin to wonder, because I don't remember little Anna being interesting in all this stuff. She says, I was gonna invite you in but I get really worked up about exams and I probably wouldn't have been very good company. What's the time? I gotta get a taxi to the station. You wanna come for a ride?'

So Einar and Anna take a taxi to Manchester Piccadilly on a mild December morning, she (the details are all I have) in a check shirt with at least one button undone, chewing her lip and refusing his whisky with quick smiles. Perhaps because he hasn't slept properly for four months, Einar's speech declines into drivel some three minutes into the journey, and it is left to Anna to fill the gaps. She talks about her elective in Kenya, and it then becomes obvious that little else has happened to her in the six years since she returned from her world tour. She speaks of one fellow medic who holidayed with her in Malta, but at the mention of a possible rival Einar begins to yawn impatiently and poke the corduroy on Anna's knee. 'I decide at this junction she is not the woman for me. Her hair is always tickling. I dunno, mate, I think you like that sort of thing.'

After dry-eyed goodbyes outside the station buffet, he took a different taxi back to the hostel to pick up his rucksack and camping things, and left an address for the forwarding of his wages. Then he disappeared into the public transport network of peacetime England, and on an unseasonably warm evening in December we found him zipped up in his sleeping bag on the front steps to Big Kimberley.

From that moment he's been making out that he always intended to come and work here, with the graverobbers and the junk merchants, even after all the sadness that has visited us since. When he speaks of Anna now, in the doorway of this gloomy parlour, it has more to do with taunting me than expressing any real desire of his own. What's interesting is the way he seems to have transferred all his love onto this grubby wooden goose. He's nuzzling it, sniffing it, turning it in his hands, as if with a little persuasion he could make it sigh out all its secrets. Surprised that such a thing could be so lovable? I wouldn't be. Whatever he's doing to it now is no more

---

Lot 2: **Antique wooden goose**, painted white except for orange feet and beak.

than I've been doing to certain memories of it for the last twenty-five years. I'm thinking about the summers before my mother died, when she and Dad would fly off to the Costa del Something for two weeks of sangria and flamenco displays, and Alison and I had the run of an indulgent aunt and uncle and ninety acres of Brink Farm. This wooden goose which, like the house itself, is gradually losing its coat of paint, is the first thing I remember from those early holidays. It was about the right size for my two-year-old frame, safe enough to require no supervision, and light enough to be carried with me on all my romps through the massive world. I know the heat it generates when pushed along the carpet, which in the early 1970s smelled of a labrador called Sammy, who was always getting into trouble with traffic and lolloped from room to room on four never-quite-mended legs. I know its texture against virgin gums, the way it floats in a tank of rainwater; with the silver armour I put on it, that goose took me into battle against more sword-wielding enemies than I had fingers to count. Perhaps Einar can detect these images in the soft grooves between the grain, where the fingers of children and adults have rubbed away most of the white paint; or perhaps he's better at reading my expression than I give him credit for. Either way, it's in my hands for the first time since April 1977, when Dad decided he would not be having any more Spanish holidays so there was no further need to burden Don and Sarah with two young children. And I'm nine again, eyes red from crying, searching through empty rooms.

Brink Farm. You begin in the small below-stairs bathroom, gazing from the window at a green May oak, drying hands on a faded blue towel; you stand in the hallway, taking light from the stained-glass window at the top of the stairs, and try to remember your way around. You wave at Finn and Einar packing crates in the parlour, put your head around the door of the kitchen and see two children waiting at the table for a meal. From the room opposite comes the sound of piano music: not a real piano, with brass pedals and keys you don't touch unless your hands are spotlessly clean, but the piano that plays the music on the television, all the songs you used to know. You leave that door closed, because it's one room you remember better than any other, and step out into the sunlight of the backyard, still littered with the plastic vehicles of children who went away and never returned. Brink Farm stretches from here up to the road, past oil drums and water butts and barbed wire snagged with tufts of wool, then another ninety acres backwards across the moor.

If there are any mysteries in my family story, one is how my aunt Sarah found her way from a comfortable North Essex terrace to the heathery wilds of Blacksheep Moor. She wasn't alone among the three children in finding marital happiness, but only Sarah found it any distance from home. She was the only one to leave the necklace universe threaded by the A12 (without doubt, said Dad, the worst road in the country, and he'd driven most of them, and he should know), to turn off and keep on driving, leave hot tarmac and steel-filled skies, kestrels and black-headed gulls, and mix our grey-green Essex blood with any other English hue.

Except they didn't mix it, did they? They kept their colours separate, preferring the contrast, while those around them merged. She and Don never stayed up late listening to the kicking of a tiny wrestler in a sack of taut skin, or writing names on the backs of envelopes and testing them out on the silence. No unearthly wails announced the continuation of the Wilton line. Brother Mervyn, with his spirit levels and power tools, was more interested in making things from brick and plaster than from his own sweat and sperm. Did they know something my parents didn't? Was there some genetic secret they were keeping from us, so that when at last a daughter, Alison, was born to Margaret and Peter Causley, followed eighteen months later by a boy called Finn, some of them could hardly bear to lift the blanket to check all the features were in place? You can think what you like. I tell myself their failure to provide us with any cousinly playmates had a simpler explanation: they had farms to run, businesses to establish, better things to do. Sarah milked the cows and took the vegetables to market in an old Land Rover. Mervyn drove his vans around the villages of rural Essex leaving barn conversions everywhere he went. And Margaret, of course, went nowhere, spent her last year in the captivity of an unhappy marriage, bust her walls at too high a velocity and died.

When my grandparents went the same way a year or so later, losing the will to live so suddenly and in such quick succession that you thought they must have been discussing it, my aunt Sarah found herself at the head of a family she had already left far behind. Apart from those two weeks every summer, we hardly saw her. She was straight-headed and practical, happier discussing cattle prices than building airports out of paper; children were as much a mystery to her as the football news. It was Don who took us out in the tractor to show us where the witches gathered, who cooked fish fingers and beans in that sunny kitchen while Sarah typed letters next door. So when our summer breaks at Brink Farm came to a sudden end, with Dad announcing we would in future be spending our holidays with him and our new stepmother, she must have smiled to think they could now grow old in uncomplicated solitude, and never regret not having a family of their own.

At fifty she watched her husband lose his mind. Unlike others I could mention, who slipped away so gradually and quietly that no one really noticed they were going, my uncle approached his fate head on, surprising it the instant before it surprised him. People who saw it tell the same story in the same hushed tones: that Don went in with his fists up, jerking and halting like a boxer, as if his death were not to be a painless switching off of the machine, but an online overhaul, a rewiring of the nervous system that never asked permission and never gave its name. Whatever it was, it made sure he stayed awake. With the same extra sense that told him when one of his animals was in trouble, he knew how things were changing, growing up, disconnecting themselves. How did he put it, one morning in this very doorway? 'Somebody's been here and moved everything. Some joker's come here in the middle of the night and switched everything for something else.'

Then the problem was inside as well as out. Pictures lit his brain, caught his eye with colour and movement, arriving from nowhere and invisible to everyone but him. Just memories, of course, but from a mind he didn't recognise, which gave him patterns of light and fleeting smells when he wanted names, addresses, facts. He rehearsed himself tirelessly, defining himself from every possible angle: 'My name is Don. I am an Englishman. I have lived in this house all my bloody life.' But then Sarah would show him a snapshot of the two of them on their honeymoon, and he'd cough and fidget and frown himself blind. 'What you showing me this for?' 'Because it's us. You know it is.' He stomped out into the yard, brown fists clenched for a fight. But there was no one there, no target for his punches, nothing but the finger in his brain, the invisible mechanic who was reaching into his skull and plucking at the wires.

And as his frown softened, he began to smile. When you've seen the same smile on many others, some of whom are as close to you as you can be to a single person, that's something you're not surprised to hear. Bliss leaves everyone smiling. As legend has it, it's the happy enigma of this smile (to use the newspapers' favourite comparison, its 'Mona Lisa ambiguity') that gave St Mary's Disease its popular name. You've heard the official explanation of the Bliss smile: that it is a muscular response to the nonspecific drugs that are used to control some of the more anti-social symptoms, and which, as a few rare photographs have shown, persists even into death. I know some of my fellow travellers have even stood under fluorescent light in a university pathology lab, scalpel in hand, taking apart someone's final expression to see the roots of the Bliss mask for themselves. They saw a grin without meaning, a random neuromuscular event. Now they could explain what was going on behind those un-recognising stares, what showed up on the PET scans as a diffuse blue glow throughout the top floor of the brain, proof at last that this was a *physical* problem, a disease of the nervous system for which no human conspiracy was to blame. They never had to consider that a smile might stand for happiness; or ask what could have caused a happiness like that, except the pleasure of not knowing what you used to know, cutting loose from history to float free through nameless impressions, forgetting everything that might possibly have caused you pain.

Am I ringing any bells? If Hen was around, she'd tell me they were ringing from our first day as guests at Brink Farm. But we had other things on our mind that summer, and I was too concerned about Hen's own lapses of concentration to worry much about Don. In fact, because I'd seen them so rarely since our holidays here had come to an end, I thought nothing had changed. He remembered how to greet a visitor, what sort of things you could talk about over dinner, how to make a fifteen-month-old squeal with joy. There were few signs of what was rearranging itself behind those deep-set eyes, nothing to suggest he was about to join the ever-lengthening list of people for whom things no longer had any meaning, whose connection with the past was quickly reaching breaking point. Only Hen noticed anything unusual, and she kept it to herself. For me, the only odd thing was the way he would stop at the window and stare out at the horizon, as if one of his animals was in trouble out there, invisible to everyone but him.

Then, almost a year after we'd left Brink Farm to set up Big Kimberley, Bliss burst in on him like a million volts of wonder, crashing his circuits and flooding them with inexplicable dreams. He was in the kitchen, emptying drawers methodically, laying out the bits of junk that had accumulated over twenty years of marriage as if they were relics from a tomb. He was trying to make sense of them from first principles, beginning with shapes, textures and smells, describing them in every detail to a wife who stood silently at the door. A letter was *folded into three equal sections and smelling of sawdust and ink*. An onion was *a round object the size of a man's fist with brown and purple papery skin*. Days were hot and windless; he swore it was hay fever and not sunstroke, but still he skulked indoors with the curtains drawn, the pictures in his head crazing the walls like film. In the end, a curious sensitivity to light meant all rooms were too bright for him, and he took to spending days underground, crouched by candlelight among the junk in the cellar, trying to reacquaint himself with things he had put there to forget.

We pack them up, these clues to a past that became too cumbersome to bear, and carry them out in red plastic crates. In the hall we found the marble horse's head that used to scare Alison and me so much. Next, a walking stick with the brass head of a dog, which Don used to take with him on walks with Sammy. A pile of cash-books tied up with ribbon, Sarah's handwriting curling across every page. Then something like a washing-up bowl, ridged at the bottom to make two separate compartments, which Einar immediately decides is a hat.

Finally we're in the television room. The walls are white with a hint of lilac, which is not how I remember them. In my mind this room has always been blue: not the deep blue of skies over Sydney, but the paler blue of baby-suits and toys. It's the same anaglypta wallpaper that attracts cobwebs and takes the shine off laughter, but the cast-iron fireplace has been taken out and replaced by brick. Stepping across the floorboards to the French windows, you can look out at the paddock at the front, separated from the house by a gravel drive. And there's my mother's car, the blue Cortina she drove to her secret meeting, shining in the sunlight. The moment is broken by events I'm trying to remember, my eyes drift off to the right for an appointment with the forbidden past, and when I turn back to see if those three figures on the back seat were real or even familiar, the drive is empty except for our sky-blue van.

> *Did you ever see a snowman*
> *Walking on the fourth of May?*
> *Did you ever see a lion*
> *Rolling in the hay?*

But what comes next? How do these songs end?

On the sideboard sits a carved wooden box, the sort you'd trip over in any junk shop, bound together by rusty iron plates. The presence of a small keyhole explains why the lid won't lift. If there's anything inside, there can't be much of it, because I'm lifting it with ease and tucking it into the bottom of our last empty crate. The next things in, once I've wrapped them in a few sheets of newspaper, are some paintings made by Don's father in an idle moment between the wars. To my untrained eye, they look like views of Blacksheep Moor.

At the back of the room is a lace-topped table covered with glass. My mother's photograph stands in a tortoiseshell frame. There were always many others – Mum and Dad on the doorstep of our house in Basildon, Mum looking uncomfortable in her yellow bikini – but a woman who has lost her husband needs the comfort of her dead sister, and all the other pictures have been packed up and delivered to her new home. I suspect she left this one for me on purpose, along with the video cassettes stacked up on the floor where the TV used to stand, all marked with the name of a 1970s children's programme.

It's what you'd call a spontaneous portrait. You would swear her hair is nearly black, but my aunt Sarah, in one of her few words to me about her sister, was certain of a reddish tinge in particular lights. Such a phenomenon would surely have been captured on a sunny day on the deck of my father's boat, somewhere between river and open sea. I like to think she's looking out at the horizon, her brain lulled by the crinkling swell, no more imagining a watery death than the one that's racing to meet her on dry land. There's no doubting what Dad admired in her. It's not just its unrepeatability that makes her smile so poignant: there is something in that tilted forehead, head tipped back and eyes narrowing against the wind, that makes her son take more breaths than he needs. It's no surprise that a sensitive boy should be in love with his dead mother, so why does he blush when Einar comes in and looks her way?

'This yo' mama?' he goes. 'So how come you so ugly, mate?'

'That's it. We're finished here,' says Finn.

LOT
3

The town of Print, robust and rarely visited, seen in its best light by drivers cruising over the rise and dropping to third for the descent into the valley, rendered in red brick and a patina of verdigris, the higher ground dominated by three-storey mills and Victorian churches. There are two ways in: you can arrive by road, bearing down on the landmark of the central war memorial, in which case you will always be a visitor; or you can be born here, in the same street as your parents and grandparents, speaking plain English and marrying young. Alternatively, if you're well-practised in this kind of deception and don't mind leaving your past wrapped in newspaper by the old town sign, you can drive in under cover of darkness, install yourself in one of these dim palatial mills and set yourself up in business, being sure to make yourself so useful that ordinary folk will wonder what they ever did (for furniture restoration, long-term storage, general building work, etc.) before you came.

To reach Big Kimberley, go right at the war memorial and follow the curve of the road up the hill. The third turning on the left is Whieldon Street, and it's up here on the right that you'll find the sky-blue van, badly parked and needing a wash, looking somewhat portable next to the neck-breaking immensity of Big Kimberley. If you'd known what to look for, you would have seen a much smaller version of it on your descent into Print, a castle spied from afar, adorning the late spring sky with fancy turrets and ironwork from another century. This is the old red mill that became a warehouse, a storage complex, and eventually a sort of home to those who worked here and a few who didn't. The main entrance is announced by a six-foot green sign and steps leading up to two sets of double doors. Ignore that for the minute: follow the building round into Hope Street, past slate-and-red chequerboard brickwork and arched sash windows, till you reach the handle of a low white door. Inside is an echoing stairwell, tiled yellow like a public toilet, and granite steps leading up to the roof. On the first-floor landing, dusty panes let light through to the selling floor, meanly furnished with wooden podium, schoolroom chairs and a roll of purple carpet. On the second floor, the words NO HIPPIES and DISABLED BADGER HOLDERS ONLY announce the beginning of the living quarters. This is the heart and soul of our brave enterprise, Big Kimberley's sprawling nerve centre, and our refuge from all the odd things that have been going on. It's also a good place to watch the world go by, at least the part of it that takes the short cut through Print.

Here she is, Mrs Enderby, did for her husband with animal fats and milky tea, the same week she matched four numbers on the rollover and blew it all on a flat-tube viewing system with wide-screen technology. She is coming back from Pricecutter with a plastic carrier in each hand, all ready for a hard morning on the phone. Look closely: neither bag contains anything but dog food tins. We're not fond of dogs, not after what Sammy the labrador did to us on that special birthday when we were trying so hard to be kind. 'If you don't like animals,' says Nina, 'I think that really says something about you as a person' – and what it says is that Nina never had to prise stinking labrador jaws from a tender young thigh while a brand new Chopper lay untested on the drive. While Mrs Enderby unpacks her shopping in the kitchen across the road, a twice-shy Finn Causley slurps from a tannin-stained mug and regrets sleeping through another alarm. Outside in the brilliant morning, house martins show off tirelessly and the sky looks close enough to stroke. This, though, is a bonus that comes with altitude: Mrs Enderby sees nothing but fag smoke and kettle steam.

A voice from the room opposite: 'GET THAT FUCKING THING OUT OF HERE!' Something soft and heavy flies across the room and hits the partition by the door, and Einar comes sock-sliding round the corner, past Finn's open door, clutching a terrified mouse to his neck. We're not fond of animals, but we make an exception for Hector, who was found starving in a house on Butcher Street and now calls home a shoebox in the bottom of Einar's wardrobe. Only Zoë has a problem with this. She lives in that room opposite, in a double bed draped with exotic fabrics, a bed which, to the disappointment of our friend Linden, never sleeps more than one. The heavy flying object was the Mexican cushion she props under her shoulders when she's sitting up to read. Filled, by the sound of it, with sawdust: no wonder she's had trouble getting off to sleep. Ever since what happened with Roxanne, Zoë has been the loosest spool in the mill, and the strain of all these early morning interruptions is beginning to tell. It's a familiar sequence: Einar sneaks into her room before anyone else is up and tiptoes to her bed. The mouse is squirming in his hands like a soft and prickly plant. He reaches out and lets Hector run onto the Mexican cushion, which has enough biscuit crumbs embedded in it to make Hector think he's in the kitchen, from which it's a logical step to nibbling at Zoë's ear.

She goes: 'Ever since what happened with Roxanne, I just can't deal with Einar and his pathetic jokes.'

She doesn't scream like she used to, just throws things and gasps for air. It would help if she didn't immediately light up and toke as if the thing was going to expire in three seconds, but we've each had to invent our own ways of dealing with tragedy, and a diet of Marlboro Reds and bio yoghurt is about the only remedy she can contemplate this year. Poor can't-cope Zoë, the only member of the team to have lost a faithful smoking partner as well as a good mate. And, as the only woman under the age of forty who still has her wits about her, the only one guaranteed to attract attention from the men. She should have known, with her long chestnut hair and her delightful studied raggedness, the mystery of all the ashtrays and empty yoghurt pots stacked up under her bed, that she was too heady a combination to be left alone for long. The door to the room opposite slams; having given Einar his daily fix of the only drug he needs, Zoë is taking herself back to bed.

Two minutes later we can hear a lovely singing voice from Zoë's room...

You won't find this place on any architect's plans. When Finn

Causley and Serge Kuczak put up these plasterboard partitions two summers ago, converting the old glass-ceilinged throwing floor to living quarters for up to ten people, there were enough awkward ceiling angles, ventilator pipes and essential support columns to make normal rectangular rooms seem like a thing of the past. And yet, if you contemplate the trigonometry long enough, you might be able to trace a path through the maze. Think of the gap between Finn and Zoë as a corridor, and see how we have spread ourselves about. On the left, joined by a connecting door to his father, the place where Robinson dreams of trains. Next is Einar's room, bare except for a white sleeping mat, a canvas wendy house and one of Kumar's chairs made of motorbike parts. Last on that side, the room that used to be Roxanne's, her drum kit still set up on a Moroccan rug, untouched since the day she left us for good.

Back in the corridor, you'll find a cordless phone and answering machine, and an exercise book for people to write down their calls. There's a washing machine and a supermarket trolley full of clothes. Following the corridor past Roxanne's room and round to the right, you'll see a bathroom with two Victorian cast-iron baths, a shower room and two toilets, which makes facilities enough even for Kumar, whose religion demands he wash himself before and after every meal. 'I like to keep myself clean,' he says. 'I love my heart, my liver, and my beautiful skin.' He's right: it's gorgeous. He puts it all down to simple vegetarianism, and although we'd never give up meat altogether, there was one flesh we never went back to after certain lazy rumours about the causes of St Mary's Disease. The alcove beyond the bathroom looked to be perfect for a kitchen, so it's here, next to our communal dining room and entertainment area, that we prepare our panoramic sheepless feasts.

On a single gas stove with four equal rings . . . Kumar is the next to wake, dreaming of women with tiny fingers. Light from the ceiling. Upside down. He's in the room along from Zoë's and, because the partition never quite reaches the roof, he's already sharing her air. Looking around, it's white walls, cacti in little pots and photographs of a fat man with a bald head who guides him spiritually from a ranch in Montana. The sound of running water from the bathroom suggests the spiritual life is not as lonely as he'd have us think. This inner room is where he brings his long-skirted admirers after the pubs have closed, where even on a cloudy night he can promise a fair view of the stars through the glass above their heads. Eye to eye with Kumar's bone structure and chestnut skin, lit to perfection by the glow of his lava lamp, it doesn't take long to coax them out of their shells. 'I really feel we should make contact,' he says, unbuttoning a Rajasthani shirt or unhooking a bra. Whatever happens next is almost completely silent: perhaps Zoë next door simply falls asleep and misses it, or perhaps they can bypass matter and make their way into each other without setting air into motion. But Kumar's morning smile, set off by nervous coughing from the bathroom, tells a certain story. 'What a totally excellent day!'

Radiant in white tee-shirt and shorts, he puts arms out and stretches, yawns, then sinks to the floor in an attitude of prayer. For the next half-hour you'll find him working through his exercise programme, which some here think is too like yoga for comfort, and therefore in clear breach of the house rules. Others would say Kumar's smirking new-ageism is all a ruse for getting his hands on more womanly flesh, and that the fat man with the bald head is not so much a guru as a second cousin from Kanchipuram with a dhosa problem. Anyway, no one can be quite sure what goes through his head while he strives for total control of his periphery, but I'm sure there's a little prayer said for each of us, an appeal to the great barrel-bellied Montanan spirit that he won't let anyone else slip out of position while our lives lie against each other in such precarious ways. Linden, in particular, has been making himself a cause for concern. Remember the fight with Jack over the Glenmorangie? Or we could go back even further, to the cruel knock-back he took from the rarely tactful Zoë, when his offer to pose for the girls' life-drawing class was met with hoots of laughter and some interesting additions to Linden's repertoire of blushes. Said Zoë: 'You've lost it, haven't you darling?' But thinking about it, some people reckon he'd been losing it well before then.

Kumar woke to find him standing in the doorway, spying on him through the wrong end of a pair of binoculars.

Einar questioned him about items found in the fridge.

Serge, leaving for home with Nina after one revolting party, found him notionless on the stairs, neither coming up nor going down.

He's been called into the office for a comradely chat. How does he feel about working here? Does he realise he is among friends? Does Einar and Jack's constant ribbing get to him, does he speak like that (tongue, lips) because he is nervous, is it a congenital condition, was he born or was he made? Is he in love with Zoë? Is that it? No, he says, not that. One thing he will own up to is a lust for travel, and it takes no great detective work to see this as a response to our endless stories around the dinner table: of all-night parties at harbourside hotels, of pill-popping in cars in South Australian campsites, of India, Bangladesh, Cambodia, Vietnam, and all stopovers you can make on the round trip between here and here. As soon as he's made enough money from his work at Big Kimberley, he'll set off on his own, with just a rucksack, a credit card and some second-hand dreams. He'll sleep on beaches and in cars. Some liquid-limbed Malaysian will cure him of his speech impediments. He'll know how it feels to get away, disappear, find the edge of the world and step off and know that no one even knows you're gone. And wake one day to find himself a traveller: tanned and wary, with a fashionably jaded smile, reading all the lessons he ever needed from the big round three-quarters-water textbook globe.

Speak of the devil and he's in the doorway, sucking his lip. The phone rings.

'There's a problem.' It's Serge, sounding very far away.

'Don't tell me. Your wife wants to kill you.'

'I tell her, You know you've already ruined me life? She goes, Well then I'm going finish the job. Reckon she knows about me and Nina.'

I hear him breathe. Linden wanders in and sinks into the armchair in the corner, an unmarked computer disc clutched against his leg.

'Look, mate, when's the sale?'

'Wednesday. You sound depressed.'

'Cath said that.'

'She's your wife. It's her job.'

'No, it's her job make me depressed in the first place. Look at me, I'm forty-four years old. I was there when all the woman stuff was happening. Cath'd be upstairs hosing down the kids and I'd tell her she should be out there doing the thing with the sisters, you know? Now she says she put the sugar in the petrol tank because I never gave her any space as a person, and I say I spent most of our married life digging tunnels for the British Army, how much space do you want?'

I take the disc from Linden and slip it into the drive. It's a collection of images from one of Jack's filthier websites, with Linden's shaggy head artfully morphed onto each medallioned torso. Serge wonders what I'm laughing about.

'All right, you'd better tell us what you want.'

'Get Linden cover for me, just for a few days. Let me get self up a rock somewhere. Get some RP nuts into some crannies and work me way up. Think a bit.'

In the corner, the porn king feels his ears burning. He knows the road to popularity begins with constant availability, and he'll volunteer for anything, as long as it doesn't involve ringing people up. Trouble is, no one knows the layout of Big Kimberley like our General Foreman, whose final marriage breakdown seems to have coincided with our monthly sale. In the terms of our standard contract, any lapse in storage payments lasting more than six months will result in the sale of property at public auction. Lest we forget, it's this so-called Bliss Clause that's making us all so rich. Most of the lots in next week's auction will have got there in the same way: cleared out from empty houses, put into storage and never collected because the bills couldn't be met. Or else we've been given the go-ahead from long-suffering spouses who, realising their loved ones no longer recognise what they once vowed to keep for ever, have made the decision to break with the past.

'Take it you'll be back in time for the sale. It's going to be a big one, Serge. And you'll have to come in and show Linden what to do.'

For the two days before any sale, the job of the General Foreman is to go around the storage bays, track down all that's to be sold and organise getting it into position in the showroom on the first floor. On the day of the auction he wanders around with a clipboard ticking off the lots as they come up. Some of this must have rubbed off on Linden, because he's the one who helps Kumar hoist stuff into the air so our customers can see what they're bidding for. In certain lights you'd think they were two angels, saying no to gravity. Elsewhere on the first floor, Nina runs the cash desk while Einar sells sandwiches and soup. Zoë, the auctioneer's assistant, sits at the left hand of Finn Causley on the podium and scans the room for bids. That used to be Roxanne's favourite job.

'I found it in the kitchen,' says Linden, reaching across to open an image of his goateed self taking a bespectacled Swede up the arse. 'He is *really* pissing me off.'

Then Zoë is standing in the doorway in a shiny black robe, not long out of the bath. Linden, at least, has an answer to his prayers. He loves her in the way he's loved her for most of the last two years: politely, hopelessly, with much fidgeting and twitching of lips. But ever since what happened with Roxanne, Zoë has been blind to the amateur dramatics of love. She walks through and flops onto the bed, dripping on the duvet cover and deepening the green. Linden remembers the picture on the screen and hurriedly snaps the laptop shut. Zoë takes a packet of cigarettes from somewhere and offers them to Linden, mainly because she knows he's giving up. Sighing, she lights one for herself and blows a cone of smoke towards the ceiling. Through the smudge he sees her big-boned face, its pale raspberry colouring, the gold stud gleaming in her nose. She thinks she's overweight, and some agree, but to Linden every ounce is precious and perfectly formed. She stretches her legs out on the bed and parts the robe over her thighs, as if there was some sun around that she was trying to catch. Somewhere in Linden's head there is a small but potent explosion; he forgets what he came to say and leaves.

Tonight, if the weather holds, we're going to have a barbecue on the roof, the first of the year.

Kumar, Serge, Nina, Einar, Jack, Linden, Zoë, Finn . . . There once were ten of us, my fellow travellers and auction-goers, but Roxanne had all that trouble keeping herself together, and Hen, who is still a sort of wife to me, found all the history she ever wanted in a private room in a clinic on Blacksheep Moor. Remember how the two of them could communicate without speaking, and you'll know what I mean when I say the two events were not unrelated. When Roxanne misread the dosage instructions on a plastic tube of pills (she always had trouble with these foreign imports, and the Belorussian print quality left much to be desired), Hen was the first to spot the angels coming down, with their big boots and baseball bats, looking to bust a mouth. It was thirteen months ago. I'm not sure if that's a long time or a short time as far as these things go; not long enough, judging by the silence that descends like light from the ceiling whenever either name is mentioned. We all knew Roxanne had had dealings with this particular substance, the one Bliss sufferers use against all medical advice because (Roxanne) 'it makes everything add up, it shows what stuff really means'. But we assumed it was no more than a one-a-week habit, a treat for breezy cragsides on Saturday nights, and certainly never imagined there'd be any grief ground into those plain white pills that smelled of nothing in particular. For seasoned travellers like us, all the warnings about variable dosages and lethal impurities stank of tabloid scare stories, of the kind they used to spread about Rona's Surfboard when that was in fashion. So none of us had any idea that, one drizzly April day when she was left to her own devices in an empty mill, Roxanne would go to such trouble to prove us wrong. No one, that is, except for Hen, who told us exactly where to find her, who from the moment she entered the building knew Roxanne would be facing the wall instead of the centre of the room (hunched, arms stretched around the knees), who was found in the same spot among the storage shelves, in the same helpless position, when her own moment came.

I'm looking at Zoë on the bed, trying to take her for a few details of that dismal April, the month Big Kimberley lost her 150-year-old smile. On the desk in front of me is the red baseball cap Roxanne left behind when she moved on, the thing Hen wrested from her improbably cold fingers, in a white room on the other side of the moor, when her grip became sufficiently weak. Perhaps it's only in the last five minutes that I've brought it down from its shelf, because Zoë's looking at it as if she hadn't set eyes on it in all this time. The third item in the catalogue features in most of the photographs of Roxanne that survive, some of which date back to our glorious summer at the Point Hotel. I can therefore put to it a number of questions about the events and circumstances that brought us here, as well as trying to find out why Roxanne, who always differed from us in secret ways, ended up somewhere else.

Its origin, at least, is no mystery: she found it among the snakeskin rucksacks and novelty sunglasses of Camden Market, where our friend spent many of her first hours on British soil. On the front

---

Lot 3: **Baseball cap**, red cotton with white nylon lining and plastic lettering on the brow.

are the words TUFF MUFF in black plastic capitals; two interlocking strips of plastic, with studs and holes that can be pulled apart and clipped together, allow it to be adjusted for any head. Judging from the way Roxanne had it fixed, she was a bit bigger in that department than Hen; I know because not so long ago my airheaded lover was spending hours at the wardrobe mirror with this same cap pulled down over her forehead, trying to bring her face back into view.

Try, Hen. Stare into the mirror. Think about the friend you lost.

She needs help. Faces appear deathly white and gleaming. There was liquorice-black hair, sticking out in wisps under the brim. Red lipstick on a narrow mouth. Roxanne? She never lost her small white milk teeth, almost blue in daylight, flashing out from rosy gums whenever she laughed or took a drag of a Marlboro Red. Try to remember her toffee-coloured eyes. Was she beautiful? Faces seem different when things make no sense. Think of tracing-paper skin, stretched tight over grinning cheekbones; the straight nose with its embryonic cleft.

(And you, Finn, think of hands closing over your eyes, fingers smelling of smoke and cunt and chocolate, her face as clear in your brain as the voice behind you, crooning in your ear:

Guess who?)

We know little of her life. There are stories of rape and sour-breathed uncles. She kicked and punched her way through a Tasmanian girlhood, making a break for the mainland as soon as she could afford the fare. In Melbourne she landed up drumming for an all-girl grunge band, bleached her hair and had limited success on the gay club scene. We met her shortly after she'd dropped out of their East Coast tour and was hanging around Sydney trying to decide on her next move. She wore cut-down dungarees and boys' school shoes. She spoke a sort of pidgin English from years of trying to communicate with foreign travellers, which Einar soon had down flat:

'Did you enjoy the *party?*'

'Where's your friend? Your *friend?*'

'You want to *do something tonight?* Okay, *my beach* or *yours?*'

The reputation was probably deserved. I once used the word 'promiscuous' in front of her, in memory perhaps of Duncan McGuinness, or some other shag-happy friend of a friend. She looked at me with twenty-nine years of scorn and asked why I was banging on at her like an uptight parent. Then the homespun philosophy: 'Better to die on your feet than live on your knees!' Never mind that it no longer rang true, that in all her time at Big Kimberley she never brought anyone home to sit on her drum throne while she stepped out of her dungarees ... Christ, she had other things to think about: faces that even in the gloomiest rooms seemed pale and overexposed, kitchen utensils whose functions escaped her, ordinary daylight from which she had to skulk indoors and hide her eyes.

Around the time Roxanne was getting known in London, Zoë Allmark was finishing an art foundation course, living with her parents in Letchworth and commuting to London for temping jobs. One Monday morning she woke up at a table next to a dodgy peroxide with cherry-red lips, who was reading out bank loan leaflets in urban Australian and, instead of folding them and tucking them into envelopes, was using them as the basis for jokes. Zoë did more than laugh: she listened to the way the stranger introduced herself ('My name's Roxanne. This job is giving me the shits.') and knew stuffing envelopes would be bearable as long as her new friend was beside her, reeling off stories about her gigs with Beaver Rescue and talking about men with foreign-sounding names as if they were books she'd read.

At this point Zoë wakes from her reverie and looks at me with terrific purpose. 'Go on, mate. Tell 'em about those little statues we made.'

Life moves fast in our great capital, so it's no surprise that Zoë and Roxanne were soon sharing a two-roomed flat. With my friend here to prod me, I can just imagine their nights on the town: huddled conspiratorially in a North London bar, hot faces almost touching, while fat Reds crackle in ashtrays and corporate jazz drifts down from speakers set in stone. Over cool bottles of white wine, Roxanne went through her address book and told Zoë everything there was to tell: who she'd fucked and who'd fucked her, who she'd fucked with, who'd fucked her about and then fucked off, who she hadn't fucked but had thought about incessantly, and all the roots and fucks and shags and total cock-ups from which she had built a rickety but free-standing life.

Back in the flat, Zoë turned Roxanne's stories into Art. Beginning with the sort of child's play clay that can be baked in ordinary kitchen ovens, and would one day give way to proper ceramic kilns and the use of genuine Etruscan marl, she moulded and coloured the Dutch engineer whose name was Gert and thanked her after sex; English Freddy, too out of it to get into it in any meaningful way, who, in a sudden attack of acid-induced paranoia, started lashing out; and Archbishop Rivaldo, who sent back the Polaroids he'd taken of her with her halo drawn on in gold paint pen . . . Each ex-contender was portrayed in his fully budded glory; the only concession to modesty was the white sheet they had crawled across to discover Roxanne. If you felt like hunting around a bit, you might find a couple of these offerings among the storage bays on the ground floor, or lined up behind a filing cabinet downstairs. But if you're hoping a familiar presence might stare out at you from the darkness – a grin that only bothers one side of the face, a prematurely expansive brow – I'll have to remind you what Bliss did to Roxanne's appetite (while those hands close again over my eyes).

Only one of Roxanne's lovers was too special for Zoë's talent. 'Not Blake,' she said; 'he's different. Don't ask me why: he just is.' She twigged this soon after her arrival in Melbourne, when a guy came up to her at a student noticeboard and wondered out loud if she was looking for a place to live. She must have said something, because they ended up finding a flat together and calling it home for a while. Because Zoë was never allowed to sculpt him, and because Roxanne was as unenthusiastic about camerawork as her future boss, I can only say that Blake was as tall and blond as any dream director could hope, and that Roxanne fell for him like trees fall for the sky. We've thought about this a lot, in that part of the evening when the conversation turns to absent friends, and we're sure this was the only time Roxanne mentioned love. Not to me, though: only Hen and Zoë were let into the secret. She told them love was a place beyond both sex and friendship; when Blake took her there it was a theme park of bright lights and stomach-churning rides, and when he went home and left her there it was a deserted stadium, to which she never stopped waiting for him to return.

In the meantime, Rox and Zoë's slow drift towards our story required certain conditions to be in place. For a start, the two friends would have to leave London and find their way up the motorway to

Print, which meant they would have to throw a counter-contractual party at their flat, to which their landlord would have to turn up uninvited and find one of their workmates on the stairway smoking a marijuana cigarette, responding with noisy indignation and receiving a punch in the mouth in lieu of rent. This would all have to coincide with the arrival of a postcard to Roxanne, rerouted via a friend's address in Melbourne, announcing the birth of the Big Kimberley Exercise in Memory Recycling; and also with Zoë's runaway desire to find Etruria, ceramics capital of the Western world, a utopia she had only read about in books. It happened, then, but it took until the following summer, when Zoë and Roxanne had already been best friends for a year, but still some time before daylight unveiled its baffling new properties and the word Bliss began to appear on our lips.

If Roxanne already had an itch for heaven by the time she and Zoë arrived at Big Kimberley, only Hen knew how to read the signs. As Mrs Matthewman's Health Ministry kept insisting, the cause of Roxanne's problems could have been anything from the number of men who'd posed naked in her bed to the fact that she never took any exercise beyond thrashing out snare-heavy shuffle grooves on her cherry-red Tama kit. The greatest sceptic was Zoë, who switched off documentaries on the subject with a scorn previously reserved for men in BMWs. 'You know, there are women being systematically mutilated in Africa and all they can talk about is this disease which doesn't *exist*.'

No surprise, then, that Zoë never accepted what was happening to Roxanne, just as she never did with Hen. Those tell-tale lapses of concentration were put down to hangovers and memories of bad trips. The three of them went to evening classes at Print College, stoned out of their heads, drifting home in giggling formation with pots that looked like spaceships, which they would then fill with petrol and solemnly put to the flame. The same team would make mid-afternoon trips to a boarded-up terrace in Etruria, returning hours later with a small bottle of ordinary jellies or drops. At first they kept quiet about the other stuff, the real purpose of their visits, and when it eventually came out that Rox was scoring a drug called Salvation in pill form, no one guessed there was any problem she was using it to solve. And her expression? We had no idea what all that smiling was about, and we'd still be guessing if we hadn't noticed the same thing somewhere else.

Now there it is on Zoë, although in her case I'm sure a smile like that should not be taken as a sign of trouble. All you're seeing are fond memories of the time the three of them tied Linden to the cooker and shaved his legs, or when they walked out of Miss Selfridge in Etruria wearing three jumpers and five pairs of knickers each, or when they dressed up as nuns and put themselves up for auction, prompting a fierce bidding war between the chairman of the football club and the two brothers who run the deli in town. She is shaking her head. 'As soon as Hen comes home it'll be just like old times. I really miss her. It's just not the same without Hen.'

Under flickering fluorescent light, Serge is making up his list. 'First,' he says, 'you got to identify your sale items.'

Linden pretends to listen. He wears tight white shorts, grey socks. Thinks: One day I'll catch her in the bath.

The auctioneer is on his bicycle, keeping to the track that runs around the storage bays. He mutters: *It's just not the same without Hen.*

'Now, do we sort this stuff by what it is or by who owns it?' Linden stares in silence. 'You tell me. Do we keep the garden furniture in one place and the ornaments in another?' Linden scratches his goatee. He sees the General Foreman crouched at his feet, his old rocker's ponytail tied up with a rubber band. Dreaming of Zoë in her shiny black gown.

'All right, I'll tell you. We sort it by owner. Like say, that means all we know about what's in the boxes is what's written in them folders.' Linden is carrying a stack of A4-sized yellow folders. Finn cycles past, head full of condiment sets and cheesy Rodin copies. Robinson follows, at half his father's speed, on his pink-and-blue trike. 'And since what it says in them folders is never right, cause most people what work here learned English out of a comic, that means we get a nice big surprise when we open it all up.'

The first folder in the pile is labelled 1017: Murdoch, Mrs E, of Etruria Road, Print. Striplights are pulled on and off as they move through the store, reading paper labels tied to suitcase handles, glued to top corners of boxes. At head height on the third bay they find two packing cases and a wooden trunk with rusted iron handles. The numbers match. The cases are lifted down, banging against the punched steel supports and threatening to tip. The two workers grunt and sweat. Then, with keys which appear from nowhere, they break the cases open on the floor between them, and Mrs Murdoch's most sacred treasure sees daylight for the first time in months.

For each item Serge picks up, holds to the light, rattles, puffs for dust, Linden checks down the list for an entry to match. Binoculars. Plastic swan. Electric clock. 'Fifty, sixty per cent of this stuff is crap. Folk only hang on to it for sentimental reasons. You know, the underpants their husbands were wearing when they snuffed it, all that sort of lark.' Transistor radio. Christmas card list from 1966. 'When the loved ones pass away they have to move to smaller houses. Get to the point where they can't deal with it no more, have to make a fresh start.' Say it's because he's in charge, but Serge can't help talking like no one else knows what goes on in this place. The bust of a young woman. A violin without strings. 'They put stuff here temporary like, forget about it, watch the bills pile up. Like say, we send 'em two reminders, and if after six months they still in't paid, that's it.' Serge grunts and wipes his forehead. 'It's all crap, though, in't it. That's why I can't understand why anyone would want to nick it.'

'Nick it?' Linden comes to life with a shudder. 'Why's that?'

'Because what's written in them folders is not what we find when we come f'get the stuff.'

'You think someone's *stealing* it . . . ?'

'Stealing it and selling it off themselves. I got my suspects. Can't say no more than that.'

An Old Testament wind passes through the ground floor, setting paper labels fluttering. Someone's left the outside door open. All movement is picked up by trim white cameras, betrayed in corners by glowing red diodes. In a small booth off the main storage area, four black-and-white monitors make unsteady light. Two views of the ground-floor storage area, one of the first-floor showroom and one of the main entrance and stairs. Einar comes down the stairs with plastic carriers full of empty bottles for recycling. He puts his head round the door and grins.

'And by the way,' he says, 'Linden must now go back to school and learn his letters!'

'What's he on about now?' grumbles Serge.

'Because I am just now in your room reading your little book, and when you say you want to put your thingy into Zooey's special pocket, you have got her name spelled up all wrong!'

A wooden letter-rack flies out of Linden's hand and smashes into the rapidly closed door. 'That's it,' sputters Linden, beetroot-red and shaking. 'I'm putting a lock on it tonight . . .'

'Good idea,' says Serge. 'All sorts of people about.'

Linden speaks slowly, distractedly, doubts and questions all over his face.

'Do you think it's . . . ?'

Einar? A thief? But Serge's seasoned face is unavailable for comment.

They sort the Murdoch relics into two piles: one for the auction room, one for the Print and District municipal tip. In the auction pile: two pigeons in a glass case with dessicated flora; a 1910 proverb calendar; Action Man with Eagle Eyes; teddy bear with glass eye-beads and stitched mouth. In the dumping pile: copy of *Radio Times* from 1973; torn fabric washbag; tin whistle; plastic knives and forks.

The phone rings in the office on the first floor. Zoë answers. 'Yes, we have space. We offer, um, video security, computerised stock control, immediate access, you name it actually! The starting price is . . . twelve pounds per hundred cubic feet, but that gets cheaper the more space you need. Right, I'll put that in the book, Mrs Cartledge, and we'll get a van round to you before, er, dinnertime Thursday.'

On the video monitor, Zoë goes about her work in silent monochrome, scribbling in the diary with a pencil and holding the dead phone against her chest. Now and then, as if she might tell if anyone is watching, she glances up at the camera, pulls at her scrunchie and takes a drag of a Marlboro Red. AND THEY CALL IT BLISS, moans the headline of the only paper she can bear to read, and then only the headlines and TV pages, not the smaller print in between. She hears shouts on the street outside and pads barefoot to the window, where the louder of Print's two traffic wardens is discussing the forecast with the driver of a yellow van. At a silent signal, both men check the sky. After a promising start, Friday is threatening rain.

The auction items are listed, and the stuff to be dumped is going back into one of the cases. The auctioneer cycles past, smiling from one side of his mouth. Robinson follows on his trike. Serge steps backwards into the aisle and the trike and Robinson crash into the backs of his legs. The General Foreman curses under his breath.

'Why in't you at school, little bugger?'

'He's only three,' says Linden.

'I'm three and a *half*,' says Robinson, backing up and pedalling around Serge's legs.

'That's old enough. Maryrose is at school and loving it. Comes home yesterday, says Mummy, why aren't you like Jesus?'

'Actually, Maryrose is almost five,' says Linden. 'And Nina is a working mum. You could hardly say that about Finn.'

'I heard that,' says the auctioneer, gaining speed as he unfolds into the straight. He overtakes his son at the next corner. Einar's face appears at the window, tongue lolling from his open mouth. Robinson sticks his tongue out in response and collides with a stack of wooden chairs. This time he stops, quivering his lip.

We're up on the roof, looking down at babies in prams, little girls in love, shirtless lads taking drops by the war memorial, senile dogs and gutter-hopping birds. Down the hill that tilts us slightly northwards, the church, its garden of mossy stones, then the green sweep of the park. Scaled down by altitude and distance, mothers push buggies along paths, boys swing golf clubs in the manner of their fathers, and small people break free from tall people to run after scraps of sunlight and invisible balls. At the fetid pond, where only a few upended benches pierce the surface, midges bounce in golden ecstasy and blue-rinsers feed ducks from plastic bags. The rain that threatened our evening has been sucked back into those clouds, swept away over reservoir and moor, leaving our finish clear and blue. Five miles to the north, the Pikes perform their balancing act for sheep and hawks and wandering witches, purpled by distance, a jagged knife-edge against the soft throat of the sky.

Kumar wears the shirt he bought in Kensington Market on the day That Woman resigned. It is pale pink with a fine paisley design. They celebrated in a pub in Covent Garden, and there was a chilli stain on his shirt before it was a day old. If only his anxiety about the future of the nation had been so easy to shift. 'And after Maggie we got the bloke in the glasses. And after him we got a bloke in glasses with grey hair. Now that sounds very strange. I mean, how do we know they weren't the same person? Or no, that it wasn't actually some other bunch of jokers who all look the same?' He grins and rocks his head from side to side. 'Is it any wonder,' lapsing into the accent of his forefathers, 'I am finding the *spi*-ritual life is *al*-together more my cup of chai?'

This weekend he is entertaining friends from London. Lavonne is a lawyer, which Einar pretends to hear as 'liar'. Serge, who is seeing more of lawyers these days than he would like, congratulates Einar on his mistake. Lavonne, in electric blue hotpants and crocheted top, tips back her head in a silent laugh. Every silky hair on her is blown around by the wind.

'Most of us are honest,' she says, 'most of the time!'

The other friend is Janet. 'Like the computer network,' she says, and they all search each other with puzzled brows. Except Linden, who used to work with computers in Norwich. 'Software, mainly. What did you say you . . . ?'

'I work for a geographical magazine,' says Janet, right hand trying to retrieve something from her hair. 'Conservation, environmental issues, all pretty obscure stuff.'

'You've come to the right place,' says Serge. 'We're all green round here.'

Einar explodes. 'I know what we are! We are people who have found a way to defrost our dreams! God our Maker says all dreams are frozen and last for ever! They live in Iceland because Iceland is the Fridge of Dreams! We come out of Iceland in our droves, carrying our drippy dreams in plastic bags! We eat and drink and listen to Genesis and watch our dreams defrost! We take off our clothes! Our dreams make us virulent! We make love like milkmen, a thousand poptarts in our pockets, more virulent than . . . But I see you need the lessons for what virulent means!' He stares goggle-eyed at Lavonne and hangs the jaw. Lavonne blows smoke.

On Linden's ghettoblaster, Robert Fripp is spraying burning guitar all over David Bowie's *Scary Monsters*. We're eating duck sausage, olive pâté, Arizona chillis stuffed with cheese and garlic. Goan kebabs are charring on a home-made barbecue, tended sporadically by Nina in a yellow apron. There are no knives or forks. We pretend it's a moorland custom, dating back to the founding of

Dieulacres Abbey in the next valley along. The city types think it's quaint.

'So what actually goes on here? I saw some furniture being restored downstairs. It all looks very arty and interesting.' Janet takes a slurp of Shiraz, raises eyes above the rim.

'We're mainly a storage company, duck,' says the General Foreman. 'The auctions is an offshoot of that. When Finn and me started we was restoring furniture, a bit of building work on the side. Then he starts bringing all this junk in f'keep here, and next thing he's got his showroom set up and we're selling it all off.' They all look at Finn, who is pulling up weeds from the rockery, watched in silence by Robinson and Maryrose. 'Me and him, we fixed this place up between us. I don't live here with them lot. You know houses out at Waterside?'

Janet shakes her head. She has never been called duck before and she's not sure how to take it. She sucks a lip and searches for an answer in her hair. 'And the children?'

'Maryrose,' says Serge, 'she's Nina's little one. Other one's Robinson, he lives here with Finn, his dad. His mum's called Hen.'

A hush, perhaps? Lavonne cuts short a tale and looks across.

'Oh yes,' says Janet. 'Kumar told me. Same thing happened to a friend of someone at work. She just went, one weekend, like a switch. Just...'

The door opens. Zoë steps out onto the roof, biggish in a white summer dress, brown frizz tied up with a rag. One pair of hands starts clapping.

'Nice one!' yells Nina through pork-smoke and spring breeze.

Zoë pushes back her sunglasses and gives a need-a-drink smile.

'What's she done?' asks Lavonne.

'She was making a statue. She said she'd only come if she finished it tonight!'

'What's it of?'

Zoë glances at the crowd. 'It's called A Nice Cup of History. It's two beauts on the hula, except one's got a teapot instead of a head and the other's got their lips around the spout. It's dedicated to Mrs Matthewman, the Health Secretary, who wants us all in hospital where we won't keep asking awkward questions.'

Nina gasps and presses her forehead with the heel of a hand.

'You all right, love?' says Serge, taking her hand and pressing it between his.

'I'm just glad she's here,' says Nina, trying to flip kebabs.

The children pedal their vehicles around the roof, keeping close to the outer railings and that fabulous view, then veering in towards the rockery and the glass roof of the first-floor showroom. If they stayed still long enough, they could look down through templed panes to the space where Kumar and Linden have been stripping a wardrobe down to bare pine. Monday will see it all cleared away, the half-dressed wardrobe shunted into a corner and the listed items moved out onto the floor for two days of viewing before the sale. For now, though, it's Friday night, and no one's thinking about binoculars or tea-sets, charcoal portraits or lithographed religious scenes.

Over by the railing, where Linden is making a mess of his fifth vegeburger, Zoë tells Janet about her recent visit to Hen. The way she goes on, you'd think Hen's problems were no more a nuisance than bad skin or a few unwanted pounds, as though Moorview Clinic was a sort of mental health farm from which she'll return, rosy-cheeked and pond-eyed, as soon as the clouds have moved on. Who'd challenge such a reassuring story? And is it any different to what she said one January morning, when she helped Hen pack her things for the drive into a new life across the moor?

'It was *strange*. She just sat there and gave a sort of running commentary on the scenery: houses, cars, what colours they were, what other stuff they reminded her of. I kept saying to him: We're her friends, why can't we look after her here? But the thing is, she *wanted* to go. Anyway, she's got her own room and it sounds like they have a laugh. If you ask me it's just a perfectly understandable identity crisis. The present makes no sense to her, so she's gone back to the Middle Ages where it's all a bit less weird. You can give it a stupid name if you want, but it didn't help Roxanne and I don't see how it's going to help Hen.'

'Can't see why they call it that,' says Janet. 'Bliss. Sounds like anything but.'

'You should see her. No really. She looks like she's on top of the world.'

'I think it's to do with the smile.' All these girl-eyes make Linden blush. 'The, um, professional opinion is that it's just a reaction to the drugs.'

'Oh, the *drugs*. You know they give you the same crap if you've got, like, schizophrenia? I mean, do you see schizophrenics going round smiling all the time?' A breath, more thoughts. 'It's funny, though, she seems so happy when I see her, I almost don't want her to get better. Is that really bad?'

No one thinks it is.

'. . . but you shouldn't make up your mind till you've taken a trip round the harbour. It's hard to believe.' A short cork-flight away, Finn recalls evenings like these on the roof of the Point Hotel, silent storms flashing on the north horizon, the city glinting like a copper dish.

'It was never really a priority for me,' says Lavonne. 'I just wanted to qualify and start earning some money as soon as I could. Besides, I like the home comforts too much. I mean, I went InterRailing with a friend and it was a complete nightmare.'

'Yeh, but that's different. All those stuffed jumpers looking for the Hard Rock Café and expecting everyone to speak English. You've got to get out there on your own.'

'Well maybe that's all right for a bloke . . .'

'No no no, loads of girls do it. Anyway, you meet people. You travel with someone for a day, get to know everything about them, then say goodbye and don't even bother asking their name. Because you know you'll meet someone else tomorrow and it'll all start up again. It's an incredible thrill.'

'Like casual sex . . . ?' Lavonne's eyes are coloured glass.

'Yeh. I . . .'

'Well, it can't have been *that* exciting . . .'

He smiles, forgetting.

'I mean you came back, didn't you? Surely the whole idea was to meet the girl of your dreams and fall in love under the stars?'

What does she mean? Did someone ever sit on a bench and look down at him with half a smile? Were the colours green, black, blue? Did someone offer him the one thing he'd always wanted and then run off with it as fast as . . . ?

'I don't think that's really the point,' says Finn.

Beyond the rockery a cricket match is in progress. They have a bat, which Einar holds like a baseball bat, and a tennis ball. Einar pretends he's never heard of this game called cricket and doesn't want to be bothering with it now. Kumar bowls an attractive-looking off-break which beats Einar and bounces off the railing behind. In among the spectators, Linden tells his new friend Janet how he fits into all of this. He's nervous, slurping from his glass. 'Um, I spent a long time in counselling but it wasn't very. She told me I was probably abused as a child which I couldn't. To start with, and then I started thinking I must have been, and then I thought I'd better. It's like this feeling you're about to die, everything's going black and you can't. Ug. And then Sonia, she was my girlfriend, was basically shagging my best friend at the same time, well I thought he was my best friend, you can normally tell. So I started on the whisky, started and I couldn't . . .'

A swipe from Einar sends the ball skimming into the food table. A Tony Banks keyboard solo is interrupted by a tinkling of glass. Robinson toddles over to add the broken pieces to his collection of shiny things, with the General Foreman in hot pursuit. The ball bounces dutifully across the table and comes to rest on the barbecue grill.

'FIVE!' shouts Einar, raising the bat like a broadsword and staring up at his old Viking companion, the moon. Serge flips Robinson upside down and dangles him by the ankles over the cooling barbecue. The boy squeals with delight, cheeks filling with blood and fine blond hair on end, cooking slowly and gazing blissfully at people's feet. Then Nina thinks it's time the children were in bed.

'Robinson! Daddy'll be down in a minute to say goodnight.'

Serge swings the boy onto his shoulders and jogs with him to the door. Maryrose stands with hands on hips.

'I don't have to go to bed. I'm the PRINCESS ... OF ... AUSTRALIA.'

'Come on, mate. No arguments.'

'Hold your horses!' says Maryrose. 'I want to see you all get drunk. I want to see you *kissing* each other. Ugh! I've seen you do that with Serge. *Every single night.*'

'Right then,' says her mother, 'I'll take you home and you won't be able to stay in Big Kimberley with Robinson and you won't be able to wait for the Friendly Monk to come.'

Maryrose bends down and touches her toes. She straightens like a gymnast, looks up at the sky and turns a slow half-circle, wrinkling her nose thoughtfully. Turns and runs inside.

'It must be handy having someone to look after them for you,' says Lavonne. 'You must have your work cut out.'

'Yeh well. I always thought I was too selfish to have kids. But when you've got them and you see them and you're so used to having them around . . .' He stares up at the sky, trying to see what the child saw, a feeling or a thought.

By the time Jack turns up, all the food has gone.

'Dog's cunt,' he shouts, 'this is the sort of party makes me glad to have no friends! Celery? Do we still eat celery in the twenty-first century? Everybody, this is Madeleine. She's about to start filming a screenplay for BBC 2, which means she'll probably take her dress off if you ask nicely.'

Madeleine shivers, bare-shouldered in a stretchy black frock. 'I didn't realise it was going to be so . . .'

'Shall I close the window?' says Kumar in batting stance. Linden laughs his head off. Linden is drunk.

In the half-darkness Zoë is lighting candles. She made the holders herself, in the studios at Print College, women with conical breasts and glossy red deltas. Here's a miracle: the breeze has dropped and the fires flicker peacefully, held aloft by angelic arms. Reflected flame gleams from the stud in her nose. Beside her Linden lights matches, staring with half a mind into the flame, then flicking it shut with his thumb. The moon is a lamp at the bottom of a deep blue pool.

'He told me his mother was dead.'

'Who? Finn?'

'Robinson.'

'What's he say?'

'That his mother's gone to sleep for ever and never coming home. She's dead, he says.'

Janet and Kumar look over to the rockery, where candles burn and people stand in pairs, talking. Where Finn Causley, who never knows when he's the centre of attention, broadcasts stories from a faraway hotel.

'. . . it was this bar called Jackson's in the Cross, and Einar's having a pretend fight with a South African guy called Jim . . .'

'What,' says Lavonne, '*this* Einar?' This Einar looks across, mock-shocked.

'I met him in Sydney. He followed me here.'

'Finn mate! I follow you round the world! Anywhere you go, I go, that's why I am called your friend!'

He lurches over, wine swilling in his glass. He looks the auctioneer up and down, gummy with disgust.

'Don't tell me. He is telling you boring stories which are not true about what he did in Australia. I don't think he has told you about Anna Ballantyne. He was so in love with her, he let her go off with another man!'

'I was young and foolish. Now I'm . . .'

'Yes, but you are forgetting what Miles says. *A stiff dick in't got no conscience!* I was speaking to Anna very recently and she has not forgotten you. She is very interesting to meet you again, I think.'

'Do me a favour, Einar. Shut up.'

'She says, I can't stay long because I have to cut off six legs before tea-time and they will take me fifteen minutes each. But I would love to talk some more about Finn Causley, that beautiful man. I say, Well, we are having a party, why don't you come along? and she says, That's handy, I am not doing anything this Friday night!'

Oh dear. Finn is staring at the darkening view, gripping the glass too tightly in his fingers. He thought he could move fast enough, far enough, to always keep ahead of what was happening, give himself time to choose. But the sky is no longer blue over Sydney, and that's not the only thing that has changed. It may be the cold, but doesn't he appear to be shivering? Or is he so angry, is there such a screaming between his ears, that the only way to hush it is to slam his fist into Einar's face? Neither of these things. He merely says, 'Right, I'll leave you to it,' and walks towards the door. Brow wrinkling, humming a tune.

'I've never ever . . . had sex with anyone on this roof.'

'So?'

'You have to accuse someone of it and they have to say if it's true. No, hang on . . . you have to . . . Shit, I can't remember.'

'You mean you've never ever had sex with anyone on this roof, or you've never ever had sex with any of the people on this roof at the moment?'

'I don't know. I've never ever . . .'

'I know a better game,' says Einar. 'You have to spell my name. Not my first name, that's easy. My second name. If you get it wrong you have to take a drink.'

'We don't know what it is.'

'Ah!'

'You have to tell us or we can't play.'

'Ahaha!'

'It's Bjornfriggerson, or something.'

'Is it?'

'Nei.'

'Okay. B. J. O. R. N. N . . .'

'WRONG!'

'B. J. O. R. N. F. R. I. G . . .'

'WRONG! All take a drink!'

The bottle moves clockwise around the circle. Einar sits across from Lavonne in nothing but a pair of shorts and prods her with his bare toes. He's calling her Lavvy to make her feel at home.

'Aren't you cold?' says Madeleine. 'I'm freezing.' She's wearing Jack's jacket, leaving him in the same shirt and braces he's been wearing since 1987.

'Not at all,' says Einar. 'In Iceland we sit outside in the snow every night. This because there are no trees to climb.'

'I read,' says Jack, 'that Iceland has a higher concentration of Nobel laureates than any other country in the world. That's the Nobel Prize for Literature I'm talking about, not arseing needlework.'

'We are Vikings,' says Einar. 'If we don't like someone we cut off his head and rape his daughters. And eat his bunny rabbit. You, Jack, are first.'

'And they also speak a language which is effectively unchanged since medieval times. So I guess,' he fawns, 'they would like my work.'

Astonished silence? Raised heart-rates? Jack has a perfect opportunity to expand.

'He's a professional musician,' says Serge. 'He don't work here with us.'

'Nah, nah. What he does, right, is he hangs round here and shows off to our visitors, specially the babes.' Kumar tries, with short-lived success, to make the cricket bat stand up in the palm of his hand.

'I keep them on their toes. Let them know what's happening in the outside world. I have this little studio round the corner where I do my recording. Wonderful atmosphere, terribly thirteenth century.'

'He plays everything himself,' says Nina. 'And sings.'

'Is *that* what you call it,' says Linden.

'Really?' Janet shuffles forward and slots hands under her thighs. 'Can we hear some?'

'Oh, I don't think so.' Jack reaches round Madeleine to press the pockets of his jacket. 'Hang about . . . here's something I was working on the other day.'

He crawls over and stops Miles Davis in mid-phrase. A pause as the tape whirrs back to its beginning, then the clunk of PLAY. It begins with the low drone of a bagpipe, then a lute tinkers with a minor chord, then sampled tabors set up a cluttered rhythm and mixed voices chant the theme. Hen used to love this stuff, but now? A changeless smile in a private room.

'Wow,' says Janet. 'How d'you get all those voices?'

'It's all me,' says Jack.

Madeleine appears to sleep. A flute spirals up towards the moon.

'It's part of a sequence based on *Sir Gawain and the Green Knight*. Actually, it's a bit of a local legend. There's pretty good evidence the poet knew the area and used it as the landscape for Gawain's adventure.'

We listen, fidgeting like kids on deckchairs, as a new sound rises over the town. Madeleine looks up, puzzled. When Janet speaks again she's almost shouting to be heard.

'For people who work with furniture, you all sound incredibly . . .'

'What the fuck's *that*?'

For minutes a low drone has been strengthening, as if Jack's music had triggered an avalanche somewhere, some mountainous slippage that moves to engulf us, gaining force with every shift in the breeze. Now it rises to a scream, and the air curdles with an unmistakeable chopping of blades.

'It's a bloody *helicopter*!'

Kumar jumps up and strolls to the rail. Jack snaps off the tape and watches the candles flatten and die. Zoë sees it first, a red light pulsing above the rooftops, a blacker outline against the sky.

'It's landing on the roof! It's coming this *way*!'

Madeleine stumbles in fear, hair in flames around her face, clutching the jacket and tugging the dress down around her thighs. The chopper moves in above her, a black ton of metal suspended in our sky.

'That's the BOBBIES!' yells Serge. 'Manchester CID! Fly out here looking for BURGLARS . . . !'

Forty feet up, the machine settles in its own storm. A hatch opens, and something drops burning from an outstretched hand, extinguished instantly by the force of the blades. Now they're falling all around us, rough clusters of fire buffeted into darkness, blown down to the roof and into the night beyond the railings.

'That ain't no copper chopper . . .' Kumar backs off, head shaking no.

We're standing now, mesmerised, bullied to our guts, numbed by wind and noise. Ash from the whirlwind stings our eyes. The aircraft dips forward in a sort of bow, showing two silhouetted figures behind glass. They watch us without a sign. The machine backs out from above us, straightens and waits, then curves off into the night.

'Jesus,' hisses Lavonne as the noise of rotors fades.

Flakes of paper, some still burning, lie littered around the roof. Kumar picks one up, flattens it and squints at it through the gloom.

'What is it?'

He picks up a handful, unfolds them and turns towards the street for the better light.

'Photos,' he says. 'Really crappy ones. Some kid's birthday party. A caravan by a lake. Mummy and Daddy and their little girl.'

He glances out at the night. Einar lifts the edge of the rug he's been hiding under and beckons urgently to Lavonne.

'Hang on, this one looks like a comet . . .'

'A what?' Lavonne ignores Einar's signalling and hugs her arms in cold.

'A comet. Yeh, night sky and all that. Real amateur astronomer stuff.'

He holds it out, peers at it from a distance, and lets it fall. Lavonne moves to speak, shoulders trembling. Hen stirs in her sleep.

'Who are your friends, Finn?'

LOT
4

'I am in the white room. The curtains are drawn because whenever it gets a chance the sun shines onto my face and hurts my eyes. My back is to the window. There's a brown chair which I'm sitting on and a bed. You are sitting on the bed with your arms by your sides like you're about to burst into tears or something. Last time you were here, you brought a little boy to me and said it was my son. As if I need telling. A man came to me with a child, he said Hen, remember Robinson. I said, Don't just stand there, bring him closer so I can get a sniff of him. You've got to make sure people are who they say they are, specially nowadays. Christ, you look pale. Come here. You smell like towels, bread, ships, houses, trees.

'You've caught me on a chatty day. Some days I do nothing but talk. I don't know, you used to come and listen to me every day but now you've got better things to do. I can't say I blame you. I'll be honest, since I came here I've had trouble making the dots join up. Or did it start before I came, when I was Mummy and you were Daddy and he was just a twinkle in the corner of our eye? There, I'm trying to explain what it's like, all this mental stuff, and some crucial bit of information is missing. But don't feel guilty, I wouldn't want you to feel guilty. Until I came here I never realised how interesting things are. How you can look at them for ages, getting their smells. Listening to what they have to say.

'Today I'm wearing a white tee-shirt and my feet are bare. I have no complaints, which is unusual for me. I'm a selfish person when it comes down to it, we all are, it's a national trait. I am an Englishwoman. I'm a lapsed Catholic with yellow hair. Why do I think I'm here? I think I was alive at some point in the distant past, I blame the Middle Ages, and something happened to me which has traumatised me ever since. That's why I hang around in here with the curtains drawn, so I can spend a bit of time thinking and finding out what happened, and we can hurry on back to where we were.

'Is this my hand or yours? The blue lines are veins. I move my fingers and the bones move under the skin. When you take hold of it, like you did when you came in, you'll see it's smaller than yours and smooth. That's because I'm a girly and you're a boy. You're my lover. You're my shag. First there was Bill and then there was Simon. You, Finn Causley, are the third. In between there were people who never told me their names, they came and went like the hiccups. There, you see, there's a danger I'm going to forget everything unless, ooh, I don't know. Let me switch this tape-recorder on.

'Ready? That's better. I have this memory of the time we first met. I'm living in the flat by myself. There's no furniture because Simon has taken it all. The walls are white. There are some bright red flowers on the window-sill, books everywhere. I pick up the phone and dial your number. I don't know you but I know you do interior work. You say, Thank you for calling Finn's Homework, we're sorry there is no one here to take your call. Every time I phone you're out. Then you come round in the evening and we tell each other lies till we're ready for bed. But we don't get much sleep, if you know what I mean.

'That goes on for a while, just you and me, telling each other lies.

'We went to Paris to see the graves. We're on this bridge, talking about the baby. You say, You know, Hen, this is what I always wanted, I just didn't realise it till now. And then I go quiet for some reason. It's because I think you're about to say something else. Perhaps you do, perhaps you tell me you've got a surprise for me then keep me guessing like the big tease that you are. Perhaps I interrupt and spoil it. So we end up having this enormous screaming match on a very romantic bridge, then we go back to the hotel and sleep head to toe like we always do when we've had a row. Next day we're on the platform on the metro, trying to think up a name for the little shit. Then a train comes by with ROBINSON in big lights on the front, and we look at each other and laugh.

'What's this you've brought me? It's about six inches tall. I'm running my fingers all over it to try and find the clues. It's made of china, and it looks like it's been painted because there are streaks. No, it's glaze, like the things I used to make with Zoë and Roxanne. You say Zo made it? She's a flash cow. There are two people in this statue, okay, one of them with a funny-shaped head. Oh I see, it's a teapot; one of them has a teapot for a head and the other is sucking at the spout. I know what you came for but you'll have to wait.'

'How would you like a cup of tea? Come on then. We call this place the House of Love, for obvious reasons. The kitchen is two rooms down the corridor. I'm limping slightly since I twisted my ankle, don't ask me how. You let me go through the door first because you're a gentleman. Hey, I bet you can't tell which are the nurses and which are the patients! We're all as daft as each other in this place. But we're not mad, Mrs Matthewman was very clear about that. Here's the kitchen. Hold the door open with your foot. As you can see, I'm perfectly capable of making a cup of tea and looking after myself generally. First I fill this jug with water then I put the electricity in the back. Then we wait. No, you wait and I go and get the teapot. You're going to laugh when you see this, see me struggling with this great big pot. You could make tea for a hundred in here and still have some left for a tramp or two. Cor. Speaking of tramps, that's Tony in the doorway. He's going to tattoo me one day. He's seen this one on my ankle that the funny African did and he thinks he can do better. I'm an artist, I already have a design in my head. If I ever get back to Print, I'm going to make paper with strands of silk.

'If you ever see Robinson, tell him he's going to grow up to be a silk-paper-maker, like his Mo.

'Thank you. Look, I've splashed some boiling water on my hands. Ow. The milk is in the fridge. The first time I offered you a cup of tea, you know what you said? You said, No thanks, I'm trying to give it up. You're a funny cunt. Excuse my language. Put some fucking milk in your fucking cup and follow me. Did they tell you what they've

---

Lot 4: **Statue**, purple glaze on white ceramic, depicting a couple of indeterminate sex in an intimate embrace.

found? I've too much white in my ascending nigrostriatal regions. Oh, I see you've got a print-out of the scan. Today we were doing visualisation exercises. We had to imagine our NTX levels were going up and up, like a balloon rising into the sky. Don't ask me what NTX is. You're the one who went to university.

'Did anyone ever tell you you're very attractive? I'm serious. You get to the point with someone where you feel your clothes are just getting in the way. Thankfully, in this place you can go round in nothing but a tee-shirt and no one bats an eyelid. I think you know what I mean. Sit down on the bed and let me sit down next to you. Come and assuage my unease. Don't worry, I'm not going to bring out the handcuffs, I know how nervous they make you. All I ask for is a little kiss. That's right, don't be afraid. Happiness is many things but it's not contagious. Thank you. Now again. This time . . . that's better. Christ, I want you. I love you. I want you and love you! I love you so bloody much. I . . . hands . . . tongue . . . cock . . . cunt . . . in . . . put it . . . in.

'What's the mattress? What have I done?

'Go on, then. Go. Just fucking go.

'Did I ever tell you about Tony? He's a tattoo artist. He's going to tattoo me one day.

'I can see you don't find me attractive any more. Don't worry, millions think the same.

'If you see Robinson, can you tell him his Mo loves him very much?'

'You are getting up to go. I've probably been talking since 1372. Have you seen this? It's the last entry in my diary: 7th March 1372. I lost a few years somewhere, unfortunate but there it is. Christ, you're so pale you're almost shining, if I didn't know you better I'd think you were a ghost! Don't worry, next time you come I probably won't say a word. I know what the problem is. You're sick of hearing me say I'm going to live for ever. You don't want to imagine what it feels like, waking up for the very first time. But one day you'll wake up too, one day you'll know how it feels. We're the two trees, remember, the two trees on the hillside, twisted together by luck. You're dressed in green so you won't forget me, the twin tree that grew up next to you, you'll never get me out of your head. You might be in love with other people, I don't know, but we'll always be out there, twisted together under the sky. No need to be sad, my little loveability. The world is full of wonder. Listen, there are people shouting outside, even though we're miles from anywhere in the middle of the moor. That's it, I've said enough. As you get up from the bed, the sun comes out behind the curtains and I can feel that little strip of sunlight on my cheek.'

LOT
5

There are two things you can do with a thing like this: take it to a rusty yellow skip at the Print and District municipal tip, feel a flutter of regret extinguished by the proper seasonal need to make space and start afresh, and bury it, with demented gulls for witnesses, among hedge clippings and ripped-out kitchen units; or, if spring cleaning doesn't appeal, you can find a child with a small enough head and a big enough desire for space travel, for whom it can double as a cycle helmet on the short ride out of your life. These are the options, unless you happen to be an auctioneer, sitting in a cluttered room on the Saturday before a big sale, trying to piece together a childhood about which, what with one thing and another, you have never really had much to say. In which case, all you have to do is park it on the desk in front of you, so your own prematurely balding head is reflected in the plastic visor, and force it to tell you what it knows. You can no longer pull it over your ears to shut out the sound of a marriage breaking apart on the floor below, but perhaps that gives you a better chance of finding out what all the shouting was about, and why, one day in 1977, it suddenly stopped for good.

There was a time in the 1970s when every child in the kingdom would have owned a plastic spaceman's helmet, before the planets and satellites of our glorious solar system began to look like a scattering of windy islands, like the Orkneys or the Falklands, which no one would have visited even if they could: I mean the days when it was still all right to want the moon. Like every child of his generation, Finn had watched the 1969 Apollo landings from the carpet beside his mother, who, along with every wide-eyed parent of her generation, simply wanted to be around when History went by. And here it was, the thing we'd been reading about for years, revealing itself in the fuzzy TV images that flickered in every brown-carpeted living room in our street. I was no older than Robinson was when we first arrived in Print, which is a contorted way of saying I remember nothing of that momentous afternoon in July. But I remember the arrival of this helmet a few years later, when there was still enough space fever in the air to fire my dreams of escape from this earth.

I was growing up in a new house in the south of Essex, which, if there had been any hills to build it on, would have granted a view of oil refineries, container docks and a scattering of orange and yellow cranes. The Thames drove through the parks and estates of its dependent industries, gleaming with an oily complexion through the haze, looking nothing like the tourist attraction which flowed under several world-famous bridges twenty miles upstream. In London it formed the backdrop for every gangland drama that ever came to a sticky end; standard urban fantasies had it dredged for bodies and accepting getaway cars at the end of implausible chases; but in districts like ours its sole achievement was to smear its dullness across the gullible sky, leach all traces of colour from houses and shopping centres and refit them in its own miserable livery. It was a filmy, alkaline grey that travelled at a fraction of the speed of light and clung to everything it touched. It was a pigment that crept into the marrow and wrote itself into the genetic code. If you can bring yourself close enough, you'll see traces of it in my blue-grey eyes and grey-brown hair, a certain green-and-grey dullness beneath the skin. I thought it might fade as I made my escape, but it's there in my blood, the ghost of the estuary, killing me slowly with its radio-active haze.

As a family, we were standard soap-ad material. There were arguments about bedtimes and TV schedules, biscuit consumption, objects borrowed and not returned. My sister Alison was a year and a half older but hated me like an equal: that meant Chinese burns, pulled hair, missiles aimed with precocious accuracy at the head.

Here, right on cue, my space helmet offers some painful evidence: this dent in the grey plastic, just above the hinge that connects the visor to the helmet, tells the story of a flying rollerskate in as much detail as any gentle heart could stand. Who knows what might have become of Finn Causley if he hadn't been rehearsing a space walk at the time that rollerskate appeared in the doorway, three feet from the ground and travelling at a galactic speed; I know Mum had no difficulty imagining the possibilities, and even Alison, who was seven and still in a vicious rage, could see she'd done something very wrong. Shortly afterwards she was seen leaving the house by the French windows (it was memory's hottest summer, and the wasps were after us like jam), a small suitcase in one hand, later found to contain nothing but a well-sucked teddy bear, a half-packet of Opal Fruits and her sleepy dormouse writing set. 'I can't stand it,' she said, already beautiful, melting like snow on the path. There were some hurtful but perceptive comments about Mum and Dad's near-constant rowing, and she curled up on the grass. I forgave her, Mum forgave her, Dad was looking at property south of the river, and eleven years later she went up to Oxford and made us all very proud.

Who says I was short of friends? My mother was already a TV celebrity, so there was no lack of starstruck youngsters who wanted to come round to our place for mashed potato slurried with tomato ketchup, before setting off to search for the big grey cameras they assumed must be hidden around the house. She made her name with *Hide and Seek*, which, as all but our youngest customers will recall, involved a family of furry animals who hid from each other in interesting places, stopping now and then to sing songs about it in unfathomable accents. At the time of her last drive she had just signed a contract for a new show called *Vlad and Bim*, which, I was once assured by two members of the original production team, did not start filming until she was several months dead. That didn't stop me watching it for the two seasons for which it ran, somehow expecting her to show up at the shiny black piano, looking no less awkward than she had ever looked in that position, but perhaps with some sign of the peace that had eluded her in her life. It wasn't that

---

Lot 5: **Plastic astronaut's helmet**, with hinged visor and injection-moulded ventilation pipes.

I imagined she was still alive (although the idea had kept me awake through all that first tear-stained May, waiting for a tap at the window or a voice from the corner of the room); I simply thought I might have caught a glimpse of her in her last hectic days, her tall frame bowed by the scale of her impending appointment; or heard a snatch of the music she was paid to play, a few bold, sunny, confident notes.

You've guessed it: she was the woman at the piano in *Hide and Seek*, the one the animals climbed all over, who smiled like a teacher and spoke as little as she could. Margaret Causley, if you never strained to catch her name on the closing credits, overbreathing with childish pride. Hers is the music I hear when I think about her lonely death on a spring-warm moor, all those cheery songs in three-quarter time about rainfall and motorcars and cooking tarts with Nan. Hers is the face I try to remember when I'm in the mood for remembering faces; it is her song I'm humming to myself when my eyes drift off and my forehead spells careful thought. She was the reason I had to come here two years ago, trying to trace her tyre tracks through the things she left behind; and if I'd understood things then the way I understand them now, perhaps I would have stepped more lightly on her trail.

They met at a dance in the mid-sixties, when my mother's life still stretched ahead of her like a motorway sunlit after rain, when an unmarried nineteen-year-old had enough time on her hands to spend evenings in church halls, eyeing the young farmers across the parquet floor, tapping her knees to music from dinner-jacketed bands. Dad has been many things in his life but he has never been less than charming, so if I tell you that Margaret was impulsive, curious and in a hurry to escape the family home, you can imagine how, seeing him cross the floor with every sign of recognising an old friend, she was bold enough to return his smile. He always says, with the slick authority of a well-worn story, that he mistook her for someone else. Who, for instance? Was anyone's look as guileless, trusting and utterly inescapable as Margaret's? Did anyone share that long medieval face and the fine crease under the eyes? Come on, Dad, and we can decide for ourselves. Was this a trick reserved for pale-armed girls who worked on poultry farms, who were told that once the clock reached twenty their time was up and they had no chance of finding a husband; or were you simply quicker than most to recognise the one true love of your life? Anyway, he pulled up short, took a high deliberate step over an invisible obstacle, and asked her to dance. Which of our slow-eyed mothers would have refused?

Whilst we're here, on this shiny dance floor, flushed with ballroom light and the closeness of a stranger's body, let's have a good look at the man who is about to sweep my mother off her feet. He was a chartered surveyor in the latter stages of his apprenticeship, who became a real estate dealer with a poor eye for an investment but an insatiable appetite for property. Rich widows and dippy temps alike have admired his delicate English bone-structure, the light colourings that side-stepped Alison and came straight down to me; level eyebrows, aristocratic nose, nostrils that flared and whitened whenever he opened his mouth to laugh. He concealed a Collier Row upbringing with an accent that was sufficiently neutral to give him all the business opportunities he needed, but just careful enough with its vowels to suggest an education he'd never had. All of which came with an unquestioning belief in the importance of what he had to say – an observation on the habits of women, a joke at our expense – which meant he could never allow himself to be interrupted. No matter how insistently or passionately you tried to talk him down, he would continue speaking, with his horsey breath and rather wide mouth, until all his relative clauses had been delivered in the correct order, then look at you as if your unheeded chatter was as charming to him as bouquets from an unknown admirer, praises he was far too modest to acknowledge.

How much of this could any girl notice after a few gin-and-oranges and a few hundred revolutions around a slippery church hall? And what was the logical next step, once the damp walls had given way to the night over the car park, and it seemed so easy to lose yourself in this night and never find your way back to where you were? I've already said my mother was impulsive, but she was also unable to let go of an idea once it had caught hold. Phone numbers were exchanged. She played Chopin for him a week or so later, no doubt wearing the look of serious contentment that shows up clearly on the videos; she accepted an invitation to spend a weekend on 'his boat', moored thirty miles away on the River Blackwater; and presumably became a woman under a coarse blanket on a narrow berth, to the accompaniment of ticking lanyards and black water lapping at the hull. Only later would she have learned that the boat really belonged to my father's friend Brian, by which time she was exhilaratingly and trustingly in love. Two months after that, having let slip certain details about her physical condition, she was proposed to in the manner she had always dreamed, and seven months later Alison was born.

Years later, the only person who will tell me anything about the events that caused me is my stepmother Joy. I've long since given up trying to get anything out of Dad, who is more than happy to tell me the name of the hotel they stayed at on their honeymoon in Majorca, or the mileage records of their first car. But on anything that might threaten his new-found contentment by calling up the ghost of his lost wife, he is famously, maddeningly silent. I've heard him say nothing but that she was brave and spirited but cursed with unpredictable depressions, making sure a rare flutter to his voice evokes a tenderness I don't remember hearing when she was alive. So I have to get my information from the woman who replaced my mother, after what some would call an indecently short interval, in my father's life. And how does Joy know so much about that murderer's affairs? She knows because she was there. Joy was the first wife of Brian Cantrell, my father's seafaring partner, whose second Mrs Cantrell was an American starlet with whom he disappeared the year before my mother's death.

Now let's just hold it there a moment. The gap between Finn's facts and Finn's interpretation is wide enough for a blue Cortina, and a story that's judged before its end should not be called a story at all. Why these creeping accusations? Why, after all these years, can't I accept that my mother's death was an accident, something between a speeding woman and a stationary tree, and leave it at that? And while we're at it (Hen/Anna/Anna/Hen), who am I to start condemning others for wanting to move on when a love comes to an end? As Dad himself once told me, people are responsible for what they do but not what they feel. The heart has its reasons, says his dun accomplice, banging the message home with nods of her demi-waved head; and someone with my susceptibility to a certain combination of physical features could not fail to agree. So why do I call him a murderer? Because when she died he put everything she was into a cardboard box and forgot about it. Because we were never allowed to talk about her. Because the same box is now on a shelf in my room, labelled with my mother's name. And because he has a murderer's eyes and a murderer's table manners and fuck it, he's my father, I can call him what I like.

For many years Peter Causley spent summer weekends on a four-and-a-half-ton Bermuda sloop named *Bonaventure*, with a man whose only contribution to my early memories was the smell of his cigars, the sound of his farts, and the knowledge that it was his media contacts that got Mum into television in the first place. Brian made his money in shipping. It wasn't as much of a fortune as some of my family have made out, but it was enough to build a stunning slab of modernity, with boat-house and open-plan living area, on the banks of the River Blackwater. It was Joy's idea to name it Greylag, even though they were Canada geese that held parties in the garden and kept the neighbours awake. And Joy chose the wallpaper, and Joy bought the classical sculptures from the garden centre, and there, you see, it's happening: as soon as I try and tell you about my mother she turns into someone else.

Joy was from Grays, which is where Essex and London resolve their differences with sovereign rings and bottle fights, and close enough to Collier Row to lend weight to her claims about knowing Dad as a child. She always looked tanned, as if she'd just stepped off a plane from somewhere hotter than here, which she usually had. Unfortunately, when stirred up with Estuary grey, no amount of personal wealth could stop her tan coming out more brassy than golden, which was only the thin end of a bigger failure to convince the world of Spanish expats and minor aristocracy that she was one of them. As Hen's parents took such pleasure in pointing out, you can take the girl out of Essex . . . but I was too loyal a stepson to let them finish. Besides, what Joy lacked in refinement she made up for with sheer enthusiasm: an unshakeable conviction that her life to now had been a sham, that ours was the family she'd been searching for all these years, and nothing was going to come between us now. Although they were thoughtful enough to delay their marriage until after Alison and I had left home, she was ready to become our stepmother as soon as the vacancy came up. She spoke of my mother as if she were a saint. In helpless gushes of appalling sincerity, she'd describe how Margaret had put up with Dad's thoughtlessness and impossible demands, with the same resigned calm she gave to a dodgy tap or temperamental washing machine. And what effect did all this stagey adoration have on the poor bereaved boy? He learned that it was better not to talk about his mother at all; the fact that Joy was the only person prepared to tell him about her was the best reason for keeping silent; and that the only safe reaction to the mention of Margaret Causley was to shake his head and look vulnerable, darken his eyes with grief, and suggest another topic with practised speed.

When it came to the mystery of where Mum was headed at the time of her accident, it was more difficult to ignore Joy's opinion. There was no mystery. Margaret had been on her way back to the hotel in Stafford where she and her husband had been taking a weekend break, had lost her way on Blacksheep Moor and come to grief on unfamiliar roads. She can't explain what journey she might have been returning from, nor why the fatal accident report made it quite clear that the car was heading north-west, towards Print and towns beyond, rather than south towards Etruria and Stafford. The idea that she might have been on her way to visit her sister at Brink Farm found no support from Sarah, nor from the observation that the blue Cortina had turned off onto the moor well before the proper turning for Brink Farm. On the one occasion when Dad, after a rare third glass of wine, suggested that a man called Mike Browning might be the person to ask, Joy's rage was instant and electrifying. She got up from the tubular armchair where she was reading a highbrow magazine, kicked out with her foot and sent her right shoe soaring into the drinks trolley at the back of the living room, narrowly missing Dad and reducing several of his best tumblers to shards. She said she took his flippant remark as a worrying omen for their own relationship, as well as a grave insult to the memory of a very dear friend. Dad gave the smile of someone who knows he can think what he likes because no one will ever listen to him, and went to bed, kicking the drinks trolley as he left.

Joy slumped back into the armchair and hid her face in her hands. Doors slammed at the top of the house.

'Who's Mike Browning?' asked Alison, fifteen.

Joy stopped crying and stared at the watch on her wrist. It was the gold her skin could never quite achieve, the same elastic-linked strap, she informed us proudly, she had worn every day for sixteen years. No, she tells a lie: she lost it once and bought another exactly the same.

'What your father is trying in his own sweet way to say,' said Joy, 'is that Mum must have been in love with the very first person she ever went out with. The dear man is so insecure! At the end of the day, he just can't see how someone as magical as her could have fallen in love with someone like him.'

That was it. We heard no more about Mike Browning. We never found out what his interest was in my mother, nor what bearing it might have had on her accident. We had our theories, of course, or Alison did. I didn't ask to share them. To try to plug the gaps with adolescent guesswork would have been to murder her memory as thoroughly as Dad had by refusing to talk about her; and when that memory amounted to little more than a half-remembered song and the contents of a cardboard box, it was all I could do to keep it safe.

According to the photocopied sheet I found in Dad's study, the official cause of my mother's death was head injury caused by collision with a tree on a high part of Blacksheep Moor. Her blood alcohol level was recorded as negligible, and there was no evidence of heart failure, brain seizure or marital strife. The first person on the scene was a farmer, Mr Bown, his red tractor contrasting gamely with the crumpled blue Cortina, who phoned the emergency services at 5.18 p.m., just as my mother's anxious face was appearing on screens all over the country in one of the last productions of *Hide and Seek*. The corner on which she had lost control of the car was noted as being a local blackspot which had seen three fatal accidents in the previous year. After a long period of dry weather, there had been rain at noon. As every careful driver knows, this meant the roads must have been as slippery as wet soap, or the memory of someone whose time on earth was as brief and unsatisfying as a dream.

After many bike trips with Robinson around the ground floor of Big Kimberley, I have come to the conclusion that my own experience of childhood can best be likened to a late-night film you watch when drunk, dozing on the sofa, steering close enough to the big cities of consciousness to catch a few disconnected scenes. There are moments of coherence when lips move in synchrony with voices, and cars make the sound they should make when they pass in the rain; for the rest of the time you have to choose between patterns of light without sound or context, and disembodied voices which, if someone isn't calling you from another room, must be coming from your own internal dead. Five minutes from the end you wake, numb and deeply buried, to see plots and sub-plots opening out to reveal their secrets, filling the screen with spectacular effects without causes, characters whose faces you will never place and whose fates you will never understand. Now, for all Joy's attempts to inform me, my own memories of my life with Margaret are no less fractured and discontinuous and creaky with significance, so that all the adult can offer as a childhood are a few poignant stills, somewhat blurred around the edges, from a mostly forgotten film.

Even those pictures that survive, when I catch them and hold them steady before me, are little better than cartoon drawings, ambiguous and imprecise. Like the animated shorts that come on when the film has ended and the TV stays on, people look as though they've been put together and brought to life by a child, with awkward hinged limbs and unchanging expressions, scribbled hair and felt-tipped clothes. When my mother speaks to me she leans towards me with her whole cardboard body and puts the O of her mouth directly against my ear. She wears a green dress, belted at the waist, with a perfectly straight hem. She smells of crayons and pencil shavings. The music, of course, is hers: she accompanies our intimate moments with waltzes and marches, jaunty songs in major keys, lovingly selected from one of the music books propped up on the piano at home. But the fact that I recognise her music doesn't make her cartoon tears, huge and blue and pear-shaped, any easier to understand. It can't quell the feeling that I'm intruding on something that has been going on since before I was born and will be going on for some time to come, and that if I already slept through so much of the story I have no chance of catching up on it now.

Sometimes I can hardly believe my luck. Just as I'm beginning to accept why the book of my childhood has so many blank pages, and it seems more honest to pretend it never happened and move on, it happens to be a Saturday, and the Print Scout Group Marching Band is in town. Nothing could help me more, as I sit here and frown at the past, than the sound of this artless drumming, trumpets and trombones and tubas all parping away to various Christian tunes. It's as if someone, knowing what difficulties I have with the years up to my mother's disappearance, had ordered them to serve me up the perfect conditions for long-distance recollection. Girls are singing, triangles are tinging; they're three streets away, two streets away, one; there are people in wheelchairs, women waving to their kids from shop doorways, and they're all marching for Jesus, banging the big drum and singing for a better world.

It begins with the sound of drumming from halfway up Etruria Road, where the purple-brick community hall marks the starting point for the day's events. They set off to an energetic march, cars and buses following behind in first gear, past Pricecutter and up the hill to the war memorial. I don't know how well the sound carries to other parts of Print, but from Big Kimberley we'll hear it, fading in and out as the parade progresses and the band makes its circuits of the town, until the traffic starts up again and everyone goes home. Zoë will find it charming for the first five minutes then steadily more irritating; Einar's lips will interpret the rhythm with astonishing accuracy as one hand pushes the hoover around the second floor; and Robinson will spend much of the day on tiptoe at his window, the TV entertaining the corner with unwatched cartoons. Later, if he behaves himself, I'll take him down to the Market Square to see the second of the main attractions, the Girl Guides' Brass Band and Choir, who will astound us all with their brown legs and their flair for public performance. After that there'll be more drumming, in crescendo and diminuendo, then all will come together for the main procession: Scouts, Guides, Cubs and Brownies in a smiling pre-pubescent band, followed by the wheelchair contingent who always look happier than everyone else, followed by a ragged parade of mums and dads and siblings. The whole town watches, shopping bags at their feet, forgetting the words to 'Kum-ba-yah' and 'Onward Christian Soldiers', reaching out to drop hot coins into the bucket which passes slowly up the street. At the end of the High Street they cross the Market Square and make an orderly turn into Manchester Road. Followed at walking pace by the floats, packed to the gunwales with elaborately made-up children, itching in period costumes and fiddling with safety pins.

If I stay at my desk for long enough, with no blond boy to extricate from trouble and just the noise from the street to hold me to the here-and-now, it won't be long before the past takes on colour and the first pictures form behind my eyes. There is no single memory that the sound of the carnival triggers; I simply take this music as a general soundtrack for my childhood, against which most of my cartoon recollections seem to fit. I had quite a nice singing voice when I was young, and there isn't a song those kids are singing that hasn't been performed by a younger Finn Causley, even if that only meant standing at the piano with Mum on the stool beside me, in her wide-lapelled blouses, making those sounds with her fingers and feet. But the world that was gradually revealing itself to me had too many secret compartments and clever switches, and I outgrew my interest in our parlour concerts at the same rate that I outgrew my shoes.

The piano was in the living room at the back of the house, against the wall opposite the window, so that, on an overcast day, her face would be in shadow as she played. A dusky green will do for the wallpaper; black can be her hair as it falls down around her face; blue can be the daylight reflected on the keys. Her fingers are as long and pale as those keys; she hardly seems to look at them, except when a high melody or rhapsody spreads her hands to either end of the keyboard, then returns them to their central chords. She looks instead at the music in front of her, picking her way from dot to dot, stave to stave, turning the page with a single swift movement of her left hand. Her shoulders are rounded, even hunched; her spine curves forward between her shoulder-blades; yet as soon as she sees me in the doorway she sits up and straightens her back, and looks at me with an expression which is one part blush to two parts smile.

There is a scent that drifts up as I stand beside her: a simple layer of perfumed soap, sharpened by piano polish, then her own warm, bready, faintly sour smell. Smells give way to smells, making short-cuts into other parts of her: the smell of the licked handkerchief with which she'd wipe my face; the smell of perfume mixed with handbag leather, with a hint of soap from the breath-freshener pills she always carried; and the related smell of her open handbag, as mysterious to me as the breeding smell she wore on certain days, the smell of pills and lipsticks, ointments, notebooks and a fat leather purse.

Usually she would pause when I came in, sustaining a chord with the pedal while her blushes faded and she made space for me on the stool. But here is something different: a day no different to any other, green black blue, except that the music continues when I walk in, as if to cover the sound she is making in her throat, or draw my eyes away from the snail-tracks on her cheeks. And someone doesn't realise that these are tears, not until her fingers stop in mid-phrase and pale hands go up to her face. Her sobs keep up the rhythm in the absence of a tune, her body flexes and unflexes beneath her patterned jumper; her hair is brown with streaks of daylight, falling down around her hands and eyes; no wonder she is upset, she cannot see, I need to turn the light on to let her see what is frightening her. A child's hand approaches her shoulder; let me call it Finn, or say, to spare myself any unnecessary suffering, that Finn is the owner of that hand. She turns and looks up. I know now that tears can make a face beautiful, but that boy Finn, as far removed from me as any dead mother, sees nothing he can call a face, just a terrible portioning of what used to be a woman into primary colours and simple grief.

I know, I know: there is nothing more tedious than other people's childhood memories, except those that come with tales of unspoken love for dead mothers, in which case they should not be wished on anyone. So I won't have to explain why I told her to stop being such a big baby, and asked why she'd stopped in the middle of that song, and by the way, where were my football boots; I can pretend instead that Finn the huge-hearted adult lived inside Finn the chicken-necked boy, and that Margaret's eyes grew watery all over again when she realised what a selfless loving son she had raised. I won't encourage our customers to waste their time drawing lines from past to present, as if they might read the secret of my personality in the resulting mess. It seems obvious: you cannot sell a memory, you can't even fix a reserve, especially when the image is poor and the subject-matter out of date. Better to choose something that stays in your hands until you feel like putting it down, something that catches the light like any other bit of junk, but which has been around long enough to reassure you that it's telling the truth.

Lot 5: plastic astronaut's helmet, slightly dented at the temple,

NASA white on Estuary grey. Shape: roughly spherical; diameter: thirteen inches. I knew what it was as soon as she arrived in our hallway with a thirteen-and-a-half-inch box in a plastic bag. I'd been pestering her about it for months, having first caught sight of it in the window of Woolworths, placed for maximum impact between a red-and-yellow stun gun and an Airfix kit of Apollo 15. 'Let's see what Santa brings,' she said. But Santa came and went on silent reindeer feet; my birthday made me five, leaving eleven months before I could next expect a present, and all I had were stetsons and cap pistols, cheap board games which I didn't understand. Although he never made a fuss in front of the children, Dad was not one to spend good money on overpriced bits of plastic when we could make do, as he had centuries before, with a few blocks of wood and a little imagination. I have to assume that was the case, because the same evening I heard them through the floor, Dad's voice increasing in volume in inverse proportion to Mum's. I should have been asleep, worn out by an evening of moonwalking around the house. But I had just spent three hours inside my new helmet, which meant that any sound to reach me now was amplified by three hours of hearing nothing at all, unless you want to count my own heartbeat and infinity's black roar.

WELL IF YOU WOULD JUST SPEND A BIT OF TIME LISTENING but Peter I do TO WHAT I KEEP ON SAYING I do INSTEAD OF RUNNING OUT Peter TO BUY THEM USELESS BITS OF JUNK but it's not it's EVERY FIVE MINUTES YOU MIGHT BEGIN TO SEE THE LOGIC OF MY

A lip of electric light on the carpet below the door. The door opened, and a strip of yellow fanned out across the floor, spreading a fuzzy illumination. My head, encased in its plastic helmet, was resting between the jaws of the only lion ever to be sighted on the surface of the moon. Margaret was there, in a pure silver space suit, surrounded by some of the animals from *Hide and Seek*. She spoke slowly and quietly to the lion, who looked as though he could do with an early night. She warned him that if he didn't start picking on someone his own size, she would take me and a beautiful space pony called Alison away to the furthest planet in the sky. As she pointed with one silver-gloved finger to a star-sized dot far out in space, a yellow sunrise appeared over a lunar plain, and the animals, who had started singing gleefully as soon as my mother had delivered her ultimatum, left the ground and drifted up towards the dark infinity of my bedroom ceiling. And it didn't matter that there were no stars to speak of, because Margaret was kneeling beside me, pressing my hand through the blanket, loose strands of hair backlit by yellow landing light.

'Why were you arguing?'

I whispered, to make sure she came close.

'We weren't really arguing. Daddy and I were having a discussion. He is unhappy about some things.'

Her watch ticks on its leather strap. As her face comes closer, I'm noticing what I can't have noticed then: this look of bewilderment at what is happening to her, which is there in every photograph of her to survive, but which tonight, after whatever has been said downstairs, is having more and more to do with fear. Years later, I'm seeing the same expression on Roxanne, catching sight of her when she doesn't know she's being watched, wandering around the ground floor of Big Kimberley in dungarees and baseball cap. Something in the way she picks things up and holds them to the light, eyes shrinking at the corners, suggests this other place is not so far away, and it won't be long before she reaches it, kicks off her shoes and begins to feel at home. As in all the photos I have tried to memorise, there is that ripple between my mother's eyebrows, which some might call a habitual frown. How much does she know? She will live for another four years. She will become famous to children across the country for her work on television, though none will ever catch her name. If she has glimpsed into the future, she will see a space rocket travelling to a planet where everyone plays the piano and wears wide-lapelled blouses, where there are no one-sided discussions or handbags with secret contents, where people die quickly, in painless anonymity, with never the bother of growing old. Now she is saying 'we' in a different voice, and I know she means herself and Dad. 'Whatever happens,' she says, 'we want you to remember one thing.'

She waits for my eyes. Downstairs in the living room, my father holds one hand up as if stopping traffic and talks back to the news. THAT'S IT. JUST RUN TO THEM WHEN YOU CAN'T FACE A PROPER ARGUMENT. JUST

But it's Margaret's voice I hear.

'It doesn't matter how someone *talks* to you, as long as they're *good* to you. That's the thing you need to know.'

When I said that Robinson would have to behave himself if he wanted to be taken outside to watch the Girl Guides with their brown legs, I meant he should pay attention to his biology lesson. 'All right, we'll begin with a little Histology. That is, History-ology, the study of History as revealed in the lives of individual cells. Histology. Pass me that bit of chalk.' He dives for the chalk and holds it up, grinning, then flops back in his chair in front of the blackboard. First thing is a diagram of a typical eukaryotic cell.

'It's an egg,' he says, always ready with a reference to food.

'That's what it looks like. This big outer circle is the cell membrane, and the inner circle is the nucleus.'

'It's got a runny bit in the middle,' says Robinson.

'Now, I want you to imagine something. Imagine this cell is a person. There are millions and millions of cells in a single human body, just as there are millions and millions of people in the world. Biologists go so far as to say that the human body is its own complete world, with its own geography, climate, systems of self-regulation, and a constantly changing population of cells. Furthermore, each cell has its own job to do. There aren't any auctioneers or furniture restorers, but there are cells that stand in a line and sweep up the rubbish, and cells with long fingers that join up through the darkness to send messages to each other. Other cells look like doughnuts and have no nuclei, which means they need someone else to tell them who they are. These are the red blood cells or erythrocytes, although in actual fact they're not red at all but a very pale pink. Perhaps we should turn the telly off.'

He scrambles across and picks up the remote control. Kneeling high, concentrating, he presses all the buttons until the screen goes blank. He gives a big floppy sigh and rolls eyeballs up to his fringe, then crawls back to his chair.

'Just as a person has to grow from a baby into a grown-up, every cell develops from something very small into something a little bigger. Development proceeds according to a plan stored here in the nucleus. The runny bit, that's right. It's very dark in the nucleus, so everything that happens is completely random and a mystery to all concerned. In the nucleus there are lots of wiggly worms called chromosomes. Each chromosome has a best friend who she hangs around with. When the cell divides, all these pairs of chromosomes line up along the middle of the cell like two football teams, except no one knows which team they're in until the last minute. Then, when the whistle blows, each chromosome in the pair is pulled to opposite ends of the cell by little fibres called spindles.'

At the mention of football, Robinson starts singing the *Grandstand* theme tune. He grips the edges of his seat and rocks back and forwards, remembering the day he was just another cell with its half-complement of chromosomes. The chair tips forwards, turning Robinson onto the carpet like an omelette made with only one egg.

'Thank you. Now, those of you who are still with us will have noticed what a close relationship there is between biology and history. Each cell lives out its life in perfect anonymity, performing its function to the best of its abilities, until a tiny packet of autolytic enzymes arrives to put it to a natural death. Every so often, though, it happens that a cell steps out of line, gets ideas above its station and stops doing what it is supposed to do. One cell might decide that cell division is so satisfying that it can't stop doing it, no matter how the neighbours might frown. The result is a growth, which turns into a tumour, which is another name for Cancer with a capital C. We have that in the family, so take that smile off your face. Another cell might let a virus through its membrane, without realising that the virus will hijack its reproductive system and go on replicating itself until the host cell bursts with the number of baby viruses that have grown up inside. This is called History. History is a list of events that happen and are given significance only in retrospect, if only because to admit they were random would be too frightening for words.'

History is this. In April 1977 Margaret and Peter Causley left their family home in Basildon for a long weekend at the Blundeville Arms Hotel in Stafford. It was not the first time they had made such a trip. Twenty years later, Finn Causley, teaching a lesson in cell biology to his three-year-old son, began asking questions about his mother's death. On the 23rd March 1759, at his partner's factory at Fenton Hall, Josiah Wedgwood discovered the colour green. Sixteen years later, a 952-piece Queensware service, in which green frogs played a prominent role, was sold to Catherine the Great of Russia for 16,406 roubles. On the 22nd April 1214, a little band of Cistercian monks arrived at the outskirts of the Manor of Print, where they were to begin work on a great abbey, known ultimately as Dieulacres.

History is a list of events that bear no relation to each other. On April 18th 1977, Finn Causley and his sister Alison were staying with their uncle Mervyn at his house in Essex. In June 1996, Don Long, of Brink Farm, Print, was given a tentative diagnosis of St Mary's Disease. The first person to receive such a diagnosis was Michael Morton, in March 1989, at St Mary's Hospital in London. On the 20th October 1538, over three centuries after its foundation by Ranulph, Earl of Chester, Dr Thomas Legh arrived at Dieulacres Abbey with his bailiff, William Cavendish. They inspected the buildings, drew up inventories and then began the work of dissolution and sale.

Biology is history on a smaller, or a bigger, scale. The cause of Margaret Causley's death was recorded as cranial haemorrhage, triggered by a weakness in the wall of a single blood vessel in the frontal region. The first erythrocyte to cross the breach in the blood–brain barrier had a short and uneventful life. The millions that followed instantly were no more distinguished. One theory about the cause of St Mary's Disease suggests a deficit in a neurochemical called NTX, resulting from damage to the gene responsible for its synthesis. The great Cistercian abbey of Dieulacres was founded, according to local legend, as a direct consequence of Ranulph de Blundeville's dream of his late grandfather, warning him to move his existing abbey to the Manor of Print. As every schoolboy knows, dreams begin as single-cell flickers in the ascending nigrostriatal system, and end as monasteries and silk mills, promises of never-ending love, car crashes on country roads.

In the evening of Monday, 18th April 1977, the phone rang in the house of Mervyn and Teri Wilton. On the line was Mervyn's elder sister Sarah, who asked whether the children were in the room. While Sarah told Mervyn the details of their younger sister's accident, Finn Causley was in his uncle's workshop at the end of the garden, making a sculpture from the grey plastic spines to which the parts of an Airfix kit come attached. He was working with the smell of glue in his nostrils, under a single electric bulb. As soon as he had attached this spine he was going to open a small pot of enamel paint and paint the whole thing duck-egg green. He never heard the phone ring. He was humming the *Mission: Impossible* theme tune. He was going to be allowed to stay up tonight to watch it, as a special treat while his parents were away. He never heard the footsteps on the path or the voices outside the door. The first thing he knew of what had happened was the sight of Mervyn in the doorway, with Teri beside him, clutching his shocked sister to her hip.

LOT
6

The kid breaks into my room. He shoves himself up on the toes of his cute blue shoes, hands flat against the white side of the door, in a slight hurry to be on the other side. He reaches the knob, turns it first the wrong way and then the right way, and topples through the doorway, three and a half and still unsteady on his feet, into a projected window of light. His hair is spun sugar, candy-floss and demerara, clinging in wisps to a china-doll brow. He brushes it from his eyes. He has his father's milky colouring and his mother's blue-grey gaze, but the plastic brain under his left arm, the device through which he interprets the world, is entirely his own.

He drops to his knees, turns down the corners of his mouth in an expression of concentration, and places the brain with precision on the rug before him. It neither moves towards him nor turns and crawls away. It is not a tortoise nor a hamster, not a living thing nor something which once living is now dead. It is not a train. It is a life-sized model of the human mental organ, with soft folds and a rubbery scent, which nevertheless failed to reach its reserve price at auction several months ago. He once left it in Linden's car, let it roll under the seat like an empty can and didn't realise it was missing until Linden was far away. Now, when he throws it at the clinic or drops it in the street, it bounces back to him like a ball.

He leaves the brain to its solitary thoughts and looks up at the faraway room. Green walls. Spotlights clipped to shelves. No glass ceiling here, because with too much light around his mother, the photosensitive object of his search, could never sleep. His eyes drift from one end of the room to the other, joining points of interest on the plaster, moving from lot to lot with the vigilance of a seasoned buyer. She is nowhere to be seen. She is not downstairs in the pre-auction showroom, nor in the office at the top of the stairs, nor lost among the ground-floor storage bays. She is not at work because the problem she has with concentrating and retrieving simple bits of information means she can no longer hold down a job. He has put his eye to each shelf of the walnut display cabinet, he has sat on men's shoulders to inspect the bigger pine shelves above his head, and all he can find are objects, things that make up his father's special collection, waiting to be catalogued and explained. There is nothing of her size or shape or colour. She has become invisible, knowable only through the handwriting on an envelope, a scrap of paper run through with silk, a box of matches, a pile of magazines.

He unfolds from kneeling, pushes feet forward and sits cross-legged on the floor. If his mother is just a memory, there is only one place to look for her. He breaks open the two hemispheres, removes the coloured components and spreads them out on the carpet. There she is, in the left temporal lobe, squashed between a purple layer of cortex and the white matter further in. He traces the shape with a finger. He follows the purple line round into the occipital lobe and down into the lateral ventricle. His mother looks up at him from the white ridge of Ammon's Horn. He joins the two quarters of the hemisphere to make a cave for her in the ventricle, so she can stay for ever in the company of memories, their light-tricks, secluded spaces and filtered sound. Then he clicks the two hemispheres together like halves of an Easter egg, and looks down on her through the hole where the brainstem should fit.

She is trapped. He will never let her go.

He makes his way to the desk and climbs up. The chair shifts on its castors, rolling an inch towards the window. He climbs up onto the desk. Things confront him: a picture of himself in an antique silver frame, a laptop computer connected by a cable to the phone socket, and a largish cardboard box, marked MARGARET CAUSLEY: 1947–1977. His grandmother is in the box. Her name is Margaret and she is dead. She does not have a lot number because she is a person and persons, especially dead persons, cannot be auctioned. He stands up on the desk, pulls at the flaps and begins to unpack it on either side. As he works, he mumbles a tune from a children's programme broadcast years before he was born.

> He finds: 'The Silk Twister', a five-and-a-half-inch porcelain figurine
> a gold ladies' watch with gold-plated elastic-linked strap
> a leather handbag, still with guarantee label attached
> a plastic carrier bag bearing the legend *Duke's of Stafford* in brown letters
> a receipt from the same shop, dated 18th April 1977, which, if he could read, would tell him 'Leather handbag, £11.99'
> a pair of reading glasses in a tortoiseshell frame
> a turquoise polyester headscarf
> a sage-green belted raincoat, with a crumpled handkerchief in one pocket
> a necklace of blue plastic beads
> assorted photographs of Margaret Causley, some in colour
> five video cassettes, each marked with the title *Hide and Seek* and dates between 1973 and 1977.

'*Here* we are!' says Robinson like a sigh. He lays the first cassette on the tabletop and extends himself to the floor. He pushes the cassette into the video recorder and presses all the buttons on the remote control. Static fills the screen. He presses another button, the biggest he can find, and a picture scrolls down into view. As the piano starts, he stands back from the set and starts to dance, taking neat steps back and forwards in time to the music, rolling his head from side to side, lifting his arms and letting them drop back to his sides.

The picture is in black and white and not very clear. In the foreground three furry animals are singing a song while trying to find a fourth who is hiding in a box on a shelf. To the left of the picture, a woman sits at a piano and moves her feet and hands. Her face is in profile, white shaded with black and grey; if you look closely you can see her lips move as she reads the music propped on the stand. She wears a white polo-neck sweater and a necklace of plastic beads. On one finger, the shy gleam of a wedding ring. Now she turns to look at Izzy, Lizzy and Joe, her head moving to the same rhythm as her hands and feet, but more deliberate, striving after an impression of control. She smiles, and a reflection from the studio lights catches in her eyes.

I promised you things, real pick-me-up-and-turn-me-over things, on the hunch that there's no object that can't tell us something about the person who bought it, borrowed it, broke it, lost it or gave it away; but if this is a catalogue, it seems to offer little more than childhood ghosts and misremembered conversations, which, I hardly need tell you, have no value in the present market or in any conceivable market to come. I blame the weather, these drizzly Sundays after a promising morning which tamper with the God-given order until everything looks soft and dreamy and hardly there at all. But let's imagine, for the fun of it, that a catalogue was a sort of story, the sort auctioneers tell themselves when they're trying to get to sleep, with a beginning, a middle and an end. And since I call myself an auctioneer, let's further pretend that this was an auction, where thoughts and ideas like these could be snapped up in as much time as it takes to flutter a catalogue and call a number from the back of the room. What, then, would I hear for the following suggestion: that just as a story would not be a story unless there was some connection between the events, so there must be some way of organising a collection so that each item bears a meaningful relation to its neighbour, while simultaneously taking its place in the greater scheme. There. Do I hear five to start? Go on, Mrs Bickerton, it's only money. The point is that a catalogue demands a classification system, with neatly labelled divisions and subdivisions; what's more, we can't start putting things into boxes until we know what sort of things they are, and the people who left them behind for us to pick up were not always considerate enough to explain their functions in a few lines of scientific prose.

   What I'm trying to get round to is this: the plastic bowl we rescued from the kitchen of Brink Farm, with two compartments in the bottom for storing two things that presumably need to be kept apart. No doubt if I'd stuck with my education I'd be able to see through it

---

Lot 6: **Red polypropylene bowl**, divided by compound moulding into shallow compartments, function obscure.

straightaway, but I've been staring at it for days now and still no ideas have lit me up. I've tried washing up in it, or Einar has, but the ridge at the bottom causes more problems than it solves. 'It's a potty,' says Robinson, who knows about these things. Then Nina, our resident gardener, whose skills gave us our rooftop rockery and hanging baskets, suggests some horticultural application, perhaps in the planting of seeds or the scooping up of pests; but when I ask for a demonstration, all she can do is wave it uselessly in the space between me and her.

Problems. What to do. A catalogue must serve as the key to the collection, something that stands beyond and above the things it describes. But since our aims are complete inclusivity and exhaustion of the data, the fact is I've got to find space for the catalogue itself. Is it a work of Art, and therefore headed for the same place as plastic space helmets and porcelain figurines? Or does it need a separate division well away from the others, a category of Catalogues, Inventories and Other Favourite Wastes of Time? But wouldn't we then need a second catalogue, a sort of glittering super-catalogue, which would swallow up both the first catalogue and all the objects described therein? And why do my attempts at airtight reasoning always end with this pain behind the eyes?

'And what about people?' says Robinson. 'Where do people go?'

Simple distinctions. One box for the living and one for the dead. But what about those in between, neither alive nor dead, who believe they're going to live for ever because they've forgotten they ever knew otherwise? What do you do when the body is there but the mind is missing? Or when you hear her voice but see her nowhere, dreaming as hard as you can? A box for the living. A simple choice. Then there are days when even the dead won't lie down, but insist on coming back to see what you've been doing with your grief. A woman stands in the shadows and hums a childish tune. A red baseball cap appears around the edge of the door, a voice from the doorway, the name of someone you never were. Warm voice, body smells, smoky fingers closing out the light . . .

'Guess who?'

It's Einar, his eyes trying to act independently of each other, stinking of stale booze and sweat.

'I'm killed. I don't come home last night. I'm really killed.'

'You telling me you got a result?'

'I spend the night in the police station. In a cell with a man from Edinburgh.'

He topples forward into the room and keeps going till he reaches the bed. Tucked into his belt is a near-empty whisky bottle. 'His name is David. He is most virulent I think.'

'What did you do?'

'Offence.'

'What sort of offence?'

'No, a fence. The sort birdies sit on. I come out of the pub. I'm pissed as a cunt of course and so is David. He says he knows where a party happens. It's miles away, almost in the city. When we get there the party is happening but they won't let us in. I say I am famous porno personality but they never seen any of my films. So we steal their fence and take it home.'

He yawns and takes a swig of whisky, which dribbles down his chin and speckles the duvet.

'Then this helicopter comes down and the joint is absolutely crawling with pigs. I'm thinking: Rox, you know, she used to keep that chopper on the roof. Then I remember the swimming pool and I'm thinking, there may have been a donkey in her head but she had a fabulous pair of tits. Then I wake up in the cells and it's all very suspicious.'

He kicks off his flip-flops and stretches out on the bed, eyes closed. 'But what do you know, you are at home all night writing your catalogue. Now go away and let me sleep.'

Jack and Madeleine are on the sofa under a pink duvet. Kumar is in the kitchen making coffee. His grin is broad.

'Lavonne,' before I can even ask.

'And Janet?'

'Spent the night in Zoë's room. They were up all night talking.'

'About what?'

'Dunno about you, mate, but I had a good night's sleep. They went into Rox's room for a bit.' Kumar wipes his fingers on a towel and stares at the charred photo of a comet propped up behind the sink. 'And yeh, d'you hear about Linden? We're all in the Monk's, right, all the girls and everything, and Jack starts on about how Linden's madly in love with Zo. She's sitting, like, *there*. I mean, it was only a joke but he stormed out anyway. The word in the hairdresser's is: he's leaving. He's gonna do that round-the-world trip.'

On the way to Linden's room, a woman's scream is followed by the patter of bare feet. Hector has been meeting the guests.

'I suppose you heard,' says Linden. 'You know Serge reckons stuff's gone missing? And I'm not talking about the odd tenner from the housekeeping pot. I mean, how do you think he pays for all that computer equipment?'

'Yeh well. Serge gets these ideas. Jack's all right.'

'No he's not. He just hangs round here and pisses people off.'

He presses a key on his laptop to reveal Jack's latest artistic effort. On computer screens around the world, a woman with Zoë's face is lowering herself exquisitely onto Linden's cock. *'Linden wants to fuck Zoë. Zoë likes it hot and hard.'* He swivels in his chair. 'Am I supposed to hang around for this?'

'He likes the atmosphere. Poor bastard, we're the only friends he's got.'

'I'll think about it,' he says.

We walk down through the park, past the bandstand and its litter of broken bottles, along the road towards the valley floor. At the bottom we turn right, along a narrow hedged road with farmland around, then across a stile onto the hill. The climb is steep. Print unfolds below us, a new view each time we stop for breath, churches and mills cutting shapes from the sky, the war memorial a lone tooth amid the slate rooftops. Dun clouds rest their bellies on a layer of wind. Kumar and Lavonne stride on through the bruised light, followed by Janet and Madeleine, followed by Finn, Robinson and Jack.

'This is where the Hunt Cunts come,' shouts Kumar, turning in mid-stride and drawing it all in with a sweep of his hand.

'What's a huncun?' asks the kid.

'It's a scoundrel in a red jacket who rides on horseback and chases foxes,' says Jack. 'Like your daddy chases girls. Look, that's where the Abbey used to be.'

He points down into the valley, at a white half-timbered farmhouse ringed by barns of breeze block and corrugated iron. He squats down and lets the child look along the line of his arm.

'Now, the farmhouse, that white building, is made from some of the actual stone that was left when they dissolved the Abbey.'

'The monks took it to pieces,' says Robinson. 'With their hands.'

'That's what they say,' says Jack.

'He knows all about the Abbey,' says Finn. 'His mum tells him.'

'And when they'd took it pieces they sold it all. In the market.'

'How *is* your mum?' says Jack.

'Dead.'

'No,' says Finn. 'You went to see her. Remember?'

'In the clinic.'

'That's it. And what was her friend called? The one with the tattoos?'

'Tony.'

'That's it. Good.'

'She's sad. Like Nanna Margaret was sad.'

We halt at the top and turn slowly on our heels. A field of rape falls away into the next valley, then rises to the bleaker land beyond. Up ahead, an evergreen copse stands naked at the top of a rise. Far traffic sounds, laughter from the pub below. To the heat-faded north, the Pikes are a distant blue.

'The skwes of the scowtes skayned hym thoght. "The very skies seemed to him grazed by the jutting rocks." The Gawain-poet was talking about the Pikes, and the way they literally seem to scrape the sky like a knife. Now if you look over there,' and Jack points to the left of the crags, 'you'll see roughly where Gawain would have travelled to get to the Green Chapel for his tryst with the Green Knight. There's reasonable evidence that Sir Bertilak de Hautdesert's castle was actually Swythamley Hall, which is the required two miles from Lud's Church.'

'You know,' says the auctioneer. 'Lud's Church. The cave, up in the hills.'

'Where the Lollards hid from the King's Men in the fourteenth century. And where brave Sir Gawain rode to meet his fate, on the first day of the year, all those centuries ago.'

'I want to hear about the monks. I want Mo to tell me.'

'You know what? Some people believe the Gawain-poet was actually one of the monks from Dieulacres Abbey. Who wrote great romances as a bit of a sideline.'

'They used to get up in the middle of the night to say their prayers. I don't say my prayers. I used to when I was a *baby*.'

'Look at that tree! Isn't it weird!'

Madeleine has stopped up ahead. Two trees, growing a foot apart, leave the ground as separate beings but come together halfway up to form a single trunk. Like all the miracles round here, Hen saw it first. The three of us, on the same hillside, shortly after our arrival in Print:

'You see, we started off completely different people, then we got closer and closer until we were actually the same thing.'

I saw her fine-boned nose, red and glistening in wind.

'But then,' I said, 'you could say we only got together because we happened to be in the same place at the same time.'

'You think whatever you like. That's fine by me.'

Madeleine is chasing Robinson across the heath.

'He's going to slip in a cowpat,' says Finn. 'And I'll have to clean him up.'

'No harm in a bit of bullshit,' says Jack. 'You're the biology student.'

'Respect the facts. I only did it for a year.'

Jack breathes hard from the climb. 'I hated Oxford for the first year. Then I realised it wasn't the be-all and end-all of my life, but just a chance to have a laugh and shag some influential women.'

'Yeh well. They're all investment analysts by now. It's great and all that but I really couldn't see the point.'

'Let me guess. You were going out with someone who thought the only point in being at university was to find a boyfriend and cling on to him for dear life. You woke one morning and thought, When I get out of here I'll have to live with the fact that I spent the best years of my life with this dull lump. You couldn't finish it, so the only thing you could think of was packing the whole thing in.'

'How d'you guess?'

'Because I've been there, negro. Except the *burde* concerned was the daughter of the ambassador to some uninteresting Eastern Bloc country, and had to return home at short notice. I suppose it goes down as a lucky escape.'

'I don't regret it. It got me to Australia.'

'And that's where you met Anna.'

We stop at the summit. Jack scans me for a reaction to the name.
'You know Roxanne knew. Though she never told me anything.'
'Nothing to tell. Go on.'
'What?'
'What's Einar been saying?'
'Only that you'd told him she was the Type you'd been looking for all your life, and *he* said she was not exactly beautiful but she had acceptable breasts and a firm body under the cotton dress.'
'I'll ask her, if I ever see her again.'
'You must have some photos.'
'I don't take photos.'
'Go on. I suppose she's a bit like Hen.'
I get as far as the dark curved hair before he stops me with his most punchable smirk.
'Okay, I've got it. She's like your mother.'
'You haven't the first . . .'
'No, that's it! You're attracted to people who look like your mother. But you can't be obvious and say how you really feel about them because you couldn't cope with the shame.'
'First of all, my mother looked nothing like the person you're talking about. Second, even if she did, so what?'
'Defensive behaviour. Denial of the symbolic link.'
'Linden thinks I should ask you to leave us alone.'
'What, and leave you without *any* kind of intellectual stimulation? Leave you to Einar's drunken rambling and Linden's polite English neuroses?'
A scuffed boot attacks a straggly clod.
'All right, but can you at least try and get on with people?'
'Do boys like cars?' says Jack.

Back at Big Kimberley there's a total of seven new messages for fc913@terry.com. The first is from my sister, who says it's all over with Andy because he was never really her Type, which means she's probably still in love with Paul. The next five are from Hen. i was wrong about the kid. he has my eyes. Then: all I want to do is touch the world and feel it between my fingers. anything wrong with that? Then: its not true about the monks. i forgot. they didnt have to sell their stuff in the market. they got a bloke called finn to auction it all off. Then: bring that boy back to me. theres something i want to ask him. Finally: hi! are you jealous? tonys going to give me another tattoo. ps. im not telling you where. its secret!!!!!

The last message is less than ten minutes old. I don't recognise the address. No surprises there, because as much junk mail travels down this phone line as drops through the front door of Big Kimberley, and I'm always on the lookout for new friends. But then a bell starts a distant ringing, then another closer in, and all the blood leaves my tripes and rushes to my heart, and I hear the sound the world makes when it's about to end.

```
from: alb732@med.man.ac.uk
to: fc913@terry.com
re: Blast from the Past
```

Einar gave me your address. He told me what's been happening. Is it really seven years? I must have changed. Anyway, he's asked me over on Thursday night. Is that OK? I suppose I'll be seeing you then.

LOT
7

The auctioneer is lost. He has found – no, has been given – what all members of his profession dread: a thing that is not a thing. For all his diligence and artistry, his eye for detail, his facility with the colours green black blue, here it is: an object for which he can find no simple description or definition, of the kind enjoyed by space helmets and porcelain figurines, that might allow his assistants in their blue overalls and his customers in their wooden chairs to distinguish it from all the other items on display. It mocks him, actually. It says: Who's so clever now? And who can blame him, when faced with this un-thing-like thing, if his forehead is not entirely smooth? Its fine trappings tell us nothing. It obeys none of the cosmic laws that are good enough for the rest of us, except perhaps the Second Law of Thermodynamics, which warns that our universe must tend towards a state of maximum disorder, so there's no point tidying up as you go. In other words, although it depends on who has possession of it at any given moment, it tends to wear out with age. For those who have to have numbers with everything, it has a half-life of more than a minute but less than a human lifetime. I have read widely on the subject and I know seven years is not impossible when the wind is favourable and nothing bigger comes to take its place.

Only under certain illuminations (moonlight, streetlight through trees) is it visible to the naked eye. But although it's only rarely glimpsed, everyone has an opinion about it. Some say it is an electromagnetic disturbance, a pattern of interference set up by overlapping lives, like the spot at which two sets of ripples meet to contemplate each other at close range. Medics and cynics would go so far as to call it a sort of disease, and think they'd clinched the argument by ticking off the symptoms: sleep loss, hallucinations, night sweats and alternate bouts of ecstasy and despair. Others who have lost their faith in science and don't have to work for a living would call it an accident in substance, a random pattern in the glaze, and therefore in the same family as sunsets and brain tumours, head-on collisions on unfamiliar roads. Some say it is a gift from one person to another, an object that can be freely given but not sold, and thus of no conceivable interest to an auctioneer. But since it takes up no space in this cataloguing room and requires no looking after, and since the auctioneer is five feet ten-and-a-half inches tall and just as human as the rest of us, it finds its way onto this drop-leaf table, under this anglepoise lamp, like everything else.

I have had to call you, Anna, because I have a catalogue to write and everything must be included, and because you made this thing, or rather we created it in the space between us, using a little more of you than me. You are responsible. You turned up at a private swimming party and put a face to my life's desire. Then you lodged yourself in the corner of an eye and remained there patiently, sitting on your hands, confusing me with half a smile. And because I have to call you, I have to call the rest of my fellow travellers, who took off their clothes for you on a hot December evening, and became the people for whom this catalogue is intended, my customers and friends. I have to explain myself. I have to account for what might be obvious to many, why I'm still talking about someone I haven't seen in seven years (she approaches, climbs into her neat doctor's hatchback, starts the car), whose voice I have never heard on the telephone, who may or may not be afraid of moths; why I'm still talking, even as she coasts down the M6 towards Etruria and Print, checking her rearview mirror for the thing that still hasn't arrived . . . why I can't forget, even though I have a child and my child has a mother and they are both innocent in all of this. That is why, my fellow travellers, I need your audience, even though I often can't tell your nationalities or make sense of your accents; because someone has to hear me try to describe this thing, sketch a few of its features and state its colour and shape, so you'll know what it's like to have it parked on your desk, quietly annihilating your sky.

It's true: nothing happened to Finn Causley that didn't happen to many of the other Margaret's children, especially those bright sparks who had already benefited from her wisdom, and therefore knew that nothing, not even freedom, would fail to come running when money called. After a year of Biological Sciences and a further year of Philosophy, I dropped out of university, confident that the house in Basildon was sold and my inheritance was safe, and blew a chunk of it on a wad of obscurely marked airline tickets which, when used in the correct sequence, would take me in a westerly direction around the world.

If any of this smacks of escape, let the record state that Finn was not the type to stay and face up to his troubles when, thanks to recent deregulation, it had become so much easier to take flight. Below that, in smaller print, let it be noted that what drove me to it was not Kant, Hegel or Schopenhauer, but a henna-haired woman named Frances Mouncey and a synthetic compound with psychoactive properties that we discovered at the same time. Frances' sentence structure vexed me more than any long-winded Germanic philosopher, her discourses on Being were more breathtaking than any of the primary sources we were encouraged to read, and the insights she gave me into the nature of love were long overdue. And Rona's Surfboard provided my escape: first over the windswept beaches of Norfolk, and then across oceans and timezones to Sydney, capital of the Southern Hemisphere, birthplace of the wonder drug itself.

Frances, then: big noisy Frances, stalwart of the University of East Anglia Christian Union, whose motherly flesh was the first I ever inspected in pornographic close-up, who relieved me of my virginity as if it were a blocked pore or a ripe scab, taking care to wash her hands. She waddles into view through the door at the end of the room, always about to say something, loosely wrapped in a polyester duvet with a brown-and-orange scale design. She first brought me here after a Stella promotion in the late-night bar, which, in the days before Rona's Surfboard, was the only paradise whose address I knew. Then a week later, after we'd walked home together from Cinema City, stopping frequently to give our feet a rest and our hands and tongues some exercise, she invited me in for a coffee (capital C and accent on the first syllable) and silently locked the door.

How was it for you? In my case the transition to manhood was remarkable only for its unremarkability: having chased this moment by torchlight, under bedclothes, through the most imaginable partings of my sister and her friends, I slipped in, out and in again with barely a sigh, conscious of no more than a little abrasion around the base of my instrument, a sense of having dropped something into a deep letter box from which I knew it would never return, and a damp patch for which we blamed each other. 'Cheer up, it gets better,' she said, rolling off me and settling her head on my shoulder, inches from my frantic heart. We lay perfectly still in her standard-issue bed, lit for mutual adoration by an orange-and-red candle from the peripatetic crafts stall, listening to 'Fountain of Salmacis' from Genesis' 1971 *Nursery Cryme*. I may have smiled. She may have said a little prayer. In time I would mourn my lost innocence, the fact that I was no longer the little boy Margaret Causley had left behind when she went off on her endless shopping trip, leaving her music on the wind. I went back to Frances for comfort. For weeks I couldn't get enough of her trembling, glassy thighs, her grey-and-yellow jelly belly and the wiry trap between her legs; in which, according to the gossip that echoed outside her room, many Christian souls had been lost.

We were careless with our love, Frances above and Finn below. She quickly learned that she didn't really like me but also, how inconvenient, couldn't live without me, without my mildly irritating and ever more closely shorn presence. She told me things about myself I couldn't possibly know. 'Arrogant. Thoughtless. Self-satisfied.' Hands flat on my chest, her breasts, recently escaped from the still-fastened custard-colour bra, magnificent and rubber-tipped. 'Always trying so hard not to be obvious. Yet so quick to put people down.' To press the point she grimaced and snatched at what I'd put inside her, just as in more public places she would grab the lapels of my doom coat and tighten the collar around my neck. 'But you have a lovely thing. Ooh.' She sighed. I put her out to sea. I let her do exactly what she wanted, if only because it would have taken too much effort to push her off and find a replacement. And since she had threatened mutilation if she ever even suspected an infidelity, and since my imaginative powers had been honed to perfection by glimpses of dark-haired strangers in shopping centres and cinema queues, I only had to close my eyes on Frances and think of a certain texture of hair at the ear, a Siamese inscrutability, and Anna's far-flung sisters were crawling over me like bees.

What kept us together, I have hardly a doubt, could be found in a two-inch bottle like this one which, when fully loaded, contained around thirty small white pills. First synthesised in a garage lab in Sydney in the mid-1980s (and soon to be known for all time as Rona's Surfboard), it was a close relative of familiar but universally proscribed phenethylamines, with just enough innovations in its structural formula to remain, for a time at least, within the law. A single pill was all it took to create that trademark sensation of movement which, when set off in the golden fields of New South Wales, felt as close to unaided flight as our wingless flesh could aspire. But since the wheatfields of New South Wales were out of the question, at least until I could perfect my escape, we made do with the barley fields and beaches of Norfolk, even when the rain blew down our throats and it was a matter of opinion whether the sky dreamed the sea or the sea dreamed the sky.

Who remembers that first time? On the beach at Holkham, early summer, when That Decade was still alive. Running with arms outstretched, roaring like fighters, tripping on roots and crashing headlong into the sand. Lying in those dunes for hours, watching clouds hit a deeper blueness and disappear, feeling the curve of the earth in your spine and never so totally alive. Nursing a hard-on as the quiet girl took off her clothes by the water and strolled into the scuzz like she owned it all. Cherry sunset, edged with blue. Frances all emotional in a gypsy skirt, found a dead fish by the water's edge and thought it was the skull of an angel. At dusk we saw fires in the corners of our eyes. It all disappeared when we turned our heads, so we didn't turn our heads, we kept them very still, propped up on a jacket or bag, facing the horizon or staring straight up at the moon. Standing at the water's edge, flying in out in out with the shining waves; out to the horizon, to hang like gulls over tankers and oil rigs,

---

Lot 7: **White pill bottle**, blow-moulded from medical grade polyethylene, with blue lettering and easy-grip screw cap.

and back into the dunes behind. Then afterwards, once someone had driven us back to an orange-and-red candle in a boxy college room, the way we clawed at each other, Frances above and Finn below, how we made our way into each other like diving into pools, how we spun out the hours while the years ticked away.

That's what kept us together, Frances: lust transformed, by a DMPA catalyst, to gulping biting love. But wasn't there something else in that chemical formula, which gave meaning to our relationship because it gave meaning to everything? Isn't this the best way of explaining why a certain relative of Rona's Surfboard is now used, against all medical advice, by sufferers from the organic brain disorder we call St Mary's Disease? And something else on which I'd like an opinion: isn't the name given to that close chemical relative as macabre in its irony as the common name of the disease it is used to control? But Salvation made people jump off buildings or simply put them to sleep in strange white rooms, while Rona's Surfboard, whatever the papers tried to tell us, put nothing but meaning into our lives.

As if you need reminding. Once, long after Frances and college rooms, after airline tickets and swimming pools, before the scare stories bit and our sources dried up, I was surfing with a not-yet-pregnant Hen on the Norfolk coast, when she picked up a stone. Flat on our backs, in the lee of a crumbling breakwater, looking down on a translucent moon. She picked up a stone and held it above her, turning it like a diamond in one hand. 'What is it?' She held it out.

'It's a stone, Hen.'

'Is it. What else?'

'It's . . .'

'It's a decision.'

I yawned. 'Nah, you got me there.'

She held it at arm's length above her, wrists pale and eloquent against the deepening blue.

'Okay, here goes. Nature, right – that's the sea, the sky, everything – has had to decide what shape this stone is going to be. Because you know it didn't start off this shape, don't you. Nature has thought long and hard about this stone and decided what shape it will be.'

'How's that?'

'Don't ask me how. It just went ahead and did it. Thanks to all the bashing and scraping and rubbing caused by being out on a beach like this all your life, it went in as one thing and came out as something else. It's like when you make a pot or something out of clay: you take a lump of clay and press it and roll it and in the end it's more or less the shape you wanted it to be. It's a decision. And so is this stone a decision, but this time it's Nature, i.e. all the forces of the sea and the sky, which has decided. Cor. Is that amazing or what?'

A gull became a star. Smoke out to sea, one of her litter fires still throwing retinal shadows. Her voice in the dusk.

'And if you look at all the other stones, they're all of a similar shape, give or take. That's because Nature is consistent in its decisions.'

She sat up, leaned back against the breakwater and extended the index finger of her left hand. 'Now look. I'm balancing the stone on the tip of this finger but I'm still holding it from one end. So which way is it going to fall? This way or that way?'

'Give up.'

She let it drop. It fell away from me, towards the sea, whence it rolled a million years before.

'There. Phew. Now *you* didn't know, but Nature did. Nature, disguised as the laws of physics, made a decision. It weighed up all the pros and cons, measured out all the ingredients, made all the calculations, and sent it off that way, towards the sea. Now you see that everything that happens is a decision made by Nature, after careful consideration of the facts.'

She was the first to take an interest in ordinary things. Now I spend bright June days without her in the room we made, looking for meaning in a pair of blue-and-pearl Raybans (worn when driving), a black hairband (pulled tight around shower-wet hair), a jar of moisturiser with silver lid (expensive, applied sparingly every night before sleep). I have to stare and stare, from this angle and that, wrinkling my forehead and letting my eyes drift off wherever they choose. And somehow they always end up here: on a cuboid plastic bottle with a circular screw cap, finely ridged for a better grip. On the label in blue capitals is the name RONA'S SURFBOARD and a cartoon picture of the mythical wave on which, it was said, you could do Sydney–Hobart–Sydney in less than an hour, depending on the weather in your head. 'Have you got the bottle?' she'd say – and there was always a bottle like this somewhere: on the fridge, between red gas bills and spider plants; in my duffel coat pocket, wrapped in a handkerchief against prying eyes; in her Rajasthani shoulder bag, among loose tampons and used envelopes from which the letters had long been binned. Always a bottle for her to rattle mischievously in public places, sparking both of our guiltiest smiles. It was our secret, our joyful love song, the killing punchline of our lives. Small enough to fit into the hollow of a fist, so she could surprise me, coming home from a job with my mind on unpaid accounts, or leaving the bathroom in the direction of TV and food. Her pale fist in the stairway, the hint of a secret on her nervous lip. And she turns her wrist, uncurls the fingers, and the white bottle wakes up in her hand.

The pills have long since disappeared, down this throat and those of many others, to be expelled as pure white dreams. We no longer spend the long comedown making love in any soft place we can find, feeling the evening breeze on our arses and tasting the light on each other's skin. If I'd known anything about chemistry I might have got onto the network and found out the formula for myself, so we might never have less than we needed, and the bottle would always rattle when shaken. But I didn't, and the bottle doesn't rattle, and perhaps it's just as well. Things have happened. The old crowd has moved on. We're back to being the people we were before it came, the people we said we'd never be, with sensible shoes and jackets hung from hooks in cars. Remember? The people who were always Someone at home, until they got home and found they were No one. Who came too late for the party and brought the wrong drugs. Who were too boring for their parents or too frightening for words. Who said *Why?* to unimportant questions when they meant *Why?* to everything, because they were waiting for a catalogue, thirty-two pages stapled in the centre, where all the answers would be written down in black and white . . .

When, at the end of the 1980s, Rona's Surfboard was banned under the 1971 Misuse of Drugs Act, all they did was make a few changes to the preparation procedure, shift the production centre to the young democracies of Eastern Europe, and a new, more potent compound was born. The new drug was called Salvation. Its active ingredient was D-DMPA, which only differed from L-DMPA, the main component of Rona's Surfboard, in being its mirror image. One was the other turned inside out. So, although they had the same chemical formula, their chemical properties were different. At least, that's one story. Others say Salvation was just an impure version of the Surfboard, cut with any filler available, including cheaper amphetamines, bathroom cleaner, ground glass, rat poison, what else. Anyway, Salvation appeared as a still-legal alternative to Rona's Surfboard, and the accidents began. Seventeen-year-old boys never came home from warehouse parties. A Melbourne woman jumped from an eighth-floor window with Salvation screaming in her head. But other accidents were blamed on the recently criminalised Rona's Surfboard, which we'd been told was the safest stuff around. The tabloids went into ecstasies. SHAME OF THE SURFBOARD CHEMISTS. SALVATION KILLED MY SON. Research into the therapeutic uses of DMPA was suspended in three countries. In England, a new prime minister announced a personal crusade to stamp out the drug epidemic and save the nation's youth from their unspeakable selves. By the summer of 1993, around the time Hen was falling silent on a Parisian bridge, you couldn't get Rona's Surfboard for love nor money. The bottle never rattled again.

I have had to call you, Anna, even though you never put a white pill on your tongue and waited for the active ingredient to enter your blood, nor laughed at any of my jokes, in the days when I still made jokes, nor got drunk enough or stoned enough to let yourself do what I wanted you to let yourself do; but because I have this object, the thing we made between us, the one thing for which I cannot find a name. And because I'm not Hen, who has forgotten that everything has a name, and so will never think to ask what yours might be, or whether it might rhyme with 'deceit', I can't make an exception for this thing. So I call it love, because it hurts so much, and I know the two feelings go together. And say that I am in love with you, that I have always been in love with you, because you made me love you, one night at a swimming pool when you looked at me for nothing but the sake of looking, and everything that happened after that. Then because my customers are, quite rightly, only interested in commodities that can be bought and sold, and since the prospect of a genuine bargain is infinitely more exciting than any vain reflections on things that are not things, I can say this: that you are in each of my dreams, in the instant before every thought, the answer to every question I have ever asked, with crashing heart and burning eyes, on cloudy days when everything stays out of reach. If it makes you laugh, it's because I should have said it seven years ago; so I'll say it again, I'll open my throat and make you laugh like I never could, if you'll only listen to me now.

They never spoke. Anna sat on her hands in the Kandinsky dress and Finn climbed out of the pool. Then, because this is real life and not yet a thing called memory, everything carries on as before. Flesh moves on flesh. Saltwater crosses the pool. Finn Causley walks barefoot up two flights of concrete steps, pretending he only ever came here to do two quick lengths while others watched; walks, wet shirt clinging, shivering a little in the close night air. No one comes after him. No one sees him stumble like a wino when he reaches the road. So no one sees him pick himself up, turn a circle on his heels and walk back to the room he shares with Wayne Norrie in the new two-storey annexe at the back of the Point Hotel.

Forty-four hours later, at the Hawaiian beach party in the ground-floor common room, she is standing by a cardboard palm tree, talking to Wayne, who has not been back to the annexe since the swimming party forty-four hours before. Who has not slept in all this time. Whose new lover, Ilse from Denmark, is trying to turn a yawn into a smile and point it at her room-mate across the floor. Anna stands between the palm tree and the door, in blue suntop and black shorts. Her feet are bare.

Two days after the swimming party, Finn leaves the room he shares with Wayne, crosses the walkway that joins the annexe to the main building, passes a game of table tennis in full swing, climbs the stairs to the hall and hears this voice inches from his ear:

'Finn mate! Roxanne wants to ask you something! About how come you never comb your . . . !'

The last word is lost in laughter. Roxanne grabs Einar's elbow and tries to slap his face. Lights flash red green blue. Finn sees Anna. He sees the deliberate stranger from the swimming pool who is listening to Wayne. Thinks: That's her.

'Oh, thanks a *lot*! Ignore him, Finn. Ah! You little *shit*!'

Einar follows Rox into the kitchen, where fridge doors hang open and tables creak with booze and food. Finn looks at Anna again. Wayne clocks Finn and swings a playful left hook. Perhaps, perhaps not, Anna looks.

'Aloha! Get into Hawaii! Where you been?'

'Where've *I* been? I've already flogged all your stuff.'

'Ah. Been touching up me Danish!'

In better light Ilse would be blushing. She turns Wayne away from the group, squaring him up for a conference to which no one is invited. Anna clasps hands in front of her shorts and looks out at the party. She fails to stifle a yawn. Then she takes a Peter Jackson light blue from the packet in her shoulder bag and waves the packet guiltily at the person she can no longer ignore.

'It helps me dance,' says Finn.

He takes the cigarette and waits. She stares out at the fun, oddly thoughtful, as if trying to describe the situation into a microphone buried in her head.

Then: 'I'm Finn. I'm not meant to be here.'

Anna puts a Zippo to their fags, takes a long drag and blows a plume of smoke at the back of Wayne's head. She frowns and looks at the back of the same head. Then she asks this question, like she needs to ask it before it drives her mad.

'Did you say Finn?'

That's it: they've met. A half-smile on her face.

'Is that an Irish name?'

'Ish.'

Starting now, every time he says something that may or may not be a joke, she straightens her mouth, scans her eyes quickly across his face, then relieves her doubt with an infinitely slow smile. Not because she finds what he's saying funny. But because someone's made a joke, and when someone makes a joke it's nice to respond.

'I think my mum read it in a book. It was about a bloke from Finland who they kept saying was a Finn. She thought it was the geezer's name.'

'So she's not Irish.'

'She might have been. She's dead.'

She puts the cigarette between her lips and pulls with both hands at a thread or zip at the back of her shorts. She frowns. She looks across the room at the glowing Coke machine, which a small Swiss man in a sailor's top has just started picking a fight with. Where the disco lights and music are, fellow travellers are trying to limbo under a bamboo cane. They shriek and stumble. It's everyone's first night.

'Snap,' is all she says.

One arm moves across her stomach, like trying to hold something in. 'I was nine,' she says. 'How old were you?'

'Nine.'

'Fuck me.' Then this breathy outburst, caught between a whimper and a laugh. 'It was my dad. I was just getting to know him. Were you like that?'

'With my mum?'

'You'll have to tell me some time. I was leaning against this wall and suddenly it was gone, just like that.'

She holds the smoke near parted lips. Her eyes start to close. She puts the filter between her lips and takes an impatient little drag. Then both blurt at once.

'What d'you think of Sydney?' says he.

'Have I seen you before?' says she.

'Sorry. Go on,' says he.

'It's okay,' says Anna. 'I just wondered why I hadn't seen you around.'

She's a few inches shorter, so to look at him is to look up. She looks up at him briefly with no expression. He sees that girl from the police show he watched one night with his hand up the curtain. He looks into the future and sees a Kandinsky dress folded over the back of a chair. She waits for him to move, to reveal the thing that will eventually come into view behind him, something much bigger than anything here.

'It's all an accident,' he says. 'I really should be somewhere else by now.'

A lanky red-head in a silver bikini slinks in with a grin. 'Anna you hopeless tart, I can't leave you alone for a *second* . . .'

'This is Cat. We just got back from the Blue Mountains. This is Finn. He's . . .'

'In the wrong place altogether.'

She checks his face, gives a slow smile, and turns to her friend.

'By the way, Jerry's not coming.'

'Oh. Duncan?'

'We're two lonely travellers,' says Anna.

Now Einar arrives wearing Roxanne's black satin teddy, carrying a live lobster in from the kitchen. He sees Anna and heads straight for her, holding the lobster like a bomb above his head. She backs up, turns and walks quickly out of the door. Only Finn watches her. Actually, there is nothing to watch. Just another lonely traveller, with difficult hair and bruises on her knees, waiting for something that hasn't happened yet.

'Who's Duncan?' says Finn when Einar and the lobster have passed.

'Her boyfriend,' says Cat. 'Well, her *Australian* boyfriend anyway.'

Finn does that thing with his face, the thing grown-ups do when they want to show they understand.

LOT
8

The Point Hotel, named for its proximity to the tip of McGuyver Point, one of four or five fingers of land that push down into the harbour along the eastern edge of Sydney's North Shore. It stood in pastel blue dilapidation a few steps down from McGuyver Road, which ran a mile through subtropical flora and genteel suburban architecture to connect the ferry terminal at the tip of the Point with the main artery of Military Road. If you hadn't seen the sign by the door, you'd be as likely to think you'd intruded on the colonial mansion of a toffee-sucking widow as a backpacker's hostel that called itself a hotel. But then you saw the tanned bodies passed out in the common room, the sound of someone tossing crockery out of the kitchen window to the accompaniment of an unwatched TV, and you knew any drooling widow would be trussed up in the cellar along with all the other day-trippers who couldn't stand the pace. From the blue hallway you could take stairs up to the first floor and attic rooms, pass through the kitchen to see Einar the housekeeper up to his elbows in suds, or take another staircase down to the basement. Down here were more rooms, a table-tennis table across which a white ball flitted tirelessly, and a concrete walkway across to the annexe at the back. This is where, as a new arrival, you would have stopped, looked around and begun to unpack, while anyone who had been in residence longer than you moved into better rooms in the main building.

I meant it when I said it was an accident. I arrived in Sydney in the dying weeks of 1989, four months after leaving Norwich, Frances and my father's long-awaited second marriage, the hopeful owner of a one-year work permit and 150 US dollars in travellers cheques. Sydney was only supposed to be my point of entry, a chance to push back my horizons to take in the size of the Australian sky, before fate bundled me on to my real destination, a day's bus ride to the south. I had an invitation from some friends of Joy's to stay with them in Melbourne while I toured the city looking for work. If this was the plan, I was staying in Sydney just long enough to buy a ticket for the first bus out.

Travellers only know what other travellers bother to tell them, which in my case meant the addresses of four hostels in King's Cross and this more expensive one on the North Shore. To someone with 150 dollars in his pocket, The Cross is Sydney and Sydney is The Cross. My road-companions only need to utter that name to conjure up the neon tinsel of all-night bars and Lebanese takeaways, gorgeous young prostitutes with gym-fiend physiques, and cheap board beds in roach-infested hostels where rovers like me could recover from long-haul flights. It was the place to head for: anyone who said otherwise was here for the wrong reason, or was sitting on considerably more than 150 bucks. But when I phoned from the airport on a gold-heat afternoon in late November, four different voices told me the first four hostels on my list were full. I tried the last number, and got a man who told me his name was Greg, and that he wasn't laughing at my accent, but at one of those things that are never as funny second time around.

'Hang on . . . heck, that's Wayne. Right. I've got the bed if you've got the earplugs.'

I took the bus to Circular Quay. It gets to you, that first trip into an unknown city, wrecked from the flight but knowing that sleep is not an option, not with a year on your visa and the *colour* of the people here. When the city gets into you as fast as you get into the city, until you realise that every hopeful new arrival has a work permit in his passport, and the olive-skinned vision next to you is getting off and walking home . . . Deep grey streets in five o'clock heat. Then the first recognisable sight: one end of the Harbour Bridge, arching up above the skyline like the beginnings of a rollercoaster that'll drop you wherever you want to go. I have never owned a camera, remembering what I want to remember and forgetting the rest, so all snapshots are in my head: first view of the harbour, so blue and beautiful it made me laugh, shining like a huge untuned TV screen on which a picture always seemed about to form. The Bridge, crossing the water to Kirribilli in a single iron leap. As the Mosman ferry backed out of its berth, moustached men in shorts and sunglasses retracted gangplanks and threw ropes with easy skill, invisible propellers churned the water into white scuzz, elegant skyscrapers strode down to the harbour to see us off, the engine coughed and raised its voice, Centrepoint wouldn't sit down, the Opera House lifted its many lids and cast shadows on the water, and no one could have tried to put a number to those wide pink steps without losing count and having to start all over again.

Fifteen minutes later I was in a sunless room with cigarette burns in the carpet, 1970s curtains: an atmosphere known only to travellers in international hostels, who unpack rucksacks onto narrow board beds and think of all the people who have lived here, died here or just passed through. I was certain of three things. One, that Sydney was far more beautiful than any major city had a right to be; two, I was wrong about it being a city (it was a playground by the sea, squirming with olive-skinned visions and healthy-looking whores; it had crept into my veins and dared me to stay); and three, although 150 US dollars weren't going to buy me many of its pleasures, I'd soon be making so many of the local variety that there wasn't a single ride I wouldn't be able to afford. Everything else was distant news. Wayne Norrie was just a motorbike helmet and a pair of dirty boots kicked over by a wardrobe. Greg's quip was still mysterious. It was only later that I learned that Wayne's snoring was as notorious in the Point Hotel as his capacity to shotgun a can of Toohey's Draught by punching a hole low down on the side with a penknife, applying his mouth to the breach, snapping the ring and sucking back the contents in one go. It's only now, seven years later, while I'm in the mood for making patterns out of my past, that the extent of the coincidence reveals itself: oh, let's see, that if I hadn't been sharing a room with Wayne, or if those other hostels hadn't been full, I would never have stumbled upon that swimming party two weeks later, when a glance was an accident and the rest you know. I would have kept my clothes on and kept control of my senses. I would have gone on to Melbourne and made a fortune doing height work. I might have fallen in love in the correct way, following the established procedures, and come up with the sort of story your grandchildren get to hear about, and nothing like the heartsick comedy that was just about to begin. I would certainly never have been sitting on a moonlit balcony the weekend after the Hawaiian party, listening to the truth about Anna Ballantyne and Duncan McGuinness.

'He's not my boyfriend,' she was saying.

'Only because you haven't given him a chance!' said Cat.

'Have you been watching?'

Everyone – Wayne, Ilse, Einar and Jim de Groot – laughed. Roxanne rose up at the top of the stairs with a crate of VB under her arm. It was after midnight. We'd been drinking since six. Before that, while Einar lay face down in the pool pretending to be drowned, Wayne and I had spent the afternoon surfing down by the lighthouse, doing tours of the city from an incredible height.

'Oh shit!' Cat is saying. 'That night you didn't come home till about seven *a.m.*? You told me . . .'

'I told you the truth.'

'About Michael?'

'About everything.'

'Who Michael?' is Einar's little wonder.

'Michael's a very sweet boy who's waiting for her at home. Her *English* boyfriend?'

Anna shares a joke with herself. Somewhere on this balcony her love life is being picked over by a bunch of strangers. Strangers? We've known each other for days. Then someone has to go and spoil it all.

'Sounds to me like you're running away,' says Finn.

No one speaks. A tinny cracks open but is not raised to any mouth. Einar looks across with narrowed eyes, rocking back on his chair.

'Not really,' says Anna clearly and quickly. 'I came here because I wanted a year off before I start my training. Anyway,' the flicker of a frown, 'I don't see why a good relationship can't survive a few months apart.'

'I wouldn't know,' says Finn.

'And what please is so funny?' Einar is asking.

But Rox has lost it. 'Einar came here because he burned the school down!'

'Two hundred little children,' he grins. 'Crispy brown.'

'Are you for real?' Ilse's face is curled up in disgust.

'You know?' he drawls, leaning forward and putting his hand on her very brown knee. 'There is only one way to find out!'

He leans back and starts to unbuckle his belt.

'Leave it out,' says Wayne.

Who forgets that once he's started something, Einar isn't easily stopped. Especially not when Anna and friends are around.

'How about you, Finn? What's your story?'

Cat quizzes him through the gloom. A lamp burns in the room she shares with Anna, behind curtains closed against mosquitoes, putting a soft yellow into the moonlight. Insect sounds in the darkness, the motor that drives the night.

'I don't think I've got a story.'

'I mean, why d'you come away?'

Some unfinished griefwork. A failed university career. A laziness in all matters of importance which, from a certain distance, begins to look suspiciously like fear. The look on Frances' face after he so nonchalantly let it drop: 'There'll be no one-bedroomed flat in a nice part of Norwich. There'll be no Habitat shelving. I'm not coming back.' Tears. Threats. And through it all, a need to find her, the deliberate stranger with dark curved hair, who he'll recognise as if he'd been staring at her all his life, to whom he'll hand over that life as if he were handing out cigarettes.

Anna Ballantyne straightens her back and waits. He guesses at her eyes, lightless apertures in the night, an invisible intelligence. He has found her and now she can find him. For the first time in his life, the people he wants to listen are listening.

'It just happens, I suppose. You're born, you grow up, you get spots, you get your Bronze Survival, you get depressed, you go to college and it's all exactly what the brochure says. You go to gigs and sing all those boring songs, you drink the lager and jump up and down, and never have an opinion until U2 have written a song about it, and never wonder why it all looks so fucking dull. Then one day the music stops and you look around the bar and realise all you're supposed to do is pick up the pieces in the same old video game, put the wife in the house and the kids in the motor and go back after twenty years and find all the other losers did the same.'

A match is struck. Cat and Wayne, staring at the dark beneath the table. Faces in matchlight, distant as stars.

'It's like when someone asks you why you're doing something, and you think for a little while, and then a little while longer, and in the end you say, "I don't know. I thought I knew, but I don't." You don't ever want to be the one saying that. So you jump on a plane, you turn up skint and aching in a city where no one knows you and you take your chances with all the others, all the crazy dreamers who got out of it while they still had time.'

Someone coughs. A pleasure boat enters Mosman Bay, an impression of music behind glass. Anna looks at Finn with quiet interest, as if he were something that has blown here, quite by accident, to land uninvited at her feet. Which just happens to have the gift of speech.

'... and *this* time, if someone asks you why you're doing it, you can tell them you're finished with stories, all that matters is you're here and you made it and thank Christ you did. Because now you can be exactly what you are, not what you've been, or what people think you *should* be. Fuck it, you can *do* it, you can go down to the Point and watch the lights of the city on the water, or sit up here with a bunch of people you've only known for a couple of days, who already know all there is to know about you: that you'll never want that safe little existence back again. Because you spent your life doing what those people expected of you, you bought those choices and saw they weren't choices at all, and now you *know* what real freedom is.'

Something stirs in the darkness at his feet. It flies up and lands in his lap, cold, weighty, a wake-up call from the world of things.

'Have a beer,' says Wayne. 'Reckon you need it.'

Finn holds it, unopened, against his leg. Einar hums a tune.

'I suppose you think I talk a lot of bullshit for a builder,' says Finn, quieter, enjoying the sound of him against their silence.

Anna is the only one who looks. Still with half a smile.

'Does it really matter what we think?'

Before I was an auctioneer I was an interior renovator. Before I was an interior renovator I worked in a pub in Norwich. And before I worked in a pub in Norwich I did my time in a bar in Darling Harbour, round a bit and along a bit from Circular Quay, picking up occasional days' labouring and serving drinks in the evenings to a young and fashionable crowd.

The search took four weeks. It was easy: I got up with Wayne at six to buy my *Sydney Morning Herald* from the kiosk by the ferry terminal, trawled my hangover down several pages of classified adverts, and arrived at a car wash at seven to find myself roughly twentieth in a queue of illegal aliens for whom the world was not full of women with imponderable smiles, and who therefore looked as though they'd had a good night's sleep. I wanted a job like Wayne's, but jobs like Wayne's didn't want me. With no prospect of employment to make up for all the cash I'd spent getting here, I walked instead of taking buses, toasted my father's new-found happiness and Frances' new-found misery with the warm yellow water from the kitchen tap, and even thought about going to sit with the old Chinamen at the ferry terminal to try and catch some crabs on a bit of nylon line, except I had no idea what I'd do with them then. Charity brought me cigarettes. By the time I started at Spooner's in Darling Harbour I was only three weeks behind in rent.

There was only one problem: my clothes. After five months of the travelling life, everything had fraying hems and holes. The staff who bounced and slid around me shunned my sort of colour scheme for the simplest black and white, and were clearly no strangers to the washing machine or the ironing board. 'You look like a pile of shit,' said Dan, head barman, punching his open palm and pretending it was the side of my head. 'What are you, Robin Hood?' He was six feet four and very persuasive. Thanks to a loan from Wayne, whose Bobcat driving was earning more than one man could spend, I could afford a white shirt, black trousers and shoes. I was twenty-one years old and all set to begin a new career. And something I wasn't counting on that first night: Cat insisting I come to their room for one final style check before I left.

'Not bad,' she said. 'What d'you reck?'

There was breeze through the glass doors, across the balcony where we'd sat the week before, perfumed by the gardens below. Anna sat on the edge of the bed, one bare leg folded beneath her, a few bronze strands stirring in the air. She was staring down at a paperback with shut lips. The nub of a single vertebra showed above the collar of her polo shirt, nut-brown in early evening light. For one deranged moment I thought it might be possible to walk over and kiss it, and thus kiss her, without a word of explanation or apology, to know nothing but this need to put some part of me against the humid, salty, fine-downed wisdom of her skin. She looked up, raised her eyebrows and let her shoulders droop.

'Hm.'

She laid the book on the bed, stretched her leg, the left, in front of her and stared for several moments at the knee. She brushed something from her shin, and her toes lifted briefly as she stood up.

'Your collar's a bit . . .'

She stood in front of me, pulled hair behind an ear, reached up with both arms and made the adjustment. Her wrists grazed my neck. Her face was inches from mine, so close I could have been there in a second: brown eyes, the left marbled with green. I died in stages, shocked stiff by her casual nearness, the tantrums of my heart clearly visible through my shirt.

'That's better,' she said, turning back to the bed. She picked up the book and slumped back against the pillow. It was *Zen and the Art of Motorcycle Maintenance*, required reading, apparently, among our generation of travellers.

'But is it any good?' I wondered.

She tipped shoulders in a meaningless shrug. She flicked the pages through to the end, as if that might tell her something.

'Now get yourself to work,' said Cat. 'We'll be along later to give you some moral support. And you can tell us where you've been all our lives?'

A few hours later, with three feet of bar between us, she was still trying to wind me up.

'Don't quote me, but I reckon you've made an impression? It was the speech that did it. Where d'you learn all that stuff?'

Just then my main interest was in seeing if I could draw a schooner of New without converting most of it into froth. Dan was hovering at the end of the bar, dumbly punching his palm.

'I mean she won't bite. You never know, you might get to like her.'

'I like all sorts of people. You and Anna, well, you're in there too.'

'Ah! So you know who I mean, anyway.'

I looked over at the one I couldn't have, who had sat down with Wayne and Ilse at a window table.

'Come on, Finn!' Cat handing me a ten-dollar note. 'I saw the way you were looking at her in Pinocchio's. Chin on the table and pure lust in your eyes!'

'No, that was the other bloke.'

Now she knew what I meant: how it was Duncan McGuinness who'd been making the moves that night, reaching across the table to squeeze Anna's forearm, ask sensitive and searching questions about her life. I'd been as discreet as any murderer. What need was there for me to show my feelings when Duncan was making such a handsome exhibition of his?

By the end of the evening I seemed to have a job to come back to. Dan said I was getting the hang of the taps. The other staff, mainly pert-breasted Eurotrash like me, set me little tasks and rewarded me with fags. As it was a quiet night, Dan let me go early, in time for the last ferry. My friends were waiting outside.

'You looked very cool,' said Anna, laughing at something. I wondered what Cat had said.

We stood at the rail, watching ferrymen drag the gangplank onto the deck and throw ropes into rough coils. A Russian liner slept in its new berth. As the ferry backed out and turned towards the North Shore, the Opera House was a space creature emerging from opalescent shells.

'You know,' said Cat, 'I've been here three months and I still ain't been.'

The breeze picked up as the ferry gathered speed.

'We could go,' said Anna.

'Is there anything on?'

'*Eugene Onegin*. By Tchaikovsky?' Anna squinted in thought and tapped fingers on the rail.

'You mean an opera?' said Wayne. 'All that bloody la LA la LA de DA?'

'Well I don't know much about it,' said Anna, 'but I'd like to go.'

Then an idea occurred to her. She pushed back from the rail, smiled nervously at no one and turned her whole body towards Finn.

'You like opera, don't you?' hugging the rail in the crook of an arm.

'Opera?'

'Yes. You want to go, don't you?'

'Obviously,' he said.

*

These days, you know, we travel up to Manchester as often as tour schedules will allow, to swoon in the aisles with people twice our age, look out at life from behind thick lacquered programmes, before settling down in ritzy upholstery for an evening of Puccini, Verdi or Bizet. But in the days before the mewling banalities of pop began to bore me senseless, before I fell out of love with the massive guitar and the platitudes of rock 'n' roll, all I knew of opera was what cropped up uninvited on drawn-out Sunday evenings, in a live broadcast from Covent Garden, and always had me lurching for the remote control. Perhaps it was something in those televised excesses that made them ham it up like the Tory treasurers on *Songs of Praise*; or perhaps it simply took that long for my ear to learn the simple beauty of a well-trained human voice. I'm sure my mother, had she lived, would have shown me how it all changes with a live orchestra, and perhaps even convinced me that the result – a shameless richness of texture, a playful sense of timing, the gut-clenching spin from whisper to roar – was not a million miles from the symphonic rock epics that were to take over from our piano duets in the soundtrack of my life. Anyway, although I've still no time for TV spectaculars or satellite broadcasts from Roman amphitheatres, I could often have thanked Anna for her off-the-cuff invitation which, delivered as it was through that imponderable half-smile, meant I would have pretended to be a fan of anything if it promised an evening spent a foot or so from her sweet, secret blood.

She paid for the tickets, on the understanding that I would reimburse her as soon as I'd settled my debt at the hotel. She was temping at a law firm in the City, which meant she could comfortably afford the fifty-eight dollars for two seats in the upper circle, and six bucks for the hefty programme we took it in turns to read. Years of experience of concept albums with gatefold covers assured me I would have no chance of following the entertainment unless I read up on the story first, which I did, in deteriorating light. I was glad to see it was preposterous. A certain combination of features had appeared at the water's edge and threatened me with drowning, and I'd given up hoping for any plausible continuation, anything Finn could say to Anna to make this more of a beginning than an end. But I sat there, because I couldn't help it, listening to the orchestra trying out its toys, and found I could discount certain possibilities.

One: she would never turn Tatiana on me and send me scribbled confessions of undying love. Two: I would never get a chance to say, like her vainly adored Onegin, that I could not respond to her monstrous passion, and so must leave her, leave her and let God be my judge. You see, Finn may have had his head up there in the lighting rig, on the lookout for the puppetmaster, but his feet were firmly under the seat in front. And how had I come by this gift of prophecy? Because, thanks to the Frances I'd left behind in a candlelit college room, I knew some things about myself. I was lazy and hypocritical. I was too concerned not to appear obvious ever to achieve what I wanted. I didn't even know what I wanted, if my patient customers want the truth. And if I thought an intelligent woman would fall for someone who cropped his hair to hide his spreading baldness, who could only say the opposite of what he meant, well . . . (and my Frances always had this smug look on her face).

We listened to the overture, or rather we watched the gauze curtain shift and billow like my flimsy heaven's walls, waiting for it to draw aside and display the facts of Madame Larina's garden, which turned out to be a varnished pine platform bordered at the back by a twiggy hedge. I kept track of the breathing to my right. There was enough light coming off the stage to expose her in the corner of my eye, so I never lost sight of her, never doubted who all this performance was for. I heard the peasants singing. It began offstage, to the right of Mme Larina's minimalist yard, and grew gorgeously richer as the chorus marched into view: men, women and children dressed in natural colours, swinging scythes and canvas bags. I have never heard a more beautiful sound than that. I wanted to stand up and shout and tell them to go back and do it again, so I could feel it once more in my heart. But I also needed to sit still and show I had everything under control, that I was going to hide my feelings until I knew what to do with them, and not cripple myself before I'd even learned to walk. It does it to you, that first live opera: brings inexplicable tears to your eyes. Perhaps it was the same for her, though all she did was look contented and face the stage, taking down the panels of my world while keeping the screwdriver hidden in her palm, squeezing down her eyelids as if objecting to the light. And glance at me, just long enough to show she was still waiting for something, and just short enough to prove she hadn't found it yet.

I laid a hand on the armrest. She kept hers clasped in the lap of a blue tie-dyed dress, twisting a silver signet ring on the little finger of her right hand. When the man in front shifted towards his wife, Anna leaned fractionally towards me, so her shoulder was touching mine and I could feel her heat through the sleeve of my shirt. I thought she might have realised what was happening and pulled away, if only to spare me from any more spectacular but flimsy hopes. But she stayed there, shoulder to my arm, until the nerves in my flesh, which until then I would have trusted with any pleasure I could think of, played a desperate, unforgiveable trick. My arm went numb. I could no longer feel if I was touching her or not. Which is to say I had to pull away, just so I could be aware of something, even if only the fact that she was gone.

At the interval we stood at the bar, sipping coffee from paper cups.

'What do you think?' I asked.

'I dunno,' she said. 'I'm trying to work it out.'

She looked upwards and to the left, at the thing that still hadn't arrived.

An hour later we filed out into the night, where the harbour had laid a black carpet for us to walk on, if only we'd been brave.

'I can't see why he blew her out like that,' she said. 'When he was obviously in love with her.'

We walked to one of the bars between the Opera House and Circular Quay, where middle-aged women swallowed oysters and planned their last champagne-dazed affairs. Anna found a table by the water's edge.

'Some people are afraid of getting what they want,' I said. 'They can only bring themselves to do the opposite of what they want.'

'But if you love someone, I mean body and soul . . . Otherwise you may as well not bother talking about love. You may as well just say people do everything completely randomly, with no', she breathed, 'logic at all.'

She had never been so animated. She seemed, I don't know, offended about something. But I went on digging my own grave as if I was being paid for it.

'Way I see it, as soon as Tatiana had declared her love, that was it.

It was always going to be one-sided. Anyway, he was a cavalry officer. It wasn't the done thing.'

'That's stupid. So tell me, how are you supposed to get anywhere if no one can ever say what they feel? I can't believe people are so trapped by what's expected of them.'

'Well they're not. But . . . you know what it's like. There's no bigger turn-off than having someone tell you what, I don't know, beautiful eyes you've got.'

Anna gave a bitter laugh. 'Can't say it happens to me very often.'

'You know what I mean. Having someone come on to you like a fucking road train. You can't say that hasn't happened to you recently.'

Now I was irritated. No one should pretend to know less than they do. It's not cricket.

'What d'you mean?' It was exactly half a question, uttered softly into her glass.

'You know.'

'What, Duncan?'

I let her smoke. She looked across at a ferry docking, the gangplank thrown down, people getting off and getting on.

'Doesn't it put you off?'

'Not really. In a way it's quite flattering.'

'So why don't you reciprocate?'

'Christ, what is this?' Flashing eyes; not angry, not now. 'Perhaps I don't . . . All right, let's just say I'm not ready for a relationship. I need to grow up a bit before I start getting involved with people again.' Her mouth drifted open. 'I'll tell you what, though. I'm glad it's only Duncan? I couldn't hack it from anyone else.'

'I'll make a note.'

'No, you're okay. You don't hassle me. You don't know what it's like!' Her bursting laugh. 'I've had enough hassle from men to last me a lifetime.'

'What it is to be young and beautiful . . .'

What it is to be shaking like a leaf.

'Thanks,' she said. 'You're not so bad yourself.'

This is how it happened. The Friday after our visit to the Opera House, we drove out to Newport in Duncan's jeep and spent the afternoon on licensed grass, drinking beer from four-litre jugs. Ilse wanted to play the Name Game. Each of us wrote the name of a famous character, real or fictional, on a scrap of paper and stuck it to the forehead of the person to their left, who then had to guess their new identity by asking yes–no questions. I went along with it, even though I always ended up as the gay bloke from *EastEnders*, or someone from a children's programme I'd never seen. Anna came out as both of the twins from *Neighbours*, to which she responded with shrugging silence. At one point I saw her talking to Duncan by the car. They spoke in turns, then looked unhappily at each other, then each said one more thing, then turned and walked back to our square of grass. She was her normal, distant, accidentally graceful self. But she made a point of sitting next to me, so I had to choose a name and stick it to her forehead as if it meant no more to me than a parcel that had to be addressed.

'Fuck me,' she said. 'I've no idea who you think I am.'

And she never guessed. I'd put her down as Tatiana Lubina, which just goes to show that someone who listens to Genesis should never go flirting with Art. No one but Einar had ever heard of her, which meant only he and I could answer the questions. But as Einar seemed to think Tatiana Lubina was a small province in Eastern Siberia whose main export was badgers, we didn't exactly agree. Anna gave up, read the name on the paper and smiled.

'How d'you work that out?'

'Because under that cool exterior there's a bit of passion, I think.'

Wayne and Einar were pretending to have a fight by the fountain, cheered on by some drunks in bikinis. Duncan had gone off for another couple of jugs.

'You don't know me very well, do you?'

Laughing: 'Is that my fault?'

She thought slowly for a while, then got a word or two from it.

'I enjoyed the other night.'

'Well then,' I said.

She lit a cigarette, charmed, as if listening to an amusing story for which she already knew the ending. Then we made a date. We'd go home and cook some pasta, we'd walk up to the bottle shop for a cask, then we'd sit on her balcony and find out more about each other, until we thought we knew enough.

'Where's Cat?' I asked at nine that evening, from the doorway of Room 12.

'She's staying with Jerry. They're doing . . . something . . . tonight.'

She was having trouble with the French windows.

'Didn't you want to go?'

'The gooseberry is not my favourite fruit.'

She gave a grunt and the door banged open. We went outside and sat down on plastic chairs. At the sight of her in the Kandinsky dress, the trees set up a leafy applause and Mosman Bay tossed its glitter into the air. She yawned and stretched out her legs.

'You need a break from people now and then. But this is good, I feel relaxed now. Actually, Finn, I think you can take some of the credit for that.'

'I bought the booze.'

Her smile rose. There, you see, I could have said something; I could have told her what she was doing to me, and it would have been a simple legitimate response to what she'd just said. Instead I poured two glasses of Barossa Valley and ran away from everything I'd ever meant.

'Maybe. Or maybe I look at you and it's not immediately obvious what you're thinking.'

'Isn't it?'

'No, Finn. You're a mystery. I can't suss you out at all.'

What could I do? I couldn't let her down.

We talked about Cat and Jerry, who were now an official item: so safe, so obvious, so much happier than me.

'I dunno what she sees in him. He's just so . . . *inert.*'

'And you're waiting for someone who'll come along and sweep you off your feet?'

'Not necessarily . . . Sex is a major part of it, yeh. But really just someone with a bit of life.'

I stood up.

'Let's go down to the harbour.'

'What about all this wine?'

'Bring it.'

'And some pillows.'

'Whatever. The city is ours.'

'And a blanket.'

'Is this a proposition?'

'I don't make propositions when I'm pissed,' she said.

There is nothing like it in the world. You take the path along the back of the Point Hotel, through clipped and sculpted gardens and flowers only your granny would be able to name, under tall shrubs and evergreens, cracking gum trees that drop down to the water on steep rocky banks. You pass the last of the lace-trimmed verandahs, turn a corner, and night-time Sydney explodes into view: the deep jewel of the water, city settled like a crown on velvet, golden-eyed skyscrapers, red blue green neon tempting God and his angels to come down and buy, the Opera House about to lift off for the stars. A ferry had just left for Circular Quay, spinning a diamonded train in its wake. Anna stopped, pillows folded under her arm. I stopped next to her, so our arms were touching and my knees were failing and I would have swept it all up in a blanket if only she'd asked.

'Let's get straight to the Point,' she giggled, and it was the only joke I ever heard her make.

We passed the steps leading up to the swimming pool. Although it no longer really mattered, now I knew how I had to behave, I couldn't help wondering if she knew where she'd seen me before.

'That's where they go skinny-dipping,' said my breathless guide.

I said nothing. She led me to a smooth flat rock that dropped ten feet into the harbour. She saw me shiver, and turned.

'By the way, I remembered something. Eugene Onegin wasn't a cavalry officer. He was just a rich layabout from St Petersburg.'

'You're smarter than you look.'

'I told you I used to study literature? I had an accident a couple of years back which laid me up for a few weeks. Everything looked different after that.'

She sat with knees pulled up under her chin, watching thoughts form on the water.

'I couldn't really see the point of studying it. You know W. H. Auden? He said, "Poetry makes nothing happen." That's it. To me it all seemed too much vague and woolly.'

'I used to sing a bit. My mum was a music teacher.'

'Yeh, she was on that children's programme. Little furry animals?'

'Izzy, Lizzy and Joe.'

'So which one was she?'

'She was the pianist.'

'God, I don't remember a pianist. Sorry.'

We looked out across the harbour, at the second city reflected in the water, stretching broken chains of colour almost to our feet.

'You asked what effect it had on me, losing my mum. I think the same as you. I think it really screwed me up.'

She yawned. 'You seem pretty sorted to me.'

'You haven't been around. Someone once told me the reason I can't make relationships work is I always assume any woman I get involved with is going to be like my mum, and disappear when I least expect it. So I end up driving them away, just so I can say I've got some control over the situation.'

'I've got the tee-shirt on that one. The fear-of-happiness thingy.'

'But you don't have any problems saying what you want from life.'

'How do you know?'

'All right. When people find you they want to stay with you.'

'How do *you* know?'

'Take my word for it.'

She looked at me through the dusk. Her eyes widened briefly and she took her bottom lip into her mouth. Then, very simply, as if brushing a bit of fluff from my shoulder, she leaned forward and kissed me on the corner of the mouth.

'Don't get the wrong idea,' she said, 'but I think you're lovely.'

She got up and was unsteady on her feet.

'God, I must be pissed,' she said. 'I'm kissing total strangers. I'll be enjoying myself next.'

We stayed there, Finn sitting, Anna swaying on her feet, for some time.

Then: 'I don't see what's so wrong with enjoying yourself.'

'You're right,' she said. 'I've absolutely nothing to lose.'

'Why d'you say that?'

'Good question, Finn. Let's see. Sometimes I'm not sure if I'm really alive.'

She was trying not to laugh.

'What do you mean?'

'I *mean*,' she sang, 'I don't feel this is really *it*. I feel it's just a sort of rehearsal for something that will happen later. So I can't really take it seriously. Sorry, but that's the way it is.'

'No need to be sorry. As long as you're happy with it.'

'I am,' she said.

And to prove it, she let me stay the night.

It was not just because I was crying, what with the beauty of the city and the deep blue of the sky, and the fact that I'd just been kissed and it had taken me by surprise, and she felt sorry for me, maybe, somehow to blame. It was because nothing that might happen now, nothing she could do to me or I to her, could have made this any more real, any less a fantasy we'd thought up in a spare moment between lives, a trick the harbour plays on you on summer nights when it tunes itself to a mirror and pretends to show you your life.

'I'm sorry,' I said, blinking. 'It's a habit of mine.'

'It's okay.' She closed the door behind us. The curtains were open, the night quiet behind glass. She made me sit down next to her in this ivory light. I put a wet cheek on her shoulder, felt the coolness of her hair, and prayed I might make an afterlife of this moment, copied, multiplied indefinitely, so it would fill time like a bucket and put an end to me, to all this hopeless wanting, this sobbing waste of breath. A kiss touched my brow. My head slid down into her lap and stayed there, a ball of acid with two staring eyes, an inch from the cotton of her dress.

Eventually she got up and put on a jumper. She stood by the window, watching the moonlit water through the trees. In the little light that reached me I saw the woman inside the dress, the shape that slammed doors and rang bells in some part of my brain, the way the fabric clung and folded and curved down over buttocks and hips.

'I'm not trying to hassle you,' I said.

'I know. I wouldn't let you stay if I didn't want you to. Like you said, I know exactly what I want.'

There was sadness in her voice. I don't know why I said it, but I did.

'Would it hassle you if I took these off?'

'Those clothes you're wearing?'

'Yeh.'

The moon shone. It shone on land and water, on closed glass doors, on a woman I thought I'd never meet.

'No,' she said. 'You carry on.'

She hadn't looked round. 'You've seen it anyway,' I said.

Once again I kicked off my shoes. Once again I took off green shirt and jeans. Then, this time knowing she was here, knowing that she knew, I turned onto my front and pushed the rest down over knees and heels. And kicked it off the bed.

'Is that it, then?'

'That's it.'

She turned and saw me. Quickly, as if responding to some ancient habit, she lifted the hem of her jumper until it was just around her breasts. Then she stopped. She sat down on the bed, staring at the dressing table, as if trying to memorise what was there for some future test. She suddenly seemed very drunk.

'What did you mean? About me seeing it anyway?'

She didn't look at me. Not like she'd looked at me from that wooden bench, when I was just another traveller who'd swum to her end of the pool.

'I mean, I'm not the first naked man you've ever seen.'

She laughed. 'Poor old Finn,' she said.

In time she lay down beside me, one woolly arm hooked cautiously across my back, and became very still. I could hear her steady breathing, a friction in the throat which in an older woman would have been a snore. Outside in the corridor people were returning home from evenings out, saying hallo to perfect strangers just because it was Christmas and we were all in this together. I thought Anna was asleep. The jumper was still rucked up under her breasts, the fabric of the dress pulled taut over her ribs. In the darkness I laid a hand on her hip. Under the cloth she felt cool and smooth as glass, something on which I could never make an impression. I was not the thing she'd been waiting for. I was wildlife, something she'd caught sight of at the harbour's edge, which she was happy enough to watch from a distance, for as long as she happened to be looking. And although I wanted to nudge her awake, lay those impossible words on the darkness and let her gather me up in her warm brown arms, I knew the sort of questions that would appear on her face. How she'd try to hide her disappointment at having misjudged me, and the ease with which I'd misjudged her. I couldn't bring myself to let her down. So I lay there, skin burning with a simple need for her, a need so great it sucked air from my lungs and bled me without cuts, and knew I would never get any closer than this. And I never did.

There is little more to tell. We spent Christmas Day on the beach, trying to keep our tinnies cool by burying them deep in sand, listening to the batteries running down on Ilse's ghettoblaster. Someone had the idea of putting on our own nativity play, to make up for the lack of television, and we were soon too drunk to see an alternative. We made a Baby Jesus from sand and pebbles and swaddled him in a plastic bag. Roxanne wrapped herself in two beach towels and tried her best to look virginal. Einar climbed up onto the rocks above the beach, dropped his shorts and stood crucified in air, a sort of bisexual naked Gabriel with sunburned face. Before we could coax him down he had launched into a speech. 'Shepherds!' he honked. 'Leave your TV sets! Come down to the beach and make a party! Iceland, Scotland, England, France, the Middle East . . .'

'Who'll be my Joseph?' cried Roxanne.

That went on for an hour or so. We got into a waving match with the bare-breasted crew of a millionaire yacht, who must have guessed we were foreigners because no Australian would be daft enough to spend the entire day on the beach in December. We all wanted to think it was snowing at home. 'We're gonna miss the Queen,' whined Cat. A woman rowed past with only one oar. 'Oi!' went Wayne, 'you've dropped something!' The sun blazed mercilessly. It touched us all, made us young and wild and not quite right in the head. 'Who'll be my Joseph?' cried Roxanne, now flat on her back under her navy blue towel, making us think she must have dropped a tab of something while we weren't watching. I looked at Wayne, Wayne looked at me, and a decision formed in the breeze. Tonight we were going to surf it down at the lighthouse, where the water tongued the salty rocks, and do Christmas as she had never been done before.

And who was that curve-haired stranger? She was sitting under a tree, in white suntop and blue shorts, watching less well-dressed antics with little to no intention of joining in. Any shock she'd felt at waking up next to a naked Finn Causley two mornings before had left no evidence on her face. I'd insisted on holding her before I left, time enough for another botched kiss on the corner of the mouth, which she took responsibly, with blinking solemnity, and me nearly toppling over her onto the bed. I can safely say I took her by surprise. She'd crept back into herself, assuming our little crisis was all over, which of course it was. Since then she'd hardly left her room. I knew Duncan was spending Christmas with family in Wollongong, and that if I was ever going to take advantage of his absence to make a mystery of myself, now was the time to act. But when we put our plan to her that evening down at the lighthouse, we might as well have been pressing poison into her hands.

'You carry on,' she said, refusing our gift with holy eyes.

Wayne, Ilse, Cat and Roxanne each swallowed a pill. A bottle of water went around, and the plastic canister rattled along the railing into my hand. The lighthouse was a hollow tower reached from the Reservation by a short railed walkway. Anna leaned on the rail with blustery hair, watching gold melt in circles on the water, one bare toe scratching her calf. I did what everyone else had done: upended the bottle into my hand, picked up all but one of the pills and dropped them back in, scooped a hot palm to my mouth.

The pill tasted the same. I felt its tiny hardness in my throat. I knew that in just half an hour, though it would feel like seconds, I would be speeding through salt wind and sea-fret, as water phosphoresced beneath me, the city blazed and all I ever wanted seemed possible and true. Except, traveller, for one small fact: that the person I wanted to be sharing it with was not in a sharing mood. After ten minutes she went back to the hotel, with the excuse that she had a headache and wanted to sit in her nice empty bed and finish her book. I watched her shrink into the foliage at the back of McGuyver Road, realising that even after moonlight and fumbled kisses I was as far from her as I'd ever been, that there was no point wondering what she thought of me, because she didn't think of me, just like she never thought of trees or cars or ships on the harbour, or any of the other traffic that life sent by.

Some time ago the sun had set over the western suburbs, leaving slate cloud on a nicotine sky. We watched a ferry tug across the corrugated mirror of the harbour, cutting through the reflected city and its million stars, towards the distant hub of Circular Quay. A breeze came off the sea, bringing the sounds of caged animals from Taronga Zoo.

'I'm gonna miss this,' said Cat.

I coughed out surprise. I hadn't been expecting to talk.

'I mean I'm gonna miss Sydney.'

'You're leaving?'

'Fraid so. We're going to Adelaide? On the train?'

It was beginning to annoy me, her ending every sentence with a rise in tone, like it was a question she was putting to me rather than a statement of fact. And me trying to sound unconcerned . . .

'When?'

'Straight after New Year. I'd have thought Anna would've told you? You seem to've become pretty good mates.'

'Shut the fuck up,' said Wayne. 'I'm getting something . . .'

But there were no fires in the corner of Finn's eye, no layer of metal on the water, just a tight burn of awareness, telling him how little time remained.

We had one more night together. I came straight out with it and asked her if she would come out with me, just the two of us, so I could come straight out with it again.

'You mean, like a date?'

She was trying to keep a straight face. The joke was the rain, the way it spanked the windows and filled the room with ozone, and the serious eyes with which we sought each other through the gloom.

'If you want,' I said.

'If I want . . .' Her gasping laugh. 'What about what *you* want, Finn?'

Christ, those rainstorms . . . How silently they steal up on you, so quiet you can hear them coming, as if the hubbubs of the city were being sucked up and held back for the impending storm. You look up into a blue mid-afternoon sky to see a dizzying cliff of cloud, so high you can't see where it ends, or if it ends, even, if this isn't the whole watery universe rolling towards you, pushing back the blue and pressing a cool humidity into the streets. The first thing is the wind. Air hurries into motion, a breeze becomes a visible gale, flags flap and stiffen, doors slam and litter spins. The first fat drops of rain, getting fatter as you watch; and suddenly you're breathing water: the sky is something that happened yesterday, rain is bouncing off concrete and melting it into yellow sheets, cloud dips down to touch the harbour, and for fifteen suffocating minutes the city huddles under electric light, waiting in doorways and watching from windows, until cracks of daylight appear behind the haze, and the hammering and the melting ease as quickly as they came.

And the evenings they leave behind . . . We sat on the bench by the bus-stop, close to the steps leading down to the swimming pool. Anna wore a brown dress buttoned at the front. She pulled the hem down over her thighs, leaned forward to poke a finger between her instep and the side of her shoe. As she did, and dark hair fell forward around her face, the top of the dress came away from the body it was supposed to conceal, and showed that under the dress there was nothing but skin.

'What happened the other night . . .' she said.

'I'm sorry. I made a prat of myself.'

'No. That was a question.'

'You . . . I stayed in your room.'

'What do you think that means?'

'I don't know. What do you think it means?'

'I thought it meant I was ready for a relationship.'

'And now?'

'I dunno. I've found out a few things since then.'

I said nothing. I assumed she'd read something in her book, telling her not to waste precious love on balding twats who are too cool to say what they feel. She sat back on the bench and looked the wrong way up the road.

'I'm confused,' she said.

'What are you confused about?'

'Oh, you know. Why people feel they have to be going out with someone all the time?'

'Nights are lonely, Anna.'

'All right, but why does everything have to be so forced? Like: Oh God, I've got to be going out with someone so I might as well go to bed with this person even though I'd rather be on my own.'

'Because people spend so long analysing things, and worrying about why they happen one way rather than another, that if anything did happen they'd be too busy to notice.'

'I'm going away, Finn. I'm moving on.'

'I know.'

'Don't you think that's relevant?'

'It depends what people want. You and the other person.'

She continued staring the wrong way up the road until the bus took her by surprise. She thought hard all the way. In Pinocchio's in Crow's Nest, over grissini and a carafe of house red, she expanded on her views.

'This is your heart, okay?'

And drew a circle with a biro on the paper tablecloth.

'And this is your head.'

'My head is bigger,' I said. 'Does that matter?'

'No. Maybe. Now, you've got two options. Either you let your heart tell your head what to do, in which case: Nightmare.'

She drew an arrow from heart to head and cut it with a small black cross. I looked earnestly at what she'd drawn.

'Or you can let your head tell your heart what to do, in which case you can never really get what you want, assuming you know what that is in the first place.'

'I can see why you're a scientist,' I said.

'Now, which one are you going to choose?'

'Neither.'

'But you have to.'

'Why?'

'Because otherwise you'd be a non-human. You'd be effectively dead.'

'That's obvious, then.'

'No, what you should do is wait. Until something happens which makes sense to both your heart and your head.'

'So what you're saying is that if something doesn't feel one hundred per cent right, you should leave it and wait for something better?'

'I don't know what I'm saying. I'm just telling you what I think.'

'Come back in ten years,' I said.

'Ten years! In ten years I'll be a doctor. And you'll be married with lots of little Finns running around all over the place.'

'Unlikely. I'll be bald in a bedsit with a dodgy gas fire, wanking over memories of my sister's friends.'

'You'll find someone.'

'Even if I did, marriage is off. It would mean making decisions. Filling in forms.'

'Same goes for children?'

I nodded. 'Enough brats in the world already. Anyway, I reckon I'm too selfish. I always want what I haven't got. And I can't be bothered to go and get it.'

'What *do* you want, Finn?'

'Spaghetti alla vongole. Two portions.'

We were both drinking fast. When the first carafe was empty Anna ordered another half. I don't know what it was doing to me, but it was doing things to Anna, and I wasn't too impressed. All she wanted to do was talk about herself, when quite obviously she wasn't the one dying minute by minute from unrequited love. I tried to tell her about Frances, but she didn't appear to be listening. If she was listening she wasn't interested. I assumed she was drunk. I wished I could be drunk as well, but it wasn't working. The conversation fell over and never really picked itself up. When it was time to leave the restaurant we'd made a mess of the tablecloth and she was having trouble with her nicely tanned legs. We stood waiting for a taxi, after a comic moment of intimacy which ended with her hands in my back pockets and her head coming to rest against my chest. As three fireworks exploded above my head and filled my night with stars, I realised three important things. First, that life this close to her would be impossible as long as she was unable to take either of us, but me in particular, as seriously as we needed to be taken. This clashed murderously with my second idea, which I could have pinched from any pop song: that I couldn't live without her, for the simple reason that I was desperately, hopelessly in love. And the third? That when I looked at the two ideas and tried to decide which to steer by, the second was the one that lit up the sky and made all other heavenly bodies blink out in shame.

When we got back to her room she couldn't find the light switch.

'Are you gonna stay with me?' she said.

'If that's what you want.'

'If that's what I want.'

'Is it?'

'Oh, Finn,' she said, flopping onto the bed like laundry. 'You're such a . . .'

'Cunt.'

'That's the thingy,' said Anna. 'Cunt.'

She raised a knee and scratched it. The dress opened over her thighs. She put her knee down and laid hands flat on her thighs, on that cool tanned never-to-be-touched skin.

'What now? Cat's staying the night with Jerry.'

'We could play cards.'

'Oh, fuck off,' she said.

He didn't see the joke. Perhaps he'd lost his sense of humour. He turned for the door, gritting his teeth.

'No, wait,' getting up from the bed. 'It's okay. We'll play cards.'

'I don't want to play cards. It was a joke.'

She looked at me from brown eyes in a suddenly serious face. I wanted to die there, quickly, cleanly, so I could take this picture of her wherever I was going next, shun Anna-less heaven and make an eternity of her face.

'You don't like me, do you?'

'I do like you, Anna. It's me I'm not so keen on.'

She sighed and closed her eyes. She swayed to and fro. Then her throat moved and her mouth said:

'Come here.'

Brown arms reached out. I stepped between them and touched her hips.

'I can't be responsible . . .' she murmured.

We kissed. I felt her opening lips, her sweet boozy saliva, a push of her nose on my cheek. Our teeth gently clashed. Some distance below, my fingers, which never understood instructions given in plain English, felt the band of her knickers through the dress.

'You've done this before.'

'Never,' she said.

I pulled her towards me. I felt the pressure of her mound against my leg, thought it felt springy, like a piece of carpet. I made sure Anna Ballantyne could feel what was bothering me in her belly, through my jeans, through her dress.

Then she seemed to remember something, enough to change her mind.

'We can't,' she said, pulling away and sucking on her lip.

I stopped. 'I dunno,' she said. 'I don't . . .'

'Heart or head?'

'Head.'

We sat down on the bed and stayed there, smoking, close but not touching. I felt very close to death.

'I still want you to stay,' said Anna.

So I did. But this time my clothes stayed on. After all, it was a cooler night. The rain had started up again; we could hear it on the window, trying to get in. It's like that, rain in Sydney: it tries to rule your life. I pulled the sheet up over us, Anna sleeping, me far beyond sleep. Oh yes, it was all for the best. There was nothing the friendly fuck could have taught us, except that the same spurt of pleasure, a sorry little ecstasy that would have torn us from each other and sent us spinning back into ourselves, could have come from any other body that came our way. To make it any different we needed time, or luck, or perhaps the very thing we were hoping to make. There were other explanations, of course, and one of them had to be correct. But I didn't find out which it was until much later; and I was asleep, fully clothed in the musk of her being, before I had a chance to work it out for myself.

Three days later we were sitting on a bank of grass down at the Reservation, watching the end of the decade take shape in the sky. Four barges had been towed out into the harbour to form the platform for Sydney's biggest ever firework spectacular, with a simultaneous broadcast of synchronised pop. Duncan was celebrating his return from Wollongong with two crates of Draught and some Lebanese hash. As Anna Ballantyne, with a nervous twitch around the eyes, accepted the spliff he offered her, someone might have remembered how three days earlier she'd refused an offer of a harmless white pill. But if Duncan had Anna (and he'd always had her, never mind what fumbled kisses and moonlight might try to tell you), then Finn had fireworks, one for every thought he'd ever have of her, every breath of hers he would imagine on his cheek, every time his lips would open around her name. And these were more than fireworks: they were as fast as thoughts and as hot as pain; the way you heard them coming, the gassy sigh as they fled their mountings and streaked invisible into the night, the way they blew like bombs and bled their colours into the never-black sky, the way they clustered and hung, dizzying the day-old crowd; or just powdered and blinked out, sowing the sky with floating embers and miniature scuds of smoke. Fireworks, Anna: how some were loud enough to set off every car alarm for miles around, while others seemed to climb twice as high as the rest and hold together until long after you'd given them up as lost; and how some were doomed to fail, slew out at too low an angle and fall burning into the water, and carry on burning as they swam towards the sea . . . But mostly it was what the music did to you, the way it shook your guts and squeezed your heart (your inexplicable tears, your sad matching clothes) and, with its heartfelt vocabulary of love and dreams and hope and pain, turned every brawling feeling into words: dry your tears, some day it will happen, you'll never feel this way again.

Later we took the ferry to Darling Harbour to count in the New Year. We stood on the footbridge over the water and watched the songful crowds below. I lost Anna on the bridge, then saw her drifting back to the ferry with Duncan, Jerry and Cat. I found myself kissed by a metal-toothed Brazilian whose last meal rose to greet me and who I vaguely recognised from the hotel. On the ferry back I asked Rox what had happened to the others.

'Ah, you mean the *Poms*. Went back to Duncan and Jerry's. Can't cope with a party, I reckon.'

It was almost a week later, only days after Anna had stood at the foot of the stairs and tied her farewell gift around my wrist, that I learned the truth. It was only when Jerry came into Spooner's with an indiscreet group of mates that I realised that this New Year's Eve wasn't the first time Anna had been back to their flat, that I wasn't the only traveller who'd taken off his clothes in a blue-carpeted room while Anna looked out into the night. But for now, as I stood on the roof of the hotel and watched the sun rise over the Heads and rinse the city with light, I assumed she'd waited until tonight to make her choice. As it was a choice I'd helped her make, I could hardly blame her for the way it had gone. She'd proved herself far more capable of hurting me than healing me, so I couldn't complain if now, in a flat on the other side of the city, she was doing the same thing to someone else.

Lot 8: **Traveller's friendship band**, blue and green interwoven thread.

Roxanne came over, spliff in hand, and put an arm around my waist.

'So what's for the next ten years, Rox?'

'Stuffed if I know. Make some money eventually and get out of here. Maybe get into a band. Want to see if England's as boring as it sounds.'

She was right about coming to England. The rest . . . well, perhaps if there'd been time. As long as she had some mates around her, a drink and a smoke and some hugs from time to time, a three-storey mill full of household junk must have seemed as good a place as any to be the person she was so good at being. How could she know any different?

'How about you?' she said, blowing smoke. She had a tee-shirt that said MAD FOR IT in thick black letters. She had six years to live.

'I'm gonna sit back and let things happen to me, the way I've always done.'

'Hey, I'll smoke to that. Happy New Decade?'

'Happy New Decade,' said Finn.

LOT
9

Notice is freely given of an extraordinary

AUCTION

for the passing on of a variety of

Ornaments, Fine Prints, Kitchenware, Domestic Appliances, Articles of Childish Amusement, Tools for the Garden, Office Equipment, and sundry items of Furniture;

to accompany the Release, at the lowest possible Prices,
of a staggering array of

Bibelots, Kickshaws,
Gimcracks and Gewgaws:

to wit, the <u>Redistribution of Significant Objects</u> among those who,
like the Ancient Etruscans,
need a little help *remembering who they are*;

all this, and more, to take place at 11 a.m. on Wednesday the fourth day of June,
at Big Kimberley, Whieldon Street, in the sleepy town of Print.

Children welcomed with open arms

Zoë designed the poster. Jack looked up the words. Linden typed it up onto his bijou laptop and printed it out on a sheet of A4. Finn took the result to Print Print on Manchester Road and paid five quid for fifty copies. In the middle of the night Einar, with his new friend David from the police cells, went around town sticking posters onto boarded-up windows, lamp-posts and telegraph poles. Now, at ten to eleven on the morning of the big sale, the lots are in place, the chairs have been set out in semicircular rows, and in comes Jack, in sunglasses and cream jacket, a copy of the *Sun* folded into a copy of the *Guardian*, and announces that the queue outside is stretching right round the corner into Hope Street.

'Well *almost*,' says Zoë, climbing over a pile of deckchairs to see for herself.

She walks among a riot of things. They hang on chains from the ceiling, spread themselves out on rickety trestles, make untidy piles in corners, cling to wall-mounted wire grids, scrum together in cardboard boxes and packing cases. The head and shoulders of an outsized classical deity preside over the selling floor. A pair of stuffed pigeons looks down from the summit of an old pine wardrobe. Linden is performing a last roll-call of the Staffordshire figurines, working his way along the shelves of an Edwardian cabinet, peering through the glass and ticking off each item on his clipboard. Everything has a lot number, including Linden, who has a label stuck to the back of his overalls but is not down in the catalogue. Kumar can't be the culprit because he is upstairs in bed, having already been yelled for several times. Robinson is at the Happy Valley Play Centre with children his own age. In one of the inner rooms created by stained-glass windowed partitions, Einar puts the finishing touches to his sandwiches and waits for an urn of water to come to the boil. Copies of the catalogue, which today is no more than a photocopied list on several stapled sheets, lie in a pile on a table near the door. Across the landing, in the glass-ceilinged showroom, the remainder of the sale items, mainly larger pieces of furniture, stand ready for a last-minute viewing before the scheduled 11.30 start.

But where is the General Foreman? Did he really phone last night from a guest house in the Lake District, to which he recently escaped with Nina, who is not his wife, and Maryrose, who is not his child, thus leaving us at least six hands short? Did he forget that this is our biggest sale for months, that it will take a good half-day to see off all these lots? Did he ever ask who would take over from the auctioneer when he needs to lay down his gavel and rest his voice?

'It should be Serge,' says Linden. 'That's what you pay him for.'

'What about you, Zo?' calls Finn.

'What *about* me?' she says, pulling herself in from the window and gathering hair back with both hands. 'Look, you need someone who knows how to do the records. Remember the time Rox was ill and Kumar took over? We had to go round *asking* everybody what they'd bought.'

'Jack, go and give Kumar a kick, will you?'

He heads for the stairs, patting Linden's labelled back as he leaves. BLISS KILLER WALKS FREE says the tabloid. On the chair beside it: DSS FIRE WAS ARSON: TWO HELD.

'Think we can ask *him*?' says Finn, picking up Jack's papers and staring absently at the headlines.

'What?' Linden looks suitably appalled. 'When he's ripping us off in front of our . . . You might as well ask Einar.'

'*Allt í lagi!*' comes the voice from the refreshments kiosk. 'I have always wanted to wear a green shirt and talk in a very boring voice!'

'Right. First hundred are mine, then we'll take it from there.'

Zoë picks her way through the deckchairs and heads for the rostrum.

'Linden. Everything ready?'

Linden holds the clipboard against his chest and nibbles lip.

'Then let them in.'

First through the door is Mrs Bickerton of Morley Street, recently widowed, dressed for the auction in a new perm, white woolly jumper, sky-blue ski pants and white socks. The day Mrs Bickerton misses a sale we'll all be looking for work. She establishes herself in the middle of the front row and fans herself briskly with her catalogue. Next is Mrs Bootherstone, turned out like a Wimbledon line judge, grey bun and bucktoothed frown. The two of them continue a conversation that began in the sunshine of Whieldon Street. The thinner Mrs Bootherstone smooths her knee-length polyester beneath her, sucks her lip down over her teeth and prepares to take her seat. She is almost beaten to it by Miss Parry-David, as mad as they make 'em, and this in a town with more nutters than County Cork. You know her: if she's not pushing a rabid Alsatian around in a pram like the proudest mum on the High Street, she's over in the park, feeding chocolate biscuits to the unshockable ducks. Behind her, an art student from Print College has long crusty hair intersprigged with strips of purple crêpe paper. A tattooed rock survivor in pigskin hat and ponytail... an Asian family of four... a young couple with fabulous cheekbones – they push their way in, bright-eyed and relaxed, stroking the furniture and peering at the ornaments laid out on the table at the front. Einar gives each a buyer's number and sells them catalogues for 50p. They take off coats and anoraks and hang them on the backs of their chairs.

'So anyway, seems one of these blissed-out youngsters went and put a knife into her boyfriend...'

'Oh yes. SHE SMILED AS SHE KILLED.'

'And now,' Mrs Bickerton scrapes her chair and shifts in her seat, 'they've gone and let her go. She's been *acquitted*.'

'Don't feel safe, do you?'

'You don't. But thing is, duck, do they really know what's wrong with her? It goes how she's been getting treatment for schizophrenia...'

'But that's not the same thing, no.'

'Hang on, I think we're starting...'

'I do hope he's going to make a speech,' says Mrs Bootherstone.

A man stands up at the back of the room, reaches his full height, grows no taller, and walks on squeaking rubber to the podium. Green jeans, a green shirt with top button undone, green canvas shoes. His skull gleams under fluorescent tubes fixed to white joists above his head. A hand rises to his nape; he raises red-rimmed eyes above the podium and draws in his audience with a single sweeping gaze. A muscle twitches rebelliously in the corner of one eye. He twists up the microphone, taps the wire casing and settles silence on the room. A shy cough from a few rows back. He stands, hands gripping the wooden lip of the podium, head bowed and throat working nervously, and makes a thin but controlled voice:

'Welcome and good morning!'

A sigh is passed around the room. Each middle-aged lady fans herself with her catalogue and believes the auctioneer is staring into her soul. And for a moment he is, seeking out each hot suspenseful face, tugging at her gaze and letting it drop.

'First of all, let me say how fantastic it is to see so many familiar faces here at the Big Kimberley Auction Rooms, for what looks like being our biggest sale so far this year.'

Mrs Bickerton nudges Mrs Bootherstone and gives her eyebrows a little trip up to the top of her head. The auctioneer settles on his stool and adjusts the microphone. A squeal of feedback is followed by the shifting of bodies in chairs.

'This is my Val Doonican bit. Right, from the number of cars parked outside, I think we can assume we've got some Etruscans in the audience!'

A hum swirls into a murmur. Grey-whiskered men cough and shuffle their chairs. The middle-aged women of Print screw round to look.

'Good to see you this far out. How's the weather back home?'

More scraping of chairs. A squeal of brakes on the street below.

'Right. You've all heard of Josiah Wedgwood.'

'Get on with it!' comes a shout from the back.

'And you know how important his ideas were in building the city that lies ten miles south of here, and bringing prosperity both to that valley and to this.'

'Oh, definitely,' says Mrs Bootherstone, who used to teach in a primary school over in the Towns.

'You could say it was Josiah Wedgwood who first understood the possibilities of ordinary household objects: how they can tell stories, give evidence, leave clues, remind, deceive. He saw how a pot can be more than just a pot, how things outlast the events that make them, how we bury them in drawers and tidy them on shelves but in the end, like the ancient Etruscans who inspired him, we're just preparing for an afterlife, filling our tombs with meaningful things. Of course, Wedgwood could only do what he did by developing technologies that would allow him to produce reliable bodies and glazes, and that took years of experimentation. But the new Etruria would have come to nothing if he hadn't had that faith in ordinary things: how they can make you laugh, make you want to throw them against the wall, but most of all, how they can make you remember.'

Kumar arrives, yawning and rubbing his head, and takes up his position at the side. NEVER THROW ANYTHING AWAY tuts the sign above his head.

'Don't believe me? Have a look at this. It's a walking stick, made of ash, about – what? – three foot long. It's not in the catalogue. It is not for sale. It belongs to a good friend of all of ours, my uncle Don Long of Brink Farm. Last time Don came to Big Kimberley, to have a look at the stuff we were storing for him while he was in hospital, he made it all into three lists: what he wanted me to sell, what he wanted thrown out, and what he wanted me to keep, as a reminder of him. In today's sale you'll see some of the things he wanted sold. Let's see: Lot 263, a meat safe from his kitchen, where he used to keep his pork before Brink Farm was wired up. Lot 264, a manual till from the days he and Sarah sold veggies from one of the outhouses. Now if you, Mrs Bickerton, were to bid for one of these lots,' (Mrs Bickerton turns red from head to toe) 'and if your bid turned out to be higher than anyone else's, you could take it home, and take Don home with you,' (her bucktoothed neighbour giggles) 'and keep him there as long as you liked, until the time came to pass him on to someone else. Because Don the man won't always be around, but his meat safe will, and so will his chairs, and so will all the rest.'

'You don't get this at Sneyd and Blakemore,' says Mrs Bickerton to Mrs Bootherstone, her eyes shining with . . . what?

'So before we get started, Zoë will give us a quick rundown of the rules of the sale.'

'No buyer's premium.' She reads from her book. 'Cheques to be supported by a banker's card. All goods to be collected by 1 p.m. Thursday, and we can't make any exceptions there I'm afraid. I should also point out that there are actually no reserve prices, so hopefully we should have some bargains today. Buyer's numbers can be had from Einar over there if you haven't already got one, and . . . who's running the cash desk?'

'Jack,' mutters Linden. 'If you get the joke.'

'Jack, over there.' She points to a table near the window, an open

---

Lot 9: **Walking stick**, with ash-wood shaft and brass handle in the shape of a dog's head.

ledger and a selection of pens. 'As usual, we're serving sandwiches, home-made cakes, hot and cold drinks from the kiosk over that side. Oh, and please don't sit on the tables at the back – they're not all that strong.'

'Thanks, Zo. We're starting with a collection of Staffordshire figurines. Number One, Child at Play. Can we start this one at twenty-five . . . ?'

By half twelve we're on to the third page of the catalogue. The bidding is brisk and festive. Unshaven men in shellsuits drift around with tea in polystyrene cups, pulling out drawers and scratching at invisible blemishes in the woodwork. Mrs Enderby has turned up with two of her dogs. Over at the cash desk, Jack is having clever thoughts and writing them down immediately in a little book. Benny the Tramp, who lives in a hole in the ground on Blacksheep Moor, has bought a six-piece china tea-set with no intention of paying for it. He stands at the back, a small republic of hair, rolls a cigarette, takes it apart and rolls it again.

'Number 97, set of brass spring scales. Where are they, let's have a look.'

Linden points to a cardboard box on Kumar's side. Kumar lifts out two coils of brass and hangs them like earrings around his face.

The auctioneer speaks. As the first tentative bid is risked, and turns into the fact that makes other bids possible, he becomes that elusive person, the one who sees daylight only once a month, who takes his place on his hand-built rostrum and speaks so clearly and freely you'd think all the things he ever wanted to say were finally getting heard. As the offers begin to flow, his voice climbs to its selling pitch (Second Rule of the Auction: the same note must be held throughout, with frequent barks a perfect fourth above), and words are pushed out in faster and faster strings, as if there were so many that he must get rid of them before they start speaking him. Gavel raised, he breaks into a sweat, his lungs punching out their improvised rhythm, accent slackening further into that South Essex soul. Twangling mouth music drifts up to the ceiling; red-lidded eyes flash around the room. Everything happens at once. People stand up and sit down, cough, wave catalogues, look out of the window, complete crosswords, chat, argue, sleep.

'. . . two, two I've got, four, thank you, four, six I've got, set of brass spring scales, six, eight, thank you, eight's the bid, someone got ten? where are you, Mr Bourne, come out without your wallet again? ten, thank you, ten, ten, ten, all done at ten, thank you, number . . . ?'

The gavel comes down. A farmer type with florid face holds up his card. A human squeal from the kiosk follows an electric one from the PA. Einar's latest trick with boiling water has been a painful mistake.

'Number 98, brass bedpan. Come on, concentrate on the job in hand.'

Linden and Kumar raise the pan, faces lifted in expectation, as if this was not an auction at all, but a collection point for lost property, and the rightful owner out there somewhere, about to yelp in recognition and reach out in relief.

'Presumably unused, though I haven't looked inside. Oh, hang about, says here it's a bed *warmer*. Put some hot coals in that, shove it between the sheets and dial 999.'

Kumar drums on the brass with his knuckles. Tears of laughter spring to Mrs Bickerton's eyes.

'Start this one at twelve . . .'

Left right left goes the auctioneer's head, eyes following instants behind. Beside him Zoë tracks the same fleeting clues, scanning for a wave of a catalogue or the raising of a hand.

'Ten anywhere? Thank you Mrs Lewis! Ten pound the bid, there's twelve against you, twelve, fourteen, sixteen, eighteen, twenty, twenty, twenty-two? come on Mrs Lewis, one more, thank you, all done at twenty-two *pounds* . . . Thank you Mrs Lewis, your life will never be the same.'

'Number 16,' says Zoë, scribbling.

'Right, Lot 99, drawing of female nude, very tasteful, don't be shy. Let's have a look at it, Linden. Come on, these people've got pubs to go to.'

Kumar flicks uselessly through a stack of paintings. Linden checks his list for the umpteenth time.

'There it is!' says Zoë, pointing to the wire grid on the wall.

Kumar lifts the picture down and holds it high. Women in the front row dream of standing naked before crowds.

'Start at five . . . Five? Three then . . . anywhere? Mr Graham, this is your kind of thing. All right, a pound . . . pound . . . *pound* . . . come on, frame's worth more than that, thank you, a pound.'

Einar and Finn swap places on the rostrum. The Icelander is pale with fright. Hector peers out from the biscuity warmth of his breast pocket, where the letters BK are embroidered in white. Einar stares down at the catalogue and moves one lip at a time.

'Shit,' says Finn. 'I knew this was going to be fun.'

Linden nibbles his goatee. 'You want me to have a go?'

'You're the only one who knows the layout. Give him a minute or two.'

Which is about as long as it takes for Einar to speak. When at last he opens his mouth, it is a very strange sound that comes out.

'My name is Einar. How do.'

Chairs creak. A baby starts to whine.

'I am from Iceland.'

'And I'm Lena Zavaroni,' comes a gruff voice from the side.

'*Skál!*' he says. 'Stop me if I go too fast . . .'

Zoë leans across and whispers something into his ear. Two police officers appear at the top of the stairs.

'Oh shit, it's the PC Rozzers. But I didn't . . . no, I am here. Hallo now, number 100. Condom set.'

Uproarious laughter. Raised heart-rates among the staff.

'*Cond-i-ment*,' pronounces Zoë. 'Condiment set.'

'But nevertheless, good for stopping the little Vikings. Unscrew the silver cap, tip out all the itchy contents and believe-you-me, one for weekdays and one for weekends.'

Ladies in the front row giggle at will.

'Ha ha ha!' says Einar up on his rostrum. 'Now who's gonna make a fucking bid?'

'Five pence!' goes Lena Zavaroni.

'Bollocks!' says Einar.

'Fifty pence!' offers Mrs Enderby.

'Ooh!' says the Second Auctioneer.

'Quid!' from the man in the pigskin hat.

'Yes mate!' says Einar and bangs the gavel.

'That wasn't a bid,' says Mrs Bickerton.

'We didn't get a chance,' says Mrs Bootherstone.

Then: 'You must be quicker, ma'am.'

Zoë scribbles, shaking her head. The young man with fabulous cheekbones stands up, stays there chatting to his girlfriend and is told to sit down.

'Next!' barks Einar. 'What would you like?'

'Look at the list, you Scandinavian twat,' says Linden under his breath.

'Lot 101 . . . Now these are the very binoculars they take from me in the cop shop, and I say no, I don't need your electric razor, there's a goat who lives in my ear and he comes out at night and I never *ever* have to shave . . .'

The audience lap it up. The two cops remove someone for questioning and get a round of applause. Mrs Enderby stands over the wicker dog basket she has had her eye on since Monday, looking like she'd punch anyone who so much as looked at it, hovering jealously in the sweet anticipation of possession. She breathes excitedly as her lot approaches, fans herself with her catalogue and opens the bidding as if she were staking her life. Einar sells a set of traffic lights to a woman in perm and pink glasses who quite obviously didn't bid. Bickerton and Bootherstone bid against each other for a brass desk calendar, in 20p increments, until Einar loses patience, climbs down from the podium and secretes the calendar down the front of his shorts.

Finn Causley ascends again. Don's meat safe goes for twelve quid to a man with a pointy moustache. Dust from a Turkish carpet, unrolled for the first time since the nineteenth century, has the first three rows coughing and flapping catalogues. The auctioneer works well. Objects turn into prices, numbers are answered by numbers, and Don Long's material legacy is broken down and distributed to the crowd. People raise their hands to bid and look away with nonchalant expressions. No one is in a mood to leave. By three-thirty, when the gavel comes down for the last time, only a dozen or so lots are left unsold.

Zoë is left in charge. She glares mistrust at him, challenging him to explain himself.

'I'm off to Happy Valley, then the clinic,' says Finn.

'Did she say she wanted to see you?'

'Did she . . . ?'

'Nothing. Look, I don't mind doing this, but don't you take me for granted. Or you might wish you had more friends than you have.'

What does she mean? 'Zoë...'

But she's walking, shaking hair out behind her, already somewhere else.

The Happy Valley Play Centre is a ten-minute trip across the northern moor. Robinson is in the sandpit with a little girl called Sue.

'Don't touch me, I'm a church,' he says, hands steepled above his head.

He follows me to the van. 'Where we going?' as the straps go on.

'We're going to see Mo. We're going to have a word with the doctor and then we're going to the white room.'

'Is she gonna be sad today?'

'She's not sad. She's just a bit, I don't know, confused.'

'I went to... to the sandpit and Sue said... *Sue* said...'

He gazes out at hedgerows, tractors, bathtubs abandoned in fields.

'Her mo's dead too. She's got a Disease.'

'Your mo's not dead. I don't want you to say that.'

'She sits there and don't say nothing. Tomorrow we're gonna have a shop.'

'Are you? What are you going to sell?'

'Things. I'm gonna be an octioner like you.'

'I think you'll make a very good auctioneer. You can take my gavel.'

'What's a gavel?'

'It's the hammer you use to close a sale. You bang it on a little wooden pad. You've seen me do it.'

His head bumps around on uneven road. Under the translucent mask of childhood, the hard shape of the adult face is starting to emerge.

'If she's not dead, why... why don't she come home? Why don't she come and live with us in Big Kibberley?'

'You know I can't answer that.' But the thing is, he *doesn't* know.

He says nothing. I have seen him scream for her, face wet with apple juice and tears, asphyxiated by rage. But I have never seen him look so perfectly alone.

LOT
10

Dr Valerie Choi is a highly sought-after professional. I've been trying to get inside her office for weeks.

'I'm sorry it's been so *long*, Mr Causley. I've hardly had time to go to the *bathroom* these last few days.'

I catch her shocking pink smile, a cheap glitter in the eyes, old acne scars stretching under rouge. She may not have been to the bathroom, but those sexless book-learned charm mechanisms are all in place.

'You got a brain lying around somewhere? Doesn't have to be real, long as it's childproof.'

She trots past fake shrubs and welcoming sofas to a metal cabinet. The kid scampers over on his knees, grabs her flesh-toned toy and starts to dismantle it at her feet.

'Robinson. Where's Ammon's Horn?'

He finds the lateral ventricle and holds it up, pointing with an unsteady finger to the white ridge on the cavity floor.

'Excellent! Does he want a job?'

She invites me into her laughter but I remain blushing at the door.

'Yeh well. Children without mothers find all sorts of ways to entertain themselves.'

Dr Choi settles in her chair and looks with terrific interest at her visitor.

'Perhaps you could tell me what's on your mind, Mr Causley.'

'It's not me, Doctor, it's the kid. He wants to know how long you're going to hang on to her. Or if you can't tell him that, you can tell him what you're doing with her.'

Dr Choi draws a measured breath.

'The world has changed, Mr Causley. We used to think that this kind of neuronal deterioration could not begin in earnest until the individual was well into middle age. But in the last few years we've had to deal with an increase in extraordinary cortical dementias among the under-forties which is quite unlike anything we've encountered before. Let me explain what I mean by that. We normally say there are two main types of dementia, depending on the part of the brain where the lesion is assumed to occur. The *subcortical* dementias, such as Parkinson's Disease, affect the subcortical structures deep down in the brain. The *cortical* dementias, such as DAT, or Dementia of the Alzheimer Type, affect the cortex, which is . . . yes, the big wrinkly bit on the outside. The subcortical dementias concern those functions we know to be mainly under subcortical control. For example, Parkinson's Disease affects one part of the motor system, leading to the well-known problem with initiating voluntary movements.'

'She making any sense to you, Robin?'

He looks up open-mouthed. I'm trying desperately hard not to sigh.

'Now what we've been faced with in the last few years is a dementia, or group of dementias, which appears to have *no associated subcortical deficits*. The problems present as entirely cortical: memory impairment, disorientation, agnosia, and so on.'

'Smiling?'

'The jury's still out on that one, I'm afraid. We simply don't have enough facts in at the present time.'

'And where do facts come from?'

'Well, that's where the problems begin. As you know, a great many of our patients have an unfortunate history of substance abuse. There is one particular drug, D-DMPA, which has been responsible for almost all of the fatalities linked to this group of dementias. Very often, by the time we can get to any brain tissue, these drugs have done so much damage that, even if we did find some post mortem abnormality, we would have no way of knowing how much of it was due to the dementia and how much was down to the drugs that individual had been using.'

'So we wait for a few more people to die . . .'

'No. What we do is try to determine the cause of the disorder by looking very carefully at what sort of people are getting it. The traditional approach is to look for some genetic predisposition, and then one or a number of environmental factors that might serve to trigger the full-blown condition . . .'

She remembers whose closest genetic relative is playing at her feet, blushes and blunders on.

'Then there's the viral angle. Viruses such as HIV, herpes and so on have long been known to attack brain tissue. But there's really no direct evidence for any such lesioning. A few enlarged ventricles here and there, some loss of dendritic spines, but no changes in basic haematology, and very little to see from the scans. Let's face it: there are things out there we just don't know about yet. It may come down to something as simple as the flu. Since the mid-1980s a whole host of new influenza viruses have been described, many of which you and I will have caught. We have absolutely no idea what these viruses might do to brain tissue under certain conditions.'

'It's enough to make you fear for your life.'

Choi looks at me with all the contempt I deserve.

'It most certainly *is* scary, and the last thing I want to do is panic people. But I also have a duty to be absolutely frank with you. The fact is that we *just don't know*. And until we do, there seems little point in taking unnecessary risks with people's lives.'

'Or sending them home to live happily with their children.' I couldn't make it sound like it's *me* who wants her home.

'You know that's unfair. Henrietta is here entirely of her own accord. We can offer her a secure environment away from the dangers she would be facing in the outside world.' Across the desk the eyes are narrowing. 'You may not be aware of this, Mr Causley, but there are people out there going around with a list of people on file at the Royal Infirmary as having an extraordinary cortical dementia, tracking them down and pushing DMPA at them for absurd prices. Bliss sufferers are prone to all sorts of secondary delusions, and one of the most regrettable examples is the belief that this hideous substance is going to solve all their problems. Now, Henrietta is doing very well with us. She has not shown the need for any serious medication. As long as she is happy here, and as long as Mr Threadgold is happy to support her, she is very welcome to stay. She can leave any time she wants.'

'Of course she's happy. The problem is she's too happy. No one should have to be that happy all the time.'

'Have you asked her if she wants to go home?'

If I wasn't such a trusting soul, I'd think this jet-haired Revlon queen was accusing me of something. I think I'll stare at her until she explains herself.

'I mean that, having talked to Henrietta at some length, there are certain things about the home environment which do not sound exactly ideal.'

'Well, there's a lot of junk around, if that's what you're getting at.'

'A lot of objects for her to puzzle over. A lot of things to try to understand.'

Remember the stone, Hen? Remember the days when things were so full of meaning you could hardly tear your eyes away?

'All right. Say for the moment she wants to be here. But it seems to me that if there *is* something wrong you should be keeping an eye on her and not letting her do whatever she feels like.'

'Can I ask what sort of thing we are worried about here?'

'Just that . . . things tend to happen to her.'

She sighs and checks the clock. 'Look, Mr Causley, even if we wanted to enforce some kind of regime, we wouldn't be allowed to. There are no pathognomic tests that we can point to here. As far as the law is concerned, St Mary's Disease, or Bliss, or whatever you wish to call it, simply does not exist. Now, if you are unhappy about her staying here, I suggest you talk to her and Mr Threadgold.'

'But what you don't know, Dr Choi, is that Tom Threadgold will do anything in his power to keep his little princess as far away from me as possible. That's what all this is about. He's trying to forget the day she got pregnant by a builder. He doesn't like the way it sounds at the golf club.'

'I'm sorry if that's the case, but . . .' The worst thing is her professional sympathy. And her smug round-up: 'Now, is there anything else you wanted to know?'

'Yeh. I want to know how you get to sleep at night. Do you just shut your eyes and it all comes to you? Or is there some clever little doctor who comes and tells you what to do?'

Hen is in the armchair, reading. Roxanne's faded MAD FOR IT tee-shirt is pulled down over her thighs. Her hair is wet. An atmosphere of shampoo and steam drifts from the daylit bathroom to mix with the curtained gloom of the room. She notices Robinson like a hallucination, some test of her sanity that she is just learning her way around.

'He looks different each time I see him. It's because when we made him we couldn't keep our minds on the job in hand. Anyway, don't just stand there, come and let me have a sniff! If you're not too sure about someone, get the nose in, that's my advice.'

Her son approaches warily. She takes his head between her hands and presses lips to his forehead, drawing in the scent of fine white hair.

'I want to hear about the monks. Daddy don't know anything.'

'What do you want to know?'

'How the Abbey burned down. Jack said . . . Jack . . .'

'Yeh, yeh.'

She picks up her book and runs a finger along the crease. As Finn leans down to kiss her – hesitant, unsure now of the rules – she breaks the spine between her hands and tracks a green shadow across the wall. How she always kissed him: eyes obscenely open, looking past him at pill bottles, handcuffs, past lovers hiding in the corners of the room, as if checking there wasn't something more interesting she could be doing, some kinky alternative to this obvious game. In the hallway, late for work; under an umbrella in the rain; kissing through the transparent shower curtain, two breaths making fog circles, two sets of lipmarks perfectly aligned. Stopping her on the stairs, not letting her pass until she gave up lips, tongue; dreaming that she'd drowned and he kissed her, and she took life in his arms. The soundless language they made: their pauses, jokes, questions, doubts; all the times he tried to kiss her away, or simply closed his eyes and wished she was someone else. They trap him, these spectral kisses, twisting around each other into a noose that ties him to the past, or hangs him if he tries to leave. And the first clumsy rerun brings them all flooding back, to mock him and what he's witnessed, this change from knowable girl-love into something cruel and inscrutable, impossible to understand.

'How do you feel?'

'I'm the happiest person on earth. I suppose you've come to make me feel even better.'

He lays a few fingers on her bare thigh. No alarm is sounded; no orderlies come running. She colours faintly and closes her eyes.

'Or perhaps you're just desperate for something. Well, tough luck, sunshine.'

She shuffles her weight in the chair. The cloth sags on her belly and folds together in her lap. This shirt, once slyly lifted to slip her flesh into his hands, then so rapidly shed to complete the spell of her nudity: her shocked breasts, her pagan paleness, the left ankle with its ice-age tattoo. The body in the chair, once so urgent in his hands, now strange and hostile and clenching him up with an infuriating, loveless desire.

'You're beautiful.'

She smiles. But it's not the smile he could never resist. It is another smile: a picture drawn by a machine, a random configuration of muscles that repeats the same empty message a thousand times a day.

'Right, you're here. I want to ask you something. Do you remember when I said, "Come on man, sort yourself out," and you said, "I'm not a man, I'm a sex machine." What did you mean by that exactly?'

'Can't remember, Hen. I think it was a joke.'

'Yeh, you're always making jokes, aren't you. You're always making jokes and I'm always laughing at them.'

A foot of blue sky through the curtains. Zoë's statue stands on the table by the bed. The desk under the window is covered with open books and sketches: Hen, naked at the mirror, standing with one hand on her belly and the other cupped around her neck. A glossy brochure: Hooper's of Norwich, Estate Agents; newspaper cuttings reporting fires in a number of public buildings; a box of tampons spilling onto the side. The computer screen glows blue-grey, in consummate imitation of the sky.

'Now, if you don't mind, I've got some research to do.'

Robinson busies himself with Dr Choi's brain. He takes it apart, lays out the pieces on the floor and inspects each one in turn. He knows it's here somewhere, the thing that has killed his mother and left this grinning automaton in her place, but all he finds is moulded plastic and rubbery paint. He clicks the two hemispheres together, places the brain upright on the carpet, then lies on his tummy and gazes into its absent eyes.

'What sort of research?' His father stares at the books piled on the desk, remembering the books he found her with, in that flat on Bristol Street: books to sleep on, books to eat off, books to trip you up wherever you went. Warm September evening, a small lifetime ago . . .

'I told you, I'm doing some research for Tony. For God's sake, he's done enough for me.'

'The one I saw in the kitchen? Fat bloke with the beard?'

'Yes, but he's not fat. He's an artist.'

She hands the book to me upside down, thumb hooked inside one page:

> The enthusiasm with which mental illness was interpreted as witchcraft in the late fourteenth century is clearly illustrated in this extract from a contemporary source: 'The woman remained seated, her face twisted in a diabolic smile which no threat nor exhortation could banish. She sought neither food nor water. When given bread she would not eat, but lifted it to her eyes and gazed upon it, with writhing movements of the hands, as if it were made of finest gold and encrusted with the richest rubies. Many were filled with great fear by her smile.'

The entire paragraph has been gone over with a yellow highlighter pen. In the margin she has written: 'Yes! Tell Tony.'

'What's so special about this bit?'

'What's so special about it is that it's important to my research.'

'But what does it mean?'

Her lips move without words. One eyelid droops over its blue-grey iris. She snatches the book and stares at the open page.

'I don't know, but there's something about this colour that gets you right in the eye. The paper, well, that smells of some sort of chemical, you know, new carpet, brand-new car. But you want to know what it *means*. You're always trying to catch me out. *The extent to which mental illness* . . .' She glances sideways at her ribbon of sky.

'It's okay, I know what the words are, but when you line them up like that and put them together, they don't add up to anything. Cor. I used to think you could learn something from books, but now I'm not so sure.'

Now the smile is wary, frightened. Many were filled with great fear.

'Hen, why do you think you're here?'

'I'm here because that's what's best for all of us. I haven't been myself recently, that's obvious. But you've seen the scan, we're getting there. I'm going to get my NTX levels up and then, who bloody knows.'

I'm remembering what Valerie Choi told me, months ago, when the first scan results came through:

'There are no pathognomic laboratory results for this group of dementias. That is, there are no specific tests we can point to as providing the basis for a diagnosis. As you can see from the SPECT scan, there are no major abnormalities. We have some evidence for increased blood flow through the ascending nigrostriatal regions, which at one time were called the "pleasure centres" because mild stimulation there was found in some species to be rewarding. At first we thought this might account for the characteristic smile and elevated mood, but we now think that what we have here is an artefact. Something else is making these patients happy. No doubt if we found out what it is, we'd simply try to reverse the process, and I don't think anyone's really interested in doing that.'

I pointed to Hen's scan. 'This bit's darker.'

'Yes, there is some evidence for decreased flow through these associative centres. This was thought to explain the problems these individuals have with imbuing their experiences with meaning: if you like, making sense of the world. It may also account for the interesting confabulations. Hen can take one of her vivid alien images – a memory of the Middle Ages, for example – and use it as a starting point for imagining an entire alternative life. You could see it as an attempt by consciousness to improve on a world which doesn't seem quite real.'

She took me through the neurophysiology with an obscene sort of pride, as if all this neuronal chaos somehow reflected well on her. She showed me the EEG, from the day they gelled Hen's skull in sixteen places and connected up electrodes and I watched her drift from smile to smile, enjoying the cheesy Doctor Who-ness of it all. What came out was a set of long scribbled lines, the kind people draw when they're testing out a pen in a shop and are afraid to write their own name. It showed, apparently, a slight reduction in amplitude, low irregular theta activity and periodic discharges. 'It's reminiscent of all kinds of dementias,' said Choi. 'It's telling us there's something unusual but it's not telling us what. Look, here's a slight delay in the P300. That could easily be an artefact of her current lifestyle. We try to keep her as active as possible, but she does spend a lot of time sitting in her room.'

'What does that mean?' Like any doting relative, I wanted the heinous pathogen that did such things to people's brains, not some vague story about lifestyle problems.

'It means that if I took a normal healthy woman of Henrietta's age and sat her in a dark room twenty-four hours a day, the result would look pretty much like this.'

She showed me slides taken from the brains of other patients: enhanced-colour images of neuritic plaques, fibrous astrocytes, foamy macrophages and multinucleated giant cells . . . 'The latter are characteristic of all the infectious dementias we know about. There's an important school of thought which maintains that this is a *transmitted* disorder.' She showed me the foam cells and sea-blue histiocytes that had been found in a few marrow samples, and I stared at the pictures projected onto her office wall at astronomical magnifications, eyes too wide with wonder to see how they might possibly connect to Hen: wild Hen, infuriating Hen, impossible half-wife. She was filling her with things I never dreamed of, teasing her apart with electron microscopy, radioactive isotopes and photon emissions, planting her internal garden with blue star-like flowers and red creeping weeds, fungoid blooms and gleaming metallic deposits, and sending the pictures back to the surface as if they were treasures from an uncharted reef, instead of signals of a fate that was as much a death as any other, but just looked better in clothes.

But I've been daydreaming. It's 1372 and the monastery is on fire.

'For two days and two nights the great Abbey of Dieulacres burns. Slabs of oak crash blazing through the roof, the tapestries round the altar become curtains of flame, smoke piles out through the windows and climbs miles into the sky. Townspeople leave their homes in their nightshirts to watch the fireworks, and dirty little children run around with arms outstretched, trying to catch a floating ember or two. The sky is filled with unearthly screams, as all the people who lie buried out the back are woken by devils in fireproof clothing and told they have to die all over again. The first townsperson to snuff it is a young woman with yellow hair who, at the great arched doorway, is too curious for her own good. Ranulph de Blundeville's grandfather is seen flying low over the scene, howling like a dog and tearing at his hair . . .'

The child's face is hot with wonder. Hen sits staring at the door, stroking thighs with the backs of her hands.

'Now you don't need *me* to tell you what all this means. There's some nights that stick with you, no matter how many times you think you've put the buggers to bed. I told you something happened to me a long long time ago, something so horrible I still get the shakes about it now and then. Well, there I am, *the girl with the yellow hair*. It was the fire I died in! I wrote the last entry in my diary and walked across the fields to my death. 7th March 1372. Cor. Well it certainly explains my pyromaniac tendencies! One day I'm going to make a TV programme about it and we can clear this up once and for all. Otherwise, who knows, maybe I'll do what I should've done in the first place: light my little match, stand well back and *whoosh!* watch the whole thing fizzle to the ground.'

The boy gazes at his mother as if she was still ablaze, as if medieval flames were still leaping in her eyes, sparking and crackling in her hair. The world runs on without us. Through all the guilt and resentment, the understanding that tomorrow brings someone who will eclipse this love so utterly that seven years' waiting will shrink to a dot and blink out; through all of this, I'm stared down by her reckless beauty, the energy that comes from forgetting who you're trying to be just long enough to be it, and responding to it in the way I responded the first night I ever saw her: with pure self-hating desire.

'D'you think Robin should go for a walk?' says the feeling you get when you can't help how you feel.

'Good idea. Let's lose the kid.'

She presses a button on the bedside table. A face appears around the door.

'Rumer, this man wants to sell me something. Can you kidnap him for half an hour?'

'We're gonna have a church,' says Robin. 'I'm gonna be a monk and put out the fire . . .'

The door clicks shut behind them. Hen stands and stretches, uncoiling like springs from the chair. If the shirt rode up any higher I would glimpse the fringe of her fur, the scribble of a temperamental pen, a pale brown spreading to straw. How proud the owner, trimming it for weekly self-portraits, talking to it at the mirror as if she was the only one who understood its code. Straightening to her full height, the hem of the shirt lifting higher, I wonder how anyone could look so alive, so charged up with the lazy power of their sex. I remember all the times I cupped her spine and waltzed her around a room like this one, as we touched down after an ecstatic flight over an English landscape; how I brushed her lips with mine and she rewarded me with a sliver of tongue. All our secret details swarm out and attack me: how I drank from the cleft spoon of her hips, how she cocked her bowl and swallowed me like an oyster, the way her belly inflated as she took me in and then tightened like a drum, sucking me home. And for a second, just for a second, an old smoothness to her movements makes me think it might be different, that we might make it work like we made it work that first golden evening; that I should forget about deliberate strangers with dark curved hair and go to her, work backwards through a million kisses, make love to her until we've both forgotten how impossible this love has always been.

'What's the mattress?' she says, settling beside me on the bed and crossing her thighs.

'Just thinking.'

'Well done. About what?'

'Oh, you know. How we met.'

'Hm.'

'And what happened after that.'

She stares at the empty chair. Her eyes open wide then click shut, photographing the moment, to use it against me when my crime becomes clear.

'Hen?'

'Hm?'

'How much of that do you remember?'

She sighs. 'I remember I was really shitty towards you.'

'Why do you say that?'

'I don't know.'

'Try. It will help.'

'Who will it help?'

'Me. You.'

A satin label pokes out from the neck of her tee-shirt. She rubs her tongue against the roots of her teeth.

'We're in the flat. You're crying. I'm telling you to forget it, it wasn't important, it didn't mean anything. You're being completely irrational as usual. I always said you weren't half the man your mother was.'

'I may have had good reason . . .'

'Shh. There's more. You're saying, "In *our* place. In *our* bed." I'm saying, "It's *my* place, *my* bed." Oh, I remember now. It was Simon, wasn't it. That absolute utter piece of shit.'

'But Hen, it *was* our place. We thought it up together and we both did the work. Remember? That's the reason I was there in the first place. That's how we got it together.'

'Hey, that's a good story. I like that.'

'It's true.' The voice is hoarse and unsteady. On these shoulders, a sudden crushing despair.

'I'm sitting there on the bed. You've stopped blubbering. You're walking around the flat very calmly, packing your things. Christ knows where you're going, you're probably going back to Australia for all I know. You can't seem to get it into your head that it was a mistake! Simon came over, we smoked a bit of hash and surfed around a bit and one thing led to another. Just like it did with us, remember? Actually, if I'd known how you were going to react I'd have kept my big mouth shut.'

Now it's my turn for empty stares. Hen stands up, shirt sticking to the backs of her thighs, and leans against the desk as if trying to shift it further into the wall.

'Look, I'm sorry. I never meant to piss you about. All I know is that I'm sitting there on the bed and I don't want you to go. I probably love you or something.'

She picks up her Walkman from the desk, turns and holds it out to me. She's staring at her hand as if she wasn't expecting it to be there.

'Autotopagnosia,' Choi once told me. 'This problem with recognising one's own body parts. Terribly distressing, of course, but not uncommon in this group of disorders.'

Hen stares at the back of her hand, brows pushed together in a tiny frown.

'This is my tape recorder. Something important is going to happen and I want to record it. I don't know what it is but I know it's important. You're going to find out something about me.'

She presses the record button. A red diode eats time. She places it carefully on the desk and turns to face me.

'Stand up.'

I step in between her arms. Her spine flexes under the shirt. She turns lips to me and I take them, heart skating, feeling the gate of her teeth and the wet life of her tongue.

'I want you,' she hums.

'What . . . what did you want to tell me?'

'Shh.'

She kisses again. Skin is cool beneath the hem of the shirt. My finger traces the crack of her arse and presses deep into the heat below. Every better thought dissolves into this scented gloom. I no longer care if I'm as hard as she ever made me, if one touch from Hen can make me forget all our harm, if I want her so much I'm prepared to say it, and damn myself to this desire. Because it's not Hen, it's Anna; this time tomorrow I'll be holding her again; it has to be Anna, or all this is obscene.

'You're still my twin tree,' I whisper.

'Okay, that's that bit.'

She stands back and quickly lifts the shirt. As it comes over her breasts and her shoulders click out to lift it over her head, I can begin to see what has happened to her. There is no scribbled brown bush. Her mound has been shaved clean. She has taken blue and purple felt-tip pens and covered the stubbled skin with pointillist lines and symmetrical shapes. It's easy enough to see what she's drawn. It's

---

Lot 10: **Portable cassette recorder** plus a selection of cassettes, dated with the same hand.

the drooping flower of the textbooks, the standard diagram of the female urogenital system: vagina, uterus, two ovaries joined by curving funnel-ended tubes. She's drawn in one kidney but not yet got round to the other one.

'I've been wanting to show you this for ages. Do you like it?'

I'm staring at her naked body, with its precise graffiti, trying to understand what she's done.

'I wanted to know where things were. Women are very complex creatures. Now we don't have to worry about all those accidental pregnancies. We can do what we do best and not worry about a thing.'

It's not a joke. I can feel myself shaking. So why this urge to laugh?

'Do you do this every time you have a bath?'

'I don't need to. It's permanent ink. Anyway, I didn't do it.'

I know this voice – lazy, cruel, the same blithely spiteful tone that told me about her night with Simon, letting it drop so calmly that I really had to wonder if she understood what she'd done.

'Who fucking did it, then?'

'Tony, of course. He's a professional. But don't worry, I don't have to pay him. What's the mattress? You don't seriously expect me to do something like this on my own?'

I can see pinpricks in the skin, spots of dried blood, the cut ends of her clean-shaved hair. Further up, the fainter guide marks for the second kidney, waiting to be filled in by the inky needle. She's right: this is one mark that will never fade. I look and look and find nothing I can understand, a voiceless screaming over every rational voice, fierce tears blurring her away.

'Why, Hen? Why do you have to . . . ?'

I'm crying now. She fixes me with her lithium smile.

Says, 'I don't *have* to, darling. It's just something I *feel* like from time to time.'

LOT
11

When Roxanne was alive – before her red baseball cap became another relic preserved for all time in my catalogue, like the liquorice-black hair and her unique way of speaking her mind – the evening after a sale was one of the highlights of our three-storey life. As soon as the front door had closed behind the last customer, the key turned twice and the video surveillance switched on, we would gather in the Board Room on the first floor, at the mahogany table rescued from a farmhouse in Schyre, and go through the accounts. There were always a few bottles of Australian champagne and some of Einar's Icelandic snacks. Roxanne would read out the statistics: total number of lots, percentage sold, gross takings from auction, kiosk and sale of catalogues; then Linden and his computer would subtract the costs and incidental expenses, and the final result would announce itself to a hushed room. It was always a pleasant confirmation rather than an out-and-out surprise: we'd seen how profits went up in direct proportion to tabloid speculation about TV celebrities and Bliss-related crimes; and as long as people were continuing to find happiness at such encouraging rates, we knew our bonuses would continue to rise. That's when we sat back and thought of all the people we could have been: the careers they'd fought for, the lifestyles they'd admired, the way they held out for the big prizes while we trod water and laughed; and wondered how those routes might have looked if we'd never known about the alternatives; how we'd have smiled, who we'd have dreamed of, what we'd be doing now.

They're in the Board Room, belching over the remains of king prawn foo yung and Chinese roast pork, drinking Co-op claret straight from the bottle because the glassware cupboard collapsed and we've not had time to buy any more. It's a while since we had champagne. It's over a year since the three girls kicked off their shoes and did their Bananarama routine, then piled into Zoë's bed clutching ice-cold bottles as corks popped and we listened to their shrieks through the barricaded door. Since then Roxanne's smile has become fixed for ever, Hen never looks at me and Zoë only laughs when things go wrong. 'I got you some,' she says, 'but the lads have scoffed it all.'

She hands me a sheet of paper headed ACCOUNTS OF THE SALE AT BIG KIMBERLEY, WEDNESDAY 4TH JUNE. LINDEN, IF THESE SUMS ARE WRONG YOU'RE IN SHIT MOST DEEP.

'It's um . . .' starts Linden.

'It's good,' shrugs Finn.

'And I trust I'm getting a cut this time,' says Jack, 'after my triumph on the cash desk.'

'I'm sure you've already taken your cut,' says Linden, an accusation that makes the accuser blush, the accused smirk and every chair leg scrape. There's an atmosphere here and it's getting worse.

'Your dad phoned,' says Zoë. 'He thought Hen was still living here. I couldn't tell him what you've done with her.'

'What does he want?'

Jack gets up and bangs his chair. 'He wants to make you feel guilty for being alive. What does any parent want? Now, can we *please* concentrate on the matter in hand? Zoë, you're going to be Bertilak's wife.'

'What's her name?'

'Get away. Women didn't have names in the fourteenth century.'

'Right then. I'm gonna call her . . . Germaine.'

'*Germaine?*'

'Or perhaps you want to find someone else to be your bimbo.'

'All right, the *burde* is called Germaine. Who's next?'

'Finn's going to be King Arthur.'

'But he's bald! Arthur had a lovely . . .'

The latecomer wants to know what they're talking about. Jack covers his eyes and turns impatiently on his heels.

'He wasn't here,' says Zoë. 'Right, look. We're putting on a production of Jack's opera. You know, the one he's been writing for about seventeen years.'

'An opera,' says Finn. 'Where?'

'Lud's Church,' says Linden. 'It's gonna be an open-air extrava –'

'Oh, no, it's haunted.' Zoë shivers tinily. 'We'll do it here, in the auction room. It'll be a scream.'

'I can scream,' says Robin, and commences to offer proof.

'Right, Einar's Gawain, and Kumar's the Green Knight.'

'But he's brown!' moans Linden.

'Am I?' He sits up and rubs an arm with a finger. 'Shit! Ain't they got drugs and stuff?'

'*Slokes!*' yells Jack. 'You miss the exquisite symmetry! Gawain, Arthur's trusted knight and some say nephew, who is lured by the stunning Germaine Bertilak and very nearly succumbs to her charms, disgracing himself so badly that, on his return to Camelot, he vows to wear a green sash so he might never forget his dalliance with the demon that is Woman . . .'

'Finn wears green,' says Zoë. 'I always wondered . . .'

The auctioneer stares angrily at Jack. Who quickly makes matters worse.

'Hey, negro, just thinking about our little chat on the hill. When did you say she was coming?'

'Tomorrow,' says Einar. 'And Doctor Anna is *my* doctor.'

Zoë fixes Finn with a tank-bending glare.

'What they talking about?' says Kumar to the kid, who extrudes fried rice from his mouth.

'Why *do* you always wear green?' says Zoë. 'I used to do that when I was about fourteen, except I wore black because that's what Morrissey said.'

'I don't always wear green. I wear it when I feel like it. I feel like it today.'

'Don't you fucking snap at me, or you'll get this fucking bottle in your face.'

Jack settles on the window-sill and hums a sinister tune. He raises a hand for silence, and looks slowly around the room.

'Camelot. The beginning of the sixth century. A New Year's feast at the court of King Arthur. The Knights of the Round Table, God's own earthly stormtroopers, sit at table with *the lovelokkest ladies that ever lif haden*. There, Queen Guinevere, under a canopy of finest Toulouse silk; beside her, the courteous and fork-bearded Sir Gawain; and King Arthur himself, the greatest lord in all Christendom, *his yong blod and his brayn wylde*. As is his custom at the New Year's feast, no food will pass his lips until the entire company has enjoyed some adventure. But,' Jack stands up and catches an invisible bird, 'it's as if the expectation of the event is enough to make it happen – for even now there is a terrible thundering at the door, and in rides the hugest, most fearsome knight ever seen by that company, coloured bright green from head to toe. His beard is green. His horse is green. His fearsome battle-axe is green and gold. When he speaks the goblets rattle on the table and the torches flicker with his breath. His challenge is this: any man of courage can take his axe and deal him a blow, on one condition: that, a year from now, the blow will be returned.'

'Told you it was stupid,' says Linden.

'No one comes forward. "Observe!" roars the stranger. "Arthur's great Round Table, cowering like babes before one man!" Which is quite enough for our valiant Gawain: he steps forward and takes the axe himself. Silence falls. In every corridor and stairway, people dread the next sound. The Green Knight bends forward and offers up his neck. Gawain lifts the axe high in the air, and brings it down so quick and hard that the steel shatters the bones and sends the head tumbling across the floor. Calmly the Knight retrieves what is his, mounts his horse and, holding his bleeding head by a mane of green hair, leaves his chilling challenge: *Fulfil your half of the bargain, and seek me at the Green Chapel, on New Year's morning a year from now.*'

The child stares at Jack with wonder-struck eyes.

'Great *story*,' says Zoë – and for a moment we could be listening to Roxanne.

But one isn't listening. The bald king pushes back his chair and walks to the door, their voices fading in the darkness of the stairs.

'So one year later, Gawain sets out on his perilous journey, through wild weather and unholy land, until he reaches the castle of Sir Bertilak de Hautdesert and his beautiful wife. And there the temptation of Gawain begins . . .'

On the roof the evening is cool and blue. Finn stands at the rail with a scroll of paper in his hand: fires in the park, distant hills like strips torn from the sky, a staring absence that can never be filled. Einar moves in beside him and props his chin on the rail.

'She's having an affair. Correction. She's fucking someone at the clinic.'

A car takes the corner with a squeal of brakes. Soft lips inside an artist's beard, the squint of concentration as needle pierces skin . . .

'You sure?' Einar takes the scan and peers at it, as if he might read the secrets of her guilt in that grainy dusk.

'Well, if she hasn't done it yet, it won't be long now. She's ill, isn't she. And I've not exactly been the perfect husband.'

'You in't done nothing.'

'No, but I've thought about it. I've thought about it and I've wanted it. What's worse: doing it without wanting to or wanting it but not doing it? I tell her I love her and it's not a lie, but it's not the truth either. It's just some very pathetic excuse for not loving her enough.'

'You don't feel guilty about what you *think*. Them's just thoughts.'

'But I do. And now I feel so angry I want to smash her fucking face into the wall.'

Einar's voice is cool, liquid, an afterthought of the night.

'This your first time?'

'First time at what?'

'Being cuckooed.'

'Gets easier, does it?'

'No. But you're not the first bloke who's ever been cuckooed. That's why there are all these little boys in Iceland who do not know who their daddies are.'

'Christ. I always think I'm the only one who's got a problem.'

'Hey, we got no problems. You just gotta ask yourself what do you want.'

He remembers a speech he once made, on a balcony outside a blue room, when he still thought he knew how to choose . . .

'I don't decide things, Einar. I just get into them and find they're deciding me.'

Lot 11: **Radio-isotope image** of a brain in sagittal section, on black-and-white photographic paper, showing some evidence of cortical hypoperfusion.

'Do you want Hen?'

'I don't know. My sister says there's this one Type we're all looking for and once you've found it nothing else even comes close. I was like one of those hawks, you know, that have this one kind of mouse they're looking for and they don't even *see* the other stuff. And I found it, I found that one I was looking for, and then, yes, I found Hen. And suddenly there's someone who seems as right for you as anyone ever seemed, and you call it love because you don't know what the fuck else to call it, but in the end it's not enough, because you're that hawk and you're blind and stupid and she's not the one you were looking for, she never was.'

'So is Anna what you want?'

'Nice try. I spent two nights with her seven years ago, then the morning comes and it's back to real life. Anyway, what *I* want doesn't come into it. She wasn't interested then and she won't be interested now.'

'Shit, Finn, you are about as useful as a hole in the arse.'

The troubled king contrives a smile.

'You gonna forgive her?'

'Should I?'

'If you can. It's not always possible.'

He's seen it, then: the mark that never fades.

'You never forgave Jim, did you?'

'Jim knows what he is doing. I tell him I cannot love someone who is using shit like that to change his brains all the time. Cause if he says he loves me I don't know if it's him or the dope. That's no good.'

'You never forgave Rox either.'

'Like say, you wanna kill yourself with drugs that's up to you. She was my mate and I miss her like crazy. But it's her life.'

He sniffs and wipes his nose on his arm.

'Tell me about it, yeh, some time?'

He puts the arm round my shoulder, relieved that he can speak it at last.

'A long long time ago, before I ever leave Reykjavík. I'm nineteen. There is this big party because someone has just become twenty-one. It's in a student hall, on the fourth floor. They're doing all this shit: hash, speed, acid, everything. I have these massive friends, a boy and a girl. They're madly in love. But they wanna try some acid. They say, "You gotta try everything or you in't really living." They say, "You take some acid and you can be anything you want." So they take the acid and they say, "We're a beautiful pair of birds. We got white wings and white feathers. We can fly around the world." So they open the window and they sit on the ledge. We say, "No, you in't birds, you just *think* you are." And they say, "That's good enough for us." And they fly out the window. He goes and then she goes. We find them on the ground, four floors down. He's fallen on some railings and they're sticking right through him. She's lying there, calling his name. Then she dies too.'

The auctioneer is still. He's watching the bats flit over the roof, and the sky curl over the bats, and his eyesight melt like a lens of snow.

'Did you tell Jim this?'

He shrugs. 'People do what they wanna do. I mean, do you ever tell Anna what you think of her? I think you are too worried what she thinks of you.'

'Maybe I was once,' says Finn. 'But then you realise she doesn't think of you, she's never ever thought of you; so what exactly have you got to lose?'

When the time comes for me to sell up everything I own and so absolve myself of History, and thus get all my forgetting over with in one fell swoop, rather than waiting for the years to drag it out of me in dribs and drabs; when that is done, and Big Kimberley is empty of anything that might ever have made a difference to me or my fellow travellers, there'll be no point asking what may or may not have happened on a particular night in that suddenly warm June, unless you happened to be fond of blank smiles and indifferent shrugs or, better still, fat-arsed lies. But as long as a blue-and-green friendship band lies curled on my desk, and a box labelled MARGARET CAUSLEY: 1947–1977 is weighing down the shelf by the door, and as long as a heart is squeaking in my chest and I'm troubled by periodic afflictions of the soul that only an erection of the penis can pacify, I'll have to keep describing nights like these: southerly breeze, tangerine evening sky, no moon over Big Kimberley, and the first sight of a woman (door opens, landing light blazes), an ordinary woman whose accident of making just happens to be recorded in my genes: older, richer, more assured, more bloodstunningly beautiful than I could ever have allowed myself to dream.

She stands by the shell-encrusted telly, seven years and fifty minutes late, in cream trousers and raw cotton waistcoat, telling Jack what she'd like to drink. Einar is cooking for ten. Serge and Nina, just back from their trip to the Lake District, are along the corridor tucking in the children. Linden and Kumar take turns at a telescope mounted at the window, trained with military accuracy on a bedroom window several streets away. Zoë and David discuss football on the sofa. Anna reads the prices on the blackboard fixed to an overhead girder (15–2 on Linden and Zoë snogging by the end of the evening, 50–1 for full sex, with marriage a 1000–1 hopeful), apologises again for being late, and accepts her gin-and-tonic with a voiceless popping of the lips.

Then she sees me (racing certainty to take everything she is and worship it to the end of my days), and what can we do but smile like old friends?

'I thought you weren't coming.'

'I got held up at the hospital. Don't become a doctor, it's not worth it.'

That's it, then: not a kiss, not even a handshake or a comforting palm on the brow. Just a polite reminder that we speak the same language, and it's as good for telling lies as it ever was.

'This is amazing,' she says, glancing at Zoë's mural. 'I can see Einar, but . . .'

Her eyes scan the wall. Seven years I drifted, filming her through a tear's-width of brine, and still I'm no more prepared for this than I was the night it all began: swimming pool, green black blue, enough, run away, move on. And because she never got up from that bench, but stayed there watching while the film ran on for ever and the stars gave up and went home, I have no trouble deciding that her hair is longer, the traveller's tan has long since faded, that I was wrong about the cut of her shoulders and the height of her forehead, because what entered my memory as a girl has come out as a woman: taller, paler, the folds of skin deeper around the eyes, looking like she might be real enough to hang around, get to know the area, and see what we can do about making up for lost time.

'Oh, *I* see you. On that podium thing, in green.'

We take our places around the table. I'm sitting opposite her. She looks at the mural and I look at her. I want to know if I'm still in love with her, if what she did to me then can be done again now, or whether these old memory-tricks will finally turn themselves in.

'So what do you do, Anna?'

'Doctor Anna to you,' says Einar. 'There, you see, I tell you it will be like coming home to meet the family.'

She smiles, touched by fish-light. 'It's okay. I've just qualified, actually. I'm doing a six-month research job on the Extraordinary Cortical Dementias.'

'Sounds like a band,' says Serge.

'What we call Bliss,' says Nina.

'What some people say doesn't exist. What some people say is all a figment of some journalist's imagination.'

Zoë has spoken; now it's the expert's turn.

'I'm really sorry. I knew Roxanne in Sydney? Actually that was one of the main reasons I took this job.'

'Roxanne didn't have Bliss,' says Zoë. 'She just did a few too many pills.'

'Yeh, but why she do the pills?' says Kumar.

'She did the pills because she wanted to do them. Don't ask me, I'm not the doctor.'

Anna swallows and puts down her glass. 'The theory is, it's all to do with this brain-chemical called NTX. We don't know whether there just isn't enough NTX being synthesised, or whether the receptors that are supposed to respond to it have somehow become less sensitive.' She glances across, forehead faintly rippled, then up at the mural behind. 'What Salvation seems to do is increase post-synaptic sensitivity to NTX; in other words, it makes the nerves more sensitive to it, so it does more of what it's supposed to.'

'Which is what?'

'Well Zoë, they basically reckon NTX is involved in the way stimuli are interpreted by the brain, you know, sounds, visual images and stuff. The idea is that people suffering from these dementias have a problem making sense of things because there isn't enough NTX around. The world is completely baffling, just patterns of light and sound with no,' she breathes, 'order to them. It's like Salvation seems to make everything more meaningful.'

'See? When your life has no meaning you take drugs to make it better. And sometimes you take too many and that's it. It's your life.'

'So what about Hen?' says Kumar. 'If she hasn't got what they say she's got, what's wrong with her?'

'There's nothing wrong with Hen either,' Zoë says. 'Or there wouldn't be, if they weren't pumping her full of chlorpromazine from morning till night.'

'They've got to do *something*,' says Finn.

That's it: she's looking. It's a whisper in the spine.

'I mean,' his voice faltering, 'people are trusting them to take care of them.'

'What you *mean*,' says Kumar, 'is that all these clinics which should still belong to the people have found a way of raking in the cash by preying on the fears of a vulnerable few. You persuade them they need to be in hospital, then charge a hundred quid a day for the privilege. What a very good scam this is!'

'Hen looks happy.'

'Well maybe that says more about this place than it does about Moorview.'

Zoë can't be smiling. She only smiles when things go wrong.

'So what's all this I'm hearing about an opera?' says Einar's new friend from the police cells, as the moment turns from desperate to worse.

'The opera?' Kumar deftly takes the pass. 'Well I'm glad you asked, David, because I'm now supposed to be Gawain and (a) I can't sing, (b) I haven't a quacking clue what I'm meant to be doing and (c) the Green Knight is Icelandic and he's going to chop my head off with a pair of scissors. So how about we just run through it a bit?'

'Temptation scene!' barks Jack, already at the door. An invisible hand flicks off the lights. Beyond their neon-lit spaceship, night falls for the fish.

A match flares. From the end of the corridor, a solitary candle flame appears. Jack, wrapped in a white sheet with a pillow-case cowl hooded over his brow, bears his candle slowly before him. An electronic lute picks at a theme. Kumar, Zoë and Einar are rooting through the darkness of the linen press and throwing costumes over each other. Jack stops at the head of the table, mutters something in Latin and pushes back his cowl, his face cupped by shadowy flame.

'This dying century is hard on a monk. The harvests are bad. The habits are itchy. The lay-brethren are always fighting, and when they're not fighting they're drinking your booze. The Black Death has done nothing for your skin, and this Papal Schism means you don't even know who the vicar is. Someone has just burned your abbey down. It might have a mite to do with the fact that your own abbot is running the nastiest little police force this sleepy valley has ever seen, and now if your average peasant even sips from the wrong side of the chalice they take him off onto the moors and chop off his pretty little heretic head.'

A crash from the corner sends the fish flying. 'Ouch,' someone says.

'Aye, it's not just your beautiful abbey that lies in smouldering ruins. The entire monastic project has been swallowed up in corruption, runaway materialism, unnatural intercourse and more than the usual spiritual malaise. That's why this story burns in your mind. You must write it at night, in secret. You must guard it like a candle in your heart. You must tell those who come after you of a time when heroes walked the earth . . . of *skere ladies* and *gentyle knightes* . . . of a valiant and courteous knight, who risked his life for the honour of his king . . .'

One lamp comes on. Kumar, in a floral nightie with one of Robinson's plastic light-sabres strapped to his waist, reclines on three huge cushions, feigning sleep. Zoë kneels beside him in her black silk kimono.

'Do I have to snog him?' she says.

'You're Germaine Bertilak. He's the famous knight from Camelot and you're supposed to be seducing him.'

She yawns ungorgeously. 'Okay sweetheart, the door's locked, the lord of the manor is off hunting and I've got a free hour before lunch.'

'And I thought I knew what boring was,' says Linden, counting his fish.

'Next?' Zoë says.

'Germaine, darling, you've got to get into this a bit. This is not just your average house guest. Your little gerbil is *hot* for him. Come on, let's see a bit of *passion* . . .'

The monk starts grinding his hips against the chair. 'Oh, I know,' says Kumar, glancing down inside his nightie. 'I'm supposed to get lift-off, innit.'

'Do you love another, good knight?'

He grabs her arm. 'Actually, I've a bit of thing for Merlin.'

'Now you ask him for a gift! But he is travelling to almost certain death and he has brought nothing worthy of such a beautiful princess!'

'Oh, right,' says Zoë, 'so I give him my ring, and he won't have it because it looks too flash, so I say, here, have this lovely green girdle, it'll save you from the Green Knight's axe.'

Off-stage, the sound of blades being sharpened.

'*For sothe!* Fearing for his life the knight takes the girdle, but when the lord returns from the hunt for the agreed exchange of winnings, Gawain fails to declare the princess's gift. Now he rides to the Green Chapel on New Year's morning, where the Knight waits, fearsomely armed, to fulfil his half of the bargain . . .'

Einar appears in Linden's green wellies, an emerald G-string and half a holly bush on his head. 'Oh goody, a knight's head for my window-box.'

He snaps his long-handled loppers. Kumar jumps out of bed and bends his neck to the blade.

'And when the Knight reveals himself as none other than the good Lord Bertilak,' Einar pulls off the holly, wincing, 'and the whole world can witness Gawain's guilt, there is nothing for it but to return to Arthur's court with the lady's green girdle, so that anyone who sees it will recall his near-fatal lapse.'

Jack winks at Finn, unwraps his last finger of asparagus and feeds it into his throat. Then Anna has a question.

'I get all this stuff about the landscape matching up. But how do we know the thing was written by one of your monks? It could have just been someone who knew the area.'

'Green, Anna. The green girdle of Gawain. What does green mean to you?'

'It means someone's about to puke,' says Linden. 'But go on.'

'Hope,' says Jack. 'The belief that a new tomorrow will rise from the squalor of today. We're talking about a colour with a central role in pagan myths of rebirth and regeneration. Think of the Green Knight, returning to life after his decapitation, symbolising nothing less than the yearly rebirth of the natural world. Think of all those pubs called the Green Man, where you sat and watched the rain on the windows and wondered when spring would come. That's what our good brother is doing: expressing a faith that his beloved Church will be reborn in brilliant colour: that the New Jerusalem will come, and when it does he'll know what shirt to wear.'

Einar is in the kitchen rescuing his top secret soufflé. Jack gets up and rewinds the tape. Multi-tracked voices chant the overture, and we're silent, feeling the music in our spines.

'I wish I could get involved in something arty like that,' says Anna. 'I used to love all that sort of thing.'

'Great, we need some girly voices for the chorus. I'll do you a tape now.'

He goes to the hi-fi and picks at the wrapper of a cassette. Anna scratches a forearm, slowly, in no hurry to think or become involved, as if to prove she still exists on a different timescale to the rest of us, and the day she stops practising and starts to live is as far off as ever. So there's no point telling her now what I should have told her seven years ago, unless I'm about to notice some change in that expression, some widening of the eyes or lengthening of the upper lip, that means she's no longer hoping for something to come along and change her life, so much as expecting it.

After dinner it's a tour of the building. I follow her along the corridor, past the room where the children sleep, through the door and out onto the roof.

Where the breeze is warm, the uplands are black, and the town below us is studded with orange light.

'Out there,' says Finn, pointing. 'The Green Chapel.'

Her hand grips the rail. All the times I'd have wept to feel her beside me, and here she is: hair curved behind an ear, a few strands playing over her face.

'This is better than Didsbury.'

'We cope.'

'*We.* You know, you never used to say *we*. Even in the Point Hotel with all those people around, I used to say: Fuck me, I've found someone who's as much a loner as me.'

'Yeh well. The single life can get you down after a bit.'

She knows that's not what I mean. Just like Choi knew yesterday, when I said she should hurry up and send our yellow-haired mother home.

'But you've got Hen. You've got your little boy. By the way, I'm looking forward to meeting him. I knew you'd change your mind about having kids.'

'You can have him.'

'God, no. I can't imagine what it's like to have a life, let alone a family.'

She leans hard on the rail, feeling the silence like a drug.

'Sorry I never got in touch,' she says. 'In a lot of ways I've grown up a hell of a lot, but not in that.'

'I never got in touch either.'

'But *I* never gave *you* my address. Anyway, I assumed you'd gone back to Frances. I thought: Oh well, everything's going to change as soon as we get back.'

She's thinking. I could say it now, and she wouldn't suspect a thing.

'So did you?'

'What?'

'Go back to Frances?'

'No. Did you go back to Michael?'

She laughs. 'God, the lies I used to tell. There was no Michael. Well, there was, but he was never . . . I just made that up to keep Duncan off my back.'

She handles the name uneasily, like it might go off in her face.

'That didn't seem to be your main aim at the time.'

'Duncan was a waste of time. I can see that now.'

'Like you said, you weren't ready for it.'

'I most probably said a lot of things, Finn. I was really screwed up.'

'When are you not screwed up?'

'Not very often.'

'When it happens, can you give me a call?'

She looks out at the hills with a sunken face.

'As it happens, I'm not screwed up now. I'm just resigned.'

'To what?'

'To having spent so much of my life being screwed up that even if I got myself sorted out, it's probably too late to do anything about it.'

Then nothing. Anna stirs in her clothes. And I'm trying to decide whether to say it now, or later tonight, or whether it might sound better on another day, like the 43rd October 2097, or whether I might need even longer to find some words I really mean.

'Christ, is that the time? I've got to be at the hospital at seven.'

'Why do you doctors start so early?'

'So we can creep up on nasty diseases while they're asleep. Look, Einar said I could stay over. If it's a problem I can easily . . .'

'Hey, we've lost entire football teams in this place. There's the sofa for starters.'

But when we get inside, the table has been cleared and Jack is laid out on the sofa, too stoned to speak. In Einar's room all they can do is laugh.

'Have my room. I'll sleep downstairs.'

'For God's sake, Finn! I think I'm safer with you than with Einar!'

In the room we take our corners, waiting. Anna sits on the bed, taking in the creaking shelves and cardboard boxes as if it was no surprise to find all this raw history in here. Years pass, but nothing changes the casual beauty revealed in the turn of a head, reaching into every box, illuminating every lost corner, touching the empty spaces with its secret light.

'Anyway, you don't need to worry about Einar. He's found someone.'

She looks up, pink under the eyes. 'This might sound really stupid, but I never realised he was, like, *bi*.'

'You must have seen him with Jim.'

'Jim?'

'Jim de Groot. The gorgeous hunk who everyone fancied.'

'I thought everyone fancied you, Finn.'

'Very funny.'

But it must be, because she's almost laughing. 'No. Ilse did. She told me. And what about Roxanne?'

'What d'you know about Roxanne?'

'Einar says she had a bit of a crush on you towards the end.'

'Then he's wrong.' Anger surprises me. Cheeks are burning; body smells; hands close over my eyes.

'She was hysterical. Remember,' she bursts, 'that time on the ferry back from Darling Harbour, when that total stranger was asleep in the chair and Rox took the lifejacket off the hook and put it on him?'

'And she lit a fag and stuck it in his mouth and called one of the crew . . .'

'Because you weren't allowed to smoke. Christ, the look on his face when he woke up!'

Anna looks across and her voice is quiet.

'We had fun, too. You and me.'

'I was someone else then, Anna. We were young and carefree, and now . . .'

'Now you've found the woman you love and you've got a lovely little boy. I've become a doctor. What's anyone got to complain about?'

She stares at her shoe. She reaches down and puts a finger between leather and instep. Then she pulls up quickly and rubs her cheek.

'Anna?'

She looks up, frightened, knowing.

'Have you any idea what was . . .'

'Don't say anything, Finn. Don't . . .'

'But I promised myself. I said if I ever saw you again I wouldn't let you go without saying it.'

Her face flickers. I'm hammering it home. But then I remember the squint of concentration, the mark that never fades, and nothing, not even Anna and her sisters queueing up to laugh at me for all eternity, can stop me now.

'Saying what?'

'That I was in love with you. That I was so in love with you I just didn't know what the fuck I was gonna do.'

She sits on the bed, hands clasped in her lap, and stares at a box on the shelf. My mother gazes out to sea.

'Is that the past tense I hear?'

She looks upwards and to the left, all her disappointment rolled into one stillborn sigh.

'Has that really pissed you off?'

'It's not you, Finn. It's me I'm pissed off with.'

'What about you?'

She pulls her foot up and holds it on her knee. She closes her eyes. She opens them and is looking elsewhere.

'Where do I start? My life, how about that. The fact that I've done nothing really in all the time since I left Aus. Okay, I've learned about the blood supply to the pelvis and the musculature of the forearm and about a million types of cortical dementia, some extraordinary and some quite amazing, I can tell you. I can now read research critically and have articles published in international journals. But what else?'

'The very fact that you can say that means . . . I don't know.'

'Not to me it doesn't. I'm lost. Christ, Finn, we used to sit on the balcony of the Point Hotel and dream about what we'd be. You wanted to be a rock star . . .'

'No I didn't.'

'Yes you did. And I thought it was all so straightforward. I really believed it would all turn out all right if I could just hang on and do this. But I'm not even sure I *know* what I'm looking for any more. I'm twenty-eight and I sometimes feel like my life is over. And then I come here and you tell me this. It's . . . Can I ask you something?'

'What?'

'Why the hell didn't you tell me at the time?'

'Because I knew what you'd say.'

'No you didn't know what I'd say.' She makes a sort of choking sound and looks away, hurting to breathe. 'Finn, I'm sick of people telling me they know what I'm going to say. Duncan was always doing that and it turned out he didn't know the first thing about me.'

'All right, pretend I said it. It wouldn't have made any difference.'

'Wouldn't it?' She stops. 'Only because there was never anything for it to make a difference *to*.'

She frowns and rocks backwards, holding her heel in both hands. I enjoy a faint kissable nub at the top of her spine.

'There's this beetle,' I say, 'which starts off as an egg in the top of a tree, hatches, climbs down the tree, goes underground, stays there for seventeen years, climbs back up the tree, mates and then dies. I am that beetle.'

'I don't see why. You've got everything. And I'm just very very tired.'

I never thought those eyes could look so sad.

'Are you still going to stay?'

She yawns. 'I've got to be at the RI at seven.'

'So we'll stay up all night.'

There it is: that exasperated laugh, lost between a whimper and a sigh.

'Do you realise I haven't stayed up all night – that is, except for working – since . . . I don't know. That New Year's Eve in Sydney?'

I could say something about That New Year's Eve in Sydney, but she's yawning, twisting the silver ring on her little finger, and I've already said enough.

In ten minutes she is asleep. I pull the duvet over her and watch her from the armchair. Her back is turned. In the morning she'll do what people always do when they wake up in a strange room: look around for a familiar face, try to remember where she is. For a moment she might forget what has happened in the seven years since we last woke up together, in a blue room on the far side of the world. She'll forget who lies asleep next door, with only three years of dreams to comfort him; and who sleeps in a private room on the other side of the moor, with no dreams left, only trapped memories, broadcast in patterns of light and sound. She'll sit up and look at me, like she did in the unnatural light of a North Shore morning, when we were both orphaned and blind. And then, who knows, we might be in with a chance.

LOT
12

Don died today, in Ward 11 of the Etruscan Royal Infirmary, a bottle of pills by his side. Of all the stagehands who fussed around his still-warm body in that first half-hour, not one of them bothered to check the label on the plastic bottle, or draw any conclusions from cheap paper and smudged print. It was an unnecessary clue. The Salvation merchants had got to him: perhaps when the hospital, in a speedy response to new findings published that week, decided it would be a good idea to send him and all his fellow sufferers home for a few days amid some familiar scenery. Never mind that the only home my uncle could mention was now in the hands of some un-cooperative receivers, and that Sarah's maisonette was no more home to him than the white room he had just left. Somehow they got to him, those men in their BMWs and Jaguars, fattened on meat pies and beer. Perhaps it was even the day he drove himself and Sarah here to Big Kimberley, and they went around the shelves together, choosing which of their stock they wanted kept and which was to take its chance upstairs on the selling floor.

'It's all in here,' said Serge, handing him the file.

Don took it and stared at it, from shorter and shorter distances, until it was an angled inch from the tip of his nose. There was no quake or tremor, no sign of disorder behind those bushy eyebrows and corrugated forehead. His eyes, almost invisible in their purple-brown slits, moved in slow circles over the card. He was not reading. He was investigating the texture, tracing how individual fibres meshed and overlapped, the way daylight gave the yellow surface a soft mottled sheen.

'He means it's written down inside, love.' With a sigh Sarah reached over and opened the file. She read from the list while Serge and Finn rooted through tea chests and plastic crates. He recognised none of his things. He picked up his dog-head walking stick, weighed it, tried its strength between his hands. 'What's that for?' said Sarah, testing him. 'The end is brass. I suppose it's some sort of weapon.' Serge pulled out a pile of old cash-books. 'Whose handwriting is this?' said Sarah, and he shook his head. 'It's mine, you nincompoop. These are from the farm. Look, twelve bales of straw, six pounds 48p.'

Half an hour and they'd had enough. Sarah blinked back tears. Neither of them noticed the absence of a wooden box, saved from the television room at Brink Farm, which, along with the photo of my mother on the deck of *Bonaventure*, now hid its secrets on a shelf upstairs in my room. We made one list of things to be sold and one of things to be kept in storage, and packed a box for Sarah with some small stuff she wanted taken back to the maisonette. Don went outside on his own. Perhaps it was then, as he unlocked the car and Sarah stayed inside checking the contents of her box, that the man with the ponytail approached and offered the cure to all confusions in the shape of a bargain-priced bottle of pills. Or perhaps it was one of the ghosts who haunted the corridors of Wards 11 and 12, baffling Don with his sub-Thames accent and never thinking to mention that the fix he was peddling would kill him within weeks.

We drove over to Moorview to tell Hen. It was a full minute before she looked up at us. The curtains were drawn. 'Who?' she said. 'Don. My uncle. The farmer.' 'This isn't the time you come.' She was fully dressed, shoes on, as if waiting to go out. Where? 'You're supposed to come at four,' she said quickly, and then we'd said enough. In the van on the way home, Robinson asked if what had happened to Don was the same as what had happened to his Mo.

'Uncle Don's gone to sleep. Mo's not asleep.'

'Where's he gone to sleep? In his bed?'

'He's in the same place as Roxanne. And the Friendly Monk. They don't need a bed because the clouds are very soft. They all snuggle up together and look down at us and have a laugh.'

'What do they laugh about?'

'What does anyone laugh about?'

He bites the knuckle of a thumb, hard, leaving tiny toothmarks in the skin.

We park in the road. The mill spins its own silence, from ghosts of women in sackcloth dresses and ten thousand forgotten things. In my sunless workshop-bedroom the computer comes to life with a whirr. There are two messages from Hen.

> ive got it. wasnt don your mothers brother-in-law? i suppose youre going to tell me you dont know. she was the most caring loving beautiful woman who ever lived and you cant even be bothered to find out what killed her. or should i say who.

The second is timed ten minutes later.

> i know how he felt. sometimes everything is so bright, so real, it really hurts. you just want to escape from it somehow. i tried once but i was obviously doing it wrong.

That? We're talking years ago, before she met me, even before she rearranged her life for Simon Hughes. When she was still borrowing cars, abandoning them in station car parks or setting fire to them on country roads. Why? She never explained why, why that, why then, what she was hoping for and how soon. But she told me *how*, in all the detail I needed. Because it was impossible to overdose on Rona's Surfboard, she'd collected a month's supply of Mogadons, lined them up on the back of a magazine, put on a Billie Holiday record and started to count them off one by one. If she'd washed them down with vodka, like they do in the films, it might have taken her where she wanted to go, but all she had in the bedsit was a bottle of peach brandy left by a man called Bill. She woke in hospital a day later with the taste of sweet puke in her mouth. Bill was there. Like any man whose lover has attempted to escape without paying for what she's taken, he wanted to know why.

'When, dear, are you going to get it into your head? This is nothing to do with you.'

One thing I can say, while Don cools on his metal table and Hen is still refusing to talk to me outside visiting hours: she never used that as a threat. It was her experiment, the thing with the sleeping pills, not some adolescent power trip. If she ever threatened me with anything, it was the day she foretold her disappearance, that first winter in the flat. She spoke quickly, quietly, as if the tickets were already bought. 'I'll go,' she said. 'I'll just pack up and go and you'll be none the wiser and it won't hurt a bit. I know what you're thinking. Don't worry, darling, if I ever find out I'm pregnant you won't see me for the dust.'

I'm meeting Anna for lunch. I'll find her at the hospital and we'll drive to an Italian place in town. The Royal Infirmary is a kind of medicated hypermarket with an orange-tiled roof that slopes down on red pillars to the pavement. She's waiting by the automatic doors.

'God, it's you. I thought it was a delivery or something.' She glances suspiciously around the inside of the van. 'I've got a car, you know.'

'Lucky you. Watch me back.'

She climbs in and holds the door open for the rear view. She has a sky-blue anorak over brown shirt and blue skirt. 'Mind the flower bed. Stop!' She slams the door and slumps back, breathless, in her seat.

'I'm really sorry about your uncle. The thing is with that Salvation stuff, you build up such a tolerance that you have to take so much of it to get any effect. And the production methods are so unreliable, you never know exactly how much is in them. I still can't believe no one got to him in time.'

We wait for green. Letters painted on an end terrace spell WELCOM TO PAKISTAN. Through the window on her side, the ruins of a petrol station, jagged mouths of glass in uPVC frames, every fitting torn out by invisible hands. Behind it, a row of new houses at the top of a ridge.

'This is it. I think there's a car park up here on the right.'

We find Luigi's at the top of a flight of linoed stairs. Anna orders wine, water, puts the menu down and shuffles on her hands. 'Now, tell me what you're thinking about. Unless of course it's sex.'

I tell her about Don's final trip to Big Kimberley: the spectacle of the yellow folder, how he looked at his favourite walking stick just like he looked at his favourite nephew, as if he'd never set eyes on it before. I say I've heard all the explanations, but I still can't believe one missing brain-chemical can do all that.

'Why not?'

'Because what you are isn't just chemicals.'

'Wait a minute, Finn; think about what you just said. That was chemistry! It was all due to chemical changes in your head, which led to chemical changes in my head, and so on. One neurotransmitter level rises and the other falls.' Her eyes flash. 'That's what love is. Come on, Finn, the other night?'

I'm blushing. Doctors do this to me.

'I knew I should've told you in Sydney, before you learned all this stuff. Anyway, I said I was sorry.'

'It's okay.' She lights a Silk Cut. 'It sort of cleared the air. All I'm saying is, it didn't say anything about *you*. All it said was something about the state of your brain at that particular time.'

'Do you get extra for being this cynical?'

'Yes. Look, let's say I had some kind of probe which would give me an instant readout on the levels of the four or five major neurotransmitters in any particular part of your brain. And let's say I stuck it into your brain at the very moment you were declaring undying love for me. Okay? So you've got your mouth saying what it's saying, your heart going pit-a-pat, and these neurotransmitters going up and down. Are you telling me some vague notion of love you've got off the telly is causing these physical changes? I know which story I'd rather believe.'

The waiter wants Anna to try the wine. I'm remembering what Choi said, about how you could take a normal healthy woman and sit her in that white room and she'd come out with the same brain profile as Hen. But a normal healthy woman *wouldn't* sit there all day, because normal healthy women have better things to do, like ruin the lives of normal healthy men. There's something they're not telling me.

'All right. But whichever neurowhatsit is dropping, it can't be NTX, or we'd all be sitting in armchairs watching things that aren't there crawling up the wall.'

'Maybe. Maybe not.'

She waits for our man to finish pouring, then raises glass to mouth.

'What d'you mean?'

'You haven't twigged?'

I shrug all my shoulders. She puts the glass down and licks her lips.

'Finn, imagine you've got a disease to deal with. You don't even know if it's one disease or a whole group of related ones. You've got a public crying out for an explanation. The easiest thing is to put it down to a neurotransmitter, or brain-chemical, whose action you don't yet completely understand. What are you going to call that neurotransmitter?'

She looks at me with dancing eyes.

'Shit.'

'I'm afraid so. All those visualisation exercises,' the bursting laugh, 'all a complete waste of time. I'm telling you, Robinson probably knows more about NTX than we do!'

She sits back and taps the table. Seven years imagining what she might have turned into, and I never imagined her like this.

'I thought they were making progress. The viral link. The fifty-seven kinds of flu.'

'You're right. There's an increased likelihood of onset immediately after a bout of flu. But there's also higher levels of SMD among ex-students, particularly those who were at college near the London research hospitals. Same for mothers of teenage children. Farmers. Athletes. What you going to make of that?'

'I think I'll ask a doctor.'

'We're all doctors, Finn, but we're as clueless as you. Have you any idea how many different theories there are about how this thing might be transmitted? It's hysterical.'

'Well, there was the sex link, that was because of HIV. But they've proved that wrong.'

'Nothing is *ever* proved. What else?'

'Bog seats?'

She laughs. 'And the rest. You know, I'm sitting there reading this stuff and I'm thinking, it makes those old superstitions about syphilis and HIV look quite bloody reasonable. There's people saying you can catch it from sharing toothbrushes, towels, wearing other people's clothes, having sex with menstruating women or women over fifty who are never going to menstruate again. There's people in Stretford pubs saying a bloke can get rid of it by having sex with a virgin and passing it on to her. I'm telling you, sometimes you have to check the date on the front of the paper to remind yourself you're not still living in the Middle Ages. And that's even before the scientists have a go.'

'There was all that talk about metal poisoning. Lead, aluminium, all that.'

'Yep. There was a theory that mercury was getting into the human food chain, crossing the blood–brain barrier and eating away at the white matter. There were people talking about mass outbreaks of candida, or what we call thrush. There was the link with farm animals and their diseases, which was supposed to explain why so many farmers were getting it. And then the scariest of them all . . .'

She pauses, eyes narrowed, death-stick poised. 'You don't know, do you?'

'Seems not. What we talking about?'

She blows smoke ceilingwards and taps ash. 'What we're talking about are the human cadaveric drugs. What have ex-students, mothers of teenage children and athletes got in common?'

I feel the green splash in her left eye.

'They all used – or used to use, before they were banned – products derived from human corpses. Women with fertility problems were given hormones from dead pituitaries to help them conceive. The London students volunteered to be controls in the trials, so they were infected in the same way. The athletes took growth hormones and other things extracted from the same sort of tissue. As soon as deregulation took hold in the eighties – you know, with the government saying it didn't really matter what you did as long as you made a bit of cash from it – there was no control over where the pituitaries came from: there were just these guys going around hospital mortuaries, whipping them out and shoving them in a plastic bag. They were being paid by the gland, sort of thing.'

'You didn't read that in *Hello!*'

'Of course not, Finn. It's a bloody great big cover-up. There was an excellent government-funded research project that had to stop because the funds mysteriously dried up. Mrs Matthewman is sitting on folders of evidence which, if any of it ever came out, would make Thalidomide look like a minor mishap!'

I've thought of Anna fulfilling many functions over the last few thousand nights, but conspiracy theorist was not one of them. The wine is tingly. She has a spot on her forehead.

'All right, so what are we supposed to do?'

'What we've always done. Use our famous British common sense. Make sure people are happy and not in any danger. Do whatever it takes to keep them off the pills. As you saw with your uncle,' she looks down at the table, colouring, 'that doesn't necessarily mean locking them up.'

But Anna, it's so *convenient*, now we've so much catching up to do.

'You don't think Hen should be in hospital?'

'She should be wherever she wants to be. Remember, plenty of people spend their whole lives trying to get what she's got. Peace, contentment, escape from all those nasty tricks the past can play on you ... They wouldn't see Bliss as a disease. They'd see it as something to work towards, something that brings out whatever good things are already there; a privilege worth paying for, even.'

'I heard about the Californian bunch ...'

She swallows and relaxes a frown. 'The Americans have got their own ideas. There's a group who think the Bliss state is symptomatic of very early child abuse, which means it should be encouraged, so the sufferer can re-experience her trauma and come to terms with it. And, yes, the Californians, who started off this self-therapy business and found it all got out of hand. That would explain the drug link.'

'The drug link ...'

'They used a particular class of phenethylamines to access higher levels of consciousness and found the world became, I don't know, more meaningful. It sort of fits.'

Remember the stone, Hen? How everything that happened was a decision made by Nature, after careful consideration of the facts?

'Did Hen do any drugs?' Anna's voice is hesitant, but with her schooled eagerness for truth.

'A bit of hash. A bit of Rona's Surfboard. Why?'

'Just a thought.'

'You telling me there's a link?'

'You know the mechanism, Finn. You know the connection between Rona's Surfboard and Salvation.'

'But they're two different ...'

'In most of their chemical properties, yes. But they seem to have similar effects on the nervous system. They've just started doing research again on Rona's Surfboard; we're getting new studies published every week. Both seem to be increasing the action of something, call it NTX, call it what you like. Over time, that seems to be causing permanent damage to the connections, so the same amount of transmitter has less of an effect. So what you end up with is an effective *lack* of this, I don't know, "meaning-creating" stuff. That's when you start smiling and forgetting who people are.'

'So the idea is that everyone who has ever taken Rona's Surfboard is at risk of St Mary's Disease?'

'Probably. Yes.'

'Which means Christmas night at the lighthouse was a pretty lucky escape?'

Her face tightens, as the past plays one of its nasty tricks.

'I'm sorry, Finn. I don't . . . But there's no point pretending. For your family's sake, I think it's better that you know the truth.'

The day we say goodbye to Don is the best so far this year. Before he left for a day among the sheep on White Peak, my observant son pointed to a bright blue sky, crossed rapidly by little-lamb clouds, chased along by a breeze that smelled of cut grass and petrol. And I said: but look at that layer of cirrus, like frost on the huge windscreen that domes over us, neither white nor blue. Then he was gone, swept up in one of Maryrose's games. We walk to St Stephen's in shirt-sleeves and sunglasses, jackets slung over shoulders or smoothed between folded arms. My father shares a joke with his second wife. That black BMW parked on the corner, whose paint job you wanted to autograph with a key, whose tyres cry out for the smile of a retractable blade? That's his, bought with the same money that paid for Big Kimberley. Joy, in a nasty maroon suit and blue blouse, pulls at the strap of her watch. The gold catches fire in the sun. The watch does what it is supposed to do: keeps her polished fingers busy, speaks volumes for the benefits of good taste and a generous divorce settlement, and fits easily onto any thickness of wrist by virtue of its elastic-linked strap. In half an hour she'll be dabbing at her cheeks with a hankie, trying to catch Sarah's eye, twisting her eyebrows at the vicar's gentle jokes. But anyone with half a soul can see she's an impostor, trying to make a place for herself in a family she was never born into and which, if you believe my sister's theories, she was always out to destroy.

'Where's your lovely girlfriend?' she croons.

I'm saying nothing. The official story is that Hen had to go with Zoë to Etruria on some unpostponable business, before joining us at the church later on. On her own instructions, no one is to know she is anything more than an out-patient at Moorview Clinic, or that she sleeps, or fails to sleep, in any other bed than mine.

'She'll be out doing some last-minute shopping. One of these days they'll find a gene or something to explain why women have to buy all these clothes then only wear them once.'

Never mind the jokes: my father is not well. Perhaps his suit is too small, or his body is too big, or else twenty years of murderous guilt is finally starting to show. He lumbers around like a horseless cowboy, breathing on one side, hands poised uselessly above invisible pistols. I want to stab him with something sharp, hear the gas hiss out of him, until he's an empty costume on the pavement and all ready to feel the stamp of my shoe. But I know he'd still be the one with the looks. Admire the neatly groomed hair, thick and dark above, ageing to silver around the temples. It never receded across his skull or clogged his comb with pale brown fluff. At parties, he never had to say his age twice, three times, before anyone would believe him. He never had to watch, day after day, as his baby-smooth forehead expanded upwards and outwards, until there was nothing for it but to curse the man who made him, take a Number One clipper and shear the whole lot off.

'Oh, we'd just buy clothes anyway. We don't need no genes to tell us that!' Joy's permatan has a happy glow. She's been treated to a tour of the building: only the second ever, thanks to still-vivid memories of what happened a few miles down the road on a slippery April afternoon, and the first for two years. She has been guided personally through a report of the last financial year, and heard a representative of BK Storage Services, of which she is easily the main shareholder, announce pre-tax profits of some thirty thousand pounds. She has suggested that profits like these might justify the purchase of a new van. And, while gently reminding us whose capital made all this possible, she has let us know that these financial details are but a necessary evil, that the money is neither interesting in itself nor of any particular use to her, but rather that the reason she has done all this is that she is a true member of the family, and this is one family that will never let its children make their way alone.

We stand at the gate and wait for the hearse. I can see Zoë's red Peugeot pulled up at the back of the church, the two girls inside, conspiring behind bluish glass, with the odd incurious glance towards the mourners. When the hearse pulls up they get out and walk up to the porch: Zoë in a black suit with hair tied up, Hen in white dress and sunglasses, the blue-green ivy leaf just visible above her left ankle. Both avoid my eyes. Sarah climbs down from the funeral car, unusually elegant in a dark blue two-piece, and watches four black-suited men pull the coffin from the hearse, lift it to their shoulders and carry it slowly inside.

Perhaps if someone else had had a send-off like this, we would not have been left with the feeling that she'd walked out without saying goodbye, and Hen would never have been found in the same spot among the storage bays, looking for something that had vanished with Roxanne. As soon as the coroner had recorded his verdict of death by misadventure, she was flown back to Tasmania in a black box with gold handles. We never got the chance to stand in St Stephen's on a beautiful spring morning and sing our hearts out to the stone angels overhead. Thanks to her parents, who had decided that BK Storage Services had already done enough damage to their daughter's memory, we never got to see her laid out in some aerosol-perfumed chapel of rest, check her lipstick, take one last look at those high wide cheekbones, or wander along a corridor of frosted glass doors, fighting back the urge to push at one or two of them, find out how many other young lives were laid out in those chipboard-and-veneer rooms. Hen insisted we hold a wake in her absence, which took place on all three floors of Big Kimberley and went on until there was no more drinking, crying or singing left to be done. Soon after that Hen made her own grand exit from the rational world. 'There's nothing wrong with her,' Zoë told me on the way back from another consultation. 'She just feels guilty about what happened with Roxanne.' True enough, Hen was the one who drove Rox to a boarded-up terrace in Etruria, lent her all the money she needed, and never said a word about the pills that would one day put her to sleep for good.

But there were other possibilities, weren't there? There was the shock of finding out, first from Zoë and then, when pushed, from me, what had happened in the last few weeks of Roxanne's life. I don't mean the lapses of concentration or the fascination with the contents of the storage bays; I mean the way she talked about us, me and her, and the unforgettable love affair we were supposed to have shared. I mean the way she, in what Choi would have called 'a textbook confabulation', managed to convince herself that I was Blake, her lost love from Melbourne, and couldn't understand it when I didn't act the part. And Hen's response to this posthumous revelation? She walked out of the building, emptying her pockets – keys, money, cashpoint print-outs – onto the street. It took half an hour on the traffic island on Manchester Road to persuade her of the truth. 'It was all in her mind, Hen. And anyway, she's gone.' 'All right,' she said. 'But if I ever find out you've been lying to me on this one, you'd better be very scared indeed.'

When it's all over, and we've driven to the crematorium and stood in the wood-panelled chapel, and the conveyor belt has hummed and the purple curtain pulled across by a supernatural hand; when Don has mingled with the smog and the birdsong above Etruria, and the singing of certain hymns has brought gluey tears to my eyes, we can all push on sunglasses and enjoy this glorious June. Sarah stands on the chapel grass, where the neat wreaths are laid out for inspection, kisses cheeks and shakes hands. She's back in control. I thought she'd lost it on the phone the other day, when she told me about the pills by the bedside, the cup of tea going cold by the lamp; when all of a sudden her voice stopped making sense and, for the first time in memory, dissolved in sobs. Now she can listen to Joy talking about my mother's funeral as if she was the only mourner there, how it was such a moving occasion that there wasn't a single dearly beloved who wasn't dabbing tears from their eyes, and so on, until Sarah forgets what all this is about and starts to smile. 'Have you been on holiday?' 'Why?' says Joy, her dipthongs turning heads. 'You look very brown.' 'Oh no, that's the sunbed, ha ha ha! But I'll tell you, Sarah, Margaret's funeral! I have *never* cried so *much* in my *life*!'

It's different with Dad. She greets him cautiously, as if doubtful that he's really here, so near to where it all happened, so many years on. She's right to be suspicious. As far as I know, he hasn't seen his sister-in-law since we all met up in Oxford for Alison's graduation, and spent an extended lunch-hour wandering gowned and ermined streets in search of a sufficiently expensive restaurant. I doubt they've even spoken on the phone. There were a number of invitations to spend the weekend with them at Greylag, but Sarah was always reluctant to leave the farm. 'You know them,' said Dad; 'they like to keep themselves to themselves.' But was it just that she didn't like to impose on anyone (Dad's story), or was this her way of telling us that our family obligations had ended the day that blue Cortina came off the road? I never really liked to ask. But somehow I can't help guessing at her suspicions: that if Margaret hadn't been in such a hurry to sell a certain Staffordshire figurine and thus rid herself of the symbol of a rotten marriage, she would never have been driving to Etruria on that Monday afternoon in April. She would never have gone astray on Blacksheep Moor, lost her grip on slippery roads, and robbed Peter of a wife, Finn and Alison of a mother, and Joy, the woman who would soon replace her at my father's side, of the sort of friend who comes along but once in a life.

We take separate cars back to Big Kimberley, where Einar has put on tea and sandwiches in the auction room. Joy insists on some family photographs. Hen, smiling and joking, tells Sarah she wants to show her something, and leads the way upstairs. I know where they're going. I left the box on the table on purpose, so she can go through it again, so often now that she could do it with her eyes shut, taking out each of Margaret's things and describing them to Sarah in the sort of detail only certain brain-states can discern. They're going to ask why the Silk Twister's expression seems so knowing and so disappointed. They're going to feed their wrists through the strap of the gold watch. They're going to speculate on what's missing: the wedding ring, the building society book showing a withdrawal of £30 on that same Monday, the clothes they cut from her lukewarm body at the Print Moorlands Hospital. And they're going to look at the photographs, her long trusting face, and ask how someone who could smile like that should have had so little to smile about, how a woman who knew so much fighting in her lifetime should not find peace even in death.

Why I am not a poet: because I know that love is not a thing, like the kitchen utensils and English ceramics that go under my hammer on the first Wednesday of every month, so that, no matter how good it might look in the colours green black blue, it can't be described in the sort of language from which a catalogue is made . . . How I know it is not a thing: because recently I've seen how the very act of mentioning it, on the top floor of a converted mill while all the auction handlers and furniture restorers are asleep, is enough to change it for ever, so it must be best to keep quiet and let it go unnoticed for as long as possible . . . Why I can't keep quiet: because she is here, discussing unfinished business in the room I made for someone else, in natural colours and little to no make-up, looking at me with the first expression she ever learned (high eyebrows, cautious tension in the cheeks) while my son sleeps next door and his mother's candles cast soft ovals of light.

She takes a sip of Glenmorangie and carefully inhales. 'The thing is, Finn, when you saw me in Sydney, I didn't have the confidence to say how I felt about anything. I was only two years out of school. I made decisions on the spur of the moment, then stuck with them because I thought I had to. That's why probably you thought I led you on. But if I'd really been leading you on, I'd have been doing one thing and meaning something else. The fact is I didn't know *what* I meant. Basically,' she consults the black night in the window, 'I didn't take myself all that seriously. I still don't, but I realise that what I do is going to affect other people. I think you should do the same. Like, how do you know you still feel that about me? How can you decide that without knowing who I am now?'

'Well, seeing as a week ago I thought I was never going to see you again . . .'

'All right. But what I'm saying is, don't say you're in love with me just because that's what you've been saying to yourself for the last *x* number of years. Because if you do, you're wrong.'

'Never said I was in love with you. Said I used to be.'

'Okay, fine. Then we haven't got a problem.'

She halts on an in-breath.

'If,' she continues, 'you're telling the truth.'

'Hang on. If you think what I say is all down to chemical reactions in my head, the question of whether I'm telling the truth doesn't come into it.'

'Yes it does. It's the truth *for you*. All right, I know that as far as the outside world is concerned all that happens to me, all I think and do, is biochemistry. But *to me*, to this body I wake up inside every morning, it has meaning. I can still feel things as much as anyone. I can enjoy the taste of this whisky. I can have an amazing orgasm. I can fall in love – well, I could last time I tried.'

This strikes me as a sloppy argument. But then we're both quite drunk.

'Yeh but Anna, you talk about your emotions, about love and everything, like it was just some small part of you, some little appendage that just happens to give you hassle from time to time. You think you know how your emotions are going to be affected and you make all these allowances for them. But you never really let them do what they're supposed to do.'

My brown-eyed darling laughs. 'The reason you're saying that, Finn, is because you've never really been hurt. You don't know what it's like to let your feelings take over and see what a mess it gets you in.'

'That's right. Everything I've ever done has been completely rational.'

'I don't mean that. I mean . . .' She shifts a pillow into the small of her back. 'Look, Michael was only my second ever relationship. I wasn't a virgin but I wasn't far off. When I met Duncan in Sydney I was totally blown away. I used to go down to the pool on the Reservation while they all were skinny-dipping, just in the hope he'd show up.'

'I know.'

'And of course the bastard never did.'

'I know.'

She looks up. 'How do you know?'

'I was there.'

'Where?'

'In the pool.'

She hears a distant voice, thinks she can, can't be sure.

'When?'

'The night you were waiting for Duncan.'

'That was before I met you. No, you weren't there.'

'I was. I turned up late. You were sitting on the bench at the deep end. I saw you, I thought: Have I missed something?, realised you'd already seen more of me than most people get to see, blushed a lot and got out of there as fast as I could.'

She's shaking her head. I'm standing up and coming over to the bed.

'You remember that night we spent in Sydney? The first one?'

She stares into her glass. Hairs on her arm are golden in candlelight. I sit down on the bed, turning towards her, and my folded knee touches her thigh.

'When I asked if it was all right if I took my clothes off, and you said go ahead?'

'And you said . . . I shouldn't worry because I'd seen it all before? And you were crying because we were talking about your mum?'

'That's it. That's what I meant.'

'You were there?'

Her smile: a thankful resolution, a relieved applause in light, flickering and rippling like the last drop of tea into a cup. It's as if something she's been looking for for quite some time has finally dropped into place.

'I was really off my face. I can't remember. No, hang on. You did a sort of striptease by the side of the pool.'

'I don't think . . .'

'Yes, you did. You were really showing off! Then you dived in and swam straight up to me with this, I don't know, *demonic* grin on your face. I'm thinking: What's he on?'

'Barossa Valley. Lust.'

'And that's when Einar came after me wearing Roxanne's swimsuit, and I was just *out* of there . . .'

'No, I got out first. As soon as I saw you I lost my bottle and left.'

'And then eventually I found out what that bastard Duncan McGuinness had been doing whilst I was waiting for him at the pool.'

Two foreheads compete in thought.

'That's it, though. I couldn't see why you went back to him after that.'

'Finn, I didn't even find out until after we'd gone! Anyway,' she touches the spot on her forehead, 'what makes you think I went back to him?'

I tell her about New Year's Eve at Darling Harbour, and what Jerry told me a week later in the pub. It meets a disappointed sigh.

'I didn't piss you around, Finn. I meant it when I said I didn't want to get involved.'

She looks across, solemn, unhopeful, then gets up and goes over to the shelf. She picks up the wooden box, presses at the corners and tries to lift the lid.

'It's locked.'

'Haven't you got a key?'

'I'm working on it.'

She replaces the box and fits the small of her back against a shelf.

'Look, I may as well tell you. After that night you and I spent together, when we went down to the Point and I kissed you just because I felt like it, I knew there was . . . I felt I understood you in some way. But I'd already made a decision about Duncan. Maybe I was flattered about what he was saying and everything. Maybe I just fancied him and couldn't say no. So I spent one night with him at his flat. Oh, it was great and all that, but it made me think: Whoa, hang on, I don't want to get involved, not just at the minute. And that's what I told you next time I saw you.'

'So all that stuff about not being on the Pill . . .'

'Oh come on, Finn!' She lets one knee drop out beneath her. 'Maybe I just deep down couldn't take myself seriously. And I didn't want anyone to get hurt.'

Now she's turned towards me, one shoulder pushed up, hands pressed against the shelf behind her back. She's wearing a white tee-shirt inside a linen jacket. She scratches an arm, and one breast is nudged up into light.

'So do you take yourself seriously now?'

'I don't know. I honestly don't know.'

When we finish talking, there's a little boy to wish goodnight. She follows me through the connecting door, a board hurting under her foot. In the faint light that sweeps before us, we can see the empty second cot, the silent telly, the blackboard with its prehistoric scribbles. He is lying on his back, dreaming of lions and space

---

Lot 12: **Rectangular hardwood box**, carved in a medieval rose pattern, on turned legs with a missing key.

ponies, arms twisted at odd angles around his face. Hen looks out at us, frozen in a rare photograph, from the table by the cot.

'He's gorgeous,' she whispers, brushing by me in the gloom.

'Have him.'

'I wouldn't know what to do with him,' and it's a sad sound she makes.

We pull the door shut when we leave. Anna stands by the desk, toeing a circle on the carpet. When I kiss her forehead she topples against me, arms loose at her sides. I hold her like a friend. The hint of apple I remember has turned into something richer, glossier, but the smokiness is still in her hair. When I try her lips she pulls away, gently but with intent. She picks up the photo from the shelf.

'I think we should take things slowly.'

'I take everything slowly.'

Her mouth turns down. My mother counts the waves.

'Don't you feel guilty?'

'Hen's got her own life. We have an agreement.'

'You sure?'

'She made a decision. You weren't here.'

She puts the photo down and looks around like she's lost something.

'Are you going to stay?'

She frowns. 'I don't think that's a great idea. I don't want Robinson to wake up and wonder who this woman is who keeps sleeping in his mother's bed.'

'I have an agreement with him as well.'

A short gasp, hardly a laugh at all.

'I'll sleep on top. You get inside.'

'You'll be cold.'

'Lend me a jumper.'

She takes off the jacket and hangs it over the chair. From the chest of drawers a yellow sweatshirt is found.

'This yours?'

I sort of shrug. She drags it down over her front, pulls hair out behind. It's an old thing of Hen's that seems to fit. Ten minutes later, when she comes back from the bathroom with a towel under her arm, I'm already in bed.

'I saw Zoë locking up. I think she was surprised to see me.'

She climbs over and lies down next to the wall. I find her lips with mine. She opens her mouth and feeds me her tongue, as hesistant and cool as the last time I felt it, but seven years more precious to me now. 'Okay,' she whispers, running the heel of a hand up my hair. It's late, after two. I set the alarm and blow out the light. One dark minute later Anna sits up and takes off the sweatshirt. I can feel her losing the tee-shirt and pulling the sweatshirt back on, her brief nakedness charging the air. Then she's fiddling with a hook and pulling her bra out from underneath. She lies down flat beside me, pushes down her trousers and throws them, bundled together with bra and tee-shirt, onto the floor. She pulls the bedspread up over her legs and settles against the wall.

'Finn?'

Her breathing in the darkness. As eyes adjust and the state of things swims closer, the bedspread slips to reveal a promise of white cotton on skin.

'Yeh?'

'Thanks.'

'For what?' A dream hand, inches from her hip.

'For giving me time,' she says.

The day comes with rain. The curtains are open on two sides of the room, letting in a wet green light. Anna is asleep with her back to me, hair ruffed up on her forehead. She looks just like she did on that last morning in Sydney, when the rain seemed to have got to us in the night and washed away whatever it was we'd made. It's as though we could go back and pick up from where we were, start building again as if nothing else had happened in all that time, or nothing that more time couldn't change.

Then I'm turning over to check the clock. It's early, not long after seven. Early waking is not a habit of mine, except when I've been drinking, and the empty Glenmorangie bottle on the floor seems to have something to say about that. Then it dawns on me that this particular feeling has nothing to do with drinking, late nights or anything else. Some discoveries are so terrible that they come with an audible trace, a hollow echo that hangs in the air and dares you to find them out. This is one of those things. It's like a steady hum, or the opposite, perhaps, a deeper silence than before, as if something had moved out of the way to make space for what is coming. Or what is gone. The connecting door is ajar. The wardrobe by the armchair is open and half of the clothes are not there. Anna's trousers, bra and shirt have been bundled up and shoved into the bottom drawer, which hangs open, mocking us in the gloom. And when I get to the door to open it further, there is quite enough light around to tell me that my son's bed is empty, his clothes gone from the chest of drawers, his blue shoes no longer lined up by his cot, and the door to the corridor ajar.

That sound outside is the sound of a car.

LOT
13

While Anna is on the phone to the clinic, I'm going to wake Einar and get him to help me search the building. I have to tip half a pint of water into his ear before he opens his eyes.

'What's this light on for, mate?'

'Was anyone here last night?'

'On my mat? Or in my wendy house? Or . . .'

'Anywhere. Did you wake up and hear anything? Think.'

'In the morning please.'

'Einar, there's not going to be a morning,'

and that seems to worry him. He scoots off his mat and into the blue dressing gown with toothpaste stains down the front. We're both shivering, me half buttoned in yesterday's clothes, Einar yawning as if the answer to the problem was flying around in the air and he could catch it in his mouth. Perhaps there's something about the situation that makes me want to laugh, some joke the mind hasn't woken up to yet; or maybe there's nothing inside but a hot emptiness the size of a little boy, and I'm trying to get rid of it, and it comes out as a laugh. Either way, we're both gasping like brats on Christmas Eve, opening doors, banging heads on shelves and tables, in search of a present (blue tee-shirt, fine white hair) that is just not going to appear.

'Who comes to Big Kimberley to steal a little boy? Why not steal a car?'

'Maybe they stole a car as well. Maybe . . .'

Kumar and Linden are asleep. A light shows under Zoë's door, sounds of movement from within. The door to the back stairs is open and the keys hanging in the lock. We take them down with us and cut through the showroom, unlock the auction room and head down again to the ground floor. No sign of a break-in, no ransom note, no small blue shoes lined up on the stairs; whoever has been here knew how to deactivate the alarm, which combination to key into the pad, and how to set it again when they left.

When he sees Anna coming down the stairs with her hair all over the place, Einar gives his first proper smile of the day.

'She checked herself out this morning just before five. As far as they know, it's your birthday today and she left early so she could get here and surprise you.' The laugh I could do without. 'She's certainly done that!'

'So they think she's here?'

'That nurse you said? She said she heard Hen order a taxi last night from a number in Etruria. I phoned the number and they said yes, someone booked a taxi for five a.m. in the name of Germaine.'

'Sounds like Zoë . . .'

'So how did she get in?'

'She's got a key. This is her home.'

Anna shakes her head. 'She must have seen us. She must have come into your room and seen me there with you. I'm sorry, this is totally my fault.'

Our crisis doesn't impress Einar, who yawns and says:

'I have a very good idea. If she is here, she is on the video. If it is not Hen on the video then it is someone else. Who is that someone else?'

Both sides of the store are locked. Einar fiddles with the keys and the door swings open. The gloom of the stairwell gives way to the brighter gloom of the store. The lens on an overhead camera shrinks to Anna's astonished gaze.

'Fuck me! You never told me you had *this* much stuff down here . . . !'

and all of it awaits her, in boxes and packing cases and red plastic crates, so many things falling silent for her entrance that it takes a full minute to get her through the door. The air is cold. She shivers in bare feet. She smells wax, wood, dust, fag-ends, something rotting in an unvisited corner. A portrait in oils, someone's great-grandmother, gazes into an Edwardian middle distance. A glass-fronted cabinet awaits her shocked stare. No, Anna, I never told you. I never told you about this collection, this whispering mass of objects that turned the ground floor of our mill-home into a living tomb. I never suggested that you, who spend all day with people for whom things have no meaning, would one day discover where your friend has hidden all those things, and that every one of them would attack us from the twilight, force us to listen to their evidence and kid us they're some kind of clue. I wanted to show you a small blond boy, say 'Here, let's take him, you and me, let's be a family,' but I never thought that when I wished the mother away, the child would vanish too.

'Come and watch!' calls Einar from the video room.

Where the picture shows the main stairway of Big Kimberley.

'Five-fourteen. That's too early. Go forward.'

The tape hurries on its capstans. Einar hits the button and black-and-white dots form the same view. 5:51. He holds down fast-forward and the stillness accelerates.

Now something's happening. Einar rewinds a bit and hits PLAY. Hen is coming down the stairs in jeans and a silver anorak, the child asleep on her shoulder. She's supporting him with one hand and carrying a holdall in the other. 'Is that her?' says Anna. 'She's not . . .' Einar waves her quiet. The figure reaches the bottom of the stairs, puts the bag down on the floor and keys a number into the pad on the wall. She is leaving the way she came, with no sign of haste and no pause to look around. We watch her unlock the front door, push the bag through with her foot and slide off into the unfilmed morning.

Outside in Whieldon Street a car sounds its horn. I go out into the store and kick a path to the window. A taxi waits, in the black-and-grey livery of Etruscan Cars. It's the sort of cab we take to the station.

'So when she leaves here,' thinks Einar loudly, 'where then does she go?'

We lock up and go back through the store to the stairwell. Zoë is coming down the stairs with two suitcases and a plastic bag between her teeth. She stops, a flicker of surprise before her face hardens into a stare.

'Hallo,' says Einar.

She lets the bag drop. 'Hallo.'

'You off?'

'Looks like it. That is,' turning her stare onto me, 'if it's all right with *him*.'

'Is the taxi yours?'

'Shit. Probably.' She drops the cases and tucks the carrier under her arm.

'So what's wrong with your car?'

'Nothing. I lent it to somebody. Okay?'

'Let me guess,' says Einar. 'H . . . H . . . H . . .'

'You lent it to Hen?'

She groans softly and leans back against the wall. 'Look, I was half asleep. She said otherwise she was going down the Market Place to get one for herself. I thought she was probably in enough trouble already.' She stares wearily at the door. 'Same problem, really. We just need to get out of here for a few days.'

'Did anyone ask Robin if *he* was ready for a holiday?'

She closes her eyes and breathes. Now we all look as ill as each other.

'Christ. She never . . .'

'Come on, Zo!' Fear turns to anger and I'm shaking again. 'Sounds like you've been working this one out for weeks!'

'I said I don't know anything about it. Anyway, if anything *did* happen to them, I can't see how it's really Hen's fault.'

She glares at Anna, who pales like I've never seen. The horn sounds again. Linden comes downstairs in a pair of silky black shorts, sleepily scratching his arm.

'Don't worry about Hen. She's okay. Anyway, I'll see you around,'

then she's pushing past us with her suitcases, tapping in the same number and letting herself out into the street. At the bottom of the steps she stops, ready for something.

'Actually, there was something else. You got some thinking to do, mate. You think you can keep us here and order us about and think we're never going to realise what you're up to. Well, you're fucking . . .'

She turns and crosses the street. The driver gets out and stows her luggage in the boot. Zoë glances up once at the face of Big Kimberley, then they're gone, turning into Hope Street in a mess of exhaust fumes.

'Has she gone?' says Linden.

'She's gone. Like everyone else.'

Anna follows me upstairs. She sits shivering on the cold radiator, bare feet tucked under the rug, pushing back a yawn with the nub of a wrist. I'm in the next room, trying to get used to the silence, the dead space where once was a sleepy squeaking boy.

'What's she taken?'

'Most of his clothes. His blue shoes and the red pair. She's left most of his books, though. And his brain's still here, so it's not like he's gone for good.'

'Are you going to call the police?'

Hen's record: bus-stop blazes, a possession bust, the odd shop window. Only cautions, long forgotten, but, to my unhinged judgement, enough to make someone with a social conscience want to pay a visit and decide that a disused mill is no place to be bringing up a three-year-old child. Which is exactly what Mummy and Daddy will have been waiting for.

'So you don't want to tell her parents either?'

'If she's there she won't want to talk to me. If not, they're only going to panic and call the pigs themselves.'

She shuffles feet under the carpet.

'Hadn't you better get to work?'

'I rang in sick after I phoned the taxi. Doctors get ill too, you know.'

The computer wakes from its electronic dreams. All right: I'm expecting a message. She's going to tell me where she is, what she's doing, what time she'll be back here with our son asleep on the seat. Then I'm going to tell her that I'm no longer in love with her, that I couldn't care less about her lies and betrayals and tasteless practical jokes, because the woman I wanted her to be is now standing here beside me and I've no plans to let her slip away again. But the one message that's waiting, timed at 4.48 this morning, tells me none of these things.

Lot 13: **Life-sized model of the human brain**, in pink vinyl with interlocking parts.

> you are holding a plain gold ring. there are tiny
> scratches on the surface so you know its old. on
> the inside is an inscription. its hard to read but
> you can just see m&p, nothing else. youd be lucky
> to get your finger through it. are you lucky?
> perhaps you should find out.

I stand back to let Anna read. 'Weird,' she says. 'Do you know what it is?'

My eyes find the box on the shelf. 'I know it's made of 24 carat gold. I know it was bought in 1966 from a shop called Cartwright's in Covent Garden. I've an idea who it belongs to.'

And the song she used to sing, at the piano in the green-and-chocolate living room . . .

> *Did you ever see a snowman*
> *Walking on the fourth of May?*

'Your mother?'

I stare through her at someone else, trying to remember how it ends.

'It was the only piece of jewellery she was wearing when she died. Don't ask me why, but that's my mother's wedding ring she's talking about.'

> *Did you ever see a lion*
> *Rolling in the hay?*

Her arm enfolds my waist. Her rainy smell, her warmth, the feel of her clothes and the body beneath. I want to stay here with her, take her to my bed until we're ready to start something, some plan of action that will push all this into the past. But some things aren't so easy to shift.

'What now?' This is like a sigh.

'I'm going to do what she says. I'm going to drive down to my dad's place and have a good look at this ring.'

'We could take my car.'

'I was thinking about the van.'

'The van,' says Anna, 'has done over a hundred thousand miles and has a top speed of fifty-five. I think anyway you could do with a bit of moral support.'

'Everything you've got,' says Finn.

What is this great English nation?

It is an island in the ocean, a land of green grass and rain-drenched soil, flat and wet and sandy around the edges, rucked up like a grey-green blanket along its spine. You won't find it in any catalogue. No merchant can offer it for sale. It is four hundred miles of motorway, from the M6 at Carlisle to the M3 at Southampton, through blasted hillsides and murderous Bank Holiday rain. It is three lanes of traffic, red rivers of tail-lights climbing to the sky, sunlight on upland and fields of blue-green wheat. I never thought there could be so many people on the move. It is the way you look, North Sea eyes and marsh-sparrow hair, snot-clogged throat and a half-arsed smile. It is one hundred thousand varieties of green. It is the sort of history you don't learn at school: a cold-horsed morning in the reign of King John, sunlight glinting on buckles and badges, a dream that became a monastery, a car crash, another dream. It is the thousand-year-old smirk, a party that finished long ago from which no one ever went home. It's what's left when you forget the tune. It is the speed you speak, so fast you can't get your mouth around the sounds, tripping over yourself in the rush to say the opposite of what you mean. It is Holkham, 1989, the best trip you ever had, driving back at dawn with the birds going off like car alarms and life one long joyful scream. It is feeling bored before you begin. It's the place you can't help coming back to, the school that prepared you for nothing else, no matter how many times you spat in its dust and vowed never to return. But most of all it is the weather: days that start off dark and get darker, a rain that sinks into you like history and makes the whole world come to pieces in your hands.

'I know one thing. She hasn't left the country. She was never happy unless it was pissing down.'

We're in Anna's car heading south. There's so much spray coming off the lorry in front, I've forgotten where the south is supposed to be.

'I don't see why. It always seems to be raining in this country and

I get really fed up with it. Anyway, Finn, you're talking about Hen like she no longer exists, like this is something that's already over.'

'Yeh well. You wanted the story.'

That was the deal: complete honesty about my relationship with Hen, in return for a day of Anna, just Anna and no one else. And I'll tell her any story she wants to hear, as long as she's here beside me, tucking hair behind an ear and lighting Silk Cuts with one hand.

'So you went round to her flat after she'd left a message on your machine and she told you all about what happened with this Simon. Next?'

'We went to the pub and she tried to get me to nick a car. Then we went back to her place and one thing led to another.'

'So are we talking love at first sight?'

'Not quite. She made me laugh and all that, but I never thought . . .'

'No, you never do. But if it wasn't love at first sight, what was it? Who seduced who?'

'I don't know, Anna. I've never been seduced.'

'But you slept with her eventually.'

'Like I said, we went back to the flat, she got the handcuffs out and before we knew it we were in the bedroom making love.'

Now she understands. A saintly horror rearranges her face. 'You mean you slept with her on the very first night?'

'Look, it wasn't some drunken shag in the back of the van. We knew what we were doing.'

No one is convinced. 'God, no wonder you feel so crap about the relationship. I'd think it was going to be all a complete disaster if I had sex with someone on the very first night!' She pushes forward in her seat, looking for witnesses to my depravity in the rearview mirror, or just waiting to pull out into the outside lane. 'And what's all this about handcuffs?'

'Oh I don't know. It started as a joke, something Simon bought her as a present. We broke them in the end. She always wanted another pair, but . . . Anyway, I never really knew if she was keen on *me,* or if she just wanted someone to help her get over Simon.'

'You should ask her.'

In the outside lane at 85 mph, Anna realises what she's said.

'Sorry. I wasn't . . .'

'No, I *could* ask her. It's not as if she doesn't remember this stuff. She spends all day with these memories, like they were videos she has to keep watching because any day now she's going to find herself sitting this incredibly important exam – and all she can do is describe what's happening, without the first idea *why* it's happening, or what it means.'

'Finn, she's ill.'

'Yeh, but not so ill she can't pull a trick like this one. Like you said, you can't make up some story about NTX to get her off the hook. And even if you could, whose NTX is it?'

'I still don't understand why you're so angry with her.'

A blur of tail-lights. Black information pads in the centre of the road announce that there are no messages, no warnings, nothing to guide me in what I have to do. Cars and lorries on the opposite carriageway flash silent messages and pass. Somewhere ahead of this universe of cars, a red Peugeot 106 hurtles through hyperspace with a small blond boy asleep in the back.

'You really want to know?'

The deal, Finn: like that other deal you made, long ago, in the flat you built together, before the phone rang and blew the roof off your world . . .

She hears how Hen and I got started, on a mattress in a book-strewn room, the clawing rush to make our forgetting more total, to fuck our way to a permanent present, with neither past nor future, nothing but Us, Here, Now. How it began to fall apart, as we knocked through walls and ripped up floors, and found ghosts everywhere we looked. The first hint that even the sex wasn't enough: those impossible phone calls, sensing there was someone in the room with her, dismissed with a joke and a lie. Anger, then acceptance, as we made the deal, moments after the blow-up, her Chinese bowl still shattered on the new kitchen floor. *The deal, Finn: if we have to do it, we just go ahead and do it, and no one asks any questions and no one gets told any lies.* So if we ever split up it wouldn't be because either of us had been unfaithful, but just because it wasn't love any more.

'Sounds pretty reasonable, Finn.'

'Yeh, but it's something else when it actually happens. And when she tells you about it herself, just to see what you'll do . . . Christ, it's no big secret. One weekend when I was down at Greylag, she invites Simon over and spends the night with him in our bed. Comes out with it in the same bed, two days later, like she's telling me what one of her kids has done at school. And ... now do you see why I'm angry?'

Silence. I must love her, because I'm remembering things I only wanted to forget. Anna stares a mile down the road.

'Okay, she should've kept it quiet. But you had an agreement. And anyway, you've done the same thing to her.'

'Have I?'

'And you didn't *need* to tell her. She could see for herself what was going on!'

'You think I set this up on purpose to get back at Hen?'

'Of course not. I'm ... But in a way you have been unfaithful to her.'

What's worse, Finn: thinking it but not doing it, or doing it without wanting to? She sits in the car and smiles.

'All right, but anything I did, she did it first. I know for a fact she was shagging this bloke at the clinic, just like she was seeing Simon behind my back.'

'Okay, so why didn't you just leave? As soon as she'd told you what had happened with Simon, you could have just cut your losses and gone.'

'Because *she* was the one who was leaving. All of a sudden she's talking about upping and moving to Scotland, and she always promised she'd just pack up and go, I should have known what was going on. Then, about two weeks after her little rematch with Simon, I get this phone call. Can you hear him? she says. He's got tiny hands and tiny feet and tiny blue eyes. He's on his way. And I thought I could keep ahead of everything, I thought I could let things happen and never have to face the consequences, but now the consequences are screaming in the corner of the flat and I've got to learn to love them like I've never loved anything else.'

LOT
14

The house they called Greylag was, in Hen's opinion, all the proof anyone could ever need that money and good taste are rare enough commodities not to occur together with any frequency, and certainly not in this part of the Essex landscape. If a house is a small city, she'd say, then this is Chelmsford: drab, soulless and a bit too pleased with itself. And Hen could say this, because Hen knew which silk emulsion made the best of a room, the precise hue of burgundy to complement a particular beige blouse, and how to arrange three bunches of flowers and a pile of books so that an empty flat looked like the scene of a great artist's greatest still-life. Clearly, when it comes to matters of taste, the owners of Greylag would be better off saying nothing at all: you turn into a private road, head for a gap in a sculpted hedge and come to your senses on a curving gravel drive, bearing down on a modern house with wood panelling up to the first storey and stone statues holding classical poses around the porch. A wide passageway between house and garage leads through to the boathouse at the back. No doubt it used to announce itself as the House of the Future, in the days when Joy lived here with Brian and the four of us were frequent visitors: I mean the days of Trimfones and Angel Delight, Crimplene blouses with albatross lapels, when a Spanish fortnight was a trip to the edge and anything further was a holiday on Mars. But now it just reminds me how even a modern man like me will look dated before the week is out, and my soul is leaking as the wheels of Anna's white Renault disturb the gravel on the drive, and once again I'm a black-hearted adolescent fulfilling family duties on a sunny Saturday afternoon.

'What time do you want me to pick you up?' Anna applies the handbrake and knocks it out of gear.

'You what?'

'I'm not coming in with you, Finn.'

Finn tries his puzzled look.

'What are they going to think of me?'

'They'll think you're an old friend of mine who's come along for the ride.'

She cuts the engine and laughs. 'So what are you going to tell them about Hen?'

'They like her even less than Ali does. They won't even ask.'

'Where's Hen?' says Dad, appearing in the passageway in neat sideburns and paint-smeared jeans, showing no surprise that we should have driven two hundred miles to drop in on him unannounced. I trot out my story about her taking the kid for a weekend with Tom and Jan, then catch him eyeing my stolen bride.

'This is Anna, an old friend from Sydney. This is my old dad.'

'Anna.' He tries out the name for himself, decides he likes it and presses some of that superior charm into her hand. 'And less of the old, thanks, Finn.' Now, obviously keen for some time alone with Anna: 'You'll want to ring your sister. They let her out of the jungle last night.'

No: he's not on form. His wife, on the other hand, can hardly keep the lid on her joy. In pale blue jogging suit and emergency make-up, she hops out from the back of the house and kisses us like footballers.

'We didn't think we'd be seeing *you* in such a hurry! So you're a friend of Finn's, are you? Anna? Doctor? Ooh, come here. Funnily enough, I've just been on the phone to your Auntie Sarah! She really is bearing up *incredibly* well . . .'

'We can't stay long.'

'Oh!' She can sound so terribly disappointed. 'And the garden's looking so *nice* . . .'

Anna follows me along the passageway. Joy flits silently in her open-plan kitchen, glancing out at us through patio windows which lay the back of the house open to the world. Dad's boat is mounted on a metal cradle at the edge of the lawn. It's the one he bought himself with Joy's divorce settlement, shortly after Brian sailed off into the sunset with his new American friend. He's doing something with a pair of ropes, taking his time.

'Wow,' says Anna. 'You don't get this in Didsbury.'

The tide is in. The river sleeps beyond fifty yards of mud flats, breaking light on its surface and reflecting it in pale loops of gold. I lead her eye across tilting boats and weed-choked buoys to the nuclear power station, veiled by a mile of haze, and explain that it was growing up this close to all such radiation that accounts for my early hair loss and extraordinary powers. 'And which powers are these?' she says, her bare arm grazing mine. But time for that later, Anna: there are things only my father can tell me, and when Joy turns up with a jug of orange barley water and four glasses on a tray, it seems as good a time as any to ask.

'Dad?'

He sits down on a plastic chair and pours himself a glass. When he thinks he's ready to listen, he looks up, eyebrows raised.

'Where's Mum's wedding ring?'

'Where's . . . ? That's quite a question, Finn.'

'Do you know?'

'It's upstairs in a drawer.'

'Can I see it?'

He empties his glass, fixing the horse-chestnut at the back of the house.

'Would it be rude to ask what for?'

'I was trying to describe it to someone and I realised I've never actually seen it.'

'It's a long way to come just for that.' He flares nostrils and pulls shoulders back against the chair. It's not enough, he's saying. You'll have to do more.

'Come on, Peter! They can see it if they want! Here, *I'll* show you where it is . . .'

Dad glares at Joy, who stops, half risen from her chair. Realising, almost surprised, that there is nothing he can do to avert what's about to happen, my father looks down at his feet, mouth loose, sweat gemming on his brow. Now the three of us are standing, awaiting some explanation for his resistance, or simply needing a word from him to jerk us into life. 'Yes, they can see it if they want . . .' – but his voice is a whisper, and for the first time in memory that looks like real despair, however quickly bitten, on his ungenerous lips.

We follow Joy through the French windows, across the open-plan reception area with its tubular chrome furniture and splendid river view, up three steps to the kitchen and dining area, then spiral wooden stairs to the first floor. In a moment we're in the bedroom, looking round at gilt-trimmed wardrobe units, a frilly white four-poster and matching kidney-shaped dressing table. Joy roots through a drawer, opening up small square boxes and putting them back with impatient sighs. And there, propped up on the glass-topped table, bringing back my old enthusiasm for breathing, is the last person I would have expected to see: Margaret Causley, fixed for all time in a tortoiseshell frame, head a few degrees from the vertical, wearing what could only be a requested smile.

'That's Mum,' says Joy, as Anna steps forward to pick her up. 'See where he gets his looks from, no question at all.'

Anna checks me against the photo. But if it's looks she wants, all she's getting is a blotchy mix of anger and disbelief. And instead of a tirade against my stepmother's abominable lack of taste, the best I can manage is:

'Don't think I've seen this one before.'

'No? I take that one with me everywhere. Now, where is this blooming thing?'

The heat licks at our eyes. Nothing but the sounds of Joy's search: drawers sliding in and out, envelopes flattened out and shaken, boxes opened and snapped shut. Everything makes sense except one thing: this photograph, which Joy knows I know about and has made no attempt to explain or excuse. Which means either she's deliberately out to taunt me, or else all the assumptions I've kept warm for twenty years – how they packed her into a box, stowed her in the attic and vowed never to mention her again – need to be thrown out and replaced with something closer to the truth. The more I look at my mother's measured smile, the seeming reverence with which she's been set apart from bottles and jewellery boxes – as if, who knows, she'd been put there to bring them luck, the first guardian angel ever to be captured on film – the stronger this feeling that I'm more wrong than right, that my search for twenty-year-old secrets is never going to turn up anything but more wrong-headed beliefs. And because these ideas are not objects with lives of their own, but are all jumbled up together in the toy box I call my mind, all those silent accusations are dragged out into the open for an audience with her doubt-dispelling smile. The accident was just an accident. A car came off the road. Dad cried, we cried, we loved her, we carried on. Because how else could he do it, look at this picture every morning, unless he loved her like we loved her, unless . . . ?

'Here we are!' says Joy, and a small black jewellery box is in my hand.

'Is this it?'

'That's it. You know, I told Peter you should have it, so all her things could be kept together, but at the end of the day he wanted to keep it here. That ring is all he's got left of her. He used to love to see her wearing that ring.'

It sits in its black velvet slot, a plain gold band with two initials, M & P, engraved on the inside. It hardly fits over my fingernail. It holds a secret, though: a snatch of that crackling childhood film that shows her in the mood I always want to remember: brimming with songs, laughing, aware of nothing but her luck in getting this far. Perhaps I can even recall the sight of it on her long white finger, cutting into the finely creased flesh, glinting under the piano lamp.

'Try it on,' I say.

A cloud passes. She pulls anxiously at the strap of her watch.

'Go on. I want to see what it looks like.'

'I'd rather not, Finn. It's not really my . . .'

She glances at me, almost angry now, and turns. At the door she stops, fills her lungs with brave resolutions and unburdens herself with admirable control.

'Finn, I don't want you to think Mum's ring is not good enough for me. If I could be one tiny bit as good a person as your mother was, I'd be the happiest woman in the world. It's just . . . I've tried so hard all these years to fit into her shoes, and there's some things you just can't ask me to do.'

She's gone, bare feet slapping on the stairs. I pass the ring to Anna.

Lot 14: **Wedding ring**, 24 carat gold, in a box marked *Cartwright's of Covent Garden*.

She turns it in her fingers, biting her lip.

'I'm sure this is bad luck.'

'Please?'

She slides it onto her ring finger. It reaches the middle knuckle and will go no further.

'It's bloody tight.'

She pushes it, hands against her chest, until it's over the knuckle. She holds her hand out, fingers splayed, and looks at it with dreamy unease.

'I'm going to need some washing-up liquid to get it off.'

She holds her hands under her chin in two loose fists. I have this feeling of being slowly brought to the boil, tiny bubbles fizzing at the edges, thickening and creaming against every possible law. I can't stop myself from kissing her face.

'You know what? People used to tell me the reason I fancied you so much was that you looked like my mother.'

'Do I?'

'No.'

'Well, I'll tell you what. Either your mum had very thin fingers, or this is one ring that wasn't supposed to come off in a hurry.'

'Perhaps,' I joke, 'we'd better ask my dad about that.'

I think my sister's love life must be looking up. It takes her about twenty minutes to answer the phone.

'Christ, little brother, you don't give up, do you?' Even outside, listening to her on Joy's peach-coloured cordless, I can tell she's out of breath.

'I catch you on the job?'

She snorts. 'If you must know, I've just got back with Andy. Takes him a while to get going.'

'How was Malaysia?'

'Nasi goreng and piped heavy metal. Not an unspoilt beach in sight.'

'Who'd be a fund manager?'

'I was going to fly home for the funeral but I couldn't swing it. You know Sarah's down with Mervyn this weekend?'

'Yeh. Thought we'd go and see her tomorrow, once we've drunk your booze and eaten all your food.'

'Wonderful. You can tell me how to work my video. I've got a new cat as well. He's called Limpet because of the way he jumps onto you and won't get off.'

Joy has dragged Anna inside to admire her maritime watercolours, an exercise that will take at least half an hour. Dad is in his chair at the end of the garden, staring out over the water as if he was about to lose it all.

'You found it,' he says.

'Yeh. It's very small.'

He sighs. I've never heard him sigh before.

'Your mother had very slim fingers. Very strong, with all that piano playing, but amazingly slender. I've never seen fingers like that anywhere.'

He looks sadly at the backs of his hands. I've a feeling that, if I ask him now, I'll hear stuff I've never heard before.

'I wish I could remember. That's what I really regret, Dad: not just that she died, but that I can remember so little about her.'

'I told you, didn't I? I sat you on my knee and I said: Sometimes she'll be here next to us, as real as this house, and other times she'll be like a person in a dream that you never get to know. But she'll always love you, because she told me.'

I tried to forget his tears. But I could never forget the feeling that he still had some access to her, behind closed doors, in grown-ups' silences, and that if I stayed close enough to him I might overhear something, the clouds might part and some of her floating soul would whisper through to me. Then silence, all those years.

'And now,' he's saying, 'there are times I can hardly remember what colour eyes she had . . .'

'Yeh well. Can't blame ourselves for that.'

'Maybe, Finn. I have my regrets, like everyone else, and it's up to me to try and live with them.'

What's this? An admission of guilt? Someone must be laughing. But his voice, this sick-hearted tone . . .

'What regrets?'

'Ask Joy. She's the one who's had to put up with them all these years.'

'No, *you* tell me.'

He frowns, suddenly older, unhappy to be caught like this.

'All right. I regret I wasn't around more. I regret I spent so much time trying to land property deals that weren't worth the paper they were written on. I regret I didn't give her the attention she needed, especially when the TV thing started to take off. I can't really blame her for losing interest.'

'In what?'

'In the marriage, Finn.'

Is it the heat? He's said more to me in the last five minutes than I've heard in twenty years.

'Why do you think she lost interest?'

'It's obvious. There were people in her life she never really got over.'

'You mean Mike Browning?'

He laughs, dismayed at what he's started. 'Look, your mother was in love with Mike Browning long before she ever met me. Those kinds of feeling are strong. They have a habit of coming back to you again and again and again.'

If I didn't know him better, I'd think he'd remembered how to cry.

'What happened to him, this Mike Browning?'

'Set up his own business in Schyre. They said he made plastic egg boxes or something. I really don't know.'

'Schyre's just west of Print.'

'More or less.'

'Across Blacksheep Moor from Etruria.'

No problem accepting that.

'Is that where she was going?'

He looks at me, squinting against the sunlight, fighting down twenty years of uncertainty and pain. All at once I understand. The Silk Twister, the loss of direction on unfamiliar roads: neither of them the real reason for that trip across the moor.

'I don't know. All I know is I wouldn't blame her if she was.'

'You really loved her, didn't you, Dad?'

But all my answers are shining in his eyes.

LOT
15

When she left me for Duncan McGuinness, who had all his hair and the six-pack to go with it, and then left Duncan McGuinness for a trip around the great Australian continent in the care of the Deluxe Coach Company Pty., the only items that would have appeared in a catalogue under 'Gifts from Finn to Anna' would have been a few fumbled kisses, two nights of edgy intimacy on a rented board bed, and a piece of paper on which I'd written my address, dreaming of that rainy day in England when she would read my name and realise what she had done with the keys to her heart. I had given her only slightly more than she had given me, and still it felt like I'd caught sight of the one lot in the showroom that I could ever truly set my heart on, only to be told it was not for sale. I suspect these auction-room metaphors will be my downfall, so I'll switch to another: in an echo of that good-natured trick that holidays play when they fizzle out in immigration queues and baggage reclaim halls, I forgot all the bad bits (the voice that went up at the end of the sentence, our collective failure to come up with any joke that made us both laugh at the same time) and kept only what I wanted to keep. I obsessed myself with her disbelieving smile, the hair that wouldn't stay in its parting, a roundish face that only became beautiful by accident, with a slight turn of the head; and all the other details that were even now fading from memory, dissolving like starlight into the dim shallows behind my eyes. I called that long delusion January. I hung around with tiresome people for the sole reason that they were friends of hers, and so might help these fading images, drawn on night air and harbour-water, to survive. Then, as I was making my own journey around the same vast continent, always nearer to loneliness than company and nearer to sky than anything else, I stopped blaming others for my Annalessness and started, better late than never, to blame myself. I should have been more obvious. I should have told her what she was doing to me with her brown eyes and her unforgiveably kissable neck. I shouldn't have been so worried that I would sound like all the others, that she would guess the darker purpose behind these brotherly smiles and treat me to the brush-off I deserved. Thankfully, there are only so many years you can go on having thoughts like these, and even the most obsessive wallower needs an occasional change of shit. By the time I met Hen Threadgold in her flat on Bristol Street, I'd finally got round to imagining what would have happened if I *had* said what I meant, if I'd swallowed my fear and delivered the speech I'd rehearsed so many times in my room. The irony was not lost. Even as Hen was making excuses for not letting me move in with her, I was hard at work on a parallel life, in which, for steadily more vivid interludes, I could pretend it was Anna's heat pressed into the sheets, Anna's clothes looped on the bedroom floor. Sometimes, when reality drove me to anger or tears, I wished I wasn't so good at it. But as my imaginary life with Anna became more real than the real one with Hen, which was already turning into a sort of story we told each other in remorseful moments after a row, it all resolved itself into a single overpowering need: to find her, to pre-empt this oncoming disaster, to hear it from her own lips: 'I didn't love you then and I will not love you now.' The rest you know. She's sitting in the passenger seat of her own car, hands flat under her thighs. London streets flash by. Now I've found her, or now that she's found me, I realise a potted history like this can never give more than half the truth, that none of these feelings ever followed on from one another like items in a sale, but were at each other's throats from the start. I was hopeful at the same time as I despaired, I was looking back at the same time as I looked forward, and if the answers come tonight, tomorrow or in the last half-minute of my life, they will come, I will listen, and they will be what I want to hear.

'I still don't understand what your mum's ring has got to do with anything.'

She looks calmly at the road, as if this was another film she's seen many times but wants to prove she knows the ending. Her fingers on the door handle, ready for a quick leap into the dusk.

'Nor do I. Unless she wanted to get me out of the way for some reason.'

'Like what?'

'So she could get back into Big Kimberley. No, I don't know why she'd want to do that.'

'Perhaps she wanted to flush you out. Get you moving. So she could come after you.'

She doesn't look round. We must be in love because she knows what I'm thinking. I'm thinking about that red Peugeot 106 at the services we stopped at earlier on.

'Why would she want to do that?'

'Find out what we're up to. You know, if we're going to sleep together tonight.'

She pulls at her top and the breeze licks sweat from her skin.

'You're enjoying this, aren't you?'

She grabs the handle and winds the window down fully. 'Well Finn, I do think you're too hard on them. I think Peter and Joy are really nice.'

I'm checking the mirror and pulling out. No red Peugeot swings into view. No bearded tattooist taunts me from the passenger seat: for once we're headed where we're headed and there is nothing behind.

'So when did you start smoking?' I've watched her puzzling over this since mid-afternoon, when we shared coffee and Silk Cuts in the services near Milton Keynes.

'When I was thirteen.'

'Okay, so when d'you start up again?'

'I never gave up.'

'You never smoked when I knew you in Aus.'

'I was doing thirty a day when I met you. Packet of Peter Jackson's, light blue.'

'God, I don't remember that at all.'

She's watching. I feel it here, in the top of my spine.

'So when did you start being so talkative?'

She yawns. 'Oh, I get bored when I'm not driving. As you've probably noticed, I'm a really bad back-seat driver.'

'You're meant to say it's because you feel so comfortable with me.'

'Finn, I feel more comfortable with you than I've ever felt with anyone. Except when you're driving.'

'So?'

'So, I think that's enough for the minute.'

By the time we've found my sister's new flat in Kensington, I seem to have proved to Anna that I'm not as dangerous a driver as her perspiring upper lip would suggest, and that one or two less-than-perfect gear changes have done no permanent damage to her precious French gearbox. She, on the other hand, has been the perfect navigator, moving from page to page of the A to Z as if it were a dissection manual and our great capital just another corpse to be understood. I wish she could tell me what to do with my life with as much confidence and authority as she tells me which exit to take off the North Circular.

'I'm a doctor,' she says, tugging a holdall from the boot and catching my surprise. 'You never know when you might get called away.'

My sister's flat is at the top of the end terrace. She waits, beautiful in places where I only sweat, in the doorway at the top of the stairs.

'Don't fight it, little brother. You know it's the law.'

I kiss her three times, as she has taught me, and she turns to the one I call Anna.

'So you're the long-lost love from Sydney. Oh Finn, I always knew you'd get it right in the end.'

The flat is sloped ceiling, skylights and doors onto a whitewashed balcony. We catch up on each other from the comfort of sofas, then Anna goes downstairs for a shower.

'So how long has this been going on?' as the bathroom door closes and the bolt slides across.

'Not long.'

'Big sister approves.'

'Not much to approve of yet.'

'No, you always were a bit slow off the mark. Anyway, Hen. You said she was ill or something.'

It's not a question and there's no question in her voice. The fact is that my sister and Hen do not mix. Last time they met they had a blistering row in an excessively fashionable restaurant, failing to agree on politics, vegetarianism and finally, finishingly, Bliss. Alison was trying to convince us it was all in the mind. 'That's pretty obvious,' said Hen. Ali thought this was a bit rich from someone who'd never even been to Oxford, and gave the first sign of knowing more about Hen's problems than she'd been told. 'Well, Hen, I'm sure you know a lot more about it than we do.' It was unforgiveable, of course, but Ali never asked forgiveness for anything. Instead she made sure she always asked after her, as if, rather than feeling bad about her cruelty, she just wanted to check Hen had survived it. I tell her what has happened since this morning. It all seems very long ago.

'You know she's all right, don't you? She'll have just gone back to Mummy and Daddy until they get sick of her and send her back to hospital. It's happened before.'

'She's never taken the kid before.'

'He's safe. Anyway, who is it who looks after him all the time? Who feeds him and baths him and takes him to playgroup? You deserve a holiday.'

I tell her about the message describing Margaret's ring, and how we went to Essex to find out what it meant.

'Did he let you see it?' She looks surprised.

'Anna tried it on. It was too tight for her.'

'That's funny. It was too tight for me too.'

She stares down at her knuckles, flares her nostrils and yawns.

'So anyway, we got talking about Mum. For the first time, you know, I think he was really saying what he felt.' I pause, testing the weight of what I'm about to say. 'He seems to think she was having an affair.'

Ali bursts like a swimmer. 'Does he now. The smarmy old cunt. It's okay, I love him really.'

'Look, Ali, I know what you think. You think because I took Joy's money for the business it means I must be on Dad's side. But I just want to know what happened. It seems to matter now.'

She sucks her lip thoughtfully. Perhaps this time, now that it matters, she's succeeded in lowering her voice.

'I don't know what happened. To be honest I don't really care. She had an accident, she died, she's not coming back. It was nobody's *fault.*'

'You don't really believe that.'

She waits. We, too, have never talked about this before.

'Okay, she was having an affair. I *think*. I don't think it got very far. I met him once – he was her Type all right. I don't know if she was going to see him that day or not. Who cares?'

'So why blame Dad? Sounds like it was Mum who cocked everything up.'

'I don't blame Dad. I just don't think she deserved to die for it. And I think if he'd acted a bit differently it might not have got that far.'

She gets up and goes over to the video, kneels down and starts fiddling with the display.

'Why might it not have got that far?'

'For Christ's sake, Finn, can't you see? I don't really want to talk about it.'

'No one ever wanted to talk about it.'

She stands up, scratches a perfect cheek and looks out at the sunset.

'Dad found out. Don't ask me how. It was 1976, that really hot summer. It was so long ago we actually had a Labour government. They had this colossal row, but it wasn't about politics. The same day Mum packed us into the car and drove us to Brink Farm.' She turns. 'You must remember that.'

'I don't remember any row. Maybe I remember wondering where Dad was. But then he was away on business all the time, so it wouldn't . . .'

'Well Dad *wasn't* away on business. He was smashing plates in our dingy little kitchen. He gave us an hour's head start and then he came after us. Mum's in tears all the way, which isn't surprising bearing in mind who she's married to. We get there, and we're sitting in the TV room having a glass of squash, and Mum's telling Sarah about what's going on, and all of a sudden we hear this car on the drive, then Dad's voice in the hallway, calling her every name under the sun. And Don's out there in the hallway, trying to calm the fucker down.'

'What was he saying?'

'Christ, little brother, were you asleep or something? He was *threatening* her. He said he was going to get a divorce and take us away from her, because she couldn't be trusted with us, because she was a dirty fucking slag etcetera. He's going on and on about a court order. So she grabs us two kids and takes us out to the car, locks all the doors, and we sit there on the back seat with our faces in her lap, waiting for him to calm down.'

'We must have got past him somehow.'

'She opened the French windows. You must remember them, you walked into them enough times.'

Brink Farm. The television room with its sad anaglypta. The gravel drive, the solitary oak, the churned-up paddock, and the blue Cortina, gleaming in afternoon sun. Three shadowy figures on the back seat: one big, two small.

'What was she wearing?'

'Can't remember. Some sort of dress. Maybe that green one with the belted waist. Anyway, Dad's pounding on the roof, screaming his little head off. I'll see you swing, you bitch, and so on. All Don and Sarah can do is watch.'

Downstairs the shower has gone silent. I sit across from her in the fading light, staring at the state-of-the-art hi-fi on the shelving unit, wondering if it has ever been switched on.

'Look, if you want to know any more you'd better ask Sarah. I know she's never talked about any of this, but now Don's gone it might be worth a try. And Finn,' she gazes down at her finger, 'don't think I don't care about Mum dying. I had to learn about sex from a Durex packet because she wasn't around.'

I laugh without laughing. 'It just sounds like, I don't know, Hen knows something I don't. She was talking to Sarah for ages at the funeral.'

'She probably knows a lot of things you don't know she knows. About your new girlfriend, for example.'

I wince. Why does she have to be so . . . ?

'Like I say, there's not much to know.'

'Except the fact that you're in love with her. That she's quite obviously your Type. That she's not a complete neurotic who can't hold down a job.'

'That's unfair.'

'Truth's a bugger, Finn.'

'And anyway, what's it got to do with anything?'

'Well, perhaps it can explain the message she sent you.'

I'm not as clever as I look.

'All right,' she says, 'assume she knows about Mum and everything. And assume everything you've found out today is what she wanted you to find out.'

'About Mum having an affair?'

'About Mum never getting over the person she was first in love with. About how pointless it is trying to make a go of it with someone when they're always thinking about someone else, always wondering how it might have been if they'd made different decisions. Hen's not stupid. Perhaps she's showing that she knows all about you and Anna and doesn't want to be a burden on you any more. Perhaps, I don't know, she's offering you your freedom.'

The idea crashes over me like a cold sea wave, which stops stinging after a while and soothes to an aching warmth. Ali hovers on the balcony. The sound of a bolt being drawn back.

'It's too late. She had her chance when we were in Sydney. And she never got in touch even though she knew for ages where I was.'

She looks past me into the stairwell, her famous complexion lit with a smile. 'Maybe you'd better ask Anna about that.'

Her hair is wet. She's wearing a blue summer dress with buttons down the front. She comes up the stairs tentatively, arms behind her back, as if she had a gorgeous secret to keep from us.

'Thanks,' standing back to let Ali pass downstairs. 'Now I'm clean again.'

We sit together on the sofa. A yellow rug of sunlight warms her ankle. A few shin hairs are pale and gold.

'Couldn't find a hairdryer.'

'You look good wet.'

'Thanks. It's a pretty special dress.'

'What's special about it?'

'Tell you later.' She touches her neck, swallows, and looks out at me through beautiful hurrying eyes.

Half an hour later we're studying the menu in the Chiang Rai on North End Road, mobbed by purple orchids and white damask napkins folded like lotus flowers. Andy is supposed to be meeting us here. 'He's always late,' says Ali. 'We'll give him till half past then I'll chuck him.' 'Again?' says Finn. 'Again.' But Andy must be listening, because in the next moment he appears in the doorway in grey suit, pink shirt and bottle-green tie, and stands there, looking around.

'Why's he in a suit?' says Anna.

'Because that's what they teach you at public school.' She sighs. 'I do hope he's not going to get on your nerves.'

'Sorry,' says Andy, grinning at us two strangers and kissing Ali three times on alternate cheeks. Ali does the introductions. Andy gives a rushed sort of bow and sits down next to me. He looks like he'd apologise for anything. He has a round, rubbery face, with two malignant-looking moles on the cheek and a clump of thick brown hair. But it's the accent that gets me listening.

'What are we having then?' He speaks too loud, like drunk, pronouncing *what* as if the *w* and *h* were reversed.

'Two of everything,' says Ali. 'And make it fucking snappy.'

'Anyone mind if I smoke?' Anna says.

'Christ, please do,' goes Andy. 'I'll sit here and sort of . . . suck it up.'

'You bastard!' says Ali. 'You're supposed to be giving up!'

Andy turns and stares at me, as if I were the referee in this little contest.

'Here,' says Anna, holding the pack ajar. Andy takes one, moaning softly, and lights it inexpertly. Anna's foot moves under the table. It crosses the cross-strut, reaches my shoe and stops. Very slowly, in smooth and knowing circles, her bare toes touch on my leg.

'How was your shopping?' says Ali.

'Wonderful. Spent a fortune in my bookshop down by Cambridge Circus. Actually, that's the reason I was late. I got sort of engrossed.'

'In a book?' says Anna, love in her toes and a dreamy smile on her mouth. 'What's it about?'

'Comets and eclipses. You know they used to be taken as omens of disaster? One story goes that drunken astronomers who failed to predict an important eclipse had their heads *removed from their shoulders*. I mean, not even our fund manager has to put up with that.'

'Tell you what,' says Ali, 'next to lunch with Chuck Kieslowski from Weissmann Müller, instant beheading sounds like an attractive proposal. He phones me from HK, right, four o'clock in the morning, says: I'm on the 76th floor of the frigging Regency Hotel, this ninety-quid brandy bottle is bloody empty, MTV Asia blaring in the background, little yellow men banging on the door telling me to shut up, so there's nothing for it, I'm just gonna have to chuck myself out the window. So I go: Go on, then, Chuck: *chuck*!' She hoots. 'Sorry, your eclipses.'

'Yes. Ha ha ha! You know, you spend a few minutes with a book like this and it completely changes the way you think about History.' He's waving hands around, pulling them together and shaking them to make a point, as if that was an invisible melon stuck between his palms. 'To me, at school, it was just this list of dates: 1066, 1538, all that sort of thing. But when you read about a total eclipse of the sun,' her toe climbs my leg, 'which took place on *March the 23rd* in the year *228*, that day, so long long long ago, somehow comes alive. Doesn't it? You can imagine the sun on the grass, the sheep in the fields, the wind in your beard . . .' 'Your *beard*?' '. . . and suddenly this wave of darkness crossing the green and pleasant at more than the legal speed.' He laughs, tapping his cigarette. We're waiting for the punchline. 'Well actually, we're not too sure anyone was watching that particular eclipse because it wasn't recorded. But we know it *happened* because we can calculate it.'

'Are you ready to die now?' says Ali.

'Sorry. I'd much rather hear about Chuck Kieslowski.'

'No,' Anna insists. 'It makes a change to hear someone sounding, I don't know, enthusiastic about something.'

Alison belches in her corner. 'I'm enthusiastic about my Tom Yum.'

'I agree with you, Anna. There are so many people in this city who do nothing but complain. They all hate their jobs and yet all they ever do is talk about them.'

'I hate *my* job,' says Alison.

'Exactly. But what do you ever do about it?'

'What *can* I do about it?'

'You could get out,' says Finn. 'You could go and live in an old-fashioned town in the middle of nowhere, where people are still called Mr this and Mrs that and a man comes round in the evening and wishes everyone goodnight.'

'What, like that grubby little sheep-shagging town you hang around in? No thanks, I actually quite *enjoy* being alive.'

'You mean you want to have two hundred different films on every night, so you can never make up your mind which one to see.'

'And even if you decide,' says Andy with enthusiasm, 'it takes two hours to get anywhere . . .'

'And the pollution . . .' says Anna.

'And all those homeless people helping themselves . . .'

'And the constant fear of being mugged,' says Ali, 'or being stopped by Sky News and asked your opinion about something. Yes! Yes! Say I'll never have to look at a cow again!'

'All I'm saying is, you can't judge how interesting someone's life is just from their postcode.'

'Unless it's an Essex postcode.'

'Hey, I'm from Essex,' says Andy.

'That's what I mean.'

Andy grins. He has a cat named Delicious. I'm liking him more and more.

The food lives up to its reputation. For the time it takes each of the blue-and-white dishes to be emptied, you can hear nothing but porn-movie moans, smothered burps flavoured with lemongrass and coriander, and earnest whispers of advice about what next to enjoy. When it's all gone, and the third bottle of house red has been reduced to dregs, and Andy's Bank of America Gold Amex card has performed its function efficiently and inconspicuously, Alison makes her announcement. She's getting into a taxi with Andy and going back to his flat and the cat they call Delicious. Which means Anna and I have the place to ourselves.

'You can have my room, but only if you *promise* to behave.' Her eyebrows make sisterly arches. All Anna can do is yawn.

'You won't know a thing,' says Finn,

and we step outside, dizzy and stumbling as blood tips from our brains and sloshes to our feet, into an evening that seems no cooler than the day. It's late: the city idles, pubs are dark and silent, all-night shop-lights softened by the alcohol in our eyes. Anna takes my arm with both hands and hangs from it, looking down into her own enchanting abyss.

'If I fall asleep on you, Finn, I apologise now. I'm just absolutely,' a yawn surprises her, 'shagged.'

She sways a little, shivering, as I open the door. When we reach the living room she offers lips for a kiss, falling forward with drooping eyelids, mocking us and this game we're playing. When my fingers reach her waist she pulls away impatiently, suddenly awake.

'Let's have a drink on the balcony.'

'I thought you wanted to go straight to sleep.'

'Oh no.' She looks very serious. 'Sleep's for *boring* people.'

The kitchen is a white booth behind a pair of glass doors. She opens the fridge and crouches, touching hair behind an ear. 'Ah. *This* is the sort of thing I had in mind.'

She swivels on her heels to show a bottle of champagne.

'Think we should?'

'She can afford it.'

She stands up and flicks through some cupboards. The dress follows her movements like a bit of sky has snagged on her, falling from her shoulder-blades to where hips flare outwards in perfect stretched curves. She gives up on the search for champagne glasses and chooses two tumblers from the draining board. She brushes away some coffee grains with the blade of her hand and puts the bottle down on the worktop. She peels off the foil and twists at the wire, blowing hair from one side of her mouth.

'I'm a bit of a spacker at this. Don't get much practice in my boring life.'

She turns half towards me and jams the bottle against her tummy. The dress lifts an inch on the backs of her thighs. She gasps as the cork flies out and hits the skylight with a ping. A white lick of CO_2, and champagne froths out and down in a wet yellow mousse over her hand. She fills the tumblers cautiously, as if measuring solutions for some sort of experiment, checking the levels for parity. Now she licks champagne from her hand and briefly contemplates the puddle on the floor.

'Oops. What now?'

Her top three buttons are undone. She waits for me to open the doors and I follow her onto the balcony.

'God, it's still really warm,' she says, resting elbows on the wall and offering the backs of her thighs to the spying stars.

Lot 15: **Blue summer dress**, with an uncomplicated floral design, buttoned from neck to knee.

'Like Sydney all over again.'

She turns. A fringe of moisture glistens at her hairline. The sole of one shoe comes to rest against the wall behind.

'I can think of one difference.'

She takes a sip of champagne. The blue cloth folds into a loosely wadded triangle in her crotch. She scratches a knee and holds a faint smile.

'What?'

'We're grown-ups. We don't have to make stupid excuses for not doing what we want to do.'

A sweep of cars on North End Road. A pigeon coos a love song on the next balcony along.

'I've lost it, Finn.'

'It's all right . . .'

Slowly, as if every movement was causing her a familiar and longed-for pain, she puts her glass down on the wall and turns. Her breasts shift under buttoned cloth. She takes my hand and puts it there, on the left, on the warm electric softness where I once found her heart.

'Go on,' she breathes.

My hand, wet with sweat and spastic with fear, moves down over the last few ribs, into the elastic gap between ribcage and hip, round and down over the turned length of her thigh. My fingers, the fabric, her skin. There is nothing between her and this half-open dress.

'Aren't you cold?'

She laughs, relieved I know her secret.

'Not cold,' she says.

My hand cups the small of her back. Desire makes me stupid hard clumsy, can't go back, can't think what to do. She moves, half pulled, half needing no encouragement, into my arms. She kisses me with lips I dreamed of all my life, rolling my lower lip between hers, licking the tips of my teeth with the underside of her tongue, leading my tongue in a slow blind chase around her mouth. Her body burns and shivers in my hands.

She steps backwards into the room, kicks off her shoes and pulls me in by the hand. Now I'm raked up in her arms; she sucks in her lower lip, fingers running slowly around the inside of my trouser waist as if searching for a hidden catch. Against my thigh, seven years since it pressed on me in a room above a silent harbour, the elastic imprint of her pubic bone.

And suddenly I'm awake, and something I never thought would happen is happening, just slow enough to understand. She's clearing newspapers from a chair and dumping them onto the floor. She's unbuttoning my shirt, pushing it off my shoulders and pushing me down onto the chair. My hands go to my belt, pull leather through buckle and wrench it all down. Suddenly I'm fourteen, getting changed for swimming, just the cool touch of the air making me hard. Anna lifts one leg over my knees and the dress rides up over her thighs. I breathe her slippery scent. I know I'm not allowed to touch her, this is not part of her plan. But she should be keeping track of my hands, because as she holds my shoulders and poises her body over mine, I bring fingers up and touch: her bristling wetness, the slick groove into which my mind is crowding, a smear of thigh on the back of my hand. Now I am this beast of the hedgerow, a sticky tear in my eye, and she's guiding me in with hasty fingers, until I'm snug inside and she can hold there, tongue scrubbing the outside of her lip, crouched like a skier above my fire. My hands move to her hips and she can't hold any more. She sinks down onto me, breath wet on my face, and I sink into her with a faint stretching pain. She looks past me with fear and pain and joy, all her weight hot and cold on my thighs. The clock on the video reads 00:00. Now she begins to move, in small slow circles, the dress crushed between her buttocks and my lap, and I'm making myself think: of swimming lessons, of the mellotron intro to 'Fountain of Salmacis', of the injection system of a Peugeot 106, of an unrecorded solar eclipse two hundred years after the death of Christ . . . Then my mind, which has always been a container of limited capacity, refuses to give me any more ideas, and I have to face up to where I am. I am naked on a wooden chair, being kindly and earnestly fucked by the same woman whose face I have spent seven years trying to remember, since the day I saw her in a different dress in a different city on the other side of the world, when I didn't even dare dream; and her wire brush is scrubbing my pubic bone, and a long knotted ribbon is being pulled slowly through the places she has threaded it, and I'm coming: one, two, three, four, five, six-and-a-half, seven, as many seconds since we started, and dark smoky hair is tumbling around my face, and potato-water tears are pricking my eyes, and Anna's face is red and terrified, two inches from mine.

'I'm sorry.'

No one moves. The balcony doors stand open, conducting our shared heat into the night.

'Finn, it was fine.' Her weight shifts and settles. 'It's the first time.'
'I hope so.'
'What d'you mean?'
'I hope I haven't blown it.'
'You haven't blown it.'
'It's been months. Hen . . .'
'I know. Same for me.'
'When?'
'Oh, last summer. One of the nurses, spur of the moment sort of thing. Nothing to get too excited about.'

I stare, excited, at the details of her dress. This moment after coming is like a mild illness, a meld of numbness, loss, a salty pain, and a chance to feel very sorry for myself. Part of me goes soft inside her, in tiny frequent twitches, until it's guesswork where I end and she begins. And someone wants to know who this person was, this nameless nurse who could get so far after one night's work, just by being confident and sexy and knowing what to say and when, and whether it counts as more proof that seven years' waiting is one way of doing it, if you're a short-haired fool who can never say what he really means.

'How d'you feel?' says Anna, arms loose around my neck.

'I don't know.' I breathe. 'Last night you were so distant, I really thought this was never going to happen. I thought you were going to tell me you didn't want to get involved. And now . . . It's like she planned it all.'

'Maybe she did. Maybe,' she leans forward and whispers it close to my ear, 'this is exactly what she wants.'

'That's what Ali said.'

'Don't feel guilty, Finn. She's doing the same thing with Tony, remember?'

'It's not doing it I feel guilty about. It's how much I want it. I don't ever want this to end.'

'Nor do I.'

Something in her voice leaves me hanging. And this silence that follows: I don't know whether to fill it or wonder what it means.

'Do I mean anything to you?'

'Of course you do, Finn. You're the man of my dreams.'

She seems to grow tighter around me, then relaxes again.

'Tell me about this dress.'

She sits back and shows herself, adjusting her bare weight on my thighs.

'It's my seduction dress. I use it for seducing people.'

'You wear nothing underneath and wait to see their faces when they find out?'

'That's the general idea.'

'Does it work?'

'You tell me. I've never worn it before.'

'Take it off.'

She looks past me at the wall. Her lips move, surface traces of thought too deep for me. She unclips two more buttons, crosses hands in front and lifts it over her head in a single elastic movement. She looks down at the body it reveals, frowning, her mouth turned down.

'I've put on some flab since you last knew me.'

'You're beautiful.'

'It's a body. It does the job.'

She is not the first woman I have seen. But I've never spent so long trying to imagine what was going on under a cotton dress, never quite believing that the Anna version, in her eventual nakedness, would stare out at me with the same astonished expression, the same crystalline skin, that simple crease between hip and thigh. Maybe that's why I'm growing hard again inside her, now I've discovered the woman inside the dream, and it's time to feel that body in my hands, gaze at it until its shape and colour are burned into my sky, until she realises this should never have happened, pulls her blue dress over her startling nudity and climbs back into her neat doctor's car.

A door slams in the building beneath our feet. Voices on the stairs.

'Shit,' dropping hands from her back.

'Don't go,' squeezing me between her knees.

Ten seconds pass. Twenty. A clattering of hearts.

'Must be the other flat.'

She looks down and parts her lips. Now it's me who's moving, grinding hips beneath hers, planing her crushed buttocks with flattened palms.

'Not like this,' says Anna, closing knees again.

She watches me, teasing, scared. I grab her arse and heave my bones on end. At first she's surprised to find herself up here, all sweat and dizzy flesh, but now she's laughing, clinging on with arms around my neck, shins hooked behind my thighs. I'm headed for the sofa. As she turns for the approach my knees fail and we crash down together on the cushions, still fused at the groin, soppy with laughter.

'Are we there yet?' says Anna, fighting for breath.

And all I can do is start fucking her again, because I've always loved her and always thought of her and now she's here, splayed out like a carved bird on this colourful fabric drape. 'Is it Indian?' she giggles, stroking the fabric with the back of a hand, 'because they get really badly . . .' and I block this with a kiss. So she moves her fingers up onto my back and plays the tips along my buttocks, joyful and tentative and making me want to sneeze in her face. One of us is not keeping time. Of course it's me, because I'm not used to being up here on top with this giddying world-renewing view. She peers over my shoulder and squeezes me between her thighs; I cup my hand beneath her spine, push my other fist against the cushion and lead her on a waltz, just the two of us, drunk and merry and smelling of sweat and cunt and come. We dance past Alison and Andy, past Linden and Zoë, past Hen and Robinson (everyone as naked as we are and gazing with approval and respect), past Cat and Jerry, and when we get to Duncan McGuinness, who is bleeding from multiple wounds, I realise what this night, this dance, means. We're back where we should have been seven years ago, the harbour black and silent beneath the window and our brilliant future in the stars. She'll never have to tell me she doesn't want a relationship; I'll never be crashing through her absence, wondering who she's with if not with me, and if not here then where. And Anna knows this, and it makes her a little sad and frightened, which is why she's looking over at the coffee table, eyes wide and lips apart.

'Where the fuck did that come from?'
'Huh?' I drop down a gear, if that's possible.
'*That* bloody thing!'
I'm looking.
It's a cat.
It is standing by the coffee table, a black cat from nowhere, looking at us in green-eyed awe.
'It must have come in off the balcony.'
'Shoo!' says Anna, shifting her hips half-heartedly. 'Bugger off!'
'It must be Ali's.'
'What's it called?'
'Can't remember. Try something.'
'Kitty! Go away! There's no food for you!'

The cat stays where it is. I'm thrusting again, because I'm a builder at heart and that's what builders do when they're on top of a woman they like. Slowly she turns her gaze away from the cat and back to a point on the ceiling. My hands slide down under her buttocks and ease them together; she squirms deliciously, throat working, toes curling on the backs of my calves. The cat seems to have brought us luck: we've found our rhythm, or at least I've learned to follow hers. The clock reads 00:00. Movement, a black leap, in the corner of my eye. The cat lands on my back with its claws out. 'Leave it,' she hisses. The cat retracts its claws and settles into a furry bomb of some weight in the small of my back. It rides me like a donkey. I can't say I hate it. Because Anna, my love, is coming, twisting her face like a bad actress, digging nails into my buttocks, shoving one or two fingers into the crack of my arse. The cat on my back has the best view of any of us, so you should ask it, not me, about the way the tongue moves in her opening mouth, blood blooms in her chest and leaves her pink and dying in my hands. No, don't ask me, because I have other things on my mind: a loosening of something fluid, some deep internal slippage that turns to a clutching in the groin and a steady surge of power in my nerves; and this time there's no need to think of anything to stop myself coming, except the fact that I love her, love the lips she chews so thoroughly, the blissfully closed eyes; I love her and I want to be with her for ever, and if that noise in her throat sounds like sobbing, it's because she feels the same.

LOT
16

We're at the swimming pool. Our fellow travellers are all back at the hotel. Anna Ballantyne is telling me what she has under the Kandinsky dress. Salt cellars, dessert plates, wooden rocking horses, Edwardian silk scarves ... 'Show me,' says the auctioneer, clinging in desperation to the side. 'Not likely,' says Anna. 'I'm waiting for someone who'll be along any minute. He says he'll give me an on-the-spot valuation.' 'Take it off,' says the auctioneer. Anna sighs and stubs out her cigarette. She stands up, crosses hands across her front and lifts the furry hem. It rises in no particular hurry, inch by inch and colouring from green to black to blue, and the suspense kills him several times over. After two minutes, just as Duncan McGuinness's body is floating ominously to the surface of the pool, her thighs are all visible and the auctioneer can just detect a single pubic hair curling out under the hem. Then the undressing stops. A shrill warbling sound is heard. 'What was that?' says Finn. 'What?' says Anna, becoming colourless against the bushes. 'That,' says Finn. 'It's obvious,' she says. 'What?' says Finn, 'what d'you mean?' But the Anna version is gone, leaving a neatly folded dress at the poolside, and anyone can see there was nothing under the dress when she sat down and there is nothing under it now.

The warbling stops. A voice is speaking into his ear.

'Ten twenty-five. Japan is dining. America sleeps. And England? Outstaying her welcome again.'

He says What? She says You heard. He says When? Eleven, she

says. He looks around. And all that is dream stands apart from all that is not dream – trembles, bleaches, stirs itself into oblivion – and shows that the woman who disappeared is asleep in the bed beside him: strands of hair over her face, cheek puffed against a pillow, more heartstoppingly real than any lot that ever passed under his hammer in a hot crowded room.

'What time did we come to bed?' Brown eyes twitch open.

'About four. We finished the champagne then crashed out on the sofa.'

She pushes up on an elbow and leans at me with sleepy eyes. Her kiss is deliberate, reassuring. Regrets? Second thoughts? A breast trembles in sunlight. It's her it's her it's her.

'How d'you feel?'

'Magic,' she yawns. 'Magic is not the word.'

Minutes we lie there, bodies waking and minds unfurling, and then she gets up. I watch her through the doorway of the en suite, passing in and out of sight, until the door is pushed to. I hear the toilet lid going up, the cistern emptying and filling. She comes out holding a green towel over her chest. She goes out onto the landing and returns with her holdall, dumps it on the bed and starts rooting through with one hand. 'Oh bugger me,' she says, drops the towel to free both hands and gives herself to my eyes. The part of my brain raised on French films and door-crack glimpses into my sister's room clicks into action and shows me its dearest image: the face that appears when a woman steps out of her clothes, whose expression never did anything but dare me to be more than I was, but now recognises me like an old friend. Yet it's not What she looks like that excites me so much as Who: and if I was so in love with the idea of her that the woman herself got less than she deserved, it's because I never saw the details behind the idea: a certain sleepiness in the way the fruits quiver and sway; a streak of dried spunk, like the track left by a snail, on the white inside of a thigh.

'You're beautiful, Dr Ballantyne.'

'Thanks. Why is it I can never find anything in this bag?'

She gives up and goes back into the bathroom. The tube over the mirror flickers on. I'm out of bed and coming after her with ambitious flesh, praying she'll still be there when I reach her, thanking every passing angel when she is. She turns and feeds her arms through mine, crushing breasts into my ribs and tickling my

thigh with her gorse. Her it's her it's her it's.
'Last night was amazing, Finn.'
'Mmm. Specially the cat.'
She sniggers. 'God yeh, the cat.'
'I remembered his name. Limpet.'
'It was funny.'
'Glad you remember it.'
'Of course I remember it. It was the best sex I've ever had.' She straightens her back and brushes my thighs with her fingers. 'I mean that.'

What can I do but blush like a bride? When I've stopped feeling quite so pleased with myself, I put my smile away and ask her a question. I ask if she still feels like she did one moonlit night down at McGuyver Point, when she told me she didn't feel she was really Here, that all this was temporary, a rehearsal for a real life that was yet to begin.

'No, Finn. This is real. Last night was what I've been looking for for really a long time.'

When Ali comes we explain about the champagne, endure her knowing grins, and take our places in the sunlight. Anna's excellent mood is only improved by finding her car intact. She drives us through hungover streets, past limping dogs and wheeling crisp packets and young professionals on their way home from corner shops with thick newspapers and bread. We talk about what it might be like to live here, once we've made the changes that will set us both free, and it frightens us more than we thought.

A pack of cigarettes lies on the dashboard. I offer them as if they were mine. 'I've given up,' she says, shaking her head. 'Since when?' 'Since last night.' I wind down the window and drop the box into the breeze. Anna can't find her sunglasses. We bicker about music: Anna loves U2 and REM and claims the one early Genesis album she heard was completely unlistenable. I can live with that. Last night is in me like a piece of velvet I can't help stroking, and I'm already thinking about what happens next, once I've told Hen that her new tattoo was quite unnecessary because I'll never be putting that part of me inside her again, and the sooner we call time on this ongoing mistake the better for all concerned.

'Yesterday was quite a day.'

She's almost singing. 'I'm glad it all worked out.'

'Well, in some ways it did.'

'Only some?' She looks across and her smile is sly. 'I've no complaints!'

'I found out some pretty awful things.'

'Oh, thanks a lot! I wouldn't call them awful!'

She can't have forgotten what I told her on the way here. 'Maybe not awful. But it's not every day you find out your mother was having an affair.'

'When you said it was quite a day,' she laughs, 'I thought you were talking about last night! I mean, it's not every day I go to bed with a complete stranger who I've only just met!'

Perhaps I'll shut up now. She doesn't want to discuss anything but us, to congratulate ourselves on what people have been doing for centuries, or just to marvel at her own good taste.

'I told you what Ali said.'

'About that bloke your mum was seeing?' She gives the steering wheel an impatient tap. 'Try not to think about it, Finn. It's not going to do you any good.'

But I can't not think about it. 'I feel like I have to find out. Then I can leave it and we can get on with our lives.'

'You mean, so we can get on with having brilliant sex!' She kills the smile and sighs. 'Okay. So what do you think happened?'

but her interest is a sham. It's the way she always smiled at my jokes, not because she found them funny, but because she thought she should. I tell her anyway: about the Silk Twister with the faint but unmistakeable expression, about the collector's shop in Etruria where she had gone to get it valued for insurance purposes, and – this new piece, still shining, just slotted into place – about the journey she never finished, the drive across an unfamiliar moor to see the one man she ever really loved.

'That's everything?'

I hum a little tune.

'I'm sorry, Finn, but I don't see the mystery. It was a car crash. You should spend a night in Casualty.'

What's this: an invitation? Will the doctor be there too?

Half an hour later she applies the handbrake and asks: 'Is it always like this?'

I can only call them chickens. There are hundreds of them and they were not here last time I came. My aunt Sarah is trying to corral them into a corner of the yard with a length of bamboo. Mervyn is laid out on a sunlounger on the patio. 'His back's gone again,' says Teri, appearing so promptly from the side of the house that she must have had warning of our coming. Anna is introduced in her blue summer dress; the beaded seat cover has left white ovoid marks on the backs of her thighs. 'Whose are all these?' she says, meaning the birds. 'Sarah brought them,' says Teri, shrinking a bit more each time we meet. 'We were going to build a hen house but then Mervyn's back went and . . .'

'Finn can help,' says Sarah, emerging from the outhouse with a roll of chicken-wire as tall as her. 'If we crack on we can be finished by lunch.'

Anna is called to the kitchen for the usual interview. My white-haired aunt is making short trips into the outhouse and coming out with fencing stakes which she lays in a pre-plotted square on the lawn. She holds them near the base while I bang them in with the hammer.

'These are from the farm. We wanted them to stay in the family.'

'Are they layers?'

She snorts. This aunt of mine was never famous for her chat, but I feel doubly doubtful of getting anything out of her today. I could be somewhere else, shutting down one life and starting up another, instead of standing in an Essex garden trying to charm secrets from the dead earth.

'Hen's taken Robin to her parents' for a couple of days.'

'I know. She told me.'

'She . . . ?' But of course she did. Hen knew I would come here, to ask Sarah why her sister's wedding ring was so tight, and that I'd have to excuse her absence with another unimaginative lie. Forget all possible sightings of Zoë's Peugeot: Hen doesn't need to follow us to know what a prat I can make of myself.

We reach the next stake and Sarah pauses, as though there's something she has to say first.

'Hen's an unusual girl. When we were up in your room the other day, she was looking at Margaret's things with such interest . . . That's Rhubarb. You get to know their markings after a while.'

I'm sort of hoping she'll give me some more on Rhubarb, but then the phone rings inside the house and Teri is on the back step, waving her in.

'Did she . . . did Hen ask you about Mum?'

'She asked about a lot of things.'

'About her ring?'

That look: it is years of unspoken hurt nudged awake by a need to bring the hurt to an end. It both warns me off and invites me in.

By the time Sarah has seen off another long-distance well-wisher, lunch is ready and we're taking our places in the dining room. I can't say I'm enjoying myself. I've a feeling my aunt wants to tell me something, but the unfinished hen house and too many sympathetic phone calls have not done wonders for her mood. Plus I'm starting to worry about Hen. If she hadn't told Sarah where she was going, I might have believed it, but now . . . And I've no idea why the kid has to be involved. I've decided to ask Anna to phone the Threadgolds after lunch, pretend she's from the clinic and find out when Hen can be expected back. But Anna just makes polite conversation and the meal drags on. As soon as the coffee steams into view on a metal tray, Sarah announces that she and I are going outside to finish the hen house. Since Anna is about to set out her own personal theories of St Mary's Disease, they hardly seem to know we're gone.

'So what do you know about the ring?' Her old hands span the base of a stake while I thump another inch of it into the earth. In the hour and a half we've been inside, the sky has clouded over and is sending down more and more fat drops of rain.

'It was tight. Anna tried it on. That's why we were at Dad's.'

'And did Hen tell you to look at it?'

'Yeh. Why?'

The question seems to miss. But when she speaks again her voice sounds closer, like I'd passed some sort of test, as if she'd moved on from where we were an hour and a half ago and somehow brought me with her.

'Twenty years is a long time to keep quiet, Finn. Sooner or later things have to be said.'

But she's not saying them. I wait. She cuts chicken-wire. Hen, from whatever vantage point, laughs.

'Do you remember,' I try, 'that day we came up to stay with you after they'd had a row, and Dad followed us? It was really hot.'

'Of course I remember. I think that was the first time I realised just what a mistake Margaret had made.'

'Do you remember what she was wearing?'

'She was wearing a green woollen dress. I remember thinking she must be sweltering in that thing.'

We move to the next stake. The wood splits and crumples under my onslaught.

'Is it on any of the photos?'

'Try the wooden box. That's where we put them all.'

'It's locked.'

'Oh.' She rocks back on her heels and looks thoughtful again. 'You know the thick envelope where we put all the business notes? The key's in there.'

She knows what I'm going to ask now. She sits back on the lawn, hands stretched out behind her, and stares at the perimeter shrubs. I sit down next to her, picking with nervous fingers at the grass.

'I need to know what happened.'

'I know you do. I wish I could tell you. All we knew was that they were having this long weekend in Stafford. She rang to say she was coming to see us, and next thing we know there's a call from Peter saying she's been in an accident. One thing about death: the news travels fast.'

'You say she *phoned* you?'

'That's right.'

'Where from?'

'No idea. A payphone, some café on the A34. She must have got lost.'

'So she was coming to see you?'

I dreamt how this would be. No words, just guileless piano music, answering my questions in three-quarter time.

'She said she needed to see me. She sounded . . . well, she sounded upset.'

'So she wasn't going to see Mike Browning?'

She winces, shakes her head.

'You think it was something to do with Dad?'

'He's still your father, Finn. And I've probably said enough.'

She hasn't finished. But the question has to be right.

'The statue . . .'

She breathes painfully and stares at the turf between her feet. 'I don't understand what she saw in that thing. Your father bought it for her the year they got married. For years she'd been meaning to take it to Etruria to get it valued.' She glances up at the rain. 'You're the auctioneer, Finn. You know the appeal of a quick sale when you're trying to forget about something.'

'Is that what she was doing that day?'

'What does Peter say? He was there.'

'He says they went shopping in Stafford on the Monday morning, then she was going to drive up to Etruria in the afternoon while he was watching the test match. She must have thought she'd drop in on you on the way.'

'Test match? In April?'

Perhaps it's listening to all those Tony Banks keyboard solos that makes me so slow off the mark. I mutter more inanities while one of Rhubarb's friends investigates the nutritional content of my leg.

'Well, I can't see why your father would lie about that sort of thing.'

This is the game we're playing. No one wants to do anything as uncivilised as blaming anyone, so we chase each other round the garden like a pair of butterflies, getting steadily drenched. Sarah flits out at me from behind a hydrangea.

'Do you know how they found her?'

'In the car with her head against the steering wheel. Is that right?'

'It was very peaceful. Mr Bown who found her actually thought she was asleep. She was wearing a brown-and-green frock and leather sandals. There was only one item of jewellery.'

She doesn't need to say what that was.

'But do you know where they found it?' she says.

'On her finger?'

A smile ghosts it across her face. 'I went with Peter to identify her. He didn't seem to notice it and I'm sure no one mentioned it at the time. Of course he wanted to take it off and keep it. Don't ask me why, because he never even looked at any of her other things.'

I wait patiently for the information. Even in this steamy gloom she seems to be squinting against the light.

'It was on the knuckle. Not where you'd expect it to be, on the fleshy part between the knuckles. But actually on the middle joint, tight on the bone.'

'Like she was trying to get it on but she couldn't because it was too tight?'

'Or the opposite.'

'You think she was trying to take it off?'

'I . . .'

'That's why she lost control of the car. Because it was so tight.'

She takes her time. 'The ring was tight, yes.'

'So why didn't she just get it altered? You can get rings altered.'

She's wondering how to tell me this.

'Do you remember – no, of course you don't – what the weather was like that day?'

'It was raining. The roads were slippery and she skidded out of control. That's what it said in the report.'

'It *had* rained, briefly. There was a shower around lunchtime. I don't mean that.' Her wise eyes frown. 'I mean it was hot. It was really hot. Don was walking around in just a pair of swimming trunks.' She looks at me with sudden distaste. 'You know what happened to your mother's hands in the heat.'

'No.'

'They used to swell up. Her hands and her feet. That's why she couldn't get the ring off. Margaret *hated* the heat. She couldn't play the piano, which meant of course that she couldn't work. She couldn't even wear her normal shoes. We had to keep a footbath for her at the farm so she could cool off.'

Photographs found at Brink Farm: woman, late twenties, in yellow bikini and seventies hairstyle, smiling against a canvas of green sea. I ask my aunt how visits to the Costa del Something fit into our heat-shy story.

'Finn, she *hated* those holidays. It was all Peter's idea to go away. Even when she was pregnant and already swelling up like a balloon, he . . . She used to ring up from the airport in tears.'

'I didn't know.'

'Of course you didn't. It was none of our business. Don said to say anything would only cause trouble between you and Peter. So we kept it to ourselves.'

'And I suppose Mike Browning kept quiet too?'

Now there's a new pain in the lines of her face: hotter, deeper than anything I've seen. 'I don't know what Peter's been telling you, Finn. Mike Browning was Brian's golf partner. He was the one who had the contacts that got her doing *Hide and Seek*. She met him once in 1973 and that, as far as I know, was it.'

'So she wasn't having an affair?'

'She found him charming, I suppose. But risking everything you value for something like that – I don't think that was your mother at all.'

She waits, tears brimming, as the belief that I know what I'm talking about walks out on me for the last time. 'I know he's your father, Finn, but she was also my sister and I think I've stood up for him long enough. It was seeing all her things the other day that did it: her scarf, her reading glasses, that handbag she bought the morning she died. The way he bundled her into a box and forgot about her, as though she was something he'd grown out of, hoping we'd all grow out of her as well. And now I see that look on Henrietta's face, going through her things so carefully that you'd think Margaret was still standing there in the doorway, and I realise we were just as wrong as he was. Your mother was no saint. She made mistakes and she didn't always take the blame for them. She never ever did what she was told. But to be forgotten like that, boxed up in the attic like a pile of old clothes . . . We all killed her, Finn, we all have a box like that in the attic; we all said nothing when we could have said something, and there's no worse kind of murder than that.'

We're driving again, through hardening rain, along the A120 to Bishop's Stortford, then fast new roads cut through limestone scarps and ancient green fields: Cambridge, Huntingdon, Kettering, west and slightly northwards across the flat midriff of our country, under dreaming pylons and grey cloud streaked with daylight, to where the M6 splits away from the M1 and continues west. The temperature drops. Every second the wipers draw their blades across a clean new world; every second the rain comes down as quickly as before, explodes and merges into quivering slicks, chased up to the top of the screen to be pushed back down on the return stroke. After Junction 9 for Wednesbury, where the headsetted occupants of the RAC Control Centre look down on another sluggish Sunday afternoon, the traffic will ease, the car in front will pull away, and the North will announce itself with waddling lorries and an army of German cars. The colour of houses will change. Life will shrink to fit people's expectations of it; old routines will pull us apart. I'll notice the spot on her forehead and the broken vein in her cheek; she'll ask for a cigarette and find I've thrown them away. And because we're both having trouble keeping up with what happened last night, when the clocks stopped just long enough to show how much catching up we had to do, she'll need to be reminded – not once: twice – to take the exit for Etruria, and not continue on her usual route, up the M6 to Didsbury, leafy closes and home.

'It's very quiet in here,' says Anna.

Rain. 'Was that a question?'

'I thought you were going to tell me what your aunt said.'

'I thought you were bored of all that.'

She chews her lip. 'Now *that's* the sort of car I want,' she blurts, meaning the black 7-series BMW that has just pulled in ahead of us,

and suddenly, against all desire or understanding, with heat in my head and an ache in my chest like a cold sponge being squeezed, I've got myself thinking about Hen. Brave Hen, foolish Hen, who would not be seen dead in a BMW unless she was stealing it to teach someone a lesson. Is it so wrong to think we should be back there trying to find her, not driving so fast the other way?

'You're worried about Robinson, you mean. Anyway, you should've brought the computer. She's most probably sent a message saying where she is.'

Her eyes flit between mirror and road.

'Sarah said she – Hen – seemed weird when she saw her at the funeral.'

'Are you surprised? Having your internal organs tattooed on your abdomen is not exactly normal behaviour.'

I wish I hadn't told her that. She flicks the indicator on but stays in the middle lane, waiting.

'Sometimes,' says Anna, 'I have to agree with those people in California. It seems to me like no one gets this thing who doesn't really want it.'

'You think she chose it? Bored of sanity so let's try the wild stuff for a bit?'

'From what I can see she wasn't exactly stable in the first place. Look, I've told you what I think of this Bliss thing. As a doctor I think: okay, so-and-so's got a problem and they need help. As a human being I don't know what to think.'

'Yeh well, let's leave it at that. I have *some* loyalty.'

But Anna doesn't leave it at that.

'What you've got to understand, Finn, is that there's more than one way of looking at all this. You've got a thing we call St Mary's Disease and you've got a thing we call Bliss. St Mary's Disease means a particular set of basically brain symptoms, too much of this and not enough of that, the sort of stuff you've seen on the scans. Bliss is what happens on the psychological level: the effect it has on *people*, the problems with making sense of objects and remembering where you are in space and time. So when the brain has SMD, the mind has Bliss. Yes? But so can it also work the other way round. The mind can have Bliss before the brain has St Mary's Disease. So it's very traumatic and all that, but in the end it comes down to what the person believes is going on. It's a sort of self-fulfilling prophecy: if you think you have it, then you have it. Simple as that.'

'I didn't hear you saying this to Sarah.'

'Like I said, Finn, just because they're psychological causes doesn't mean they can't have physical effects. It's no good pretending the mind is some magic thing which has nothing to do with the real world. Your uncle was unlucky. If he'd never heard of this thing called Bliss then he most probably would never have thought he had a problem. Bliss never killed anyone: it's the stupid things people do when they think they've got it.'

'That's not much help.'

'What's no help is when people are afraid to express their opinions. Anyway, you're going to have to talk to her. I'm going back to Dids. I'll come over as soon as you've sorted it out.'

That's it: she's satisfied. For a moment I'd forgotten who's to blame for all this.

'So what else did your aunt say?'

She goes on watching the road, one eye on the speedo, the other checking the mirror for police. No, she *is* the police: she may have let me inside her body with gay abandon, but she won't let me feel anything she doesn't think I ought to be feeling. So I've no choice but to tell her: about the ring and whereabouts on the finger it was found, about Margaret Causley née Wilton's well-known aversion to the heat, about the rushed phone call to Sarah, promising a visit she never lived long enough to make.

'So she was trying to take the ring off?' She's interested now. 'She must have been upset about something. I mean, *really* upset.'

'Really upset.'

'Yes. I mean, what would you do if you thought your marriage was over?'

But I've already thought of this. I would try to rid myself of the one thing that reminded me of it, particularly if it was a five-and-a-half-inch Staffordshire figurine with some value as a collector's item. And if I really thought it was over I'd lose the ring as well. 'But I think I'd wait till I'd got wherever I was going.'

'Well I think that depends how upset you are.' She gives a cleverer-than-you smirk. 'If you were *really* upset you might not be able to wait. Rings are very powerful things.' She holds up her left hand to show the silver signet ring on the end. 'My dad gave me this a few weeks before he died. If I ever take it off for any reason I feel totally lost until it's back on. It could easily work the other way. You get to the point where things are such utter shit you just can't bear to have the thing on you any longer. Maybe your mum thought that.'

'But what could be that bad? They were supposed to be on holiday. What do people do to piss each other off so much?'

'I'm sure Hen's got some idea about that.'

The mill is deserted. Zoë has gone. Jack is down in London with his Latin-speaking friends. Kumar is cooking macrobiotic Sunday lunch in a dingy flat in Manchester with the football on in the background. In the upstairs corridor, a red light on the answering machine tells me a message is waiting. I thought someone might have slipped a note under my door to explain this deathly quiet, but then I remember that I never slipped a note under anyone's door, never took the time to explain my new sleeping habits to the people who deserved to know, so their silence is all I can expect.

She bites a nail in the doorway while I switch on the computer. There are 136 new messages, all from the same address. The first is timed at 12.47 yesterday; the latest came at 3.19 this afternoon. I read the first then scroll through at speed. Phrases fall out at random, ideas without context, mental smithereens. i am five feet six inches tall with fine yellow hair. i am an englishwoman. i am different things to different people. Then: a few more hefty history books and i find out what all this is about. Then: he is lying on the bed. his eyes are closed. his hair is white and brown. i just wanted to get to know him better. Then: why is the silk twister smiling? Then: did she have to be called anna? couldn't she be called melissa or jemima or something stupid like that?

Anna walks through and sits down on the bed.

'What does it say?'

'It says they're alive.'

She starts on another nail. 'She knows, doesn't she? About us.'

'She knows. She knew before we did.'

The phone rings. After four bursts the machine in the corridor switches on. It's Einar. He's drunk. A TV provides covering fire. He says something about the Icelandic chess team, damp squids deserting the Fridge of Dreams, then the line goes dead. I switch off the machine and rewind. The other voice on there is nervous, uncertain of trusting its message to a machine.

'Finn? It's Sarah. There was something else I didn't mention. They didn't go to Stafford on their own. Peter said they felt sorry for her because it was just after Brian had run off with the American woman. They stayed at their usual hotel. That's it. It probably means nothing, but I thought it might help if . . .'

Anna lies back on the bed and stares up at the ceiling. The auctioneer sits at the window, an index finger at play on a cheekbone, musing over an empty street. Mrs Enderby, her dogs, the traffic wardens, the ducks on the pond: all rounded up and tortured to death.

'I bet she hates me,' says Anna. 'I know I would.'

But the auctioneer isn't listening. He stands up and goes over to a shelf. He takes down the cardboard box marked MARGARET CAUSLEY: 1947–1977 and begins to unpack it onto the desk. He finds:

a leather handbag with guarantee label attached
a turquoise polyester headscarf

a necklace of blue plastic beads
a gold ladies' watch with gold-plated elastic-linked strap

His face ripples and settles. What did *she* do, when she found this watch in the glove compartment of the blue Cortina, coming back from her shopping trip with her hair still wet from the recent rain? Or did her blindness last until she stood in the doorway of their hotel room, unbuttoning her sage-green raincoat and wondering why the TV was on and no one around? How long did it take to recognise who it belonged to, and make the short trip down the corridor to try one particular door? And there see something that made her forget why she had come, that made the blood quit her brain and begin its final journey back to her heart, a sight that made her stuff the watch into her coat pocket (to be found, years later, by her inquiring son); leave her sobs on the landing, her tears on the stairs, her breath on the mirror as she gets into the car to drive: drive, in brown-and-green dress and leather sandals, her sobs keeping the rhythm in the absence of a tune, heart sick and pounding for a release which comes, which comes. Drive: too fast for these country roads; too fast for trying to remove a gold ring from a heat-swollen finger; too fast for this heel-dragging earth.

His voice is calm. Those are not tears in his eyes.

'You've seen it before. She bought another one exactly the same and never stopped going on about it. She was wearing it yesterday, playing with the strap.'

Anna's mouth is opening. He wants to tell her more, ask if she too can hear the song that's playing, but then someone smiles at him from the doorway and all at once he is years behind.

Lot 16: **Gold ladies' watch** (Müller of Lausanne) with self-winding mechanism and elastic strap allowing it to fit any wrist. Popular in the 1970s with the ex-wives of shipping magnates, now sadly overlooked.

LOT
17

They find Robinson on Monday morning, in the favourite restaurant in his three-and-a-half-year-old world, the McDonald's on the A14 near Huntingdon, where, by some obliging coincidence, his father and his father's new lover almost stopped on their way home the previous afternoon. You can't miss it: set high up at the top of a slip road, disguised as a red-and-grey flying saucer from a 1950s B-movie, with a radial passageway leading to the restaurant at the hub. They ate chicken nuggets and fries. Then Hen must have told him she was popping to the loo, but instead of coming back to pick up their life together where they left off, she went straight outside to the car, got in and drove off in one of four possible directions. The staff watched him for twenty minutes and then someone went over. On the table, amid crumpled serviettes and cartoon packaging, was a piece of card with two phone numbers written in red felt-tip. The first was the private number for Big Kimberley. The second was Hen's family home in Fleet and, hearing nothing but a recorded message from the second floor of Big Kimberley, it was Tom and Jan who got into their maroon BMW and drove up to Huntingdon to pick him up. As there was still no sign of Hen by the time they arrived, and as the answering machine on the second floor was repeating the same message well past the point of boredom, they had no choice but to take him back with them to Fleet, unlock the room at the back of the house they had always intended would be his, and set him up amid blue wallpaper, dinosaur mobiles and two big windows with an interesting but untraumatic view.

And where was Finn Causley, while the answering machine in the corridor was switching on and off, having committed nothing to tape except imperious bleeps and samples of Tom Threadgold's voiceless wrath? Was he slouched on a bench in the park, having recently taken up smoking again after a brief respite, trying to find the sleep he failed to find the night before? Was he back on the motorway, writing blistering speeches in his head for his next confrontation with the Greylag Two? Was he in bed with his new lover, a deliberate stranger who looked wonderful in the shower, attempting to improve on their performance of Saturday night? None of these things. He was in an airless terrace on Jubilee Road, net curtains in neighbouring houses still twitching from the arrival of the sky-blue van, in a downstairs room where no sun ever tried to shine, rooting through cupboards and drawers, cardboard boxes stuffed with curtain fabric and children's games, for anything that might justify his effort in next month's sale. Einar is with him, his piggy eyes thoroughly bloodshot, the stale whisky in his veins adding effort to every move.

'So did she . . . ?' He rolls eyes, raises hands above his head and makes his oily cormorant wail. A cat slides from a corner to stare.

'She wasn't yawning, Einar.'

He gives that lost look. I should toss him the details, every gasping squelching fact, so he can have his chance to say he never really fancied her, he actually thought her rather boring, all that chasing around the swimming pool was for her entertainment alone. But things have happened since my improbable night with Anna Ballantyne, and I'm in no mood to brag about what he seems to be able to guess for himself.

'This is why I am drinking all weekend. Because I know what you and little Anna are up to. I see her in that blue dress with no panties underneath.'

We work on in silence, adding the smell of our sweat and last night's garlic to the general death-fug we have intruded upon. Nothing speaks but signs of hurried abandonment: objects laid out on tables in a last attempt to make them yawn out their secrets, drawers tipped out onto carpet, photographs and letters sown thickly on an upstairs bed. As red plastic crates pile up in the hallway, I hear the latest developments from home. Linden caught Jack loading some boxes into his jeep, repeated his accusations of theft, and heard Jack suggest he'd be better off concentrating on trying to find a girlfriend with the normal complement of limbs. Einar is expecting trouble. As he talks, I'm supposed to be calling out items for him to write down on his clipboard, but this doesn't seem to be happening. I've become that vanished owner on his last trip around the house, staring at things without understanding, putting them back without learning anything at all.

'You are thinking about Hen. I know this. You are wondering: What in the name of Baby Jesus am I gonna do when Hen comes home?'

Last night, while I was trying to persuade her not to go back to Didsbury but to stay one more night in my arms, Anna looked like the only thing that could protect me from what I knew. I'd spent the best part of an hour staring at Joy's watch, the conspicuous trinket whose message I'd been blind to for twenty years, as if I could discern the style of my father's treachery in the faint scratches in the gold. Why hadn't I seen it before? Why hadn't I *understood*? I heard it again, that howling sound from low down in the back of the head, a hot drilling roar, like the pigs I heard slaughtered in Goa, screaming and screaming behind a palm-mat fence and me wondering how anything could take so long to die. 'Do you know you're doing that?' she said. 'What?' 'Humming.' She had found Hen's self-portraits, charcoal on Daler board, and seemed to want to talk about this other cunt, so deftly portrayed at the mirror, to fence it off as a slightly obscene historical curiosity with no bearing on Us or This. But I'd made it quite clear that she wasn't going to get through to me, and no matter how much I wanted her, how great my faith that one more night of Finn and Anna could banish all our harm, her car was waiting, her keys were changing hands and she could think of no more reasons to stay.

'You don't think it was a mistake?' I said, holding her by the car.

'The only way it's going to be a mistake is if you try and pretend it didn't happen. You have to tell her, Finn. Otherwise it won't mean anything at all.'

Lot 17: **Collection of charcoal drawings**, seated female nude, unsigned. Also Polaroid photographs of the artist, naked at a mirror, with striking yellow hair.

I stood in her rising fume cloud until I could taste her smog no longer, then walked across the road to the park. I saw a man sitting with his two sons, down in the valley between two grassy banks, a miniature cricket set, stumps, bat and bails, discarded at their feet. The older boy was throwing a tennis ball into the air and catching it. A plastic carrier was blowing away in the breeze. I guessed the younger boy was supposed to be chasing after it and packing up the cricket gear, because the more he clung to his father's neck the more the man tried to push him away. 'Help me, Dad,' this boy was saying. And all the man did was punch him, hard, much harder than you should hit a kid that size, and again, because he wasn't doing what he was supposed to be doing, or he was doing it the wrong way. It made me think that I too would like to be hitting someone, the more innocent the better, preferably someone who didn't deserve hitting at all. The kid began to wail. Was that Finn down there, the tearful child who went on clinging to what was hurting him, hoping he might catch a whisper of his mother's love in the spaces between his father's lies? Or could I be the father, the balding thug who could only show what he thought of love by acting it out with his fists? Answer: I was both. But I was also the person who sat by and did nothing, too lazy or too afraid to intervene. The howling again, the dry machine-like howl, so loud and unrelenting that I was having to make this noise in my throat just to blot it out.

'Stop that fucking foolish noise,' says Einar, and today, in a death-scented terrace on Jubilee Road, I'm still doing it: humming a song whose tune I can only guess at, because the person who taught it to me died before I could learn it properly, and is still dying even now.

We load the crates into the van and drive back to Big Kimberley. The light on the upstairs machine is flashing, but someone has hung up several times without leaving a message. Of the latest messages from Hen, one in particular seems to hang there on the screen. tony and i are no longer friends. he left because i wouldnt sleep with him. i told him i was saving myself for my twin tree. as for the kid, i looked after him for ages and he never even said thank you. thats men for you, i suppose.

I hit reply. If what she says is true, and I was as wrong about her and Tony as I've been about everything else, then ... But the question makes no sense. If I'm wrong about this then I'm wrong about everything. If I'm so far wrong about the things that really matter then it doesn't really matter what I say. My fingers choose the keys. The words that seemed so fitting in my head look wet and fatuous on the screen. `I'm sorry`, it begins, but because I've no intention of saying what I'm sorry about, it's not the sorry it would like to be. It's the sorry of the Englishman who bumps into someone in the street, when there was no harm done and no one at fault, just the need to say something, if only to acknowledge the occasion on which Something Occurred. It's an apology that admits no blame or wrongdoing, the reflexive politeness of someone who has no idea what he has done wrong. `I'm sorry`, it goes, `but when you say you didn't sleep with him, do you mean you didn't fuck him? Or were you so busy fucking you couldn't actually get any sleep?`

The phone rings. Tom Threadgold's anger, captive in his neatly shaved throat since the day he first let a suede-headed builder into his family home, hisses through three small holes in the plastic at my ear. He doesn't want to know where I've been all morning. He wants to know what has happened to his daughter, his unstable, vulnerable daughter who I was supposed to be guarding with my life. I can hear a woman shouting in the background, and something in the pitch and tone makes me think it must be Hen, and they've found her, confused, angry perhaps, but alive. But it's Jan, not Hen, and here's the anger I always imagined behind those horsey grins and brimming eyes. 'You might be interested to know about your son,' says Tom, and tells me about events in McDonald's, of Hen's second disappearance, their one-and-a-half-hour mercy dash around the M25 with their engine tuning itself four thousand times a second. He says it looks as though the little chap's going to be staying with them for a few days. I can't think of any arguments. My voice is probably too calm. 'Can I talk to him?' 'NO!' howls Jan, collapsing onto something soft and patterned and sliding into gin-laced sobs. But grandfathers play fair, and a moment later he's here, mumbling, not speaking into the receiver, but breathing at least.

'Hi, kid.'

'H'lo.'

'We're calling the police!' shrieks Jan. I guess they've left the front door open, because I can hear traffic, or heavy artillery, or nuclear meltdown, beyond and behind everything else.

'Mo went to the toilet and never come back. She's gone dead again, in't she?'

'No she's not. She's all right.'

His breaths are heavy. I never thought he'd learned how to sigh.

'Are you a bad man, Dad?'

'What do you think?'

'I dunno.'

We both try for better answers. In the fake mahogany background Tom and Jan are planning their retribution. It will have halogen lights and a fifty-megawatt speaker system. Everyone will know who is to blame.

'We're gonna make some paper. With silk. When Mo comes home.'

'Good idea. We can all have a go.'

'But we're not gonna be in Big Kibberley, are we? Because . . .'

Now there's silence in their lovely Hampshire home. A family holds its breath. Glassy eyes, the smug smile on her furry puckered mouth.

'Mo says everything's different. What's different? When's she coming back?'

But this time I have nothing to say.

I've often had the feeling that the peace at Big Kimberley was a sort of strenuous pose, that things were happening off-camera that the most vigilant director could know little about, and that one day the hand holding the camera would slip, a shocked silence would descend from the translucent ceiling, and it would all flood into focus in the shape of a horrible truth. Last year we thought we'd done our grieving well; we thought the tears we'd shed for Roxanne, in small groups scattered around the second floor, would be the last; but since then it's been hard to escape the feeling that one of us would one day say the wrong thing, and we'd lose another friend and team member, maybe two. But I wasn't expecting it tonight, on top of the message from Hen, the phone conversation with Robinson, and my brief telephone interview with DC Clements of Hampshire Police, in which I explained why I didn't actually know the registration number of the car in which Hen made her escape, but if DC Clements were actually to phone this number (Zoë's) she could actually ask the owner of the car for herself.

'And if we hear anything you'll be first to know,' I told the plain-clothed wunderkind, fistfuls of fingers crossed behind my back.

We're in the Chapter House, panting off a massive bowl of Jack's Sicilian pasta and several bottles of rustic red. Pharaoh Sanders is making terrifying noises five thousand miles away in a smoke-filled basement. I've hardly eaten. Anna is only here because I swore I'd messaged Hen requesting a meeting as soon as she was ready to give herself up. Earlier, in the park, she was testing my sincerity with the bluntest probes, seeing how far I would go in Hen's defence, how much of the blame for this mess I was prepared to take upon myself. I said I didn't want to discuss Hen any further. 'I'm not surprised,' she said. 'People never want to discuss anything which forces them to make an emotional decision about anything.' I reminded her of what she'd said in an Italian restaurant some seven years before: about how, before making a choice between heart and head, you should wait until all the evidence is in. 'What evidence do you need?' She sat on the bench and lit a Silk Cut.

'I thought you were giving up.'

'As you know, Finn, some things aren't so easy to give up.'

I'd never seen her like this before. I told her that.

'That's because all you've ever done is stare at me from a distance as if I was going to disappear in a puff of smoke if you got any closer. You never really tried to get to know me.'

'You're right. I'm . . .'

'I don't see why you're sorry.' She stared deliberately at the sunset, having sensible thoughts.

It was better after that. We discussed the business: I told her about today's house clearance on Jubilee Road; how it all began, how I became a junk merchant on the back of the same disease she was trying to understand; how, in a sick kind of way, we both served the same employer. She seemed never to have thought about what I did for a living. 'Don't you feel a bit criminal, going into people's homes like that and taking their stuff?' I remembered her surprise at stumbling across the storage bays, how she must have wondered what Finn was up to, whether he thought he could stand for every person who ever lived by hoarding up what they'd left behind. I tried to bend her to the thrill of the auction: the sea of expectant faces, the first tentative bids, the constant motion of objects and prices, the way a good sale has the festive feel of a major race meeting, except that people are betting on inanimate objects which never go anywhere except back into the past. At the centre I placed myself, resplendent in green with infra-red eyes, coaxing the price upwards like a feather until it reached its true level and the biro pinned it to the wall. This, I explained, is where the jokes come from, the need to please the Bickertons and Bootherstones of this earth; how if I talked so little on non-sale days it was because I was saving my breath for that auction world; and she listened, and little by little forgot her doubts about the morality of my profession and lost herself in half a smile. I kissed her, for the first time since yesterday, on the bench by the tennis courts, just as Miss Parry-David was passing with her pram.

Now that she has some idea of what goes on in this cluttered palace of ours, she can witness the vitriol that's sloshing around between Linden and Jack as if it was just another part of the show. According to the blackboard above the table, the odds on it coming to blows by the end of the evening have shortened to 5–2. Jack wants to talk about his opera; Kumar thinks there's little point now Zoë's gone. Linden is trying to perform surgery on the TV, which hasn't worked properly since a flying Einar touched down on it six weeks ago. It doesn't help that Jack is firing a potato gun at him with considerable accuracy.

'Can you stop that please,' says Linden, picking up the remote control and failing to get a picture again.

'He's a spy,' says Jack. 'You know what happens to spies.'

Einar appears in the doorway with a pair of knickers pulled down over his face. 'I find them on the stairs,' puffs the white cotton where his mouth used to be. 'Someone here is not wearing any is my believe-you-me conclusion.'

'No wait, Linden,' Jack is saying. 'Let's be friends. Look, I've written you a poem. It's called *Sir Linden Smeglund and the Shagge that Scarpered.*'

'That's not my name,' says Linden.

'Oh, but it *is*,' says Jack. 'You see, you don't really exist until someone has written a poem about you. And if they happen to write Smeglund rather than Smedlund, then that's your entelechy.'

A piece of A4 emerges from his waistcoat pocket and unfolds

before our eyes. He retrieves his Lennon glasses from another pocket and hooks them behind his ears. Kumar puts an end to Pharaoh Sanders and closes the linen press doors. Jack clears his throat, lifts his chin and basks in imagined applause.

> 'Sythen swete Sonia hat her siker knyghte spurned,
> And he on ful hyghe heles hastened hat
> In Ford Mustang in paynte of penis redde
> Thurgh wynde and wylde wederes of the worlde aboute
> To come clene to this aunciain burgh of Print
> Quer luflych lorde, lustige ladies als,
> Did muffen and mulen ful mony a day,
> Wo wohned that wyght that wonne his herte,
> That was fayrest in felle, of flesche and of lyre,
> That ever he syye. Stript woulde he stande
> His peinture her to paynt, his pricke to pamper,
> Bot Zoë loved him not, nor pumped his pipe
>   With blow;
>   Hir lyppes laid no kysses,
>   Hir buttokes gave no show,
>   And quen off she pysses,
>   A-wanken he must go.'

'What d'you think?' says Jack. 'I'm not sure about the break in line ten.'

'Is it supposed to be funny?' says Linden.

'I couldn't say.'

'Well what does everyone think?' he says, rocking back on his heels and glancing angrily around.

Silence and uncomfortable smiles.

'When I was at Oxford . . .' begins Jack.

'Look, you never fucking went to Oxford so why don't you stop fucking pretending?'

This is interesting. He's removing his glasses and nodding to himself.

'You know what's really sad about you, Linden? Now Zoë's gone, not only have you blown your last chance of ever getting your dick sucked, but you seem to have lost your sense of humour as well.'

None of us has ever seen Linden really lose his temper, so when he does we're all looking the right way. First he hurls the remote control against the wall, leaving a dent in the plasterboard which he stares at for several seconds. Then he spins round on his heels, crouches for the instant it takes to get his feet into position beneath him, and leaps across the room at Jack, who goes down in fits of laughter with arms crooked stupidly around his head. Linden is clutching him by the shirt and banging his head against the arm of the sofa. Soft with giggles is Jack. Then he seems to remember where he is, and contrives to roll Linden off the sofa and onto the floor, where his own head collides violently with the table leg. Now they're really fighting, punching each other with wire-muscled arms and groaning like constipated boys. The fish stop swimming to stare. Kumar, who looks like he's been intervening in fights all his life, steps in to break it up. Over by the telescope Dr Ballantyne watches it all with her uncertain gaze. Einar has taken advantage of the diversion to drop his shorts and climb up onto the ledge above her for a better view. He sees Linden over Jack, fists clenched and poodle perm bouncing around his face, quivering and sobbing with rage. Jack is staring at the underbelly of the table and mumbling an inconsequential tune. His lip is bleeding.

'That's it,' goes Linden. 'I can't . . . ffffucking . . .' He storms out of here with writhing lips and blazing eyes, kicking the shelving unit so one of Zoë's statues topples over and smashes on the lino.

Jack doesn't move. Einar is now wearing the mystery knickers and concealing a boyish bulge.

'Was that really necessary?' says Anna.

'He had it coming,' croaks Jack mysteriously.

'Is it true you never went to Oxford?' says Finn.

'Huddersfield Poly. Binned it after two years, like you.'

'So why d'you say you went to Oxford?' says Anna.

'Oh, I don't know. I say things for a joke and people take them to heart. I wouldn't mind if people lightened up a bit. Ah, it's so depressing.'

Anna sees what Einar is wearing and coughs explosively. 'Don't laugh,' he says. 'The pants are yours.'

'It's no fun any more,' says Jack. '*Dryghten wot*, maybe I should think about moving on.'

A stolen road-lamp makes us yellow in the gloom. No one begs him to stay.

In the corridor she has something on her mind. She stops outside Roxanne's door and stares at it, shaken by the stillness after the fight. I wait at her shoulder until I can hear the air suck up into her lungs.

'Is it me, or is Jack a complete wanker?'

The door makes no reply. I've an urge to open it, find the pills in the drawer and show Anna how it used to be, when time didn't bother us and all things had meaning and we hung like gulls above beaches with fires scattered in our eyes.

'I know what he means.'

'Do you?'

'I do it too. Say the opposite of what I mean, if it sounds more interesting.'

'I used to think you were just showing off. Remember that speech you made on the balcony?'

'I was on drugs.'

'Were you?'

'I was a prat then, Anna. But now I'm cool.'

She shakes her head, as tired of my lies as I am. From Linden's room comes the sound of objects flying about. He is standing at the bed, stuffing clothes into a rucksack. He hears a cough and looks up, a masterpiece of embarrassment.

'Cairo. Delhi. Bangkok. Kuala Lumpur. Australia if I've still got any cash.'

'You driving?'

'You can't drive to Malaysia. I checked. Anyway, you don't need to be sober to drive a penis-red Mustang. It drives itself.'

'So that's it?'

He nods his fluffy head. By tomorrow he'll be gone, his outrageous car turning heads from here to Birmingham, rear washer adjusted to squirt those last few traffic wardens before he takes off for busier towns. 'Look after the fish,' he goes. 'They'll come back to haunt you.' And if we never hear him say goodbye, it's only because we can't believe he's really gone.

On the roof the moon has started without us. The wind waits in the trees.

'You okay?'

'I've had better lives.'

She leans on the rail, looking at a pool of pale night over the town.

'I got a message from Hen this morning. She says she never even slept with Tony.'

'Is that right?' A knee drops out beneath her and jerks her upright. 'What do you want me to say?'

'Well, it shows I was wrong about her.'

'And that makes you feel guilty about sleeping with me? Come on Finn, this isn't some sort of game. I slept with you because I wanted to, and you did the same too I hope. Anyway, if Hen tries to make you feel guilty then she's a complete hypocrite.'

'Is she?'

'Okay, so she never slept with him. But he must have got pretty close to do a tattoo like that. I mean, think about it.'

I'd rather not. 'I'm sorry,' she says: 'let's leave it.' But:

'It's just this feeling I'm wrong about everything. About Hen, about my mum, everything.'

'What *about* your mum?'

'I don't know. Maybe I've been jumping to conclusions,'

and I point out all the loose bricks in the argument, like: How do I know Joy didn't give Margaret the watch as a present? Was it really such a secret about Joy going with them on their trip? She listens in silence, smoking and pulling at a thread on her sleeve.

'In which case, why was the watch in her pocket? Why wasn't it on her wrist?'

'How do you know it was in her pocket?'

'You said. All the stuff they took off her at the hospital, your dad just bundled it up and put it in a box in the attic. He never even looked at it. Anyway, Sarah said the ring was the only bit of jewellery she was wearing. She never said anything about a watch.'

She turns and feeds her arms through mine. Her hands tug thoughtlessly at my belt.

'What you need,' she says, pulling back from a kiss, 'is some brilliant sex.'

'Who were you thinking of?'

'Well, Einar was looking a bit bored earlier on.'

She still isn't smiling. I love her now and I want to love her

269

everywhere; I want to put a pill on her tongue and run with her out into that forgetting night.

'Here.'

'What?'

'Let's do it.' I've found cool flesh under the skirt.

'Out here?'

'Yeh. No one's going to come.'

'No thanks. It doesn't turn me on.'

'Why not? No one's going to come.'

'You've said that.'

I take my hands out from under the skirt and hold her, pressing a sort of apology into her bones.

'Is that what you used to do with Hen?'

Hen, day or night, up against the shell of the stairwell, jeans and knickers mocking us from the asphalt, her feet jammed up against the railings and slipping out of her shoes. Wet wind on my arse, making me stand out miles. Afterwards, her leaning on the rail and shouting, in her mad high voice, for all the town to hear: 'Oi, you lot! We've just had sex and it was fucking great!'

'It has been known.'

'Well, I'm not Hen.'

Hen, on the carpet in the auction room the night before the sale, to wish us luck, if you like, make the sale go better, with Kumar or Linden or Jack or Einar always walking in on us, and none of us giving a shit.

'Of course you're not.'

She leans against me, arms limp by her sides, forehead at rest on my chest.

'I hope I'm not too boring for you.'

'You're not that.'

'I just get so knackered with this job. Maybe I should give up drinking and take up running or *something*.'

'Anna?'

'What?'

'I love you.'

She stays there, soft against me, until I think my passion has been met by instant sleep. Then she pushes back with her palms on my chest and looks up.

'Is that present tense?' she says.

The knickers are pinned to my door. Anna pulls them off and throws them down the corridor with a laugh. Inside, Hen watches us from a charcoal self-portrait propped against the cabinet. Just as I'm starting, Anna wriggles out from beneath me, walks in her own knickers to the drawing and turns it against the wall. I fuck her there, against the glass-fronted cabinet, with Hen watching us from the table, the shelves, all the drawings and photographs we never got round to making because nothing was permanent, everything was just for now. She always liked the way I worked. She likes the way I do it to Anna because it's the way I used to do it to her, when I used to imagine *she* was Anna and she never did anything to let me down. But now there's no need to pretend, and I'm so achingly hard as I remember who it is I'm inside, whose throat the gasps are pushing up from, whose flesh is melting in my hands. I throw her onto the bed and let her pull me to her conclusion, blood spreading through her chest and drugging us with its bitter scent.

'I love you.'

'Say it again. Keep saying it, Anna . . .'

'I love you too.'

'. . . Anna . . .'

'I'll *always* love you. I love you so fucking much.'

LOT 18

According to the typed inventory in the relevant yellow folder, the envelope I'm looking for is in a box marked LONG4/270597. Counting in from the stairwell, Don's stuff is halfway down the third aisle. I almost trip over Robinson's trike as I come in, dressed for my task in tee-shirt and faded green jeans, the locked wooden box clutched awkwardly under my arm. No sound of hammering or sawing comes from the workshop under the outside stairs; no carefree laughter filters down from the office on the first floor. Serge is out with the family at the new retail park in Etruria, Einar is taking Hector through the contents of the fridge, while Kumar lazes in front of the Jubilee Road TV, tee-shirt pulled up over his beautiful brown belly, watching the rain fall at Trent Bridge.

 The key I want is at the bottom of this manilla envelope, among handwritten receipts, magazine cuttings and typed business plans. It fits the lock. In the box is a smaller envelope, and inside this are photographs, from broad glossy sun-snaps to tiny sepia cameos. Here she is, in yellow bikini and winged sunglasses, almost as tall as Dad, hair shoulder-length and wet from the sea. Now they're in a hotel restaurant, facing each other across an expanse of paella; the flash has made eyes red and everything cheap and Christmassy. Their hands crawl towards each other across the linen tablecloth; my mother's wedding ring, the only bit of jewellery on her body, gleams between the knuckles of her left hand. I move towards the window for the light. Now she's alone, caught in black and white on an East

Anglian beach, six inches of North Sea foaming around her ankles. One hand holds a flowery skirt up around her thighs, while the other reaches down to touch the water, fingers splayed.

This is the one I'm looking for. It's the green dress my aunt mentioned, which used to slip by like felt under my fingers in the days I doubted her and had to prove her solidity with touch. It is not turquoise nor khaki, not the green of traffic lights when they're telling you to go, but the green of uncut lawns, or the candlewick bedspread she pulled over me every night as her watch ticked on its leather strap. It clothes my mother's long body as she leans back against a tree, one knee lifted, hands sandwiched behind her back. You recognise the tree. It's the Brink Farm oak, which budded exuberantly in the first week of April and filled our summer sky with magnificent green. Green, the colour of things you knew without knowing, the light that makes everything clear. There's the old Cortina parked on the gravel, the chewed-up paddock sprinkled with straw. The dress matches the leaves. Green is now a symphony, an agreement, a concord. It means listening to both sides of an argument, and sometimes admitting you're wrong. The hem draws a line around her knees. It's hot: she's kicked off her black patent leather shoes. She smiles, sees Peter Causley's finger move on the shutter, then steps forward, brushing bark and moss from her hands.

They go inside the white farmhouse. Years pass.

Now there's shouting from inside the house. A man's tantrum, a man's fatuous pride. French windows open, sunlight flashes on glass, and out steps my mother, heaving us forward like shopping, one child in each hand. There's Finn, blond and blinking in the sunlight; and Alison, wiping her eyes and stamping her feet. Piano music is heard. Margaret opens the back door of the car and pushes me in. Then she climbs in, pulling Alison after her, and pushes down the locks on all four doors. She's crying, with straight-backed dignity, staring straight down the drive to the hills beyond. 'Why are you crying?' I bury my face in her lap. Green. Her hot bready smell. She gets into the car and dies. Green these days is all I see: it's a kind of blindness, but the void is not black, not death, not casual oblivion, but this perfect happy green. Her body hot under the dress, tears dripping from her chin and landing, cool and improbable, on my neck. A green monster pounding on the roof and roaring words I don't understand. Green. A jealous colour with murderous tendencies. The colour a mother leaves, like the reflection of trees on water, when she disappears. 'Don't leave us, Mum,' says Alison, yet I know that's exactly what she's going to do. And when she does, one day, when she gets into the car and dies, I will never speak her name, never mention her, no matter how the questions might probe; if anyone asks me about her I'll just stare into the distance, forehead crumpling in a frown; but I'll make up for her, I will wear her colour, when the mood is right and the weather feels like spring. If anyone asks why I'm wearing it I'll say I can't remember, leave me alone please, it's just a quirk of mine, not something that needs to be punished or discussed. I'll hear them crying at night, for people they themselves have lost, and I'll cry along, I'll weep with the best of them and no one will ever know why. He lost his mother. She gets into the car and dies. But I'll never forget the release she yearned for, forbidden to shout or scream; the colour of her hope and her sadness, the simple certainty of her tears; and the afternoon she taught it to me, her smell blotting out the edges of my world, her sobs giving time to mine.

Einar stands by the window two aisles down, watching.

'I think Tony is here.'

'What?'

'Tony. I think this is his name. The man who cuckooed you.'

I stuff the photos back in the envelope and lock it all in the box. 'Where?'

'Upstairs. In the showroom. Come see.'

But instead of leading me upstairs for a violent confrontation with the man who ruined my life, he pushes past, polishing a key on the leg of his shorts, which he then uses to unlock the video suite.

'I watch him from the office. He has a beard and heaps of tattoos.'

The monitors flash on. A man stands by a pillar with some part of a disassembled motorbike in his hands. He peers at it, drops it back on the pile and turns away from the camera, to an ornamental sword rescued from a Bliss-struck brigadier several months ago.

'That is him?'

Lot 18: **Assortment of photographs**, monochrome and colour, none less than twenty years old.

'I only saw him once.'

'He is smiling. Has he . . . ?'

'He wasn't in Moorview for the company.'

The danger person waits in the middle of the room, gazing up at the glass.

'Maybe he wants to kill you. He is here all morning.'

We lock up behind us and climb the stairs. I watch from the doorway, not brave enough to enter but not happy enough to look too hard for an escape. He has scuffed bike leathers and a denim cut-down. I think of those ink-stained hands on Hen's bare stomach, carefully marking her for life. It makes me sick. He has picked up the sword and is smacking it against his palm.

'Mr Causley?'

'This is him,' says Einar, pushing me forward into the room.

'Thank Christ for that. Thought I'd got the wrong piggin place.'

He grins. Many were filled with great fear.

'Is she all right?'

'Who?'

'Hen.'

'Hen Threadgold?' He pulls out a piece of paper and reads from it. 'Muz Henrietta Threadgold?'

'Is she all right?'

'Sort of hoping you could tell me!'

'Don't hurt him!' squeals Einar.

He stabs the sword playfully in Einar's direction and takes a step forward.

'Put down the weapon!' Einar says.

He lays the sword on a table and shows several chipped teeth.

'Graham Perse. I think we got a mutual friend.'

My murder can wait. This man is paid to ask questions. But will he tell me my crime?

'So what's he paying you for?'

'Put the kettle on,' he grins, 'and we can find out.'

I escort Graham up to the Chapter House, where Kumar sprawls in semi-trance on the sofa, an old copy of *TV Babes* tented over his face. I remind him that he's due to help Einar with a house clearance in twenty minutes, and he leaves us with a transcendental sigh. I boil water while Graham privately investigates the room. Zoë's statue lies shattered where it fell. No one here has the heart to clear it up.

'Stayed in a place like this once. Donington '87. Bunch of mad hippies and a half.'

I make tea in two mugs and put them down on the table. He stands by the linen press, head tilted, reading down our CD stack with interest.

'Who's the Genesis freak? Lost their touch after the Gabriel departure but the genius is still in evidence.'

I murmur assent. Graham picks up his mug and sniffs at it.

'Wrote a letter once. Phil Collins, Charisma Records. Said if he didn't stop acting such a fackin ponce with that tambourine I'd come round and break his fackin legs. There he is, greatest drummer that ever walked the earth and he thinks he's Julie Fackin Andrews.'

'I thought you were a friend of Hen's.'

'That Tom Threadgold's told me nothing. I'm gonna have to have it all from you, Mr Causley, all the juicy circumstances. Mind if I kill myself?'

He pulls a plastic pouch from the pocket of his cut-down. The last thing I want is to go through this again. But he looks as if he could kill me without feeling a thing, and my life's one moment of courage has passed. I let him roll one for me.

'What about the police?'

'It's not illegal, Mr Causley.'

'I mean Hen.'

He lights our smokes with relish. 'Trail's gone cold. They give it twenty-four hours and then it's sorry, we got reports to write. Because it's not a recognised disease, they say they got no powers anyway. Buncha fuckwits. You heard about the car?'

I squint at him through smoke.

'The car she borrowed? Your mate's red Peugeot? Well they find it all right, in the drive outside your mate's house. She's upstairs in the bath. They ring her up and say, We found your car, and she says, You clever things, because it's parked outside my house. Your girlfriend must've taken it back Sunday night. I love that. You clever things, because it's parked outside my fuckin house!'

He laughs and coughs and laughs and coughs.

'Is Zoë in trouble?'

'Nah. They never had piss all to go on and now it's even less. Muz Threadgold will have got on a train and fucked off somewhere. Probably in France by now.'

I blow the idea back at him in a cloud. Memories of our famous trip to Paris mean she won't be in France, not in this lifetime. She'll have found a car in the next street, coathangered it standing up with her back to the door and made her escape with the slightest squeal of brakes.

'So what do you want to know?'

He pulls a notebook from another pocket and flips it open. 'Start with money. How's she financing all this?'

'She's got accounts. The police will have checked that out.'

'Told you, not interested.' He makes a note. 'Suppose you haven't heard from her?'

'Only messages on the network. She's got her own laptop. But . . .'

In the room he spends some time flicking through what's left of Hen's clothes while I check the latest messages.

```
im in this white place. theres no furniture
because someones taken it all. theres some flowers
in a vase on the windowsill, i think theyre
tulips. i sit here all day and the phone doesnt
ring once. any minute now someones going to walk
in here and change my life.
```

I stand back to let Graham read. He smells of roll-ups and patchouli. I explain about the flat.

'Yeh, Bristol Street. Mr Threadgold told me you done it up.'

'But they sold it when we moved here.'

'Not according to him they didn't.'

He keeps on shaking his head until I start shaking back.

'Don't you lot ever talk to each other? Mr Threadgold kept it on as an investment. It's still in your girlfriend's name.'

'The flat? You sure?'

'I'm too beautiful to make mistakes.'

At this point in my life I should be used to improbable revelations, but this one takes a while to sink in. Down below, one of Mrs Enderby's dogs is being blinded for fun.

'Is that where Tom thinks she is?'

'Nah. It's being rented out to stoodents. Has been since you lot moved out.'

The brochure on her desk in Moorview: Hooper's Estate Agents, Norwich and King's Lynn. When she caught me looking at it she seemed to return to where she always was: alert, suspicious, aware of everything, as if Bliss was just an act she was putting on for a purpose none of us could judge. Then she blinked, her eyes settled on the door and it was back to her medicated stare.

'Unless,' I say, 'she's been in touch and told them to clear out.'

The number I want is in my address book. When I get through to the main Norwich office and pretend to be interested in Flat 2, 17 Bristol Street, I'm offered a number of alternative properties. When I persevere with my inquiry, I'm told they have no such property on their books. When I ask whether they have ever had such a property on their books, I am told they cannot give out such information on the phone, but that if I would like to call in to the office they will certainly do their best to help.

Impressed, Graham glances at his watch. 'Four-thirty. I'll be there first thing tomorrow. I love Norwich. Some fuckin mental fuckin hippies there. Reckon we'll have this sorted by tomorrow night.'

Do I sound enthusiastic? Does my voice fail on the edge of speech?

'You want her back, don't you?'

'Maybe we'd better talk about that.'

In The Monk's Pleasure, with his phone neat and silent on the table between us, Graham tells me what a certain 1972 Genesis recording means to him.

'It has to be the most crucial album ever committed to vinyl. I mean, look at what's going on in a piece like "Get 'em out by Friday". Banks is laying down jaunty pipe soundscapes over a rampant on-the-nose bass line from Rutherford with Hackett feasting on his trademark Les Paul volume swells. Then Collins moves to his rides and drops it all down, big and baggy, Gabriel's flute drifts in over what is actually a very pastoral mid-section, and he sings that bit about how all humanoids are to be restricted to a maximum of four foot in height. Now, you know what really gets me?'

'No.'

'Look at the gatefold. The place: Harlow New Town. The date:

18th September 2012. Now I was born *in Harlow*, 19th September 1962. We're talking *the day before my fiftieth birthday.*'

I want to show that his enthusiasm is mine. But I'm worried he's going to get on to a close reading of 'Supper's Ready' and then neither of us will be going home tonight.

'Did you go to their house?'

'Fuck me, what a pile. That Threadgold's a stuck-up cunt. But can't complain about what he's paying me!'

He laughs and grabs our glasses and heads for the bar. When he comes back, I wonder if he saw a little boy with blue shoes.

'Hen's kid? Sorry, your kid too. Yeh, he's good. Got two myself. I tell you I was married?'

'No.'

'She's a fuckin scream, my wife. I fuckin love her.'

I'm fourteen years old. My skin is bad and my voice is breaking. But there's this question I have to ask.

'How . . . I mean, when did you know? That she was . . . ?'

'Milton Keynes. You believe that?'

'The '82 reunion? First gig I ever went to.'

'Was it raining? Had her brother just died and was she lonely and sad and getting into those dynamics like she didn't know how long she'd got? It was hurting her and it was hurting me but it was real, you know, it was more real than fuckin both of us. I'm thinking, Her brother's just died and all that but I can't keep my fuckin hands off her, and she walks four miles in the pissing rain cos I'm ratarsed and she won't come on my bike, then all of a sudden I'm scared of my dreams, I'm scared of going to sleep cos I know she won't be there.'

'You knew that from the start?'

'Took a few months. It's not a fackin pop song! But then you know, you look at her and you look at yourself and it all starts making sense.'

Did I shake my head? Or did I just say nothing when I could have said something, and show how close to nothing I was?

'Well mate, you've got a kid. You know how it feels when you want to stick with someone.'

'I know when it seems like you've got no choice.'

His eyes expand and he does a very good impression of Tom Threadgold.

'So, Mr Causley, what is your relationship with my daughter?'
I laugh unhappily. 'She's Mum and I'm Dad.'
'But you're looking elsewhere.'
I look elsewhere. I don't know if I want Hen, or if I want a friend who understands that I don't want Hen, or that I do want Hen but can't admit it, or whether I'd rather not be thinking about this at all.
'I've started seeing someone else.'
'And that's why you're not sure if you want her found.'
'I do want her found. I'm just not sure what I'm going to do when she is.'
'Look, tell you what I'll do. Soon as I hear anything I'll let you know. Give you a bit of warning. Same goes for you.' He takes a card from his wallet and writes his hotel number on the back. 'Room 319. I'll be at that flat first thing tomorrow. I can almost *smell* her . . .'
He winks and pockets his phone. For a moment he seems like my only chance of finding Hen. And for a moment that makes him more precious to me than anything on earth.

The thing about tragedies is that the reason for calling them tragedies isn't always obvious. A real tragedy, like a really good song, takes a few listens through to get the idea.
Tragedies, like photographs, come in all shapes and sizes. Some are wide and detailed, drawing all generations of the family into their frame of horribleness, and then it's impossible to pick out any single fact that makes it a tragedy, rather than a stretch of bad luck which has gone on longer than is fair. Others are no less cluttered, but the clutter and complication are only background to a very simple truth. Out of the tangled wreckage of circumstance and consequence, from all the traffic that has plunged headlong into the fabled gulf between reality and desire, there is one sore detail that can be pointed to, circled with a pen, peered at, taken out, admired. There, you say, there's the tragedy. It took me years to see it, but in the end it's very clear.
The real tragedy of my mother's death is not that she was expecting something else, or that a man called Peter was unfaithful to her or that she might have been unfaithful to him. As my medical friend has insisted, it doesn't matter whether her accident was really an accident or the inevitable consequence of inevitable stress; it

makes no difference that the person who was at fault was not the person who lived or died as a result. No, what sets my forehead wrinkling and my voice-box humming is not the thought that it might have been prevented, if only people had acted differently, if someone had been a bit more considerate to someone else. The real tragedy of my mother's death is the fact that it happened, and in happening could never be undone. It's the fact that Dad never got the chance to speak to her, explain what had happened, or apologise and beg forgiveness, or simply say he loved her and leave it at that. She was already gone. We have the story now: how she drove the twenty miles to Blacksheep Moor (and of course she never stopped in Etruria: the Silk Twister should immediately be renamed the Red Herring and scrubbed from the catalogue), drove to Blacksheep Moor with the gold watch ticking in her pocket, turned left too soon onto unfamiliar roads with a stubborn ring on an inflamed knuckle and the sun blinding in the west. In a studio in London, the opening sequence of *Hide and Seek* was ready to roll. A screenful of sunlight bleached her brain, a hand slipped on a vinyl steering wheel, the blue Cortina changed direction for the last time, the song stopped in mid-verse, a single red blood cell burst through a weakened vessel wall, and anything Dad might have wanted to say to her was lost on the dandelion wind. We had already survived her. The thing about tragedies is that no one really understands them at the time.

Usually, on leaving The Monk's Pleasure after more real ales than are good for me, I'll head straight back to Big Kimberley, check on my sleeping child, read my messages and spend twenty minutes in front of an Abba video making conversation with my right hand. Tonight, though, I'm headed for the park, through streets whose only sounds are the odd lorry passing through on Manchester Road, green shoes on tarmac and that unfinished tune in my throat.

I'm thinking about several things.

I'm wondering what was going through my father's head in the first minutes after my mother left, as he hugged his knees in Joy's hotel bed, breeze through the open window and Monday afternoon traffic on the street outside. (She'll be okay. She's gone to Sarah's. I'll find her and explain.)

I'm wondering what Joy thought lying beside him, shocked at what she'd seen but somehow pleased with herself for being here, in the thick of it, secretly glad to be involved. (She'll get over it. I got over it. I wish it hadn't happened like this, but there you go.)

And I'm thinking about Hen, alone in our flat on Bristol Street, thinking not in words but in objects, textures, patterns of light, smells, contours, sounds. Wishing that someone, even the madman who disfigured her for a joke, was there with her, just so she wouldn't be alone.

It was the night of Roxanne's anniversary. She was home from Moorview for the weekend, to help us remember what had happened and see if it made any more sense a year on. We got drunk in the pub and staggered home. She stood in the doorway with her hands up on the frame, making the small comfortable movements that had made me mad that first September and got me into something from which I'd still not found an escape. A silence still clung to her, the silence of the white room, but behind the stare was the stirring wildness, the urgency that made me want her without wondering who it was I was wanting, whose pale body was stepping out of whose clothes. Yet as soon as I was inside her the picture changed, and all I could see was the tissue in Choi's micrographs: sky-blue flowers at grotesque magnifications, fibrous bundles and metallic plaques, the salty circuitry that drew the lines on the scans, this entire fragile ecosystem which my obvious little spurting could only wreck and infect. 'I don't want to hurt you,' was my strongest imaginable urge, but I went on hurting her, until it happened and it felt so good we could almost believe nothing was wrong. That was two months ago. Now, on the bench overlooking the pond, with pissed teenagers crashing through the shrubbery behind, it's the same urge to explain myself, but it's drowned out by that inhuman drilling, and at last I hear the words that go with the howl. 'I don't want to hurt you.' *'What?'* 'I never wanted to hurt you, Hen.' But the reason for the howling is that it's already too late: she's gone, we've survived her, she gets into the car and dies. There is a statue with my face on it. There are things I don't understand. I see Roxanne's face, flushed and gleaming with sweat, saying, 'Let's keep it to ourselves, yeh? and no one will ever know.' Hands close over my eyes. And I don't know what I'm remembering, but I wonder if this kind of treachery is hereditary, whether you catch it from your father at the precise moment he cheats on someone else, or if it's just something you pick up when you've hurt enough people enough times. Roxanne turns to Hen and hands her a white bottle with blue lettering, saying, 'If things are getting you down, Salvation can bring you round! By the way, if anyone ever says your lover fucked me while you were out shopping, they're lying. It was me who fucked him.'

So I'm running now, to a place called Big Kimberley, where the lights aren't on and there's a message on the computer from an address I know.

```
its a small plastic container which rattles when
shaken. inside theres something which will make
all my troubles go away.
```

'Room 319,' I tell the man who answers the phone.
'Yeh?' says Graham on the nineteenth ring.
'It's Finn. I want to come with you.'
'Why?'
'Do I have to give a reason?'
'Yes you fuckin well do.'
'Because I love her and I have to find her and there's something I have to tell her. Because I can't bear the thought that I'll never see her again.'
'Pick you up at nine,' says my new friend.

LOT
19

When, my fellow travellers and fat-walleted customers, I claimed to have learned my first lessons in sexual love in the arms of my sister Alison, I meant more than glimpses of flesh-toned biodiversity on the landing outside my room, which, repeated lovingly over the course of a long and boring adolescence, helped train that shadiest part of my brain in what to look for under summer dresses and layers of winter clothes. I meant that, although my dreams were blessed by no shortage of quickly naked women, only the one starring Alison came to any satisfactory conclusion; while others would have me squirting before I was even out of my clothes, Alison was the only nude darling I ever had time to penetrate, and thus the only one who could ever say whether or not she enjoyed my intrusion, or look up at me with the kind of slit-eyed wonder that my young mind wasn't concerned to understand. It happened in silence and with cheering predictability. I would catch her coming wet-haired out of the bathroom, tug the Marks & Spencer's underpants down around her ankles, and make dull and hectic love to her right there in the corridor, with much grinding of teeth and knocking of heads against the banister, while she squeezed the spots on my back and hummed the *Match of the Day* theme tune through lips that stayed tightly closed.

Shame, like any other emotion, has its own devices, its own ways of disrupting proceedings in order to make its point. As soon as I had panted to my soul's release and Alison had closed her eyes as if in death, I would wake – not gently or magically, but forcibly, as if ejected from a fast-moving vehicle – to a slick of tepid jelly on the sheet against my thigh, the blue-grey light of an Essex dawn, and a feeling of having committed a more appalling crime against nature than I could have come up with in any number of boring English lessons. Why Alison, please? What was wrong with all the other curve-haired beauties I encountered in the bright-lit corridors between sleep and sleep? What prophecy was being made: was I to believe that no matter how many women were jigging around me like balloons waiting to be punctured, I would never fuck any except the one I didn't want, the one I should not even think about, just because the bits – my sister is a beautiful woman – were so obviously in the right place? At breakfast I could hardly look at her. She would be staring at the nutritional information on the side of a Frosties packet, twirling a black lick of hair and sucking milk from her exquisite lips. Would she have sat so comfortably if she'd known my secret, the vile truth about what I'd been doing to her in my dreams? My *dreams*? I doubted the lino beneath my feet. Couldn't I have crept into her room, an oily-skinned incubus in nothing but a Jethro Tull tee-shirt, peeled back the duvet and impregnated her in my sleep? I hated us both. I hated her brazen sexuality and my own gullible lust, and the way the contents of her dressing gown kept bringing the two together for laughs. I longed for thoughtful women with troublesome partings, who wouldn't scare me to death every time they stepped out of their shape-concealing clothes. I wanted . . . but there was no one else to want. I thought with terror of our child, the sort of pale-eyed mutant that only incest can deliver. I heard it sighing, stirring in her belly, passing its unspeakable horror over us like a cloud.

The reason I'm reminded of this now, fifteen years after I last made love to my sister on the landing of our Essex home, is that last night the dream came back to me; came, gave its silent lesson and fled, leaving the same blue-grey horror in its wake. It wasn't Alison this time, nor Anna, nor even Hen. It was Roxanne. She was spread out on her hospital bed, blissfully conscious, pulling me into her with her strong drummer's arms. And just as those landing-dreams shocked me with their horribly possible truth, so I can't help thinking that this too is a kind of prophecy: a proof of something I refuse to remember, like the red baseball cap I have taken down to stare at for the millionth time, as if, just maybe . . . and those hands close again over my eyes.

It's well after eleven by the time Graham phones. 'Met some Arabs who want to play poker. Up till fuckin five o'clock.' I wonder where he is. 'Whieldon Street. Couldn't find the fuckin doorbell.' I grab my jacket, set the answering machine and go down the main stairs. Graham is sitting in the middle of the road on the nastiest motorbike I have ever seen.

'This,' he says, folding the phone into his pocket, 'is a Honda CBR 900 Fireblade. This little black beauty is gonna get us from here to Norwich in about an hour and a fuckin half. Here.' He lifts a helmet from a pannier and dunks it onto my head. Then he thumbs the start-button and the air between us seems to melt into sound.

'Thought you had a car!' I yell. 'A nice little private investigator's hatchback!'

'You jest,' he goes, letting me climb on behind.

'No, cars are very useful. They have plenty of seats and . . .'

'Yeh, but you can't do *this* in a car.'

He lets out the clutch and spins the throttle, and we leave the normal stationary world with a lurch and a squeal of rubber which, if I ever see this town again, will probably stretch from Whieldon Street to the junction with Derby Road. I have a sensation of lifting straight up into space, towards my own five-seater hatchback heaven, at something close to forty-five degrees. I'd like to tell Graham there's been a change of plan and I don't want to go to Norwich after all, but the message comes out as 'Hang on, I've left . . .' and all he does is look back and nod his head. I consider the irony of the situation: on our cross-England mission to rescue Hen from a lonely flat and lethal drugs, I and my new friend meet an articulated lorry on a bend in the road across Blacksheep Moor, are sent skimming several hundred feet down the tarmac like a couple of schoolboy's bags, and have our life-support machines switched off early in the next century after failing to regain consciousness. I cling to the leather heap in front of me with a passion that my relations with women have sometimes lacked, and pray that death will come quickly, that it won't involve any more painful decisions, and that my last heroic though uncompleted deed will not go unnoticed when I stand before the clockwinder in my bloody green clothes.

Life improves when we hit the motorway. Graham holds a steady ninety-five, skipping between middle and outside lanes with slalom verve, until I finally stop fearing for my life and start enjoying it. But the scream – long and joyful, drowned by engines and hurtling air – is not just for me: it's for Hen, who'd have climbed up here uninvited and zoomed straight back to her car-borrowing days. It's also for Roxanne, God's first delinquent, the biggest speed-freak of us all. Her turbocharged dreams: how, when she'd made enough money at Big Kimberley, she'd buy herself the meanest motorbike she could find and take off for Europe, Africa, the Middle East ... And Hen, across the room from her, feet up on the sofa, always had this longing look in her eyes.

Last night's dream. Roxanne's hot face, her small white teeth tinged with blue. *If things are getting you down, Salvation can bring you round!*

I'm thinking of Roxanne, our dead friend, and the things she said.

I'm thinking of the red baseball cap, the words TUFF MUFF emblazoned across the front, two strips of plastic clipped together behind. *If anyone ever says your lover fucked me while you were out shopping, they're lying. It was me who fucked him.*

I'm thinking of hands, woman's hands with a familiar smell, warm and dark over my eyes. *Guess who?*

Roxanne ... How many times have I thought about her death? Last year's all-nighters, every photo we owned spread out on the table, talking about her just for the sake of talking, as if talking could keep her here, in smoke-tinged memory, for a few hours more. We were thorough in our grief. We regretted everything there was to regret, and more. So why is it that now, with my own death a speed-melted road a few inches from my feet, my forehead is wrinkling, my eyes drift off to the right, and I have the feeling that the story is incomplete, some vital piece is missing, and the gap is somewhere between me and her?

Because ...

Because something happened. Because I wasn't who I said I was.

The first time the name was mentioned was in January last year. We were in the Chapter House, talking about that day's sale. Roxanne was trying to light a spliff and I'd hidden her matches. We'd made some money that day.

'What've you done with them?'

'What've I done with what?'

'Give!'

'What? Tell me what!'

'Oh cut it out, Blake,' she said, and fixed me with a look meant for someone else.

'What did you call me?'

She thought for a moment. Her lipsticked lips bunched and twitched.

'Blake.'

'Why?'

'Cause you look like him. Shit, I don't know.'

Then it was in my room, a week or so later. I was on the floor, dusting the shelves of the walnut cabinet, taking things out and putting them back. The word was formed so carefully, it couldn't have been a mistake.

'Why do you keep calling me that?'

This time anger, hurt. 'Why do you just ignore me? Why do you say you love me and then act like I don't *exist*?'

Soon after that Zoë and Hen persuaded her to go to the Royal Infirmary for an interview. They came back with a tentative diagnosis of St Mary's Disease. 'They're all *tentative*,' said Zoë. 'It means they haven't a clue what's wrong with her.' But what was there to know? My uncle Don, who had spent the previous summer at Brink Farm taking things out of drawers and describing them to himself in a hurried monotone, had yet to be told his fate. Only Hen took the diagnosis seriously. It was she who read the leaflets we were given, made sure Rox avoided stressful or emotional situations, and followed all the other advice that seemed so hopeful at the time. What she didn't do was keep her off the drugs. They drew up a weekly ration of 50 mg of D-DMPA, which, depending on the batch and country of origin, could mean anything from one to eight small white pills.

By March we thought the worst was over. The smile, that enigmatic turning-up of the mouth that was starting to appear on faces all over the country, was the same one she'd always worn. She talked about Blake as much as ever, but none of us had the trousers to accuse her of lingering on among out-of-date loves. 'Better to live yesterday in colour than today in black and white' – and the way she said it, you had to agree. She'd sit on the sofa, curtains drawn and kimono pulled tight across her, giving blow-by-blow accounts of her time in the flat in Melbourne, laughing at things Blake had said to her and she'd said back, occasionally glancing across at me as if we should have been somewhere else by now. I watched her wandering around the storage bays, or pedalling Robinson's trike with her knees absurdly splayed, stopping every few yards to pick something from a shelf and turn it in her hands. 'You guys should try this. There's so much . . . *meaning* in this place. I could live here for ever, just looking at stuff. Hey, maybe I will.'

Then came that febbish day in spring, sun trying to break through, when we realised how wrong she was. We'd been out buying supplies for the kiosk and assumed Rox was sleeping late. As soon as we were through the door Hen tensed, like she always did when she was about to say something inexcusable. 'What's up?' 'Oh, you know.' The others went up, laughing at something Einar had said. Hen stood at the foot of the stairs, staring – we watched it later on the video – at the entrance to the store. 'She's in there.' I came back with the keys and opened the door. Roxanne was crouched on the floor, facing the wall, arms clasped around her to ward off invisible blows. Beside her was that month's *TV Babes*, a few white pills lined up on the back cover, and a plastic cylinder with an illegible label. In one hand, the red baseball cap was scrunched up like a message she didn't want to read.

She died forty-eight hours later, in the Etruscan Royal Infirmary, without ever opening those toffee-coloured eyes. According to Hen and Zoë, who took turns to sleep in the plastic armchair in the corner, the smile never left her lips. They sang and told jokes, straightened the baseball cap on her head, tried to remember every stupid thing the three of them had ever done. They talked about the bike they would buy when Rox was better. They said: 'You little shit, don't you die on us,' and thought her eerie grin might have deepened for a moment, and reflected something more than the white walls of a coma. Then, so quietly that neither Hen nor Zoë noticed, it happened, or rather she stopped happening, stopped being here and started up again somewhere else. 'Like putting down the phone,' said Hen that night. 'Not something to get all spooked about.' Then dawned that smile, the look of wonder I'd seen on so many beaches, saying that whatever she'd seen she knew it couldn't hurt her, just like it hadn't hurt Roxanne.

A few days later we were around the table in the Board Room, remembering the last time we'd seen her alive. The three girls, with Einar and Linden in tow, had gone out on the Monday night to the Monk's Pleasure, where nothing untoward had happened, no lapses of concentration had been noted, no inappropriate remarks had been made. When the question came round to me, I shrugged shoulders and seemed to forget.

'Must have been Monday. She was hanging round the mill, looking for something to do. She seemed all right.'

Then we were on to something else. Only Zoë looked at me as if there was more to be said. Suspicion? I couldn't tell. But it's Zoë who's with me now, as I hurl down the motorway on the back of Graham's bike, every bone in my body vibrating at 5000 rpm. It's Zoë who stands on the bridge above us, staring down through a storm of hair. 'Go on, mate. You remember. Tell us about the last time you saw her alive.'

Since the pillion position on Graham's motorbike seems so conducive to high-speed recollection, shaking loose memories I never knew I had, let me ask the following question, and see if any answers fly back at me out of the wind. Something happens between two people. One of them dies. There is no physical evidence of what took place, no object left behind as a clue, no documentation, photographic or otherwise. All that exists is an image in one person's head, what sentimental types might call a memory – as if a memory was a thing like a teapot or a shoe horn, highly sought after in provincial sales. No, a true object can be given, taken back, dismantled, discussed; it proves its nature in any number of different lights. But an image in someone's head? A memory that fades with time? With no one else to share it, how can anyone say, 'Yes, this happened. He ... She ... Yes, I'm sure'? Fellow travellers and auction-goers, what sort of object is it that becomes less real each time someone has a look at it? Not the sort from which history is made. History can be bought and sold, sought in airy warehouses, read in the hinge and the grain; which is why you come to me with your chequebooks and your empty cars, because otherwise it's the belief that *anything* might have happened, and there's no medicine for that disease.

You see, I did see Roxanne on the last full day of her life. She was doing more than hanging around Big Kimberley looking for something to do. She was looking for Blake, her long-lost love from Melbourne, and for some reason she thought she could find him in our room.

'Go on,' shouts Zoë, poking her head out of the window of a receding van. 'What did she do?'

Let me also make it clear that I never really forgot it, this event for which there can never be any proof, but it's only now that I realise how it fits in.

'Go on!' yells Zoë through her bushy new beard, turning round to grin at me through her visor. 'You shag her or what? What's it like to fuck a dying girl?'

So quickly it is dark. Moist warmth, salty softness: human flesh. Fingers, smelling of smoke and other things. They fold across my eyes and make me blind. A wild giggle, then the voice says, 'Guess who?' And I say, 'Roxanne,' because I know it's her, she's done this many times. 'That's right, you little shit. And who are you?' 'Finn,' says Finn. 'Oh no you're not.' 'Oh yes I am.' 'Your name's Blake,' she says, 'and you're the only guy I ever loved.' 'Prove it,' I say.

'Okay,' she says, and the hands fall away from my face and drop to the back of the chair, and they swivel the chair round through half a turn, enough to show me Roxanne, wearing nothing but her TUFF MUFF baseball cap, hands on her hips and that misplaced affection on her face.

'How about it? For old times' sake?'

'Rox, you don't know what you're doing.'

'Reckon I do.' She grabs my elbows and tries to pull me to my feet. She's strong: drummer's muscles thicken her arms. I smell her cumin sex, old sweat, a hint of shit. A nipple scuffs my cheek. The cap is knocked sideways in our sluggish fight; she lifts me like a metal dress, growling and puffing hair from her mouth. With nervy laughs I manage to break her grip and roll back to the window.

'Oh Blake,' coming after me, 'you're *such* a tease . . .'

and she's straddling the chair, arms clamped around mine, kissing me like a fire she can only put out with her mouth. One hand pulls at my zip. She finds flesh, grates her cunt against its heat, and for one aching second I don't care, I'll have her, I'll go along with it and see what it's like! But only for a second, because a twice-shy Finn has pinned her arms to her sides, an obscene hug in which she can only struggle and grind her hips. She becomes limp, following my movements with her curious face, patiently trying to make eye contact. 'It's okay, I can take a hint.' Her cheeks burn. I watch her weaken, from curiosity to resignation, then the simplest sadness I have ever seen.

'Blake's gone,' is all I can think to say.

I wrap her in the duvet and walk her to her room. I watch her fall asleep. By the time Hen returns with bags of shopping and her usual astonished grin, the duvet is back on our bed and the cushions lined up on top. Two days later they're moving Roxanne's bed towards the window, as if the sight of those beloved hills might creep into her brain and put some mindlife back into her smile. And even though I know the rules have changed, and other forces have got hold of her – even though nothing that happens now can turn a cause into an effect – I'm still wondering: if I'd played along with her game, if for a minute I'd been who she wanted me to be, might . . . figurines, ironing boards, silk ties?

For some reason I thought that when we arrived at the flat, Hen would open the door, pull her old spin-eyed smile at the repeating absurdity of life, and all my troubles would steam away into the kitcheny sky. But once we've turned off the ring road and are scooting past overgrown churchyards and avenues with tiny-leaved trees, I realise it will take more than a glimpse of the cathedral, the smell of a familiar pub or two, to tie up what has come undone.

A pillar box marks the turning into Bristol Street. The picture blurs for some seconds then clarifies like a zoom shot on a slow-motion replay, as real life matches to memory through the visor's smoked lens. Road inclines to sky. Two lines of bay-windowed terraces study each other across the street. Here, at the junction with Exeter Avenue, is the converted end-terrace we called home for nearly three years, the bats in the belfry of Dr Chakrabarty, who spent the days watching daytime telly and wondering when the life it advertised would squeeze the brakes, assume the crown of the road and turn the corner into our street.

While Graham tries the doorbell I inspect the house from the outside. The upstairs curtains are closed. Round the corner in Exeter Avenue, our kitchen window is covered by a yellow blind. At the back is a tight passage between Dr Chakrabarty's and a lock-up garage. Beyond that is a taller garage and the screen of our bathroom window, showing nothing but reflected sky.

'If she's here,' says Graham, 'she's surely washing her hair.'

A net curtain twitches downstairs. Graham goes back to the house and knocks on the window. Birds gibber in silver birches and lorries boom on Unthank Road. Graham knocks again. The window opens and a face swims out from the gloom. Dr Chakrabarty stares out at me with no sign of recognition.

'If you are from the council,' he roars, 'then I will ask you please to answer my letters and not come round to my house!'

'We're not from the council,' says Graham. 'We're looking for someone who used to live in the flat upstairs.'

'And if you are a traffic warden, I will tell you that you are a great waste of the Public Sector Borrowing Requirement!'

'Her name is Henrietta Threadgold. This is a photograph.'

'Men who live in this house are fools! They are threads of shit, not threads of gold! No one lives in this house but shitty people who tolerate all kinds of waste of public affluency! And most days there is no one here at all . . .'

'You've been most helpful,' says Graham, slipping the photo back into his pocket and turning to the street.

The head of Dr Chakrabarty cranks out from the window and scans the street for further wastes of public affluency. He glances up at the sky, glares at us for the last time and withdraws, pulling the window shut behind.

'Next move?' I ask.

'Come back tonight. Still no answer, go up and have a look.'

'You mean break in?'

'I mean gain access to the premises using any means available. We could do it now, but I don't think you'd like prison food.'

On the way to Graham's favourite pub, which I've never heard of but he's sure is around here somewhere, I bravely resolve that if anyone's going into the flat tonight it's going to be me. 'I know where everything is. And if anyone turns up I'll show them that

293

superb bathroom and say, Look, I *built* the bloody thing.'

We find the pub and a table by a pinball machine. When Graham comes back with the beers, he wants to know everything I didn't tell him last night.

'So this new bird of yours, you got the beefburger but you ain't told Hen?' I pat it away. 'So it's not like you don't want to find her, it's just you're shitting yourself about what you're gonna do when she finds out?'

'I just want a chance to explain what's happened. I'm worried something's going to happen before I get round to it,'

and I tell him about Roxanne, about Don, about a drug called D-DMPA and its links with St Mary's Disease, and about last night's message from Hen, in which she described a small plastic bottle in such detail that I could almost see those white death-units twist off the cap and line up on the back of a magazine.

'Salvation? That's like The Surfboard? I used to do that shit. Off it all now though. Kids, responsibilities. This great fuckin job!'

'So's Hen, as far as I know.' I'm shaking. My voice! 'But no one thought Don was doing it either. Except the bastards who were selling it to him.'

Graham takes out his pouch and starts rolling. He's shaking his head. 'You say that's the last message you got from her?'

'There were two this morning, just before you turned up. Something about the bathroom window.'

'So she was all right this morning. And we know she's at the flat. Fuck!' He bangs the table. 'She's probably out shopping or something. That's where we usually find them, in Dorothy Perkins, all dreamy among the fackin lanjeray. But I ain't paid to take no chances. We'll be in that flat tonight.'

Somehow the great thug with his bulldozer logic has convinced me that Hen is safe. This is where I start believing I'm going to see her and tell her all the things I've been wanting to tell her. This is also where I stop worrying and start hyperventilating. Tell her what, exactly? That all that stuff about loving her for ever was just vowel practice? That in all our years together there wasn't a moment when I wasn't thinking of a Kandinsky dress at the side of a swimming pool? Or would it be more truthful to admit that as soon as I'd slept with Anna I realised nothing had changed, the purpose of my life hadn't suddenly written itself in fiery letters on my sister's ceiling, and that all that has happened since, rather than showing me the meaning of love or any basic facts about it, has only shown me that really loving someone is not something I should be thinking about as a career?

'What do you really want from life?' Dad would ask me, and I would spin in circles, hiding behind a lopsided smile.

She was a dream: I wanted her to be one. I wanted that far-eyed girl with difficult hair, who hid her womanness under baggy clothes and loose summer dresses, who would never squeeze the spots on my back or ask irritating questions at moments of great spiritual intensity. I wanted that girl from the police show and her pen-sucking cousins, frowning in dingy kitchens around the world. But instead I found Hen, who disgusted me for the same reason my sister disgusted me: because she was obvious, because she made me want her without wanting her, because she never looked upwards and to the left with that enigmatic swimming-pool smile. When she was available I wanted her out of reach; I'd watch her step out of her clothes and wish, just for once, there'd be nothing there. But now I've heard the sound of her absence, the stellar echo at the end of the phone, and I begin to realise that mixed in with all those things I hated – or not mixed in at all, but just the same things seen in different lights – are the things that made me love her, a love so huge and ordinary I never knew it was love until now. But I also realise that I've made a choice, and that, as Jack would say, is my entelechy.

Anna, in my room, half a lifetime ago: 'Don't say you're in love with me just because that's what you've been saying to yourself for the last seven years. I've changed. So have you.'

Anna, in my bed on Tuesday morning: 'Did you think it would be easy to say goodbye to Hen? Or did you never really think about what it would involve?'

I watched her dress. Today she was shy, wary, in a hurry to get out of here, away from all this talk of treachery and loyalty and back to the hospital, back to simple matters of life and death. She would catch me looking at her and frown, pulling hair behind an ear and peering down at the buttons on her shirt. All I ever wanted was to watch her, to spy on her from the closest possible vantage point, like I spied on her from that swimming pool on the other side of the world. But I'd already made myself known to her, in the way I'd always wanted, with much chomping of shoulders and nibbling of lips. I had never imagined what it would be like to wake up next to her, feel her heat on the pillow and the smell of her sex on mine, and find nothing either to excite or irritate me, nothing to prove she was any more real than she'd been in my dream. I'd been longing for her to say something – not a joke, because she couldn't remember jokes, except the one about the grizzly bear and the bunny rabbit that wasn't funny the first time – but there was only one question on her lips, by now a sort of habit: when was I going to tell Hen? 'I love you,' I said. 'I love you too.' And swept past me with that mile-long gaze, the one that used to speak of wonder at a world that wasn't quite believable, but which now had more to say about exhaustion, boredom, fear, or nothing at all.

I tell Graham some of this over several pints of Ruddles County. He thinks I'm right to be confused. 'When I started seeing my Linda I was still shagging someone else. Remember thinking it was wrong at the time, having a crack at something new like that. But if you're licking it you might as well be dicking it, know what I mean? Well, fuck me from here to Hammersmith! If it ain't Bodwin from the fackin Lotus team!'

'Strange days in the Eel and Merchant!' goes Bodwin.

'Unholy mischief on wilder shores than this!'

and so on ('Will she or won't she?' 'She with the 50cc box!') until I head off for another round. After telling us all we need to know about life on the Lotus team, Bodwin takes us round the corner to an 'F1 Mexican place' where we can fuel ourselves for our break-in. I'm not eating. It's not the prospect of being hauled up for breaking and entering that's turning my guts to oil, but the thought that I might get away with it, just long enough to hear what Hen has to say. How much does she know? What did Roxanne say to her in the pub that night, the last night of her conscious life? *They were lying. It was me who fucked him.* I see Hen sitting alone in her unfurnished flat, just as she was the night I first set eyes on her, when she stood up and stretched in shape-hugging yellow and a rush of blood changed my life. 'I always knew you'd betray me. You did it with Roxanne. Now you've done it with this other woman, what's her name, while I was saving myself for my twin tree. Perhaps your aunt's right, perhaps cheating runs in the family. Perhaps it's in your genes.'

It's dark by the time we get back to the flat. Blue light flashes in Dr Chakrabarty's living room. Upstairs the curtains are still closed. He rings in short bursts, standing back and waiting for something to happen, then joins me by the gate. 'Sure you wanna do this?' I'm sure. He says okay, he'll sit down on this wall and sing. One song will mean trouble and the other will mean proceed. Songs I'll know? 'We're not talking about the fuckin Beatles!' I leave him smoking on his perch, trying to hum his way through some immortal mellotron, and entrust myself to the darkness behind the house.

A thoughtfully placed kitchen window shows Dr Chakrabarty in the folds of a TV lullaby, several cans of superlager empty at his feet. The plan is to retrieve his wheelybin from its upended position in the garden and push it up against the garage wall. I quickly rechristen the wheelybin a scrapybin when a loud grating noise is heard. My heart makes clumsy love to my voice-box. Just as I reach the darkness of the passage, my lookout bursts into song . . . A green ironing board folds itself against the wall. Three teenage girls pass, slapping each other and cackling. I push the bin into position and clamber up. Then I climb up onto the roof of the garage and wait.

Small and leathery beneath me, he sings of hidden glades and forest pools. I cross to the next roof and crawl to the window, heart labouring towards an orgasm that spells the end of this and everything else. A back door opens and eighties pop is broadcast to the world. Dogs bang, bin-lids bark, and all Finn has to do is raise his head, raise his head and look through this window, look through this window and see

Hen, crouched on the bathroom floor, arms clutched around her knees

Hen, stretched out in the bath, pale flesh in a rosewater pool

Hen, dead Hen, with purple lips and hanged stare, one last accusation smothered in her eyes.

The waters are disturbed! The naiad queen Salmacis has been stirred! Legs are numb, asphalt cuts my knees. I need to stand up. So I do that, stand up, hands on the sash conducting my fear-spasms to earth. No dead face stares back at me. The bathroom is the one I know. But there's liquid, glistening on the surfaces, scrawling floor and walls with messages too dark to read. Through the door the walls of the flat gleam yellow, as if a host of candles were burning out of sight.

Down on the street, Graham's singing has taken an urgent turn. Fortunately I have a plan. It doesn't involve smashing any windows or drawing any attention to myself. It involves a builder's patience and a few careful thumps on either side of the sash, as detailed in the last message I got from Hen. you tell me that window is a security risk. i prefer to think of it as a promising opening. you just have to bang on it in a certain way and you can come and go as you please.

I open the window and climb in, stepping down on the toilet seat and pulling the sash down behind.

Back in our old bathroom, with a surprisingly tuneful Graham running through the Genesis back catalogue on the street below, I spend a moment investigating the markings. I was right: it is writing. Curly handwriting, with no capitals or apostrophes, rendered in a silver paint pen. Hen's handwriting. On a floorboard by my feet: *you did this. it was my idea but you were the one who got all dirty pulling up the old boards. you looked like a miner when youd finished, there was so much dirt on you.* On the side of the bath: *my choice. you wanted peach or avocado but i said its got to be white. as white as the innocence of our love.* On the mirror above the sink: *do you ever look at yourself and wonder who you are exactly? like you didnt recognise your own nose and cheeks and eyes?*

The ink is fresh. I turn to the door. Yellow points of light gleam in the gloss, betraying fine latticed brushmarks. On a poster from the Musée d'Orsay: *we went to paris to argue and shop. we're standing outside this kinky junk place and im saying, if you ever decide you want to spend the rest of your life with me, forget the diamond solitaire, THATS the thing i want.*

The living room is lit by maybe fifty candles, stuck with blots of wax to tables and floor. I guess they've been burning for a couple of hours. Everywhere I look there is more writing, all in the same silver pen. On the radiators: *installed by finn causley the week before he moved in, to replace the old ones which never stopped humming.* In the kitchen: *its a fridge, my little loveability. they have fridges up north, dont they?* On the walls, clippings from various papers, some of which I recognise from her room at Moorview: BLISS LINK TO MUSEUM FIRE ... BLISS

ARSONIST CLEARED . . . WHEN WILL THE EXCUSES STOP?

The door to the bedroom is closed. *in this room, in the year 1372, a boy called robinson was made. before he decided he needed to have other children by other women, his father brought him to see me. he has my eyes, i said.* Inside, a double bed is freshly made. A white plastic cylinder, with cap grooved for ease of opening, makes its own dent in the duvet. The label has been torn off and overwritten with silver pen. *to finn, from your twin tree. dont worry, plenty more where these came from!!!!*

In the living room I'm out of breath. Candles crowd and flicker: one for every day we lived here, one for every time I wished her gone. I want to feel something but my heart has pumped itself dry. A bitter dryness in my stomach, dryness in my eyes. Then tears, the tears of someone who should have started crying long ago, smearing the pointed light into clusters of fire, dripping from scorched cheeks to splash on the skin below.

'I'm sorry, Hen. I'm just really fucking sorry, okay?'

No one answers. She was here and then I wished her away. I notice two things. First, a paperback with a familiar cover. Then the computer, her tiny laptop unfolded on the table. I reach across and press any key. There is a click, the hard disc whirrs, the screen glows dark then light grey. On the screen is her last unsent message. `ok i admit it. you and me, blah blah blah. so whats the best way to forget and start again? i can see you need a clue. its this thing which is not really a thing. its yellow orange red. it makes smoke, like a candle, except its much bigger and harder to put out. flames lick the sky. beams crash burning burning. ranulph flies and dies. when you want to forget something what do you do? when youve so much junk in your house that you dont understand? easy. you go in there, you say a little prayer and strike a match or two, and you burn the whole damn lot to the ground.`

Lot 19: **Paperback copy of the medieval English romance**, *Sir Gawain and the Green Knight*, with an inscription inside the front cover reading: 'To Hen from Jack. Good to have you on board.'

LOT
20

Getting back from Norwich is no better and no worse than getting there. No better, because Graham has drunk six pints of Ruddles County over the course of the afternoon and evening, and shows no sign of slowing down to compensate. No worse, because I have also drunk six pints of Ruddles County, enough to make the world seem pillow-soft and pleasant to collide with, which is just as it should be, since my love affair with life is entering the phase of slammed doors and chilly glares. Graham is taking the back way home: fewer miles on the clock, but slower progress on lonelier roads. Our light finds ghostly relief on overhanging trees: tall, grave-silent, fading instantly to black. The sodium glow of out-of-town shopping centres, timber yards, petrol stations where no one has bought anything for hours. Somewhere in that darkness Hen hurtles towards disaster in a stolen car, thumping the steering wheel and pressing lips till they hurt, while her brain is captive to a late-night phone-in from a station whose name she'll never catch.

In a part of the sky called Lincolnshire I thump Graham and signal for him to pull over. He kills the engine, tugs off his helmet and starts rolling cigarettes. I ask if I can use his mobile. Wondering how a flame-melted phone sounds to the caller who has not yet heard about the fire, I dial our private number, on buttons that glow in the dark, with an index finger that won't keep still. Kumar answers. 'Keep an eye out for what?' Hen's face on a Norfolk beach, gilded in the light from her own fires. 'People with matches,' and I listen to him breathe.

'You mean Hen? I'm picking up some real unlove between you two.'

I can't say any more. After tears, a need to do less than nothing, to drift back and see how the done might be undone. There is a wailing noise in the background.

'Einar. His mouse died. He's gone all religious about it.'

By the time Graham drops me in Whieldon Street it is well past midnight. He yawns extravagantly and treats me to a brief outline of his plan. In a minute he's going back to his hotel to try and win his money back off the sheiks. Tomorrow he's going to stick around and wait for Hen to turn up. 'Piggin shame she's on the train. Makes it well harder to track her down.'

'Can you keep a secret?'

'Is Tony Banks a genius?'

I tell him about Hen's earlier career as a borrower of cars, her skill with hairpin and coathanger, the astounding night vision that allowed her to pull the correct wires from a gap in the steering column while pretending to be scratching a foot or feeling for a ladder in her tights. Graham is all plans. 'First thing tomorrow, find out if any vehicles went missing in Letchworth Sunday night.' There's one last thing I want to ask him. 'Did you tell Tom and Jan about the flat?' His head-shaking reaches new levels of vigour and he fastens the helmet under his chin. 'Nothing to tell. They probably think there's still stoodents living there. Stoodents! I tell you I went to university?'

'No,' I say. 'But thanks.' Then he's gone, disappearing down Whieldon Street in a haze of brake lights.

Upstairs, more candles raise soft tents in the gloom. Einar is legless on the sofa, a bottle of Scotch balanced unsafely on his thigh. Jackesque chants spill out from hidden speakers. Hector is laid out in a piece of sky-blue oven-to-table crockery, skirted by thin slices of cucumber, a dozen closely placed candles warding off the dark. Kumar stares at an Italian strip show with the sound turned down, one hand down his trousers and the other propping up his face. All he wants is an excuse to leave. 'The frequencies are wrong. My head's picking up too much junk.' He yawns and stands up. 'By the way, your girlfriend phoned. Left a message on the machine. Matchgirl didn't show, but hey, there's always tomorrow night.'

He switches off and wanders down to his room. I take the bottle and pour myself half a mug. Einar rolls over and puts an arm around my waist. I touch a hand to his ribs, blood quivering in recognition of his warmth, and we lie there, in shared grief and unvoiced longing, until one of the candles gutters out. He leans forward to replace it, then changes his mind.

'How did it happen?'

He thinks for a moment, biting back tears.

'Vacuum cleaner. I am doing my shores. I nearly suck the poor soldier's eyes out.'

'I'm sorry.'

'I lied. It was a natural death. It comes to us all.'

He slumps back on the sofa and stares up at the ceiling. One piggy eye seeks me in the gloom.

'Stay with me.'

'I'm not going anywhere.'

'And I'll stay here with you . . .'

But he won't. He'll be off like everyone else, back to Iceland or beyond, wherever things move a little more smoothly and the past doesn't pile up in the cellar to trip you at every move. I pour more whisky and wait for him to fall asleep. It occurs to me that I might try to find the instructions for the security alarm, so I can change the combination and keep drug-crazed arsonists, even those who mean more to me than anything in the world, out in the night where they belong. But the instructions will be down in the office, lost for ever in Zoë's labyrinthine filing system, and anyway the irony would finish me off. For the last twenty-four hours I've thought of nothing but getting her back, talking to her, hearing her witter on for hours about topics of astounding insignificance, taking her up to the roof and letting her love me beneath passing stars – and now I'm doing my best to keep her out, save my antique goods from her firestarting hands, without realising how much I've already done to keep her away.

Einar can keep snoring on the sofa and the candles can burn on down. Alone in the corridor I hear Anna's voice: cheerful, nervous, pitched to sound interested without appearing to intrude. 'I suppose you're out somewhere.' She pauses, wondering if I'm here and listening. 'Um . . . Give us a ring some time.'

A message on an answering machine; a couple in the first uncharted miles of a love affair, with no history or secrets, only the need to test each other, establish jokes, fair topics and taboos. No reason to doubt what they're doing, or think it should have waited for less complicated times. A face in firelight. A familiar hairband on a peg above the phone. I feel a bursting regret, some loss I do not understand, a taste in my mouth turning to briny heaviness below. It follows me into my room and sinks me into a chair. A charcoal drawing. A white telephone. In a moment I will hear it ring; I will pick it up and hear her voice, her mouth never quite moving fast enough for her brain, ribbing me, failing to listen to what I've been doing, criticising the dress sense of two women walking past, or telling a funny story and getting the crucial information the wrong way round. A red baseball cap. A small white pill. I stare out at terraces trimmed in Victorian iron, roofs of rain-wet slate in rough oblongs, alchemised by streetlight to a muddy gold. Wind rattles the door of the van. She is out there, in a phone box or parked car, her lips unpainted, her body forever scarred, waiting, like me, for the gust that will finish all this, the finale we'll only recognise when it comes.

A gold watch. A crumpled handkerchief. And so on and so on through drawers stiff with yellow folders, handbags, walking sticks, the things we keep to fill the spaces people leave behind.

Two years ago I wondered how we could ever fill a place like this. Even when Serge and I started work on the second floor, there were corners our voices never reached, spaces that no amount of second-hand furniture or tricks with plasterboard could ever make like home. We cluttered the gaps and spread ourselves thinly, shocked – after the cramped flat on Bristol Street – by how easy it was to lose ourselves. Robinson learned to walk on hard floors in echoing halls; we'd find him caught up in a stack of old chairs, or in the stairwell, blue and silly, taking one sheer step at a time. But then we lost Roxanne, and Hen's lapses of concentration took on a sort of urgency of their own. We would find her in the store, hunting through crates and boxes and muttering strange audits into the gloom. We thought: the store, because that's where we found Roxanne. Perhaps something of her dead friend was still there, baseball cap pulled down over her forehead, browsing the aisles between this world and the next. It drew her in, calmed her avid mind and soothed her with appearances, and there came a slowness to her movements that I hadn't seen since she was pregnant, sweating in the heat of that summer with one eyelid drooping and her nose always cold. Yet in bed, with me, she was in a hurry, as if nothing could matter so much as getting back downstairs, to her world of eloquent things, where Roxanne was speaking to her, weaving overheard stories between the punched steel shelves.

I can't say exactly when she changed her mind, when the size and clutter of this place started getting to her and making a ghost of her smile. But when we found her down there one morning, arms around her knees and this same red baseball cap pulled down over her eyes, we could guess what she was trying to say. She'd taken nothing, of course; there was no rattling poison, no synthetic compound from Belarus melting synapses and turning her blood to jam. The professionals whose offices we dragged her through all said the same: that she was simply trying to get back to Roxanne, to find out where the party was and why she hadn't been asked along. All agreed on a change of scene. 'It's doing my head in. All that stuff just sitting there on the shelves. It's like a room full of thousands of people, all screaming their life histories at you. I can't hack it, doc.'

Which is how I came to be standing by the van, one sub-zero morning in January, waiting for her to come down. Two suitcases on the pavement. Hen upstairs finishing her make-up, turning one last circle around the room we shared. She came down the steps, shivering in her blue coat. 'Just for a day or two,' I said. She smiled, past me rather than at me, as if – 'Yeh?' – she'd already moved on. Zoë appeared. 'She's coming with me. For mortal support.' She looked up at the three storeys of the building, arms stiff in her pockets, an orbital terror in her slaty gaze. 'You mean moral?' 'No, I mean mortal.' Only then did she show me that smile. 'We'll get it right one day. When all that stuff is sold. We'll make a ton of cash, have the biggest party you ever saw, then' – and the light was sodium in her eyes.

Friday morning is only morning in that the sky grows lighter and the traffic starts up again. Finn Causley sits in the same chair in the same clothes, thoughts captured in an empty whisky bottle, looking out at beauty accessories, timepieces, letter-racks, all that a violent night has shaken down from shelves and frittered across every surface in the room. Where he's been you wouldn't call sleep. Where? Try a stony beach in Norfolk, watching sun filter through the aftermath of the smoothest surf trip ever, a yellow-haired lover dozing by his side.

The phone rings. Tom Threadgold's polished voice intrudes upon the silence, speaks volumes on these stacked disorders, fag-ends and cardboard boxes and lists and plastic bags.

'We need to pick up some things for Robinson. It's seven now and we're leaving at nine.'

And he must have had his finger on the button, because the line goes dead before I've even had a chance to sigh.

Graham calls. He says three cars were reported missing in the Letchworth area between Sunday and Monday lunchtimes, and he's a smart idea one of them is now in Print. 'And if we don't find her today, a signed album from the US *Lamb* tour says we'll have her – quack! – by cocoa-time tomorrow night.'

Tom and Jan arrive just after midday, bearing my son between them like a trophy, the spoils of a battle I never lifted a finger to win. It seems right that I should lose him as easily as I found him: with a silence-heavy phone call, an initial misunderstanding blooming slowly into realisation: that something has happened that can never be undone. He wears new dungarees and trendy red shoes. A rubber brain no longer follows him on a string. He was too much of a dreamer but now he's too afraid, glancing hauntedly around, his trust of this place and all that happened here now poisoned by their uncontested lies. Jan's handing me a piece of paper is excused by watery smiles.

'We need these things,' she says, her own vowels paining her.

I leave the list flapping in her hand. 'His room's through there,' my voice green, fag-rough. 'Just let me have him for a while.'

Both hesitate, breathing from the stairs and shocked at the mess they've found. Jan's powdered cheeks deepen to pink.

'You know Hen wants us to have him. She thinks he'll be . . . *happier* with . . .'

'People who know how to look after him?'

'Yes.'

305

'Have you spoken to her?'

She stares.

'Then shut your fucking cunt of a mouth.'

Tom steps forward, knuckles whitening on his fists. I'm unshaven and still drunk. He seems to totter. Something thuds to earth. Robin! A headache announces itself with flashing lights and sirens.

'If you were a man . . .'

'Oh, I'm a *man*. Only a *man* could get your precious *daughter* up the *duff*.'

He glares at me, grabs Jan's arm and hurries her next door. I kick the door shut after them and turn to him, my little troublemaker, the cause of all my fighting, I pick him up and hug and hug him till he stops wriggling and starts to sigh. I slump almost voluntarily to the floor and there I hold him, as he twists his head from side to side, craning to see through the clutter to the thing he has still not found.

'I was so worried about you. So worried . . .'

'Where's Mo? Nanna says you know where she is but you won't tell.'

'I don't know where she is. We're gonna find her soon and then we're all gonna be together again.'

'Here?'

'If that's what you want.'

'Grandad bought me a train. You put it on the tracks and it goes round and there's a tunnel for it to sleep in. He says I can have all the trains in the book.'

'He can afford it. That's important.'

'You smell.'

'I haven't had a bath since you ran out on me. Robin?'

'Nut.'

'What was Mo talking about when you were away?'

He stares at a reflection in the mirror, every muscle in his face alive.

'We went to McDonald's. I had a chicken.'

'Was she talking about fire?'

'She was saying about the monks. The abbot was a wimp and they was all drunk all the time. Then King Henry wanted to get married but the Pote wouldn't let him so he told all the monks they had to go and live in holes.'

I hold him to my ear, to listen to his heart, to hear what it sounds like to be alive.

'What's a wimp?'

'A wimp is someone who knows what he has to do but isn't strong enough to do it.'

'Do *you* know what you have to do?'

The door opens. They stand there, flushed, still angry, but finished here for now.

'If I didn't,' says Finn, 'I'm learning now.'

'Is that it?' Anna says. 'Are you going to just stand back and let them take your son away from you?'

Now it's Saturday. Anna came over last night and I haven't told her about Robinson till now.

'They buy him trains. They go to church and stuff.'

'So? If he was my son I wouldn't let him out of my sight. I told you, I couldn't cope with having kids. I'd be panicking about them all the time.'

She slides out of bed and pulls on a shirt. She stands by the open window, biting a thumbnail and looking out onto far blue hills.

'Last night . . .'

'Shh. It happens, Finn.'

Hair stirs in a rooftop breeze. She stands amid the clutter, locking a knee so the leg is straight and pushes her up an inch, then aimlessly, crushingly, letting go. It seems incredible, after what a moon saw on the balcony outside her blue room, that I could know who she is without it meaning anything, that I could fail to raise anything but schoolboy curiosity in what I put under the microscope with dutiful care, that nothing could rouse me in the stir of her breasts or the yawn of her hips, her finely mosaiced skin or her slow trusting musculature, or make me chase what I remember through the places she left open, her bristly mollusc or its stubborn pearl. Nor that she could be so little bothered by it, dressing for another hospital drama, so indifferent to my loss of heart.

Midday I get up and spend an hour in the bath. At threeish my leathered saviour calls, panting like a fat boy. 'Told you I'd find it. I'm on . . . hang on . . . Brindley Street, outside the Conservative Working Men's Club. That's a joke, I like that.'

I cross town in a daze of heat. Hen winks at me from every shop window, burns in every sun-crazed mirror, chases sweat through every crease in my skin. I find Graham peering through the window of a yellow Fiesta, jotting things down in his book.

'This is it. E62 KLP. Lifted from Letchworth town centre Sunday night.'

In the back, stuffed down behind the seats, are boxes in red-and-white plastic bags. On the dashboard, a black elastic hairband curls.

'Any ideas?'

'The bags are from Milton's. Otherwise, yeh, it's her.'

Milton's plays piped pop songs. Milton's people make you smile. Milton's is hardware heaven: kitchenware, dog snacks, paint, electrical goods, wallpaper, gardening utensils . . .

'Candles,' says the ragga lad with tyre-tracks up his nape. 'She bought about twenty boxes of candles.'

Graham folds the photo back into his wallet and waits for the punchline.

'I thought, perhaps she's having a birthday party, sir.'

On a corner a yellow-haired woman smiles. Graham retires to the Working Men's Club to await Hen's return. When I get back the phone is ringing.

'She's gone, in't she. The fuckin car's gone.'

I'm thinking about an evening on a beach in Norfolk, fires burning out of sight, fingers closing around a stone.

'That's all right then, is it?'

It's a decision, Finn. You drop one of these and it all makes sense. But what about the things you left behind, that made you mad with ten thousand shouted stories, now scattered and forgotten behind that door?

Graham's voice is urgent in my ear. 'Look, I've had to tell Threadgold. But I know for a fact they're not leaving Fleet for another couple of hours. He says they're gonna drop the kid off at his auntie's then drive straight back up here.' He pauses for effect. 'We got maybe five hours.'

Shops close and the nearly-thirties get ready to go out. Anna turns up, gauche and unexpected, black-eyed and hurt and quiet. She almost blushes when I tell her we've found Hen. 'What do you want me to do?' she says, pulling back from my rehearsed embrace, our small doomed heaven reflected in one eye. I kiss her, to say that what she's doing is all I could ever have hoped she would do, until something shining on the table catches my eye.

'What's this?' I ask her, just wondering what she'll say.

'It's a stone, Finn.'

'That all?'

'Yes. Unless this is some kind of test and I've just proved I'm not the person you want me to be.'

She sits down on the bed and starts picking at a thread on her dress. Einar comes in with tea and anchovies, followed by a shirtless Kumar and some suntopped hippy whose name I forget. You can tell there's a crisis because we're all in here sweating quietly, staring at the junk and feeling absences like a fever, the next move an impossible joke. Finding comfort in science and confidence in her comfort, Anna takes us through today's main news: Mrs Matthewman's latest refusal to include St Mary's Disease in the list of disorders covered by the 1983 Mental Health Act. 'It's political common sense.' She brushes fluff from a thigh and looks up. 'Basically, if you're going to run a country you've got to have people responsible for their actions. Plus the fact that as soon as you recognise it as a disorder each one of however many thousand sufferers immediately are eligible for full invalidity benefit. And amongst all the *Daily Mail* readers who think the only problem with people like Hen is pure lazy-boneyness, that's not exactly going to go down too well.'

'It's about time someone pulled the batteries out of that woman.'

'But it's more than that, Kumar.' She scrubs her knee and frowns. 'The fact is there's too many people see this as something to be *aspired* to. D'you remember those adverts in the eighties, trying to keep people off heroin?'

'Lanky blokes in gutters looking ill?'

'Yes. Do you remember what happened to them?'

'Lanky blokes with AIDS sitting in gutters looking ill?'

'No, before that.' She gathers looks. 'They became fashion items. Kids used to see these things and suddenly stop eating and washing,

---

Lot 20: **Pebble**, grey streaked with amber, from an East Anglian beach, several hundred million years old.

just so they could look like the people in the pictures. They used to cut them out of magazines and stick them on their walls like it was a band or something. Now it's the same thing happening with Bliss. All the trendy rave magazines are running cover stories on this weird happy state with the spooky drug link. You know, I'm seeing people dying out there and I'm thinking, My God, this can't be happening. There's people going round faking the smile, staring at things and describing them over and over again, just so's people will think they've got it.'

'You reckon Hen might be faking it?' says Kumar.

Anna looks at me with sudden cruelty, or irritation, or maybe no intention at all.

'What do you think, Finn? Is Hen the sort of person to fake things?'

Cruelty. I sit back and sweat. I remember blue-and-green friendship bands, scraps of paper with names written on them, small white freedom-giving pills.

'So where is she then?' says Kumar.

'You say she bought candles. What do you think she's going to do with twenty boxes of candles?'

'Maybe she's expecting a power cut,' says the hippy.

Einar totters to his feet. 'We have no power cuts in Iceland. This because we have no electricity. If we get cold we go and sit in a volcano till our faces are glowing and we are full of happy songs. But these songs,' he frowns, 'I do not remember what they say.'

But the auctioneer remembers. Stocked up to recall what everyone else forgot, equipped to read clues in every telling object, every cheerful song in three-quarter time that ever lost itself on a moorland breeze ... He is picking up a book from the desk, glancing at the dedication and flicking through the pages with wrinkling thought. Towards the end he stops, leafs back a few pages and folds the book out flat. A passage is marked in silver pen:

> Hit hade a hole on the ende and on ayther syde,
> And overgrowen with gresse in glodes aywhere;
> And al was holw inwith, nobot an olde cave,
> Or a crevisse of an olde cragge – he couthe hit noght deme
>   with spelle.
> 'We! Lorde,' quoth the gentyle knyght,

'Whether this be the grene chapelle?
Here myght aboute mydnyght
The dele his matynnes telle!

'What does it mean?' says Anna.
An eye twitches. 'It means we can ask her ourselves.'

We reach the bottom of the stairs just as Tom Threadgold's maroon machine corners into Whieldon Street, followed by Graham on his bike. 'We'll take mine,' says Anna: 'I'll meet you round the back.' She walks her blue dress into the silvering evening, confidently past the man on the motorbike being interviewed by the man in the car. I go back upstairs and cut through to the back entrance, where Anna's engine is running and doors unlocked. Jan puckers her lip and watches us, puzzled, as we drive out. We take the road north out of town, past old mill-owners' houses and retirement homes, down a steep hill and up a steeper one, so Anna has to drop to third and then to second and keep her foot to the floor. Buildings, a pub, a sorry petrol stop, then the endless green emptiness that pulls roofs off houses and kills within hours. To the north-west, the Pikes rise in purple, peaks lit with the last of the sun.

'Why do you think she's in a church?'

We turn left off the main road and push up through winding forest until the road is a single straight track. She listens quietly to my lesson. Land drops away to the left, stealing our eyes away over the reservoir and blanketed outskirts of Print. Rightwards and above, great stacks of granite overhang us, balancing a million tons of doom.

'Don't look now,' she says, accelerating, 'but I think they're following us.'

A mile back the twin headlights of the BMW puncture the gloom. I have to get out to open a metal gate, watch Anna drive through then close it behind. A hundred yards on, another gate stays open. At the end of the track she slows to walking pace and I hear her daunted breaths. The yellow Fiesta cools in sandy shadows of impending stone. We have seen no other cars.

'I'll wait here,' she says. 'If anyone asks . . .'

and I'm out of the car and running, up a walled track, over a stone stile and down, down into the river-veined valley, where Gawain went down one New Year's morning, and monks in white robes announced the green man's coming with the hammering of iron on stone.

With the bank on my left and the river rushing out of sight, I follow the signs to Lud's Church. Roots are treacherous underfoot. I slip and fall, push to my feet and run, past collapsed trunks in hollows plush with last year's leaves, nets of branchwork, weedy flowers in spots of yellow and mauve. I don't call out; I don't need to be heard. Like those before me I want the cave that is not a cave, three holes in the hillside where you can hide all that shouldn't see day, where legends tell of a strange man in Lincoln green, Lollards outwaiting law in the fourteenth century, and a young woman with yellow hair waiting on a rock for her lover to arrive.

There are two ways into Lud's Church. You can stick to the path until you meet a hole in the hillside on your left, or you can follow me up above the path and climb down from the ridge, where the sky is near and sugary and light rises vaporous and pink. A crack opens in the earth, yawns to a fissure, cuts down through spindly grasses and alien ferns to sheer sides of gritstone and hanging scrub. And candles: melted onto rocky ledges, balanced in mossy tufts and softly gilding the giddying abyss.

'This is a private party. Ramblers not invited.'

I look up. A strip of sky is fringed with grass. High up on a ledge, dropped by careless wind or crow, Hen crouches in jeans and primrose shirt, boxed in by green-brown sides of rock.

'Hen, it's me.'

'Oh yes, I remember. You don't ramble, do you? You just blunder.'

It's enough. All the love I tried to smother bursts from my throat in a searing tearful breath.

'Hen, I'm sorry . . .'

'Pardon?'

'I'm sorry. Can you just come down and we can talk about it?'

Something flies up into the air, bounces off the rock face opposite and clatters to the ground. It rattles, white and plastic, in my hand.

'Those are for you. Yummy. I've already had mine.'

'Hen . . .'

She breathes deep and shuffles on her heels. 'This is the story of a girl called Lady Lud. Her grandfather was Walter de Ludauk, a follower of Wycliffe the God-botherer, who used to hold secret church services in this very cave. One night the King's men came upon them when they were at prayer, and in the ensuing punch-up Alice, Walter's yellow-haired granddaughter, was shot with an arrow and killed. There. The oak at the entrance marks my grave. Always knew I'd be a fourteenth-century heroine when it came down to it.'

The voice won't hold. 'For Christ's sake, Hen, what have you done?'

'Only kidding. I got too interested in the magazine to remember to take the pills. Anyway, you needn't have worried. I could never do what Rox did, I haven't the *concentration*.'

'Come down. Please?'

She stands up, careful as a drunk, and descends unhurriedly to the next rock. Stones break away and thud to earth. She crouches, almost slips, saves herself on a root and sits down, swinging her legs.

'Great venue. Only one tourist in all this time. I told him I was a witch and I'd fallen off my broomstick. He was German, I don't think he understood but he scarpered none the less.'

I watch her, desperate to care for her, catch her, hold, love.

'Why did you do it?'

'Do what?'

'Run away. Take the kid.'

'I just wanted to get to know him better. You used to bring him to see me every day but then you got bored. And I thought I was being talkative.'

'I didn't get bored. I thought you were bored with me.'

'I thought blah blah blah etcetera. That's Finn for you. Somehow there's a reason for everything but it's never anything to do with him. Shame you never had a reason for staying with me.'

'I did. I have.'

'I'm listening.'

(Once, on a bridge in a foreign city, he might have come closer than this.)

'I loved you.'

'Speak up.'

'I love you. I still love you.'

The silence almost topples her. For a moment I suspect she's given in to gravity and my punishment is to watch her crash. But then she straightens arms against the rock and regains her balance, pulling in her feet.

'I'm in this green room. It's getting on for dawn. It's familiar somehow, the wardrobe, the chest of drawers, the bed. The box on the shelf with my writing on it. There are two people in the bed. I know one of them . . .'

'Stop . . .'

'But the other one's a mystery. She's wearing my jumper. She's sleeping where I usually sleep, with the person I usually sleep with. But she's not me. I don't know, the mirrors are broken and it's seven years' bad luck all round. You see doc, I don't know who's me and who's not me any more.'

At last she looks at me, arms tight around her stomach, a puzzled crease above her eyes. If she fell now she'd probably break a wrist.

'The point wasn't to hurt you.'

'Oh, don't worry about the *point*. I knew you'd do it sooner or later. Why do you think I left that big place? As soon as I heard about Roxanne I . . .'

'What did you hear about Roxanne?'

'As I was saying, as soon as I heard about Roxanne I realised . . .'

'What did you hear? Think you could maybe tell me?'

She swallows and stares, bites invisibly, features strengthening at my tone.

'Oh, you know. That you cavorted naked with her on the last day of her life, when she should have been informing her bank and sending back her credit cards.'

'How do you know that?'

'Because she *told* me, Finn.'

'She lied. I pushed her away. She thought I was Blake and she tried to . . . I didn't let her.'

'Cor, such a big head and such a tiny little brain. I know you didn't fuck her as you like to put it. Why do you think she killed herself? Because Blake, i.e. you, had rejected her. Cruel, heartless Blake, the only man she ever loved and he goes and knocks her back like that. I heard that and I thought, There he goes, trying to do everything properly and getting it all wrong.'

'You saying I should have done that and you'd have been happy knowing?'

'There's other ways of caring for someone, Finn. Anyway, I wouldn't have known, would I? Oh, unless you thought you'd invite me along. Yeh, come in, Hen, stand in the doorway and watch how I do it with someone I actually fancy. No, you didn't come up with that idea till later.'

'Hen, you're ill.'

'Well if you say so, darling. But actually I think you're the one that needs help. You're obviously never going to really love anyone.'

'I *am*. I *do*.'

'Oh do me a favour. You think you've come up with a real emotion just because your eyes are red and your little voice is quivering. Then if at last you ever *do* feel something, you just carry on with whatever unobvious thing you were doing before. When you can see perfectly well what your father did to your mother you make that stupid smarmy Clark Gable face and start humming that stupid song. I mean, did you actually *believe* that story about Mike Browning? All the fairies are dead, Finn. And don't think you take after Margaret either because you don't, she was a mountain and you're just a little hump. No, in fact do you know who you remind me of? You're your father, Finn: a bit pathetic, a bit cowardly, turning a blind eye to everything because it's easier than admitting what's actually going on.'

Now the auctioneer reaches for her, but she is far above and beyond, and she stands, brave, mocking, and he falls to his knees, to dead leaves and shattered rock.

'Anyway, there's more to being faithful than just keeping your pants on when someone you fancy walks in. Love is about being true to someone in your *head*. For example, when you're in love with someone else and always have been, I mean coming out and maybe *owning up* to it.' She sways, steadies herself. 'I'm not blind, sweetheart, I've *seen* the little bracelet she gave you. It's the lies, Finn, not the fucking. I could maybe have lived with that.'

I'm holding the bottle, gripping the cap and turning it, mind in circles and sky already speeding overhead.

'Go on, one won't hurt. Fires on the beach? You and me in love? Take yourself on a wonderful trip.'

A white pill on a palm, our old temptation, the way back to the way it used to be. I stare and stare but it gives no instructions, only promises happiness I know too much to sustain. I drop it and crush it with one heel into the rock.

'Have you been taking these?' The bottle seems full.

'Get away. Those days are over, if you hadn't noticed. Anyway, I've been getting quite enough excitement zooming around in Tony's mate's helicopter. You know, Rox would've *loved* it up there.'

She sits down again, ruddy with emotion, hips rolling and skin gleaming between her buttons. 'How's the kid? I presume he's with Mummy and Daddy.'

'He's fine.'

'And what about that private detective bloke? Dr Chakrabarty told me all about him. What a star!'

'He's fine too.'

'So everyone's happy.'

'No.'

'Oh dear.'

'Come home.'

'I'm sorry, darling, but that's just not a good idea. Apart from the fact that three is an awful lot of people to fit into our little bed, I've got this nasty brain disorder and it means I'm not responsible for anything I do. Doctor says it's all those pills I took when I was younger. Or should I say, all those pills *we* took.'

'Hen, we can sort this out. Come . . .'

'No. Anything else?'

A rustle of clothing at the far end of the cave. I haul to my feet, pocketing the bottle and brushing dirt from my knees. Anna is breathless from running, glancing with dry lips at the candles, self-conscious and refusing surprise. She registers Hen like furniture and a bastard in me starts to shout.

'They're coming,' she announces flatly. 'I just thought I'd better tell you.'

'So this is Anna,' barks Hen from her ledge. 'She looks different with her knickers on.'

Anna glances up, frowning, then turns dully to me.

'I'm going.'

'No, wait. Very sorry. Won't mention your knickers again.'

316

'Have you told her?' Anna says.

'I . . .'

'You haven't. Okay.'

'He has,' says Hen. 'He's told me he doesn't love me any more because he really loves you. Has done since he met you. We were just winding things up, talking about old times, before science, before NTX, doctors who thought they were gods.'

Anna stares past me into the cave. She breaks a thought and walks over, anorak rustling, one arm pulling at my side.

'Are you okay?' Outnumbered like this, just when I thought I was making a choice.

'Oh I forgot! You're a doctor too!' Hen fidgets, rocking gleefully on flattened hands. 'I've got this funny pattern on my tummy. It's agony when it rains. What do you think it might be?'

Love looks at me without understanding. Love watches us both with amused contempt. I'm losing them both, the one I had and the one I wanted, the fact that became a figment and the dream that leaned forward into the real. Anna starts to speak but Hen is moving, standing up and turning back the way the uninvited come. Different voices, the flirt of a torch, small rocks breaking away from bigger piles and settling their differences with earth. Two figures appear at the lower entrance, all voices suddenly hushed.

'Oh fuck,' says Hen. 'It's Hampshire's Finest.'

Her mother's face is stitched with grief.

'Henrietta!' shouts Tom, starting forward over unsafe rocks.

Then a sort of inevitable calm. 'All right, all right,' and we watch her, dazed by candlelight, pick a way from ledge to rock to earth. They swallow her, crush her with their decencies and make her a child again in their arms. Jan sees me – '*No!*' – Tom grabs Hen's arm and pulls her back, but love escapes, turns to me, spinning her eyes like I'd always been in on the joke.

'Wait for me on the path. Go on, I won't be long.'

So they're turning, battered shadows, sliding into the dusk beyond. Anna has disappeared. My other stands before me, my hands pressed in hers, staring at my wrists with a heartbreaking wonder that I could still be unfamiliar after so long.

'Who do you love?' she says.

'You. I love you.'

'Oh dear. Wrong answer.'

'I mean it.'

'Since when?'

All the times I said it as an excuse for not meaning it, all the days I tried to wish her away, and now she stands here, softened by time, her birdish energy humming in every nerve, her complicated eyelids holding tears. And her humbling resilience, a look of having come through some terrible ordeal with the important thing intact.

'I always loved you. I just maybe didn't realise it.'

She shivers, as something quits her and loops into the night.

'What's wrong with Anna? She doesn't laugh at my jokes.'

'That's because they're not funny.'

She huffs and smiles and on the surface I laugh, I laugh.

'D'you remember when you asked me to marry you?'

'Hen . . .'

'Well you were about to anyway. We're on this famous bridge in Paris and you're acting funny, like there's some big secret going on. Has he bought them? I wonder. Has the clever boy been back to the shop on his own? Anyway, after you broke that first lot I always said we should get some more. Then, I don't know, I must start chatting on about something else and never get to hear the big plan. Shame, really. I could have looked great in a meringue.'

'So why didn't you ask me?'

'Because I knew what you'd say.'

'Yeh?'

'Yes.'

(Once, on a bridge in a foreign city, he held something in his pocket that would have answered her questions for good . . .)

'HENRIETTA!' shouts darkness. Bats flit in fear. I stumble into her, knees failing, and she catches me, gasping, her life hard against mine.

'We could do it now. Tomorrow.'

'It's a bit late.'

'Don't say it's too late.'

'I will if it is.'

'Hen . . .'

'HENRIETTA!'

'You'll get over it. Think of it as a mad fling that went on a bit too long.'

Tears. 'Don't I mean anything to you?'

'Of course you do. You're the love of my life.'

'So . . . ?' I crush her closer, clumsy, frightened.

'You don't get it, do you?'

That's it: I don't get it. She holds me for the last time. She kisses me, afraid of herself and the hurt she might disturb, quick eyes searching for an escape. The next thing is calling her, hurrying her to prepare, rousing her duty to tackle life like a simultaneous equation or a thousand-item memory test. She turns, picks a quick path over the rubble, pushing down on knees with both hands.

'Hen?'

'Yes darling?'

'Keep in touch.'

She holds there, frozen in mid-step, one last doubting smile on her lips. A thought clouds her eyes. For a moment I think she's going to change her mind, that we can walk back to the old room and pick up our life where we left it, the three of us, for all the ever that remains. But I'm already forgotten. I watch her climb the rocks to the path and turn off into a tree-thick dark.

Night is an absence, a gap no future can fill. Anna comes with deadened footsteps, testing the gloom for a body to stand against.

'What now?'

'I'm going home to do my job.'

She laughs. 'What does that mean?'

'An auction. Like no one's ever seen.'

'But . . . what are you going to sell?'

Something must be frightening her, because when I want her to look at me she flinches, halts, looks up and left into a green black blue past.

'Everything. The whole fucking lot.'

'Do you mean that?'

He looks at her in the fading light of candles, the broken vein, the anxious body in the blue dress, and there can be no mistaking the certainty on his face.

LOT
21

'You are each holding a catalogue. It comes to you in permanent green, bearing the name of the maker and his watermark, to please the three-colour artist, the list-maker, the incorrigible hoarder and the casual connoisseur. It has been put together in little more than a month, in a small room above our heads, to the rustling of paper in boxes and much humming of misremembered tunes. For those of you of a green persuasion, I can tell you that every fibre of it is recycled: what used to be someone's life story is now a brief guide to modern things. In this little book, fellow travellers and customers, entire histories can be divined. What's more, it has cost you nothing; it's the only thing here that is not for sale. Buzz the pages, get a little high on fixative and ink, and remember that even those who only sit and watch will not be going away empty-handed. From the people of Big Kimberley to the citizens of Print: a few of our favourite things.'

An expectant murmur, as if the room were picked up and gently shaken, building at the edges and rippling through the audience in tides. Junk hangs from ceiling hooks, clutters tables, piles up in the spaces between feet. Print people stand with arms folded in the

---

The Catalogue: printed on sixteen sheets of acid-free paper, folded to produce a thirty-two page booklet, wire-stitched into a laminated green cover. At the centre, several fine black-and-white photographs depict items from the sale. On the cover, in black capitals: BIG KIMBERLEY AUCTION ROOMS. GRAND SUMMER AUCTION. 2 P.M., SATURDAY JULY 5TH.

wings; pale Etruscans lean against columns or perch on gritty sill-tiles behind. A high haze of fag smoke is stirred by a longed-for breeze. Beyond the glass, above cast-iron snow-guards and verdigris hatches, the sky is circus blue.

'Thank you. Now, before we get started, a few words on today's sale.'

He stands on the rostrum, in the deep green of his profession, scalp flashing under a single fluorescent tube. A cigarette burns in a yellow saucer. He casts raw eyes over his audience, clearing his throat with a succession of cold-engined coughs. Four rows down on the left, a sunbed tan, a clean-shaven property dealer, a greying builder and his diminutive mate, and a white-haired widow guarding an empty seat. Across the aisle and back, the jet-haired financier with the striking complexion hides her boyfriend's hand. A phone call, a cryptic plea. Delicate blackmail disguised as innocuous chat. Two hundred miles on a Saturday morning, on roads that get worse the further north you go, a land where you don't understand what people say the first time so you have to hear it once, twice again. Still none of them knows why they're here.

'First of all, sorry there wasn't time for a proper viewing before the sale. But if you're the sort who likes to cop a feel before you buy, Kumar and David – welcome to the team, David – will be passing some lots round as we go.'

'He could pass me round any day,' says Mrs Bickerton, as her friend sucks sweat from her lip.

'A note on the catalogue. Inside the front cover you'll find the usual rules of the sale. Then, on Page One, a list of categories. Mrs Bootherstone, perhaps you'd like to read them out.'

'Me?' She starts in fright.

'Yes. If you don't mind.'

She wipes her lip and frowns. 'One: SOMETHING GREEN. Two: CHILDHOOD MEMORIES. Is this what you . . . ? Three: ARTICLES OF CLOTHING FOR IMMEDIATE PERSONAL OR DOMESTIC USE. Number Four: LOVE IS NOT A THING. Five, no thank you, REMINDERS OF THE BEAUTIFUL DEAD. Number Six: SONGS TO LEARN AND SING. Seven: WAYS OF GETTING WHAT YOU WANT. Eight: TOOLS FOR THE IMPROVEMENT OF SIGHT. Nine: PRECIOUS LITTLE EVIDENCE. Ten: THINGS THAT ARE DONE WITH. Eh . . . that's it.'

A breeze of applause. Fame for Mrs Bootherstone, her saffron embarrassment deepening with every clap. Her friend speaks angrily to the man behind.

The auctioneer blows smoke. 'Categories. A brief guide to modern things. Those with a restless urge to understand will see the appeal immediately; the rest can take the questions in any order, buying and selling as they go. But buying *what*? What is it, this Thing that can be bought and sold? Something with a name. Something that *is*. Something that exists, and carries on existing when you're not looking at it. Something that gets lost. Something you thought was lost and then turns up in your bed, smirking like an angel, and makes sure nothing is ever the same. But more: what?'

'It's a memory,' says Mrs Bickerton. 'That's what you said last time.'

'A memory. An object is something that *remembers*, and does so a damn sight better than your average husband with his strange brain disorders and his fascination with blank walls.' Zoo-like stirring from the floor. 'But that's only if there's someone around to *read* that meaning, preferably someone – sorry Linden – with a mind of his own.'

'What's *he* doing here?' says Serge on Artwork and Misc.

Linden slurps his Fanta. 'I'd booked my ticket and everything . . .'

'Don't worry, I promise you'll get paid this time. Anyway, a thing only has meaning as long as someone can take it as having that meaning. In fact, if I were to say the word *thing* to a Viking,' (the Second Auctioneer pricks up his pointy ears) 'he'd say it meant a *meeting*. Simple. Look it up. An object is where the mind of the maker and the mind of the interpreter sit down together for a chat.'

'Are you actually selling anything?' says Mr Koliaczek from the doorway. 'Because I've got a garden to dig.'

'Yes, I'm selling. All crates must be cleared!' He pulls on his filter and coughs. 'So if an object is something that *means* something, then a collection of objects, like the one we're looking at today, is a Collection of Meaningful Things. And what do we call a collection of meaningful things?'

'A museum,' says Mrs Bickerton.

'I like that. A friend of mine used to say this place was too much like a museum for anyone's good. But not what I had in mind.' He hears silence and raises his eyes. 'Here's a clue. If I didn't have so much crap to look after, I wouldn't be wasting so many of them now.'

'Words!' says the young man with the cheekbones.

'And? What do we call a collection of words?'

'A story,' says his beautiful bride.

'A story. A collection of meaningful things tells a story. It can tell you how this led to that and that led to this, and some were sorry about it, and some may even have been to blame. But as long as the finished product had a beginning, a middle and an end, a few flecks of blood and gristle, a hint of sweat and sperm, I for one would be proud to call it a story and tell it to my fellow travellers on a sunny Saturday afternoon.'

'Is he wonderful or is he wonderful?' says Mrs Bootherstone.

'He is,' says Mrs Bickerton. 'He really is!'

And that wonderful trusting smile! 'To show you what I mean, let's have a look at some of the lots that are up for auction today. First category: SOMETHING GREEN. In a moment you'll get a chance to bid for a five-and-a-half-inch Staffordshire figurine, 'The Silk Twister', fired in 1966 at the Royal Etruscan Manufactory, after an unusual nineteenth-century design. Kumar is passing it round as I speak. It depicts a scene that would not have been uncommon in a place like Big Kimberley in the early days of steam: a woman at a throwing wheel, twisting tirelessly for buttons and pins. It's the expression that gets me, though: the sense of an outrage that has been silenced for long enough. What has she seen? What knowledge could be so shocking that even the dead can't find peace? If anyone out there knows something, let's hear about it some time.'

Kumar's instructions are to take the Silk Twister down the left aisle and hand it to the woman in the fourth row. Joy Causley, glowing gently beneath her spectacular perm, smiles as she always does when she thinks she's getting special treatment, and passes it quickly to the man at her side. No one notices his uneasy recognition, the bitten irritation in the lips, nor the way the Silk Twister returns his stare, her glazed accusation unfaded by two decades of attic dark.

'What's next? CHILDHOOD MEMORIES. Kumar?'

Kumar checks his list, reaches under the table and pulls out a light grey plastic sphere. He walks to the fourth row and hands it to Joy, who glances at it like TV.

'Is there anyone here who hasn't once begged Santa for a plastic spaceman's helmet, or dreamed of walking off this planet and taking his place among the silver-paper stars? Note, please, the dent in the temple region, just above the visor hinge. Someone, way back in astral time, must have caught a chunk of flying debris. Question is: did the child survive? What is he doing now?'

The auctioneer sweats. His eyes keep returning to the white-haired woman in the fourth row, who seems to be trying on a smile.

'D'you think he's all right?' says Mrs Bootherstone. 'He looks a bit, I don't know . . .'

'Three: ARTICLES OF CLOTHING FOR IMMEDIATE PERSONAL OR DOMESTIC USE. A few bits for you to look at, when you're ready, lads. Sage-green belted raincoat, still with a handkerchief in the pocket. Then, from the same box, a turquoise polyester headscarf and a necklace of plastic beads. Could they add up to a woman? Forget it: there's no story here.'

When Peter Causley sees the raincoat, a twenty-year-old note of recognition is torn off, crumpled tightly and dumped where all unanswered messages go. His wife whispers to him but gets no reply. A few seats down, his first wife's sister makes a note in her catalogue and shares a joke with the empty seat.

'Remember, anyone can bid for these lots. The ladies may display their taste in a thousand ways! Now, we always promise surprises, and that's exactly what we get with LOVE IS NOT A THING. It's a wooden box, bound with iron and carved to a pleasant rose design. The mystery is that it's locked. There may be nothing inside. On the other hand . . .'

'It might be treasure,' says the daughter of the Asian family.

'Who wants to find out?' He hiccups and checks the clock on the wall. 'Next category I've called REMINDERS OF THE BEAUTIFUL DEAD. Kumar? Red baseball cap? Interclipping plastic strips?'

Kumar sits back and shakes his head.

'Oh no,' says Einar from the rostrum. 'You are not selling this.'

'But lads, anyone can make a bid! It's worth whatever you want to pay.'

The cap moves hesitantly to David who, having no other instructions, passes it to the home-dodger at the end of the front row. She reads the badge and gives a scandalised little laugh.

'Tell us, Einar, do you really need this more than Mrs Biscay over there? Anyway, you'll find one on every schoolkid. This next item is far more revealing.'

Kumar rummages in a box and comes up with a red plastic bowl, which he holds one-handed above his head and tilts this way and that.

'Any ideas?'

'Looks like a potty,' says the Asian girl.

The ladies at the front laugh and fan themselves with their catalogues.

'Not quite. Anyone else?'

'It's a footbath,' says Benny the Tramp, who, because he's had no bath of any kind since the abolition of National Service, always gets a corner to himself.

'A footbath. Look inside and you'll see it's split into two separate compartments, one for the left and one for the right. Who lives in a footbath like this?'

'Someone with smelly feet,' says the Asian girl. 'You fill it with water and wash them . . .'

She fades out, face twisting in shyness.

'Not necessarily,' says Mrs Bickerton. 'You might have feet what swell up in the heat! Mind you, haven't seen one of them things in years.'

'Twenty years,' says Finn. 'Twenty years . . . Which brings us to our next category: SONGS TO LEARN AND SING. Kumar, when you're ready.'

'Five video tapes,' says Kumar. '*Hide and Seek, 1973–1977*. Isn't that . . . ?'

'Izzy, Lizzy and Joe,' says the better half of the beautiful couple.

'Take them gently, for they are attached to my heart. If anyone wants to watch a clip or two before they make up their minds, that can be arranged. Just one question, though. If I remember anything, *Hide and Seek* was still going out when Our Lady of Grantham arrived to save us all. So why do the tapes only go up to 1977? Did someone lose interest? Or did something else happen that year?'

It's getting hotter. Expressions range from peering interest to attitudes of sleep. The auctioneer adjusts the microphone and is answered by a squeal of juice from the PA.

'All right, WAYS OF GETTING WHAT YOU WANT. David is handing round a leather handbag, as fresh and glossy as the day it left the shop. Suspicious? Look inside. There's the receipt, headed *Duke's of Stafford* and dated 18th April 1977. That year again. Questions. Why was the handbag bought and never used? What happened to the woman in the green raincoat, whose feet swelled up in the heat, who took such an interest in the children's programme *Hide and Seek*?'

'Perhaps she kicked the bucket,' says Mr Koliaczek. 'Is that what you're extrapolating?'

'Comes to us all, Mr K. Perhaps her hands swelled up as well as her feet. Perhaps the irritation drove her off the road, so to speak.'

His father blinks and stares. Joy's smile begins to slip. Mervyn and Teri make delicious puzzlement, as the white-haired widow muses into her lap.

'What the bloody hell are you on about?' goes Mr Goldstraw.

'Stop playing silly buggers!' yells Mr Kopffüssler, tilting for a fight.

'Customers are free to depart whensoever they wish!' barks the Second Auctioneer. No one moves.

'Category Seven: TOOLS FOR THE IMPROVEMENT OF SIGHT. Don't bother with the tortoiseshell reading glasses, Kumar, they could be anyone's. Let's see where the gold lies: an Ordnance Survey map of Print and environs, marked at one place by a single red cross. Mrs Bickerton, would you tell us where the treasure is buried?'

She takes the map from David, opens it up and presses it onto her knees. 'Ah, here it is. That's road to Schyre. X marks the spot!'

'What are the features of the landscape at that point, Mrs Bickerton?'

'Ooh, not a lot. There's . . . what's this? A footpath. No houses, no telephones, nowt.'

'Perhaps she had an accident,' says her bucktoothed pal. 'Them joyriders are always down there wrapping themselves round trees.'

'She had an accident. Her car came off the road at exactly that spot and hit something much bigger than she. It was that day in 1977, the day she bought the handbag which, like its owner, never had the bother of getting old. An unseasonably hot day.'

Joy's bliss is melting. Peter's eyes are hot stones.

'Aren't you reading a bit much into this?' says Mrs Bickerton.

'A hot day. A woman whose hands swell up in the heat. Kumar, PRECIOUS LITTLE EVIDENCE.'

'Lot 14. Says here: Thanks to Alison for borrowing it and bringing it along. Who's Alison?'

'I'm Alison,' says Alison. 'Listen, we're the kind of family who like to help each other out.'

Now Peter Causley is turning in his seat and glaring at his daughter across the room. Sweat gleams at his bloodless hairline. He turns back and stares into the seat in front, nostrils white, muscles working in his cheeks.

'There's an inscription on the inside,' says Kumar, 'but . . .'

'Mrs Bootherstone. Perhaps you'll have a go.'

She takes the ring from Kumar and peers in. 'No. Can't see a thing.'

'Then perhaps you'd like to try it on.'

Mrs Bootherstone looks slowly at the gold.

'Superspicious?' says Mrs Bickerton. 'Give it here.'

She swaps the ring for her own. A scraping of chairs, as folk on all sides stand up to watch. It slips easily over the first knuckle, but at the second it stops and will not budge.

'It's tight! And I've got tiny fingers. My Doug always said . . .'

'The ring is tight. And if it's a hot day, and the person who's wearing it has a problem with swelling hands, it might be more than she can manage to get it off. It might be enough to make her lose her grip on the steering wheel, go straight on when she should have turned a corner, and maybe . . .'

'She'd have to be in quite a hurry,' says the mother of the Asian family, the first time we've heard her speak.

'Perhaps she was upset about something,' says Mrs Bootherstone.

'Happen she were being chased by Christians!' offers Benny the Tramp.

'I couldn't say,' hums the auctioneer.

The hubbub drops. Kumar crouches and delves in a brown envelope. The fourth row watches it like a dream.

'Is it going tell us what happened?' says Mr Koliaczek. 'Because I've got a garden to . . .'

'Da-DA!' says Kumar, holding up the gold loop of a braceleted ladies' watch.

An animal cry, immediately stifled, from the end of the fourth row. Joy Causley sits up for the view, frowns, opens her mouth, sinks back, closes her mouth, turns to her husband and forgets every word she wanted to say.

'Yes, my fellow travellers and customers, we should all be crying now. It may be a little late, it may not seem like the weather for it; you might think all this stuff should be forgotten, these junk-cluttered stories from so long ago. But we should cry anyway, for the woman in the sage-green raincoat, whose fingers swelled up in the heat. You have this friend, you see, who goes with you everywhere, who knows what you're going to say before you say it, who can let you know what she's thinking with just a look – yes? – or a smile. So when, at the end of a spring weekend at your favourite provincial hotel, you come back from a shopping trip and find your best friend's watch on the table by your bed, you think she's left a sign for you, some faint message scratched in the gold. But when you go round to your best friend's room – customers, I'm only selling, you'll have to fill in the gaps for yourselves – when you push on that door and see what struggles so lovingly under a candlewick bedspread and a tassel-shaded light, you think more of treachery than friendship, more of universal abstracts than brand-new handbags, reading glasses, strings of plastic beads. If you know one thing you know you have to get away, far and fast, on a hot day when your hands are burning and not even the ring he married you with will loosen its grip, when the sky is blinding and the things the world throws at you are just too quick, too huge . . . And that's why the Silk Twister has that look on her face.'

For a moment no one breathes. But how much is a moment? How long does the truth take?

'That's not true!' screams Joy, standing up and lashing at her husband's hands. 'You know nothing about it!'

'That's it!' says Miss Parry-David. 'You are making all sortses of conclusionses on no evidences!'

The sky falls in. Chairs bang and voices clash. Now Peter is standing too, and the two are trying to force their way out along the line and through the violent crush at the sides.

'Please!' says the auctioneer. 'Customers can leave whenever they want!'

'We supposed to believe you?' roars a purpling Mr Goldstraw. 'Junk don't tell stories! You're just making the whole thing up!'

'It's all true.'

'Why should we believe that?' Now the crowd turns on him, murmuring.

'Because,' comes a clear voice from the back, 'it's his mother he's talking about.'

At the door the father turns, his whole body broken, staring at the table in despair. The man who never had any trouble finding a joke, the man who would not be talked down by anyone, has nothing to say. One last glance at his daughter, the wild astonished crowd, and he's gone, down the stairs and out into the heat.

'What, your mother what's dead?' says Serge.

'There's only one.'

'You're selling your mum's stuff?'

'Let's say I'm letting it find its way on the open market.'

He sees Sarah in the fourth row, head raised high, her old face bright with tears. Teri leans on Mervyn's shoulder, facing down on an empty seat.

'Well I'm not buying none of it,' says Mrs Bickerton. 'He should keep it. Then the little boy will know who his grandmother was.'

The voice is quieter, measuring a greater grief.

'Finally, THINGS THAT ARE DONE WITH. No longer of any use. Nothing to show you, I'm afraid, though you'll find full descriptions inside. A few bits of furniture, home-made cot, stuff no family can be without. A life-sized model of the human brain, suitable for any interested toddler; a personal tape recorder and a couple of boxes of cassettes. Some charcoal sketches, clay statues and assorted women's clothes. I'm keeping the telly, though: never know what old nonsense they're going to repeat. And last but not least . . .'

But there are some things that will not be sold. As if all the trips he ever took were piling up in his bloodstream and threatening to efface him in a single chemical flood, the truth of what has happened seems to overtake him. An artery flicks in his forehead. He stares at the scrap of cloth in front of him as if nothing had ever made such wonder, picking at threads of blue and green, trying it against his wrist, feeling the ghost of her knot, the shape of her fingers in the frayed cotton curls. How long did he wear it? How many people could see the harm it made? He hears a woman's tears, quiet at his ear, someone who never hurt anyone but suffered all the same; he turns to the doorway, but the face he remembers is gone. He wanted the world to look away, never wonder at the lies passed down from man to man, but the dead cry over everything, they are children, they will not be consoled. His humming finds a tune. Then, as tears split light and blind him with his shame, he pushes the tattered friendship band into a pocket and steps down from the podium. For every one who stands down, there is another waiting to take his place.

'My name is Einar. I am from Iceland. We have no auctions in Iceland. If we want something believe-you-me we simply go and take it. Don't laugh, Mrs Biscuit-Eater, I am already been to your house. Now, first lot is the lady with the wheel, she is so pretty, she spins and spins until ... Ooh! What a lovely duvet! We start the bidding at twenty quids ...'

'I can't believe you did it. I can't believe you really sold all that stuff.'

'Not all of it. I think the speech might've put some people off.'

They stand outside the hospital on a blue evening. Anna looks edgy and tired. She hears about the sale, the things that passed before him in that hot auction room, and what sort of prices his father and stepmother offered when they realised exactly who was being sold.

'Why d'you do it, Finn? It was really cruel.'

Once there was a reason for everything. Now there's just a scrap of cloth in a pocket, a message on an answering machine, a promise to meet someone on neutral ground and carry on as if nothing had changed.

'I'm thinking, maybe he's trying to forget everything that's happened and start again on his own.'

Once – oh, long ago – he saw this accidental beauty, the way she pulled hair behind an ear and glanced down at him with no intention at all, and it was all he wanted in the world.

'Is that why you didn't want me to come?'

'It was you said you were working today.'

'It's okay. I don't mind. But ...'

The last obstacle is anger, from the irritable self he leaves behind: that she's still saying these things after so long.

'If we're going to be together, I need to feel I'm a bit more part of your life. I've still never seen what you do.'

'Well I've never seen you chop people's legs off but I'm not complaining.'

'I don't chop people's legs off. I wish you wouldn't say that.'

'If we're going to be together,' says this disintegrating Finn, 'you'd better learn what's meant by a joke.'

She looks past him at the departing world, long-sighted and marble-eyed.

'I'm sorry.'

'So am I. I'm sorry I don't share your unique sense of humour. I'm sorry I always forget to laugh.'

A hand gathers her arm. She frowns to feel him but lacks the effort to pull away.

'I don't know.' She breathes. 'Maybe it doesn't matter. But I need you to tell me a few things. Like, what do you want? What do you want from life? What do you want from *us*?'

'I don't want things, Anna. I wait for them to want me.'

'Be serious. This is serious. I don't know if I can . . .'

He stares in breezy fascination at the brickwork, one hand in his pocket, picking at the fraying blue and green threads until they start to pull away.

'All I ever thought about was finding you. That's all I could ever get my head around: in Sydney, in Norwich, when Hen was pregnant, when Robinson was growing up, when we moved into Big Kimberley and started the business. Every tearful bedtime and every pissed bathroom trip, every bit of junk that came and went: all of it was you. You know how much of your life that takes up? And now I've found you, and we're here and everything's different and that's all really great.'

She frowns and rubs an eye. 'Oh God, Finn. I don't know whether to laugh or cry.'

Not now, Finn: soon. They stand there, arm in arm, watching an ambulance reverse into a space.

'So what's different?' she wants to know.

'Everything. That's the problem.'

'I don't see why it's a problem.'

'It's not a problem. It's just that what seemed right then looks ... different now.'

'And I was what seemed right then but I'm not what seems right now? Just say it, Finn, and I can get back to my boring life.'

But he doesn't say it. He hears insistent rhythms and ghostly guitar, sees the face that was once seeded in his blood made strange by an ethereal fire, as what started in the auction room catches up with him again.

'I want things to be how they were. That night at the swimming pool.'

'But Finn, this is me. I'm sorry if you don't like it, but there it is.'

The light seems to hurt him. 'You sound like someone I used to know.'

'Well, I wish I *could* be more like Hen. Because it's obviously Hen you want now and who you've always wanted.'

'No.'

'Really?'

Insistent dream-sounds, the burning landscapes of her skin! And now it comes, the change from symphony to song, the tender undemanding music of a soul falling backwards into space, as a screen slides back to reveal two things to choose from, and one chance to choose.

'No.'

She bites her lip and looks around, sighing. 'Okay, I believe you. But don't keep going on about that night at the swimming pool. We were both really drunk. You never even stayed long enough to get a proper look at me.'

'I did. I was in the water for ages, watching you. I couldn't take my eyes off you.' He shivers, forgetting. 'It was like I'd been waiting all my life to meet you, and now you'd just walked in and sat down without a word. When you left, I was going to run after you, fall to my knees and say something very stupid about love.'

'Hang on,' her eyebrows arching under damp strands of hair. 'Run that by me again ...'

There is no other way. 'But by the time I'd got my clothes on you'd disappeared. I wasn't going to knock on every door in the hotel, though it crossed my mind.'

'Are you sure? It was ages ago, Finn. Like I say, I was really off my face.'

So he's talking, like he never talked in any auction, forehead wrinkling in a tender reflection of her frown. The last thread comes away from the knot. He tells his story: how he surrounded himself with junk in the hope she'd turn up somewhere and they'd be together like they always should have been; how for seven years all his thoughts were about her: what she was doing, how he could find her, what he'd say to her when he did.

'And now,' he turns to her, blind and strange, 'it's all come true.'

'Has it? Really?'

'Look at me.'

She looks.

'This is happiness, Anna. For the first time in my life, I'm that happy I . . . I don't know . . .'

She finds an uncertain smile. But it's nothing next to the smile seen on the auctioneer. Ah, that smile! How would you describe it? Is it the same smile he used to see on her, in all the years he carried her around with him in his head: the smile that waits for something breathtaking to come along, as if she'd heard of a real world behind this apparent one that would one day push through the gaps and hook itself into shape? No, that's not it. Is it the contrary smile of his youth, half amused and half hating what's amusing him? It's not that smile either. Is it the smile a father keeps for his son? A son for his mother? Or the sort of smile that warms the hearts of government ministers, looking down from Whitehall windows on a nation at peace with itself? What would count as proof? It stretches pale lips across a gleam of teeth. It sinks tiny trenches in the corners of his eyes. It is the smile left behind when all else is forgotten, when pictures dissolve into the water on which they were drawn, with a trembling hand, at the beginning of a possible life. It's the smile of someone who wakes from a long sleep and sees a new world in its wonder, and never has to ask what any of it means. If it was a colour, the colour would be . . . but you already know. And because it's the auctioneer who is smiling, and because all his yapping pasts have been boxed up and sold off to the highest bidder, you know this happiness is no pretence. They can do what any young fools can do: stick together because it's better than being alone, change the past to fit the future and crave each other like they were born to do. And think about nothing but the night they met, when love kicked away his knees and showed him a sky crowded with stars, when she took off her cotton sundress and joined him in the water, and she swam to him and he swam to her, and they clung to each other's naked body as though their lives depended on it, and kissed like trying to suck up each other's soul, and never had to wait seven years to see how it would turn out.

Last Thing

The way winter comes to Big Kimberley, with thin skies and stinging rain, a wind that gathers speed in empty rooms and slams around downstairs like a drunk, blue light on the walls and masking tape on the windows to keep out the draught.

Waking on New Year's Day to the hum of central heating, the throb of cold engines on the street below; ordered around in the dimness by stacks of newspaper and bright red petrol cans, or lying in bed and looking under the curtain, peering up the skirt of the day.

Postcards: Reykjavík, Melaka, Sydney, the last written in a hurry from the neuroscience department at the University, hoping the fact that you never seem to answer the phone means you're getting over that bad patch and getting out more . . . Actually beginning to think that this time apart is probably the best thing for both of you, knowing it's hard blah blah blah to keep things going at such a distance, some regrets about that very last phone call but really optimistic about coming home.

A most auspicious auction: October 20th, 1538, offered by His Majesty's servants Thomas Legh and William Cavendish. For the glory of St Mary and St Benedict, *halfe a dozen of oulde Antyke clothes, 1 fayre table of alerbaster, one sute of vestments of blue sylke, 'mbroderyd wyth goulde; fether bed, boulster, pyllowes, coverlett; great brass pottes, choppyng-knives, chafyng-dyshys and hoggesheads.* What the bailiffs miss, the monks take with them and hide in holes on the moors.

The last message on the computer: when decorating, is it best to wait until the new units are in before painting, or should the splashy bits come first? The truth is she never liked your colour scheme for the living room, and now the bed is in there it's finally going to get the gopping yellow it's been screaming for since 1372. Glad to report that your suggestion about the avocado jacuzzi has been treated with the contempt it deserves. And by the way: the kid loves his room.

Lying on bare floors in semi-darkness, trying to understand the sky.

The face on the man from Sneyd and Blakemore's when he announces that he has found a buyer for this unique industrial property, and his client is hoping to exchange contracts by the end of the month.

Seeing your own name on the insurance documents and trying not to smile.

An audio cassette, dated earlier this year. '. . . but then I don't expect you to break the habit of a lifetime and actually *do* anything, so I go quiet and stare down at the water and years later you think: Hen, going funny for no reason, that's where all the mental stuff began. I won't describe the object in question because it would do your reputation as a raging sex machine far too much good. So we're stuck there on this unpronounceable bridge and you're *still* trying to make up your mind about something. Which I don't know, makes me think you're about to do something we're all going to regret, it's only a baby after all, so I start on about something you'd actually rather I shut up about, and we prove to the whole of Paris just what a perfectly matched couple we are. Then the next day we go back to the kinky junk place and look in through the window and the bloody things have gone. Cor. Is that a sign or what?'

The metallic smell of the electric fire you find among the storage bays, the soft harpsichord of springs as you carry it upstairs.

To an empty fish tank, an abandoned telescope, the red light on the answering machine that never stops flashing.

The smell of her hair on that Parisian bridge, when you hold something in your pocket that is too huge and ordinary to show, so you hide it and then bury it and never look at it again. The way that regret comes back to haunt you, until you have to do something just to stop the drilling in your brain.

The *you* in 'I loved you'. The *you* in 'I love you still'.

The drilling in your brain.

Catching sight of her in a steamed-up mirror, blithe and pink behind the transparent shower curtain, and the thought of losing her all over again.

A cardboard box. A plastic can. The look on your mother's face when you tell her you've remembered her tune.

A chance malfunction in the smoke detection system, discovered during a routine check of the premises and met by an uncomplicated smile.

The smell of petrol soaking into old wood, as you stuff paper between the bars in the way she taught you and plug the time-switch into the wall.

*

A walk on the moors! Unbelievable how cold, that first step into daylight, after a last trip up to the roof to view the extent of the snow. You cut across the park and down towards the Abbey, through thin trees and abandoned houses, streets as dusky-pale and strange as the backs of your hands. Climbing up over the forest, a rubbery taste in the mouth and a need to shit, earth frozen underfoot and your breath on the air in clouds. Her gift in your fist is a muted rattle which only those who've travelled it can understand. Past the trees you stop and look down: at the layer of mist you've climbed through, the way sunset higher up makes amber light on the tips of grasses, and the distances you've come to, sharp beauty of rocks and rolling miles of sky-blue snow. Silent cows and calling crows.

Do it, says the bottle. The clatter of the pill as it tips through into your palm is like a solitary applause.

The tiny hardness tastes the same. That's the first thing you remember: the time it takes to get started, the final blasts of memory as your whole world burns, until the wind stiffens and earth shifts beneath you and you blur through it one last time. Then you remember who the *you* is that it's happening to: a certain sea-eyed gaze, greenish tinge beneath the skin; how she'll find you, all the places you'll reach her with all the love you tried to hide; and for all these futures happy, as the face that seemed so strange in the mirror becomes this body you're waking up inside. Halfway up this slope is a tree: two trunks leave the ground and join after a foot or two, and the next thing you remember is that you came here for a reason, and it stirs in your gut like fear. The hollow is wet with leaves. Six inches down earth gives way to plastic; more scrabbling and the plastic is free, and inside the bag is a thing that will make you cry out in wonder, that you ever should have buried it, or that you ever could have left it so long. Nothing else is needed: it begins. Ground turns again beneath you, and that instant of imbalance is enough to make you airborne, and no saltwater memory can stop you rising further, on a flickering wind with green canvas wings, a birth that hangs you up among the kestrels with your love gleaming in your hands, turning, moving, to an uncertain home, away from the fire in the valley to the faint hills beyond.

A pair of gold-plated handcuffs, engraved *La Belle et la Bête, Paris* and showing no sign of use, strong enough to carry someone with you from here to Arkangels, or as far as you want to go.

ACKNOWLEDGEMENTS

The possibility of a connection between the author of *Sir Gawain and the Green Knight* and the monks of Dieulacres Abbey is examined by Ralph W. V. Elliott ('Staffordshire and Cheshire landscapes in *Sir Gawain and the Green Knight*', *North Staffordshire Journal of Field Studies*, 17, 1977). The history of the Abbey is detailed in Michael J. Fisher's *Dieulacres Abbey* (Churnet Press, 1989). Several of the ideas concerning cultural attitudes towards Bliss were inspired by Richard Davenport-Hines' *Sex, Death and Punishment: Attitudes to sex and sexuality in Britain since the Renaissance* (Fontana Press, 1991). Asa Briggs' *Victorian Things* (Batsford, 1988) has been a valuable source of information on collectors, catalogues and classification systems. My thanks are due to my agent, David Grossman, for his constant help and encouragement, and to Katie Owen, for her wise and patient editing; to my family, for love and support that have never failed; to those who read and commented on the book as it was taking shape: James Wood, Matthew Diggins, Nic Regan and Ewa Maciejewska; to Chris Currie, Fr. Michael Fisher, Lisa Sargood, Richard Osbourne, Don Brechin and everyone else who answered questions; and above all to my wife Lizzie, whose love made it possible.